PRAISE FOR

THE MAN FROM BERLIN

"I'm reminded of Martin Cruz Smith in the way I was transported to a completely different time and culture and then fully immersed in it. An amazing first novel."

—Alex Grecian, author of *The Yard* and *The Black Country*

"From page one, Luke McCallin draws the reader into a fascinating world of mystery, intrigue, and betrayal."

—Charles Salzberg, author of *Devil in the Hole*

"Set in 1943 Sarajevo, McCallin's well-wrought debut . . . highlights the complexities of trying to be an honest cop under a vicious, corrupt regime . . . Intelligent diversion for World War II crime fans."

—*Publishers Weekly*

"Luke McCallin's first novel . . . is nothing if not ambitious . . . Because every surface appearance in the Balkans is deceptive, setting his novel there makes Luke McCallin's maiden effort an even more notable achievement. Despite such potential pitfalls, the author has produced an extraordinarily nuanced and compelling narrative."

—*New York Journal of Books*

Berkley Books by Luke McCallin

THE MAN FROM BERLIN

THE PALE HOUSE

THE PALE HOUSE

Luke McCallin

BERKLEY BOOKS, NEW YORK

THE BERKLEY PUBLISHING GROUP
Published by the Penguin Group
Penguin Group (USA) LLC
375 Hudson Street, New York, New York 10014

USA • Canada • UK • Ireland • Australia • New Zealand • India • South Africa • China

penguin.com

A Penguin Random House Company

This book is an original publication of The Berkley Publishing Group.

Library of Congress Cataloging-in-Publication Data

McCallin, Luke, 1972–
The Pale House / Luke McCallin.—Berkley trade paperback edition.
pages cm—(A Gregor Reinhardt novel)
ISBN 978-0-425-26306-8 (paperback)
1. Germany—Armed Forces—Officers—Fiction.   2. Intelligence officers—Fiction.
3. Civilians in war—Crimes against—Fiction.   4. War crimes investigation—Fiction.
5. World War, 1939–1945—Yugoslavia—Fiction.
6. Sarajevo (Bosnia and Hercegovina)—History—Fiction.   I. Title.
PR6113.C3585P35   2014
823'.92—dc23
2014006608

PUBLISHING HISTORY
Berkley trade paperback edition / July 2014

PRINTED IN THE UNITED STATES OF AMERICA

10   9   8   7   6   5   4   3   2   1

Cover art by Danielle Abbiate.
Cover design by Richard Hasselberger.
Interior text design by Tiffany Estreicher.

To my wife, Barbara,
and my children, Liliane and Julien.

All my love.

ACKNOWLEDGMENTS

It all began when my editor, Amanda, asked me if I could deliver the second Reinhardt within a year after the publication of *The Man From Berlin*. Given it had taken me eleven years—give or take a few months—to write the first book, I was more than a little nervous. So, it turned out, was Amanda! Writing *The Pale House* has been a source of immense personal satisfaction, but also a testament to how much encouragement and help I've had along the way. Far more than for *The Man From Berlin*, writing *The Pale House* has needed quite a bit of both.

I would like to thank my friend Chelsea Starling in particular for introducing me to Jordan Rosenfeld, a writing coach whose course on plot helped in focusing and refining my understanding of how stories work and come together. For anyone wondering or interested in such courses, look no further than jordanrosenfeld.net.

Thanks again to friends and family who read and commented on the drafts, in particular—as always—to Mum and Dad and my sisters, but also to Severine Rey, Marina Throne-Holst and Marina Konovalova, Jean Verheyden, Ben Negus, Miriam Lange, and Mike Flynn. Thanks to Jennie Rathbone for not only reading the draft, but for putting me in touch with the good people at World Radio Geneva. Special thanks to Professor Emily Greble, who took the time to answer my questions about Sarajevo, to Franz Bottcher for going beyond the call of duty in researching German Army judicial proceedings, and to Tamara Simidrijević for setting my Serbo-Croat straight!

A special thanks to Pamela Cramer and her daughter Anna who, while walking down Lexington Avenue in New York, snapped a picture of a gentleman in a car reading *The Man From Berlin*, and who was promptly christened the Man From Manhattan! The picture is on my Facebook page for anyone who would like a look at it.

Thanks again to Ryan, Tamara, and Loris at Geneva Fitness for always setting the bar high and keeping me on my toes!

I have been moved by all the reaction to the first book, and hope *The Pale House* lives up to expectations. I have thoroughly enjoyed meeting so many people through Sofie von Staplemohr's and Monique Bouvoir's reading groups, and thanks as well to Xavier Huberson at Payot Books and to Helen Stubbs at Off The Shelf. It has as well been a real pleasure to hear from, and interact with, all those readers who took the time to contact me through the website or on Facebook.

A big thank-you to my agent, Peter Rubie, for keeping things simple. And last, but not least, I want to thank my editor, Amanda Ng, for always pushing me to consider and reconsider Reinhardt's journey. It was hard, but I enjoyed it, and I hope you all do as well.

Note on Pronunciation

c	"ts" as in *hats*
č	"ch" as in *starch*
ć	"tch" as in *hatch*
Dj	"dg" as in *fridge*
Dž	"dg" as in *hedge*
J	"y" as in *you*
Lj	"ly" as in *million*
Nj	"nj" as in *new*
š	"sh" as in *shut*
ž	"zh" as in *measure*

COMPARATIVE CHART OF SS, GERMAN ARMY, AND BRITISH ARMY RANKS

WAFFEN SS	WEHRMACHT	BRITISH ARMY
Reichsführer-SS	-	-
-	Generalfeldmarschall	Field Marshal
SS-Oberstgruppenführer	Generaloberst	General
SS-Obergruppenführer	General	Lieutenant General
SS-Gruppenführer	Generalleutnant	Major General
SS-Brigadeführer	Generalmajor	Brigadier
SS-Oberführer	-	-
SS-Standartenführer	Oberst	Colonel
SS-Obersturmbannführer	Oberstleutnant	Lieutenant Colonel
SS-Sturmbannführer	Major	Major
SS-Hauptsturmführer	Hauptmann	Captain
SS-Obersturmführer	Oberleutnant	Lieutenant
SS-Untersturmführer	Leutnant	Second Lieutenant
SS-Sturmscharführer	Hauptfeldwebel	Regimental Sergeant Major
SS-Stabsscharführer	Stabsfeldwebel	Sergeant Major
SS-Hauptscharführer	Oberfeldwebel	-
SS-Oberscharführer	Feldwebel	Staff Sergeant
SS-Scharführer	Unterfeldwebel	Sergeant
SS-Unterscharführer	Unteroffizier	Corporal
SS-Rottenführer	Stabsgefreiter	Lance Corporal
-	Obergefreiter	-
-	Gefreiter	-
SS-Sturmmann	Oberschütze	Private
SS-Oberschütze	Schütze	Private
SS-Schütze	Gemeiner, Landser	Private

CAST OF CHARACTERS

IN THE GERMAN ARMY IN SARAJEVO

IN THE MILITARY POLICE, THE FELDJAEGERKORPS

Captain Gregor Sebastian Reinhardt: a former detective in the Berlin Kriminalpolizei (Kripo)
Colonel Scheller: commander of the Feldjaegerkorps in Sarajevo
Captains Lainer and Morten: decorated veteran officers
Lieutenant Max Benfeld: a young Feldjaeger officer from Alsace, known as "Frenchie"
Sergeant Priller: a machine gunner
Corporal Ossig: communications
Priller, Bader, Pollmann, Triendl: Feldjaeger

IN THE MILITARY POLICE, THE FELDGENDARMERIE

General Herzog: commander of military police in Sarajevo
Major Neuffer: liaison officer to the Feldjaegerkorps

Sergeant Ibel: a patrol officer
Private Günsche

IN THE 999TH BALKAN FIELD PUNISHMENT BATTALION, UNDER THE CONTROL OF THE FELDGENDARMERIE

Colonel Pistorius: commanding officer
Major Erwin Jansky: chief of staff
Lieutenants Brandt and Metzler: officers in the penal battalion
Kreuz: a soldier sentenced to the penal battalion, a recidivist and informant
Thun: a documents clerk
Alexiou: a Greek, a "hiwi," a foreign volunteer
Kostas and Panos: his twin sons
Georg Abler, Carl Benirschke, Otto Berthold, Bruno Cejka, Jozef Fett Werner Janowetz, Marius Maywald, Jürgen Sedlaczek, Christian Seymer, Ulrich Vierow: soldiers sentenced to the penal battalion, their fate unknown

IN THE SARAJEVO GARRISON

General Kathner: general officer commanding in Sarajevo
Judge Felix Erdmann: chief of army criminal justice in Sarajevo
Judge Marcus Dreyer: serving in the War Crimes Bureau, an old friend of Reinhardt's from Berlin
Colonel Wedel: in charge of the army's defense plans for Sarajevo
Captain Langenkamp: army liaison to the Ustaše
Doctor Henke: a military doctor
Captain Prien: an officer in military intelligence

IN THE CITY—THE OPPOSING FORCES, THE CITIZENS CAUGHT IN-BETWEEN

IN THE PARTISANS

Vladimir 'Valter' Perić: chief of the Partisans in Sarajevo
Simo: his right-hand man

IN THE USTAŠE

General Vjekoslav 'Maks' Luburić: commander of the Ustaše in Sarajevo, a man of fearsome reputation
Colonel Ante Putković: his deputy, known as "the Gambler," an old adversary of Reinhardt's
Captain Bunda: an Ustaše of imposing size and temper
Captain Marković: Ustaše liaison officer to the German Army
Nikola Marin and Franjo Sutko: Ustaše torturers
Labaš and Zulim: Ustaše soldiers, friends with Bunda
Jovan Buzdek, Svetozar Trpić, and Branimir Zulim: Ustaše officers, brutal men, of particular interest to the Partisans

IN THE CITIZENRY

Suzana Vukić: one of the directors of Napredak, a humanitarian organization, and mother of Marija, whose death Reinhardt investigated in The Man From Berlin
Inspector Bakarević: a detective in the Sarajevo police
Almira and Suljo Blagojević: an elderly couple, refugees rescued by Reinhardt from a massacre
Neven: a boy rescued by Reinhardt at the same time as the Blagojevićs
Anica: a woman working at Napredak
Safet Kafedzić: a playwright

ELSEWHERE AND ELSEWHEN . . .

Carolin: Reinhardt's wife, died of cancer in 1938

Friedrich: Reinhardt's son, lost with the German Sixth Army at Stalingrad

Captain Koenig: officer in the Vienna garrison, a member of the German resistance

Rudolf Brauer: Reinhardt's former partner in the Kripo and his oldest and closest friend

Colonel Tomas Meissner: Reinhardt's mentor, and regimental commander during WWI, a member of the German resistance, his fate unknown

Major Hassler: former deputy to Colonel Scheller, killed in action in Montenegro

Doctor Muamer Begović: a senior Partisan, a friend of Reinhardt's, known as "the Shadow"

Inspector Andro Padelin: a Sarajevo policeman and Ustaša, partnered with Reinhardt in *The Man From Berlin*

PROLOGUE

VIENNA, NOVEMBER 1944

"*Tell me again,*" the Gestapo officer said. *The one slouched behind the desk. "The bit about the car crash. Tell me that bit, again."*

Reinhardt's mouth felt gummed dry, the blood in his mouth sticky and heavy. They had given him nothing to drink since they had dragged him in here. He breathed heavily through his nose. "We were attacked south of Brod . . ."

"*On the way to interrogate General Verhein.*"

"No," said Reinhardt. Something felt wrong in his mouth. There was space and movement where there should not be. He focused on the floor. The tiles were mismatched, different colors, different sizes. He focused on one, fixed his eyes on it, tried to ignore the pacing of the second agent. The one who prowled and struck whenever he wanted to. "We were lost. We ended up going south by mistake."

"*So you weren't looking for Verhein?*"

"No."

Fingers snaked into his hair, and his head was yanked back. The other agent measured him with his eyes.

"*So you were looking for Verhein.*"

"No."

"*The crash . . . ?*"

*"I told you," he slurred, gagging against the blood in his mouth
as his head hinged back. "One moment we were driving, then there
was firing all around, and the next thing I remember we had crashed
off the road."*

"You were alone?"

*The other man let go of his head, shoving it forward. Reinhardt
leaned to the side and spat weakly.*

*"My driver was dead." He spat, again, watching a tooth roll
across the floor.*

*The interrogators laughed. "A tooth, Reinhardt? You need to be
careful with them. Still, there's plenty more where that one came
from, right?!"*

"Captain Reinhardt."

Reinhardt pulled his eyes back from the past, lifted them over the
glass standing untouched between his forearms and the second glass
standing brimful across the table. A cigarette burned slowly between
his fingers, and a harsh line of light lay across the inside of the tavern.
It pulled form from shadow, flowed across the other men in the bar
and pushed up against the cigarette smoke that roiled and twisted in
the pull of air.

"Captain Reinhardt."

His back tensed up, and he looked around slowly, looking across
the tavern at a sergeant of the Feldgendarmerie standing by the door,
his gorget bright across his chest. A second Feldgendarme, a lieutenant, stood to one side, and Reinhardt's stomach clenched, wondering
if they had found him at last, and if the man he had been waiting to
meet had had anything to do with leading them here.

"Captain *Reinhardt*. Identify yourself." The Feldgendarmes' eyes
turned steadily across the room, eyes swinging from face to face,
pushing and probing.

"I am Captain Reinhardt," he said, turning and standing.

The two Feldgendarmes turned toward him as one, and Reinhardt
felt real fear. They were not Feldgendarmes. They looked like them.

They wore uniforms like a Feldgendarme's, with metal gorgets around their necks, but on their left arms, which had been hidden from him, they wore red bands, with black lettering stenciled across them. On each of them, the Iron Cross shone dully on their left breasts.

They were Feldjaeger.

"You will come with us," the sergeant said.

"Why? I have done nothing wrong."

"We have orders to deliver you to Feldjaegerkorps headquarters."

The bar went even quieter, if that was possible. Reinhardt said nothing, then swallowed hard at the lump that squatted suddenly in his throat. Had Koenig betrayed him? Had Koenig been trying to get to him to warn him of this?

"What does the Feldjaegerkorps want with me?"

"Ask someone who knows what we're talking about," said the lieutenant. "Get moving, Captain, and come with us."

Only the Feldjaegerkorps could speak like that, a junior officer ordering a senior one in that fashion, but whatever pride Reinhardt felt might have been hurt, he ignored it. He looked at his drink, imagined knocking it back, imagined wincing at its burn across his mouth, but he just stubbed out his cigarette and shrugged into his coat, hoping neither of the Feldjaeger would wonder why a man sitting at a table alone would have two drinks in front of him. He picked his way carefully through the silent bar, between the tangle of legs and over puddles of cloth where greatcoats hung over the backs of chairs and spread gray skirts across the tiled floor. The two Feldjaeger split to each side of the door, passing him through, their faces expressionless as they followed him under the dim glow of the entrance light and up a flight of stairs to the darkened streets and into a heavy, wet cold.

Reinhardt's stomach rumbled and he ran his tongue around his mouth, all thickened and sticky, probing the gap in his back teeth. He clenched his jaw, drawing in a deep breath of cold air. It punched through his teeth, waking him, rooting him firmly. The lieutenant stepped in front of him, and the sergeant put a firm hand on his back and escorted him over to a black car, its outline pearled in the

damp air. The lieutenant opened the back door and followed Reinhardt inside, the car rocking and swaying on its suspension. The sergeant clattered the engine into life and then hauled the car out onto
the road.

Reinhardt stared out of his window as they drove, the darkened
and blacked-out streets sliding past like a sunken city beyond the
sparkled pane of the window. His mind turned over and over what
might have happened to put them on to him but could find nothing.
They had done nothing, their so-called resistance cell, since July, when
the world had seemed to stand still in the aftermath of the attempt on
Hitler's life. They had watched as others elsewhere had taken their
chance. They had waited as the machine they had hoped had been
dealt a death blow had stuttered and then roared back into life. Then
they had hoped and prayed for the best, until one of their number had
vanished into buildings of concrete and steel and never come out
again, and then a second, and the cell had scattered after rushed and
furtive good-byes if there were any good-byes at all, eyes hooded far
back beneath darkened brows.

Days, then weeks, then months, almost no news of the others, and
no one had come looking, or knocking, until tonight. Reinhardt's
mind turned over and over, and he wondered at last, battening onto it
with a sudden desperation, why it was the Feldjaeger who had come
for him, and not the Gestapo, or the SS.

The car hammered its way through the wet night, down the wide
boulevard of Stubenring, up to what Reinhardt recognized as the old
Austro-Hungarian defense ministry building, now one of the main
German headquarters in the city. A huge swastika flag hung like a
crimson smear down the front of the severe gray structure, all vertical
lines and ornate stonework under a copper-colored roof. They drove
along the side of the vast building and around the back, weaving
through barricades and skirting a spill of rubble from a part of the
building that had collapsed in a recent bombing raid.

The lieutenant motioned Reinhardt out of the car, and he shivered
once in the cold. He followed the lieutenant inside, past a pair of Feldjaeger on sentry duty warming their hands at a metal brazier. It

seemed even colder inside as he followed the Feldjaeger through the warren of the building, up stairs and around landings and farther up until the lieutenant knocked at a door and opened it, ushering Reinhardt into an anteroom.

A corporal, his tunic studded with decorations, took Reinhardt's coat and knocked at a second door. A muffled answer came. Reinhardt walked into a long office, a desk standing at one end in front of a fall of heavy curtains, and a lamp with a green shade burned on the desk, carving the face of the officer who sat there into harsh lines of light and shadow. The rest of the room was dark, and it took Reinhardt a moment longer to realize there was a third man in the room, sitting in a deep chair far back in the shadows.

"Captain Reinhardt," said the officer at the desk, as the corporal shut the door with a whisper of wood. The officer indicated a spot in front of the table, and Reinhardt came to attention. The officer was a major and, like all the Feldjaeger he had seen and heard of, wore a clutch of decorations, starting with the Knight's Cross at his throat.

"Captain Gregor Sebastian Reinhardt," the major said, reading from a file on his desk. "Born 1898, in Köpenick, Berlin. Father, university philosophy lecturer. Mother, housewife. No siblings. Officer cadet school, 1914 to 1916. Active service on the Eastern Front. Transfer to Western Front and induction into stormtroopers in 1917. Served with distinction in Operation Michael. Won Iron Cross at Amiens, 1918. First- and Second-Class Crosses the same day." The major paused, looking up at Reinhardt, his eyes focusing on the Iron Cross. Reinhardt felt desperately uncomfortable under his scrutiny, and that of the other man he could not really see. His skin prickled with sweat, and he forced himself to breathe slowly, evenly, ignoring the slight tremor as he took each breath in.

"Severely wounded," the major continued, speaking of Reinhardt in the third person, "and honorably discharged with one third-level invalidity in December 1918. Joined Berlin police force as detective in 1920 and rose to the rank of chief inspector. Posted to Interpol here in Vienna 1938. Resigned from Kripo 1938, joined Abwehr. Assigned as intelligence officer in the invasion of Norway. Won Narvik Shield.

Participated in invasion of France, 1940. Invasion of Yugoslavia, 1941. Assigned to Afrika Korps as divisional intelligence staff. Invalided out of Afrika Korps 1942. Assigned to Abwehr office Sarajevo, Partisan counterintelligence." The major paused again, frowned, turned a page, then let it fall back. "And this is where a fairly good career derails. Fell afoul of a Gestapo investigation following his role in a murder investigation. A general was implicated, who later died in action." The major looked up. "Rather a lot of people were upset with you over that, were they not?" Reinhardt was not sure it was a question, and so kept quiet, focusing on a spot just over the major's shoulder, and pushed his tongue into that gap in his teeth. "Wounded in action again, questioned . . . intensively . . . by the Gestapo. Acquitted. Obviously. But no one seems sure what to do with you. Reassigned from Abwehr and posted in August 1943 as an intelligence liaison officer to 1st Panzer Division in Greece, then to 12th Army in Belgrade. Pretty dull stuff. I think that was the point, no? But it didn't stay that way, did it?" The major's eyes needled at him, and his skin prickled tight again. "Evacuated to Vienna from Belgrade in October 1944 following the Soviet offensive. Mentioned in dispatches for extreme bravery in covering the retreat from Belgrade. Received the German Honor Roll Clasp in November this year."

There was a creak of leather as the third man rose and stepped into the light. The third man was a colonel with a head of cropped dark hair shot with gray, a round head balanced on wide shoulders. He stooped over the desk, almost delicately taking the page from the major and turning it back. He read a moment, then looked up at Reinhardt.

"That investigation into General Verhein. In Sarajevo. Tell me about that."

"What exactly, sir?" said Reinhardt, surprised to find his voice steady.

The colonel pursed his lips, straightening up. "At a wild guess, you were told to stop that investigation as soon as you had a general in your sights. But you didn't. What happened?"

"I pursued an investigation to its end."

"Meaning?"

"I went where the evidence took me rather than where expedience suggested."

"Tell me about the retreat from Belgrade." When Reinhardt said nothing, the colonel seemed almost sympathetic. "What was the mention in dispatches for?"

"Covering the retreat of the main field hospital." The colonel said nothing, indicating with his silence that Reinhardt was to continue. "I received late intelligence that part of the Soviet advance would threaten the hospital's withdrawal. Communications were down, so I went out to warn them."

"And you gathered together a ragtag bunch, including walking wounded and stragglers, and fought off the Russians long enough for reinforcements to arrive. Quite something. First time going up against the Russians?"

"Since 1917, yes."

The colonel snorted, and the major smiled, a flicker across his lips. "And?"

"And I'd be perfectly happy going another nineteen years before tangling with them again."

The colonel stared at Reinhardt, then down at the major. Something imperceptible seemed to pass between them, and the colonel folded himself back into the shadows. The major closed Reinhardt's file and rustled a sheet of paper across his fingertips.

"Captain Reinhardt, effective immediately, you are transferred to the Feldjaegerkorps."

The major's words fell into a heavy silence. Reinhardt stood unspeaking, not believing what he had just heard.

"Are you familiar with the Feldjaegerkorps, Captain?"

"Yes, Major." Reinhardt swallowed. "Somewhat."

"Enlighten me."

"Military police."

"Go on."

"But with a difference."

"Correct," said the major. "The Feldjaegerkorps accepts only deco-rated combat veterans. Officers and NCOs, no enlisted men. We re-port directly to the armed forces high command. As such, even a corporal has more authority, should he choose to exercise it, than an officer. We have independent tasking, and full authority to maintain discipline in the army's rear areas."

"Full authority," repeated Reinhardt. Something seemed to snap inside, that small part of him that could not help but prod and poke and provoke in situations like this. "Drumhead courts-martial and on-the-spot executions."

"Sometimes, yes," the major replied. "There's more to it than that, though."

"It's about being a policeman again," the colonel said, quietly, from the shadows. "What you used to be, no? What you still think you are."

"But a *military* policeman?"

"I would remind you we are both military policemen, Captain," said the colonel.

"Yes, sir, I apologize," said Reinhardt, straining to bring himself under control. "It's not what I meant. I meant . . ." He trailed off, his eyes searching for something, anything, in the blank walls and the long, ink-dark folds of the curtains. "I mean, this morning, I woke up and I'm still a divisional intelligence officer."

"Imagine our surprise as well," said the major, dryly.

"Sir, may I ask, who recommended me for this?"

"Indeed," said the colonel, standing and stepping back into the light. "Your commanding general was rather persuasive."

"Sir, do I have any choice in this?"

"None." For the first time, the colonel's voice and face firmed, hardened, a boundary against which Reinhardt saw there could be no compromise.

"Very well," said Reinhardt, straightening. "I am grateful for this honor, sir."

The ghost of a smile flickered again across the major's lips. "Don't overdo it, Reinhardt," he murmured.

"Where are we to be posted?"

"We are being detached from Feldjaeger Commando III, here in Vienna. We're going south. Very soon. The southern front's a mess."

The major came around the table and offered Reinhardt a piece of paper. "Your transfer orders. Be back here by noon tomorrow, with your pay book. We'll get that updated soonest. And put this on," he said, offering Reinhardt a folded piece of red cloth, wrapped around something heavy.

The red cloth was an armband wrapped around a crescent-shaped gorget. Reinhardt paused, then wormed the armband over his wrist and up on top of his sleeve. It sat there, red on gray, black letters stenciled across it that denoted the unit and the source of its authority— *Feldjaegerkorps, Armed Forces High Command*—and it seemed to tighten, and grip, like a manacle, and something shifted abruptly deep inside him, but what it was he did not know, and could not wonder at now.

"Welcome, Captain," said the colonel, extending his hand. "I am Colonel Scheller. And this is Major Hassler."

Reinhardt shook hands with them both before Major Hassler walked him to the door. He paused as it opened, the corporal standing just outside with Reinhardt's coat over his arm. "Sir," he said to Scheller, "if I may ask. I am sure you do not welcome all recruits to your unit like this. So, why me?"

Scheller nodded. "You are not quite the officer we normally take," he said, walking slowly over toward Reinhardt, his hands in his pockets, "and so we wanted to have a look at you. But your record is good, and we will value your particular experience in the Balkans and your police background. Think of it like this: We also go where the need takes us, not where we'd always like to go." He stopped and pursed his lips, his upper lip folding down into the lower and his eyes fixed on Reinhardt's. "Like I said, you do come highly recommended."

There was another driver for Reinhardt downstairs waiting beside a *kubelwagen* with a canvas roof, a tight-lipped corporal who nevertheless grunted a brief welcome and remained mercifully silent as he drove Reinhardt back through the city to the barracks hard by the Donau Canal. Reinhardt stood in the dark as the car pulled away, looking up at the blank façade of the building, before turning away and walking across to the waterfront. He lit a cigarette, closing his eyes against the flare of the match, and stared down at the dull, leaden shift of the canal, blinking against the trickle of water in his eyes left by the drizzle that had begun, trying to make sense of it all. He leaned against a carved balustrade, his fingers curling and clenching across the cold metal of the gorget, and started to shiver as the stress began to flow out of him. No arrest, no accusations. Only a transfer. With shaking fingers, he lifted the cigarette to his lips, before lifting his face to the night sky and realizing the cold he felt was the night wind across his tears.

"Reinhardt?"

He turned at the crunch of steps. A shape pulled itself out of the dark next to him. "Koenig?"

"It's me," Koenig said, his uniform showing him a captain of infantry.

"You shouldn't be here," said Reinhardt.

"I know. The others . . ." Koenig paused, his voice low. "I saw you being driven away from the bar. We . . . we were worried. They asked me to watch for you. What happened?"

"A transfer happened." Reinhardt offered him the paper, then struck a match, watching the surprise bloom fast across Koenig's face in the wavering light before it flickered out.

"*Feldjaegerkorps*?" breathed Koenig, huskily, from out of the new dark. "My God, Reinhardt . . ." And was that a hint of jealousy in his voice?

"You want it, you can have it."

"Reinhardt, don't be a *fool*," hissed Koenig. "The Feldjaegerkorps is a powerful unit. It has powers and access. In it, you will be beyond suspicion. You will be in a privileged position. You are still one of us. Are you not?"

"Of course."

"When you woke this morning, still an intelligence officer, you were also one of us?"

"Yes."

"A member of the resistance."

"Yes, I said."

"Then don't forget it."

"God forbid I'd forget that," snapped Reinhardt, still rocked by this news. "I mean, just look at all we've accomplished."

"Ah, Reinhardt," sighed Koenig. "Still looking for that white horse."

"No," snapped Reinhardt. "That horse bolted a long time ago."

"Then in the Feldjaegerkorps, you might just find it. Look for what you can do where you will be. And should one of us need you—or another comrade who thinks like us—then you will be able to help him."

"You really think so?"

"Ah, Christ, Reinhardt." Koenig removed his cap, running his hands over thin hair plastered wetly to his head. "What do I know? What do any of us know? I'm just a glorified administrator, pushing paper all day long. How did they find out about you, anyway?"

"They told me the general recommended me."

Koenig snorted in the darkness. "That cunning old bastard."

"I suppose he thinks . . ." Reinhardt trailed off. He did not know what the general thought.

"I suppose he thinks he's doing you a favor. And maybe he is. Gets you away from here. Gets one more of us away from him."

"So. It's over."

Koenig nodded his head. "It's over for now. Here. We're all done here, Reinhardt. Not that we ever did much. I suppose you have that much right."

"*Attention!*" A flashlight flickered on, sweeping across the hanging streaks of drizzle in the night air. "You two over there! What are you doing?"

Reinhardt started, looking around. A Feldgendarmerie patrol had come to a stop next to them. "Talking, thank you."

The Feldgendarme lieutenant at the head of the patrol bristled at the affront he heard in Reinhardt's tone. "What are you doing here, I said?"

"Just talking, Lieutenant."

"About what? Sir?" the Feldgendarme said, coming close enough to see Reinhardt's rank.

Reinhardt looked back at him, squinting past the flat glare of the Feldgendarme's flashlight, at the slant in the man's eyes, at the harm this man could do, and saw himself, standing there looking back at someone like that Feldgendarme, and for a moment he grasped a sense of the possibilities that could open to him as a Feldjaeger. The possibilities Koenig had hinted at. He swallowed hard, his mind reaching after that sudden glimpse, and offered his transfer orders, making sure to pass them with his left hand. "About that."

The Feldgendarme's flashlight fixed on the paper, reflected light casting his face into macabre relief. The light wavered, sought Reinhardt's wrist, back to the paper. He handed it back to Reinhardt, straightened, and saluted.

"Very sorry for disturbing you, sir. And . . . and good luck."

They watched the patrol walk away, and then Koenig extended his hand.

"You are right. I should not stay. Who knows how that might have turned out?"

"Yes. You were right, I suppose." Reinhardt gave a small, tired smile to the darkness, shook Koenig's hand. "It has been an honor."

"Apology accepted, Reinhardt," Koenig replied, a smile in his voice, as they shook. "Do us proud. And don't forget, this is not all that we are."

Reinhardt walked slowly down the canal's embankment and thought of Sarajevo, of the long riverside walk there, the Ottoman bridges that arced over the froth-flecked rush of the Miljacka. He felt himself losing control, felt the sting of tears, and he could not tell whether it was fury or the sense of impotence that triggered them. His hand stole to his breast, to the Iron Cross pinned there. He gripped it until his hand hurt, his mind awhirl between the needling cold of a Viennese winter and the sodden chill of that French field where he had won it, and as the Cross's edges bit into his fingers he contemplated, for the first time, getting rid of it.

"This is not all that I am," he whispered, echoing Koenig's last words to him, their group's motto. Every time he said it, he wanted to feel ridiculous, trite, but every time he did, he felt the truth of those words, and he realized then, truly, how angry he was. With himself. With everyone. Angry at what, he could barely articulate, standing there in the darkness with the hum of the water next to him, feeling more alone than he had felt in a very long time.

Hurry up and wait, he thought, turning further in on himself. He had been doing a lot of that, lately. They all had. As much as he and the others—good men all, who believed they could do something worthy of what could be called "resistance"—had wanted to act, and as much as he tried to believe otherwise, he had accomplished nothing. None of them had, and it was so far away from where he had been that night on a Bosnian mountain when he had felt a new truth settle into him, filling all those places he had known were empty, and showing him that all those other places within he had never known had emptied out as well.

How fast those possibilities had faded before the dead weight of the world, though, and how sharing his dreams with like-minded men only for nothing to come of them save furtive talk, tentative plans, and a creeping itch that someone was watching them had worn him down. What use was resistance that never declared itself, he asked himself, again? Not much good, he answered himself. Again. Despite all their talk about dissent, to opposition, to resistance, Reinhardt was powerfully aware he had failed to take the step he might have, and perhaps should have. And now, where before he had fancied life would sometimes catch on the frayed edges of his character, now he felt sanded down, slumped, like a candle that had all but burned itself out.

He looked at the canal a long time as it unfurled before him, then up at the sparkle of rain out of the deep dark of the sky, and wondered how it had all come to this.

PART ONE

Blood on a
Dying Tree

SARAJEVO, LATE MARCH 1945

O n the trail of rumors of a band of deserters, the Feldjaeger came across the massacre toward the end of the afternoon. The valley lay hunched into a bitter wind, wet and raw with the promise of rain beneath a heavy sky of mottled, gray clouds. The little column of cars lurched down a muddy trail, through the earthen reek beneath the trees, and into a wide clearing. Forged iron-hard by the winter, the ground was heavy beneath their wheels, rutted, strewn with rocks and stones that turned the vehicles from their paths as they slid and slithered to a stop.

In the front car, Reinhardt raised his hand and engines clattered still, the silence of the forest flowing in and over them. He stood up slowly, pulling his scarf down around his throat and resting his hands on the *kubelwagen*'s windshield. The clearing was wide, well more than a long stone's throw across, sodden grass slumped this way and that across its trampled width. One side of the clearing, the downslope side, had been extensively logged, the forest pushed well back from an expanse of stumps and mud all tangled with broken branches and scattered foliage, and looking for all the world like what Reinhardt remembered of no-man's-land. Three huts stood hard against the forest, little more than shacks, doors kicked in and rags hanging from the windows. A row of shapes were mounded on the grass, bodies, heaped one beside the other. Smoke dulled the sharp lines of the trees, rising up from somewhere behind the huts.

A *kubelwagen* was parked by the shacks, four Feldjaeger gathered around it. One of them stepped forward as Reinhardt climbed out of his car. No salutes were exchanged. It was not just the fraternity within the Feldjaeger that limited it, but out here, where anyone could be looking at them, a salute was just another way of painting a target on your chest.

"What do you have, Frenchie?" asked Reinhardt.

"It's not pretty," answered Lieutenant Benfeld. A Franco-German from Alsace, he was a tall young man, taller than Reinhardt, very solid, hair cut close to the block of his head and his cheeks flushed red from the cold.

"You think it's them?"

"Shall I show you?"

Reinhardt turned to give an order to his sergeant, then nodded as Benfeld hitched the strap of his StG 44 assault rifle over his shoulder. An engine revved, and Reinhardt glanced back to see the Horch swing out of the line, trundling to one side with Sergeant Priller crouched behind the mounted machine gun that he began tracking across the clearing's edge.

Reinhardt followed Benfeld around the side of the huts to a roughly square-shaped expanse of ashen earth, bounded and studded with the warped and blackened stubs that were all that was left of the walls of a hut. Smoke curled up around the wood like flowing water, and heat shimmered the air, making ripples of the forest beyond. Three bodies lay across the middle of the hut, debris heaped around and across them. The bodies were charred black, the skulls twisted back and up and the mouths open in silent rictus, and the smell of burned meat and cloth was heavy in the air.

Kneeling by the first body, Reinhardt gently placed his finger on the hole in the center of the skull's forehead. He shifted the body over to look at the back of the head, spotting the smaller hole there, where a gun had been pressed up against the man's head. A similar hole starred the bone of the second, and when he looked over at Benfeld, the other man nodded, his finger circling the forehead of the third.

Reinhardt put his hand on the corpse's shoulder and pressed, tamping down a jolt of nausea as he did so. The skin felt hard, cracked and crisped like baked earth, and there was no give beneath the pressure. Nothing came off but a smear of ash that traced the whorl of his fingertip.

"Slightly overdone, wouldn't you say, sir?"

Reinhardt ignored Benfeld's macabre humor, pushed his fingers into a pile of ash, and watched the prints they left, figuring the hut had burned down no more than a few hours ago. He ran his eyes slowly around and over all he could see, looking for he knew not what, until he saw it. Twisted, coiled, blackened, a closely wound pile of . . . something. Not wood, or stone, or metal. Not flesh. He peered closer, lifting up what he had seen between thumb and forefinger.

It was clothing, a piece of a sleeve. He frowned, squinting closer, feeling the weave of the cloth. He spiraled a finger through the ash, feeling something hard and firm. He pulled it out, whatever it was crackling, cracking. He went more slowly, blowing it as clean as he could of ash and filth. Some kind of stiff fabric, burned black.

He looked across the corpses, then over at Benfeld.

"What else did you find to call this in?"

Benfeld gave a small smile. "This, sir," he said, holding out something warped and blackened.

It was roughly the size of his palm, twisted up at both ends.

"If you ask me," said Benfeld, "I'd say that was a piece of a German soldier's tunic. There. See? The raised pattern? It looks like an epaulette."

"I think you're right," said Reinhardt, quietly.

"And these," Benfeld added, holding out his hand. He held a handful of buttons in his palm, burned black by the fire. Reinhardt picked one up between his fingertips, rubbing his thumb across it. The button was metal, the surface pebbled. Then another.

"These two are strange, sir," said Benfeld, pointing them out.

Reinhardt picked them up, looking closely, rubbing away the covering of black ash. "This one has Roman numerals. And this one standard numbers." He bounced them on his palm, looking at the lieutenant. "Interesting."

"That's what I thought too, sir. The numbers denote infantry companies. The Roman numerals . . ."

". . . are for artillery batteries," finished Reinhardt.

"More than one unit, sir. Deserters. Almost certainly."

"Probably." He turned in place, looking toward the other bodies. "What about them?"

"Any of our business, sir?"

"Won't know until we look, will we?" answered Reinhardt. Benfeld still made Reinhardt nervous as there were two sides to him. A happy-go-lucky one, and a cold, focused one. It was the focused one that had won him an Iron Cross at Sebastopol, and the Knight's Cross at Kursk, and it was that side that looked out now.

Reinhardt turned away and walked over to the bodies, glad to put Benfeld's eyes behind him, glad as well for the cold that held the smell of blood and waste down, somewhat. He stood and looked, his mouth bunched tight. There were maybe a dozen bodies there, lying faceup with bullet wounds across their torsos. They were, it seemed, of no particular type, other than they wore the rags and had the look of refugees. Their skin was etched with grime and chapped with cold, and their faces drawn long with hunger. Some had been old, some younger. A few had been men, more had been women, and there was one girl, barely into her adolescence, lying hunched into the body of an older man, maybe her father, as if in the last moments he had tried to shield her. Reinhardt looked at her a moment, hoping her end had come fast, and her killers had not taken their time with her.

Reinhardt let out a long breath he had not realized he was holding and knelt by the body nearest him. He put a finger to the blood that had welled and spattered around the wounds in the chest. The blood was thick, but it was still liquid. He put the back of his hand to the neck, then squirmed and slid it under the clothes the body wore, feeling across the torso. He lifted one of the arms, moved it, bending it by the elbow, did the same to the next two, then duck-walked across to the next, repeating his examination. He shifted one of the bodies onto its side, then another, checking for signs of lividity, an indication as to when they might have been killed.

His eyes moved slowly across the massacre. He looked at the bodies, trying to work out who they had been, but he could not even tell from their dress what their confession had been—Catholic, Orthodox, or Muslim—which might have given some insight, however small, into who might have done this. His eyes passed slowly from body to body, as if he sought to give them some final measure of respect, or remembrance, something more than the blind stare of the slate-gray sky above. His gaze moved from body to body, face to face, coming to an elderly man with a goatee, passing on, then back. He looked at the man a moment longer, then stepped back, eyes tracking across the row, seeing how and where they had fallen. He stepped back farther still, looking left and right through the grass, until he came to a spot not far from the bodies that seemed more trampled. He moved sideways and knelt to worm his hands through the grass, his fingers finally closing around something cold and cylindrical.

Steps whispered through the grass, and Reinhardt looked up as Benfeld stopped next to him. "Any of our business?" he asked, again.

Reinhardt felt cold. Benfeld was hard, single-minded, a good soldier, but he was new to the Balkans, and he could not see what Reinhardt saw, nor understand the memories that surged suddenly across his mind.

"Sir?" asked Benfeld. "Mind telling me what's going on?"

"I'm trying to . . . I'm wondering what happened, here, Lieutenant."

"Why?"

"Professional curiosity."

"Professional . . ." Benfeld paused, his lips pursing as he looked around the clearing. "You can make more sense of this than a bunch of civvies in the wrong place at the wrong time?"

"This may be depressingly familiar to you, Lieutenant. To all of us. But, fundamentally, this is a crime scene," Reinhardt said. "As such, it has things to say." Benfeld said nothing, although the question was writ large in his eyes. "I used to be a detective, Frenchie. Berlin Kriminalpolizei." He watched the change in the way Benfeld looked at him. "It's been a while," he said, "but some things never change."

"Like?"

"They're not long dead, for starters," Reinhardt replied, fishing through his pockets for his cigarettes. "A few hours, no more. And the one with the goatee is interesting."

"The what?" Benfeld's eyes tracked across the bodies. "What's with him?"

"Look at him," said Reinhardt, lighting a cigarette and tossing away the match.

"An old man."

"The man's cheeks are barely covered in stubble, and the goatee is thick and white. It's looked after. The man shaved, recently. He took some care of himself. Can you imagine a man living up here who would try to keep a goatee in such conditions? And then look at his clothes. Quite different from the others. Worn, but not ragged. Dirty, but not filthy. Of a better cut and quality." City clothes, he realized around a deep lungful of smoke, not the bundles of rags and wool the others wore. Reinhardt frowned, kneeling next to the body, looking closer. "He's wearing a wristwatch. Which no one's pinched, by the way. And his hands," he continued, turning them over. "Soft. He's no refugee. Or if he is, he hasn't been one long. In any case, he's most certainly not a peasant. He's from the city."

Reinhardt stood up, pointing with both arms along a rough line that ran along the feet of the dead refugees. "See how they lie? Firing squad," Reinhardt said. "Shell cases there. There. There," he continued. "Those are just the ones I can spot." He opened his hand, showing what he had picked up. "Nine-by-nineteen-millimeter. Parabellums."

"Anyone could have fired those bullets," said Benfeld, shifting his hands on the strap of his assault rifle.

"I didn't say otherwise, Lieutenant," said Reinhardt, a small smile on his face, taking another draw on his cigarette. "But the chances are those people were killed by bullets fired from an MP 40. More than one, I would think. I wonder, though . . ." he said.

He walked back over to the three burned bodies, knelt by one of them, and, clamping his cigarette into the corner of his mouth, placed the shell casing against the hole in the back of its head, trying to see if it would fit. "Too big," he muttered, squinting around the smoke that curled into his eyes. He took his pistol out of his holster, ejected the magazine, and removed one of the bullets, doing the same thing, twirling the shell into the hole, tamping down on a moment of squeamishness as he did so. The bullet fit much better. He tried on the other two as well. "Pistol shots, most likely," he said, glancing over at Benfeld.

"What is it you think happened, sir?" asked Benfeld.

"A guess? There's two different sets of murders. Possibly even three," he said, as he put his pistol back together. A last draw on his cigarette, and he tossed the butt away.

"*Murders*, sir?"

"Yes, Benfeld. Murder. That's usually the name we give to the unlawful and often premeditated killing of one human being by another. Something about that strikes you as odd?"

"Well, sir . . ." The big man seemed at a loss. "It's just . . ."

". . . One of those words that seems to have fallen out of favor?" Reinhardt interrupted. "A term that's lost the power to shock. A definition that's all but meaningless . . . ?" Reinhardt looked around, sighed. "All of the above, probably," he said, quietly. "But that doesn't change what it is."

"No, sir. You were saying?"

"Those burned corpses in what's left of that hut are one set of murders. Then the civilians. Refugees. Whatever they were, are a second set. At a wild guess, these refugees were . . . probably . . . in the wrong place at the wrong time."

"Witnesses?" said Benfeld.

"Probably."

"Poor bastards."

"The ones in the hut are more important. Someone wanted to hide evidence of something, and from the evidence you found, they were wearing German uniforms."

"That does not make them German soldiers, though," said Benfeld.

"No. It does not."

"But someone went to some effort to cover their deaths up," said Benfeld.

"Go on," motioned Reinhardt.

"Someone . . . a falling-out, perhaps? A disagreement?"

"I don't suppose we'll ever know, Lieutenant."

"You said three, sir? Possibly three sets of murders."

"That old man. Him, there. City dweller." Reinhardt chewed his lower lip, then stroked that gap in his teeth with his tongue. "What's his story . . . ?"

Although the woods stood on the cusp of spring, the winter had been harsh. The ground and trunks were slimed with mud and damp, and though the trees stood thick, the pillared spaces between them were sheeted with darkness more than new growth, and that was how the boy came so close with no one to spot him.

One of the sergeants did, though. He clicked his fingers with quiet insistence, and when Reinhardt and Benfeld looked at him, he motioned their eyes over to the boy who stood partially hidden at the clearing's edge, staring blankly across to the huts and what lay around them. A quick motion to the soldiers to act normally and Reinhardt was moving before he thought of it, long strides across the hard ground, into a position where he was hidden from the boy. Then he was running, pushing past the pain in his knee, and still the boy had not moved until suddenly he leaned around the tree and saw Reinhardt, and his eyes widened. One, two steps backward, and he was turning back into the darkness of the woods, but Reinhardt was almost on him, even if the boy ran with a terrified desperation.

Hard on the boy's heels, Reinhardt followed a lurching line through the scissored prospect afforded him by the lean and slant of the trees, pinpricks of white stabbing down through the green darkness. He caught the boy quickly, as he knew he had to. There was no way otherwise, not with this knee, and this gloom. The boy's arms flailed wide as he found his way blocked. He dodged back around Reinhardt, wriggled past one hand but not the other, stumbled and fell in a tangle of limbs. Reinhardt gripped him by the neck, pushed him down, breathing heavily as the boy writhed against the wet ground, a thin keening all the sound he made as his little fingers made fists of the earth.

"It's all right," gasped Reinhardt, swallowing, chasing the right words across the edges of his memory. "*U redu. Sve je u redu.* It's all right."

Reinhardt knelt by the boy, pulled him up to his knees. He was caked with grime, and his eyes rolled left and right. "Hey, hey," said Reinhardt, taking the boy by the shoulders, feeling how desperately thin he was beneath the clothes he wore, tattered and torn to worse than rags. A hard edge showed through the back of his coat and, lifting the fabric away, Reinhardt found something long and thin wrapped in leather and thrust down the back of the boy's trousers. "What is happening? *Šta se događa?*" he asked, the Serbo-Croat coming slowly. "*Zašto se bojiš?* Why are you scared?" He unwrapped the leather, revealing a long, heavy-bladed knife, like a butcher would use. The boy's eyes fastened on it hungrily. The blade was clean, and even in the dim light beneath the trees the edge glimmered sharp.

There was a confusion of voices, angry words, and Benfeld came through the trees with a pair of Feldjaeger behind him as Reinhardt wrapped the knife back up and pushed it through his belt.

"There's two more," Benfeld said, looking blankly at the boy.

"Two what?" Something in Benfeld's flat gaze made Reinhardt draw the boy closer.

"Survivors. An elderly couple. They must have been with the boy. When he ran, they came out of the woods. Maybe his grandparents?"

Reinhardt stood, picking the boy up in his arms. He weighed nothing, just a tight bundle of skin and bones, and began to walk back through the trees. By the huts, an old lady cried out as they came out into the clearing, her arms outstretched to the boy. Reinhardt put him down, watched as she gathered him into her arms, pushing his face into her shoulder. An old man stood behind them, a tattered woolen cap riding high atop a thatch of matted gray hair, and his gnarled fist tight around the handle of an old, square suitcase, *Blagojević* stenciled in black across it.

"You speak German? *Govorite li njemački?*" The man just looked at him, his eyes flickering up to Reinhardt's face and down to his gorget, widening each time they did so, but the woman's eyes came up, and he looked at her. "What happened, here? *Šta se . . .*" he gritted his teeth, frustrated at the way the Serbo-Croat skittered away from his tongue, as the woman put her head back down, sobbing quietly into the boy's hair. "*Šta se dešava ovdje? Šta se . . .* Partisans? Ustaše? Was it the Ustaše?"

"*Molim vas, gospodine, molim vas,*" she wept, over and over. "*Milosti, gospodine, molim vas, milosti.*"

"I'm not going to hurt you," Reinhardt said in response to what he understood were pleas for mercy, but the woman just went on, darting her eyes up, then around at the old man, back to Reinhardt. She said nothing else, just repeated herself, over and over, pulling herself and the boy closer to the man, and Reinhardt had enough experience of victims to know not to badger them.

"They'll know," said Benfeld, gesturing at the three refugees where they stood in a tight huddle, the man staring at nothing, the woman pressed up against him, the boy buried in her arms.

"They probably do."

"So? Why aren't we asking them?"

"Give it time," said Reinhardt. "Anyway, aren't you the one said it wasn't any of our business?" He looked into Benfeld's cold eyes, measuring the moment the lieutenant would answer back. "We've wasted enough time. The rest of the unit's probably reached Sarajevo by now. Call in and give them our estimated time of arrival, then let's get moving. Put them in the Horch. We'll take them down to the city. Hand them over to . . . someone. I don't know."

The cars shuddered to life, bouncing heavily laden down the track where it plunged on into the forest on the far side of the clearing. The track wound through the trees for some minutes, then opened out onto the side of a hill. Like a rough-hewn template, the ground hacked as if by a crude maker's tools, slopes rose in forested blocks to broken peaks all around them. The mountains stood painted in shades of gray and green, their shadows a dark purple where they inked the land. A faint radiance outlined where the peaks ran against a dirty sky that seemed low enough to reach up and touch, like a smoke-blackened ceiling.

The driver lurched the car down the slope, Reinhardt holding himself squared against the heave and roll of the road. That faltering rhythm began to lull him, so their arrival at what must have been one of the last defense lines took him almost by surprise, the column winding through a barrier of trenches, barbed wire, sandbagged emplacements, and gun positions, a pair of tanks hull-down in their berms. The post's commander stood by the gap in the defenses, muffled up against the cold, most of his face hidden behind a thick scarf, and his eyes were hard and distant. He stopped Reinhardt's car as it came through.

"Message from your commanding officer," the man said. "Rendez-vous at the main barracks. At Kosovo Polje."

"Thanks."

"You it?"

"Am I what?"

"The last?"

"I don't know," said Reinhardt, looking back along the road as it snaked up and away across the face of the hills. "Very likely." There was no one there but Partisans now. This was the very edge, he knew. The edge of what they had taken and called theirs, now slowly furling in on itself like a leaf against the heat of a fire. All around the fringes of what they were told was a thousand-year Reich, men were standing like them, watching, looking, feeling the edges of the times they were in fold up and around them, feeling the iron weight of things still to come shifting closer and closer.

"Indian country, then," said the officer. Reinhardt looked at him strangely. "You never watched those Westerns? Before the war?" Reinhardt shook his head. "Best get your men in. It'll be dark soon."

"A moment," said Reinhardt. "In the last day or so, who has been up this road?"

"Christ knows," the commander said. "Pretty much everyone. Up and down."

"Ustaše?"

The commander considered a moment, then nodded. "Yesterday," he said. "And today. A small group of them. They came back in a roaring good mood."

"Anything else you remember?"

"I remember a lot of things, Captain, but I'm not sure I know what you're getting at."

"There was a massacre of civilians up there," said Reinhardt, pointing back up the mountain.

"So what else's new?"

Reinhardt was about to answer when he saw the futility of it, the man's disinterest, and so he said nothing, motioning his thanks and instructing the driver to carry on. The *kubelwagen* wound slowly through the lines, past a squad of laborers—from the look of them, men from a penal battalion under the guard of a Feldgendarme with his hands scrunched deep into the pockets of his coat—past the last of the barbed-wire entanglements, and then the slow lurching drive down the mountain continued. It rained shortly, the cars driving through sleet that angled out of the dim gray light as if aimed at each man. The weather-beaten span of the old Goat Bridge went by, down in its cleft, and then, atop a cliff of cracked rock blasted the color of bone, the white walls of the Ottoman fortress up on Vratnik loomed above them. Reinhardt stared at them, tension rising in him—as it had been all day—at the thought of seeing Sarajevo again.

He had been close enough, but the Feldjaeger had stayed out of the city, up behind the crumbling front lines, these past few weeks as the army retreated, slowly at first, now a rabble, and always the indiscipline to deal with. Soldiers who ran amok, soldiers who refused to obey orders, and those who melted away and formed organized bands, terrorizing the countryside when they did not simply vanish or go over to the Partisans. It was a band such as that which Reinhardt and his men had been chasing rumors of for the past few days, which had led them to that forest clearing, and of all the things he saw there, that memory of a man with a goatee beard and a girl in the arms of her father would not leave him be, and so he was again caught off guard by the sudden squeal of brakes as the car lurched to a stop, and he looked up at a stopped column of trucks.

Faintly, beneath the rumble of engines, he could hear something, and it sent a shiver down his back. It was the sound of a crowd. It was the sound of frightened women, he corrected himself. Nothing else made quite that high-pitched note, that shrill of fear or despair. Reinhardt climbed out of the car, his feet cold and stiff. With a shouted order to Priller to watch their rear, he and Benfeld began to slide down past the trucks, each one filled with men slumped bone-tired into the trucks' stiff canvas coverings, such that the sides of the vehicles made a series of humps. The road opened up a little and he could see that all traffic was stopped at the last curve into the city. Three more trucks stood swaybacked farther down the road, surrounded by a milling mass of soldiers and, here and there, clutches of civilians.

A gunshot cracked across the morning, and the crowd of people shuddered, shifted in the strange way crowds do. Another shot followed it, flatter, sharper, a pistol shot. Reinhardt frowned as he hurried on past the numb gaze of the soldiers. As long as the firing was in front of them, not behind, they were not overly concerned. He walked as fast as he carefully could, his knee sore and his feet cold and heavy until, just before he came to the head of the column, he came across a *kubelwagen* parked with a handful of Feldgendarmes in it.

"What's the holdup?"

All eyes in the *kubelwagen* swiveled toward him, dulled with a sort of lazy insouciance.

"It's the Ustaše, sir," the driver answered, eventually, a lieutenant. "They've got themselves a checkpoint at the entrance of the city. Fighting's just about emptied the countryside and everyone and his mother's trying to get into town."

"Can't say I blame them," said Reinhardt.

"Well. No. Of course not. But the Ustaše are checking everyone and everything."

"And not being particularly gentle about it," said a second lieutenant, sitting next to the driver. He had a heavy face, his jowls flushed pink by the cold.

All the men in the car laughed, all except the major in the backseat who just smiled, a sardonic curl of his lip.

"There's been a couple of executions, sir. I'm afraid the road's totally blocked."

"What've you tried?" Reinhardt looked from blank face to blank face. "To get this unblocked. To put a stop to what's going on."

"Are you new here?" This from the major, eyes narrowed, flicking back and forth between Reinhardt and Benfeld.

"Relatively," answered Reinhardt.

"Then you'll not know better."

"Than what?"

"To leave heaven to the angels, as the famous poet wrote. To leave the Ustaše alone, *Captain*." The major leaned forward. "Is there something wrong with your acknowledgment of authority?"

"None," said Reinhardt. "Sir."

"Just who the hell are you, anyway?"

"Captain Gregor Reinhardt." He fished inside his coat and pulled out his gorget. "Feldjaegerkorps." He watched the men in the *kubelwagen*, watched the way their eyes fastened on the gorget.

"Well, Captain Gregor Reinhardt, *Feldjaegerkorps*. Be patient. It'll all be over soon. Right, gentlemen?" he said, bringing the other Feldgendarmes into it, those lips pursed out into a simulacrum of a smile. "Unless of course you'd fancy having a crack at them yourself?"

And why the hell not? Reinhardt clenched his jaw, drawing in a long, slow breath of cold air. It punched through his teeth, waking him, rooting him firmly. He unfastened the catch on his holster and pushed off down the road, threading his way between soldiers, down to where the field gray of uniforms began to give way to coats in dirty browns and blacks. People clustered together in families, huddled around what little baggage they had been able to bring with them. He pushed them apart with his hands on shoulders, murmuring words of apology as he passed through until his presence began to seep into the crowd and it began to part before him, people drawing back and away. He heard the sound of raised voices, a woman crying, and a space opened up in front of him.

An old man knelt in the road, a hand clutched to a bloodied forehead. A woman stood behind him, a hand raised. A suitcase had been spilled open, linen lay crumpled across the road, and a picture lay curled and ripped in a smashed wooden frame. In front of them stood a huge man in a black uniform with a spiked club in his hand, the end a slick of blood, and something darker, heavier. Behind him a pair of trucks were parked nose to nose across the road, each manned by a black-uniformed machine gunner. More Ustaše stood here and there, some going through piles of baggage, two more standing over a handful of bodies lying by the side of the road. From the quick glance Reinhardt gave them, at least two of the bodies had had their heads crushed in by that club.

The Ustaše officer looked up as he felt the crowd go silent, and his eyes fastened on Reinhardt. He had a face whose features were clustered close together and much too small for a man of his size, as if they were an afterthought to the proportions of his frame. Little, dark eyes over a slit of a mouth, a wide nose that twitched as he looked at Reinhardt, and Reinhardt felt a stab of fear at the sight of this man, a stab that followed quick on a hard thrust of memory, from the last time Reinhardt had seen him, lumbering after him through the darkness . . .

"You're blocking the road," said Reinhardt, in German. The woman looked between them desperately as the old man put both his hands on the ground and coughed out a weak dribble of spit and blood.

"What?" said Bunda.

"The road. You are blocking it with this checkpoint."

"I'm controlling traffic. Checking for 'saboteurs' and 'infiltrators,'" he said, enunciating each word slowly, carefully, then aiming a kick at the man on the ground. His foot caught the man's arm, and he collapsed onto his shoulder. The woman cried out and tried to cover his body with hers.

"Captain, right now, I doubt any Partisan needs to come down this road disguised as a farmer in order to get into the city."

"What the fuck d'you know?" Bunda snarled, flicking his club at him, and it looked like a stick in those massive hands. Something flew off the club, spattered against Reinhardt's coat. The Ustaše drilled his eyes into Reinhardt and for a terrifying moment he thought the man had remembered him, but then his mouth curled, twitched, as if a sneer stuttered on the edge of something he suddenly knew for truth. "In any case, I don't take no orders from no Germans. We don't do that no more. We're done when we're done."

"Captain," Reinhardt said, glancing at the man's epaulettes, but the man did not let him finish.

"'Captain' nothing!" He snapped an order at his men, and two of them stepped forward, pointing back up the road as they unslung their rifles. The huge Ustašc had already turned his attention away when Reinhardt heard the safety go off Benfeld's assault rifle.

"Get back, German, wait your fucking turn," said one of the Ustaše, a thin, narrow-faced man, a scar worming its way down the side of his jaw and under his collar.

"Is there a problem, sir?" Benfeld asked, quietly, locking eyes with the Ustaša. The man's scar went white against the strained red of his face, and the air crackled between them all. One wrong move, Reinhardt thought. One wrong move would be all it would take.

"Captain," said Reinhardt, again, taking a slow step forward, keeping his tone easy, trying to make it a conversation between the two of them. "I have no real wish to embarrass you, or for this to end badly. But I will not stand idly by while you abuse these people, and if I lose men because the Partisans come down that road behind me, and I'm stuck with you in front of me, I will kill you first, then your men, before I turn back and fight them. Do I make myself understood?"

Reinhardt wondered if he did. He wondered what words penetrated the Ustaša's thick skull, that obvious sense of power and entitlement his size and uniform afforded him. He ran his tongue around his mouth, probing the gap in his back teeth where the Gestapo had knocked one out. He pulled his tongue back. More and more, he did that when he was nervous, and he hated it for the sign of weakness it was.

All three of the Ustaše fixed their eyes on Benfeld. Bunda licked his lips, worry seeping across his pinched features as he pointed at the lieutenant. "Who are you, German?"

Reinhardt turned, saw what Bunda was pointing at. It was Benfeld's armband, lying stark around the gray of his tunic.

"Feldjaegerkorps," said Benfeld. Reinhardt's own armband was under the sleeve of his coat.

"*Feldjaegerkorps*?" said Bunda, as if trying the word for the first time, and staring now at Benfeld's assault rifle, at the curved banana magazine, as if he had never seen one, then more closely at their gorgets. "Not Feldgendarmerie?"

"*Ni je sa nama*, Bunda."

Reinhardt twisted, seeing the major standing behind him, looking at the Ustaše.

"I think you should listen to the captain," the Feldgendarme said.

For a long, long moment, all was frozen, but the Ustaše nodded, finally. Reinhardt inclined his head in a gesture he hoped the other man would find courteous. The Ustaša's face twitched once more, and then he was snarling orders at his men. They heaved themselves into their trucks and lurched them off to the sides of the road. Bunda gave Reinhardt a last, long, venomous look, then took himself to one side, glowering as, around him, the crowd began moving step by shaken step down into the city. One or two walked hesitantly over to the bodies. A man darted out from the crowd to help the old man to his feet as the old lady shoved what few possessions they had back into the broken suitcase, pausing, turning, and daring a quick nod of thanks at Reinhardt before she hurried away.

The major watched them go. He was a slim man in a good leather overcoat belted tight around his waist, his eyes swiveling back and forth as the crowd moved past, then settling on Bunda. "Not wise to rile a bear when his blood's up."

"That particular bear's blood's always up."

The major raised his eyebrows. "You know Bunda, then?"

"I know the type," said Reinhardt, keeping his answer short and his eyes on the major. "Lieutenant, let's get the column moving." Benfeld slid back up through the crowd.

"*The heart of man by griefs oppressed, in life's storms stricken sore, can never hope to gain true rest until it throbs no more,*" the major said, suddenly, the flow of his words at odds with the way he stabbed his eyes across the people as they shuffled past.

"Johann Salis," said Reinhardt without thinking as a window in his mind opened. He saw his father's study, the shelves heavy with books, and his father's lined face shone up happily at Reinhardt from where he sat in his armchair, an old book of poetry open on his lap.

"A learned man," murmured the major, one eyebrow tilted at Reinhardt. "Johann Salis, indeed."

If it was an invitation to say more, Reinhardt's silence declined it, savoring instead the umber lines of that small memory as it faded.

"So, have you Feldjaegerkorps chaps come to save us, Reinhardt?" the major asked, turning, eyebrows raised. He moved toward Reinhardt with the stiff-backed walk of a martinet. "We could always use the help. Don't think otherwise, Captain."

"I'm sure we'll do our best, sir."

"Where have you come from, then?"

"Up from Montenegro, most recently."

"Dreadful place," muttered the major. "Nothing but bloody mountains. Had much trouble?"

"Some. We came across a massacre this morning. Quite a recent one."

"Really? Doesn't surprise me at all. Those forests aren't fit for man nor beast, now. Not with the Partisans crawling through them like bloody termites."

"'*Ni je sa nama.*'"

"What?"

"'They are not with us.' That's what you said to the Ustaše."

"I did?" The Feldgendarme's mouth shrugged itself into a lazy curl as he glanced at Reinhardt. "Well, self-evidently, you are not."

Reinhardt's *kubelwagen* came to a stop next to him. He waved the rest of the cars on. The other three *kubelwagens* passed by, then the Horch, with Priller up on the machine gun, and the three refugees huddled tight and low on the rear bench. Bunda saw them as they went by, and he straightened, stamping into the road.

"*WAIT!*" he yelled, hammering a fist on the Horch's hood, shouting at his men who gathered around him.

"Who are they?" shouted the Ustaša with the scar, his rifle poking into the car at the refugees. Benfeld and several other Feldjaeger jumped out of their cars, unslinging their weapons.

"*Captain,*" Reinhardt called.

"Answer me. *Who are they?*"

"Refugees," answered Reinhardt.

"What I tell you about spies?" spat Bunda.

"Them? A couple of old peasants and a boy?"

"Partisans can be anywhere. Be anyone."

"They can be. But not these ones."

"Yes?" asked the major, coming to stand next to them. The woman had begun to cry, clasping the boy to her, rocking and repeating *"molim vas, molim vas"* over and over. The man just sat straight, his case on his lap, and his bird-bright eyes fixed on the red tumble of the city's roofs, just ahead. "What makes you so sure? Where did you find them?"

"They survived a massacre. That one I mentioned to you."

"Did they, by God," said the major. "Lucky for them you came along when you did."

Bunda's face had gone blank, and then his mouth twisted as if around something foul, and he stepped back. "Massacre? Where?"

Reinhardt shook his head, puzzled by Bunda's change in tone and stance. "I don't know where, exactly. I am taking them into the city to find help for them."

"Is the German Army a humanitarian organization now, Captain?" drawled the major.

"You take a risk, German," grated Bunda, his eyes fixed on the refugees. "You take a risk bringing them here. You embarrass me. You will learn . . ." He stopped himself, his lip curling, and then was gone. Reinhardt watched him storm away, the angled frame of his shoulders hunched tight around his fury. He roared an order at the Ustaše, and then they were all piling into their vehicles, thumping them down the hill with clouds of black diesel belching behind them.

"You'll learn, Captain, that if you're going to do well here, then you're going to have to do better with them," the major said, pointing at the retreating Ustaše. "Call it a fact of life. And with that, the very best of luck to you, Captain." The major smiled, although his eyes remained hard and focused. He looked at the refugees, and the old woman cringed before him, the boy staring fixedly at him from the crook of her arm. "Want me to take care of them for you? I know where to take them."

"I've an idea as well," answered Reinhardt. "Anyway, they're my responsibility."

"A man of conscience." The major smiled as his car pulled up.

Reinhardt watched him go, the silence sudden.

"Bloody chain dogs," Benfeld muttered, eyes heavy on the Feldgendarmes as they drove past. He looked at Reinhardt. "Did you see their badges? They're from a penal battalion."

Reinhardt had not seen and did not particularly care. He looked at the refugees. "What did you see up there?" he asked, quietly. "*Što ste . . . vid . . . vidjeli?*" But the woman just repeated her litany, and the boy said nothing. The man turned his head slowly, his cap perched at an absurd angle and height atop his hair. He looked at Reinhardt, as if seeing him for the first time, then looked down at his gorget, and the man's eyes widened and he blinked once, then looked straight ahead.

A last turn, and then they were driving past the dirty froth of the Miljacka where its course forced the road close against the bone-white cliffs. The road passed underneath the banded walls of the Town Hall—the Rathaus—in the cellars of which Reinhardt had spent those several days being questioned by the Gestapo after the affair with Verhein, through the Oriental warren of Bentbaša before curling around the northern end of Baščaršija, the old Ottoman square with its fountain, artisans, coffee shops, and mosques. Crusted dark and filthy in the shadow of the Rathaus, snow and ice still lay heaped high to either side of the road and filled the tram tracks. Buildings had collapsed, doors hung open, and much of the glass in the windows was smashed. The crowd of refugees bunched up as they came to Baščaršija and began spilling off to the side, joining a much larger crowd that milled across the square.

Reinhardt stopped his vehicles on the square and walked back to Benfeld's car to order him and the others on to the Kosovo Polje barracks on the far side of town. He watched them go, then looked out at the tidal swell of people across the square, ordering the civilians out of the Horch. They stood, shaken and uncertain by the side of the road, staring out across the mass of heads that shifted across Baščaršija.

They were new to the city, he could see. They would have been blinking and wide-eyed at the best of times, and these were not them.

"Wait here," he said, as the Horch drove away. "I will see if I can bring you some help."

He walked carefully across the square's icy cobbles, searching for something he had only heard of, that the city's humanitarian organizations had a presence here on the square to offer what little help they could provide to the refugees. The city was choked with them now. Winter and the heavy fighting of the last few weeks along the approaches to Sarajevo had emptied the countryside. Those who had not fled to the Partisans had washed up here, and here was precious little. The people he passed seemed listless, ground down by the war and the cold. Many stood in lines, waiting for he knew not what: a ration ticket, perhaps, maybe shelter, a chance to be examined by a doctor but with no hope of treatment. Despite the cold, the smell on the square was heavy and sour with sweat and filth and mud. The smell of a Balkan winter.

Their desperation and, if he was honest, his loneliness had sunk into him, he knew, these past few months. He missed Koenig and the others. Even if not much had ever come of what they wanted to do, the company of like-minded men was a valuable thing. The Feldjaeger were a tight-knit unit, but they were hard, hard men, most of them, and individualists to a great degree. They reminded him, Reinhardt knew, of himself when he was a stormtrooper on the Western Front in the first war, and God knew he had no real wish to be that man again.

Despite what he saw, he realized he was happy to be back as he climbed up onto one of the benches around the fountain so as to be able to see better. Labyrinthine, claustrophobic, a place of hidden secrets and beauty, Sarajevo was all that and more, but it was the place where he had awoken to himself after too many years, and he found he had missed it more than he thought he would.

He spotted what he was after not far from the café where he used to take his coffee. When he reached the old coffee shop he saw it was closed up and the windowpanes showed nothing but darkness inside, just the faint outline of the ovens where the owner had once stooped over his big, black kettles. Next to it, a sign on a tattered white banner indicated an office of Napredak, the Croatian cultural organization. He eased his way through the crowd outside, worming his way into the front office. The place reeked of damp, and the sweet odor of sickness. Behind a rickety wooden desk, a woman in coat, hat, and gloves was taking down a list of particulars from a refugee. She stopped what she was doing as he came in, looking at him wordlessly like they all were.

"I brought in three people," Reinhardt said to her. "Two elderly people, and a boy. I found them in the forest. Can you help them?"

The woman blinked back at him. "Help them?" She swallowed. "Help them," she repeated. She looked around the room, back at him.

Reinhardt could understand her, but he had no time for this. He had other duties, for which he was late, but he had assumed a measure of responsibility for those people and he would do what it took to meet it. "I have three people who need help. Can you help them?"

"We all of us here need help, soldier," someone said. He did not see who, but that was another indication of how this city had changed. Before, no one would have dared speak so to a German soldier.

"Is there someone else I can talk to?"

"Someone else?" The people in the room shifted at the shrill tone in the woman's voice. It had a crack running through it, Reinhardt could hear, and madness squirmed within it. "There's no one else. There's only us."

"What is going on here?"

Reinhardt turned. Another woman had come into the room, dressed in a long black coat, with a spill of gray-blond hair across her shoulders. He stared at her, for a moment speechless, as if he had seen a ghost, and as he watched her, he saw recognition bloom in her eyes, too.

"Captain . . . Captain *Reinhardt*?"

"Mrs. Vukić."

Reinhardt straightened, pulled off his glove, and offered his hand. She took it; they stared at each other, then seemed to remember at the same time they had an audience. She blinked and stepped back, releasing his hand. "I will deal with the captain, Anica," she said to the woman at the desk. "This way," she motioned, showing him back outside. He breathed deeply, pulling that chill down as deep as it would go. She came out with him, pulling her coat tighter around her. People waiting in line stared at them, and there was again that moment of silence between them.

"Captain. It is . . . You have been well?"

"Thank you, Mrs. Vukić. Quite well. Yourself?"

"Busy," she said, with a flicker of a smile. "Busier all the time."

"It is valuable work," Reinhardt said after a moment, leaving the *at least* unsaid, but she looked at him quizzically a second, as if she strained after words she thought she had heard.

"What help do you need, Captain?"

"I picked up three people. I found them. It seems they survived a massacre. Up in the forest."

"A massacre? And . . . ?" She stopped, pointing at his coat. He looked down at a smear of something dark and red, and remembered Bunda's club, the bloodied muck at the end of it.

Reinhardt shook his head, scraping at the stain. "No. God, no," he said, terrified suddenly she would think him responsible. "This is something else. When we arrived it was all over. It must have happened at least a day ago. Only an elderly couple, and a boy, seem to have survived it. They haven't said anything of what happened. They've said very little at all, in fact. I don't even know if they're related. But I wanted to make sure they got whatever help there was. I realize that . . ." He tailed off, again, and they both stared at each other, but it was the milling helplessness across the square they both saw.

"You did the right thing, Captain. Perhaps you will take me to them?"

"This way, then," he said, leading her off across Baščaršija. It was starting to snow, just a little, flakes wending convoluted patterns through the air. They picked their way through the crowds, and whereas the people parted for his uniform, they washed across her path. Many knew her. Hands reached out, people stepped toward her, her name was called. She moved slowly, taking each hand offered, touching each person's shoulder who stepped in front of her, answering the names of those who called her, a gentle word here and there, but she did not stop, and they did not try overmuch to stop her from going.

They broke into open space at the edge of the square and paused a moment. She looked back across Baščaršija. "They are more and more each day," she said

"It is fortunate for them you are here," he said, remembering, suddenly, that her first name was Suzana.

She smiled, wanly. "Prosvjeta for the Serbs, Merhamet for the Muslims, Napredak for the Croats. They were supposed to be organizations dedicated to cultural enlightenment. Some charity work for the communities they served. But not this. Not . . . scraping together aid rations and handouts. But the city's got almost nothing, and the Ustaše. Well . . ."

"They're getting worse?" Vukić hesitated, then gave a little nod. Reinhardt shook his head. "As if that were possible," he said, almost to himself, remembering that checkpoint and Bunda's appalling assurance that what he was doing was not only right, but sanctioned.

Her eyes were very blue as she looked at him, as if she weighed him against some measure of her own. Her face hardened, although if at him he could not say. "It's possible," she said, at last. "They sent someone from Zagreb to, as they said, 'take things in hand' down here. His name's Vjekoslav Luburić. They call him Maks Luburić."

"I have heard of him."

"Well, it's all true. All of it. And more."

She shivered, from the cold or from their words he could not say, and he realized how tired she looked. Her hair was still blond, but shot through with gray now, and there were lines at the corners of her eyes and mouth. Her shoulders were hunched round and tight beneath her coat, worn shiny at the elbows and waist.

"You are busy, and it's cold. I must not detain you longer." She smiled again, briefly, but there was warmth in it and her face lightened. "Here are the people I mentioned to you." Vukić greeted each of them, and she knelt to put her hand on the boy's shoulder, his head turning out from the old woman's embrace slowly.

"Thank you again, Captain," she said. She looked at him and offered her hand. "It was . . . good to see you."

Her hand was small and very cold. He pulled off his gloves and offered them to her, very conscious of the eyes of his driver and the people he had brought in. "Please. If they don't fit you, perhaps someone else could use them?"

She smiled again and took the gloves from him. "You were very kind to me, Captain. I have never forgotten that. Thank you for these." She turned away, leading the people down into the square. He watched her go, running her words over in his mind. Vukić stopped, turned back. "Captain, perhaps, if you have time—perhaps you will tell me how it all ended. That investigation. Marija's death. I never knew in the end if you . . . found the person."

Reinhardt frowned. "No one ever told you?" She shook her head, and, with a last small wave of her hand, she was gone, her arm around the boy. Before they vanished back into the crowd, the boy turned, looking back over his shoulder. Their gazes locked, and Reinhardt felt a shiver as he remembered the two boys from his nightmare of that winter field at Kragujevac. Moving without really thinking, Reinhardt took the boy's knife wrapped in its leather, and offered it back. The boy took it, a quick, firm movement, blinked, and they faded back into the crowd, and when Reinhardt turned back to his car Bunda was standing behind him.

Up close, Bunda was enormous, bigger than he had seemed at the checkpoint. His bloodied staff was stuffed behind his belt. He was looking at Vukić as she moved through the crowd; then his little eyes flickered shut and when they opened he was looking at Reinhardt.

"'Ello again," he smiled. Reinhardt said nothing. "You know, I thought you looked familiar. And now I've remembered." Reinhardt still said nothing. The man engendered some kind of primeval reflex within him. Fight or flight, though neither was possible. So he stayed very still, just pushed his tongue hard into that gap in his teeth. "Captain Reinhardt. In't it?" He looked at Reinhardt's gorget, smiled again, reached out and touched it. Just touched it, but Reinhardt could feel the massive weight behind that blunt finger. "You caused us a bit of bother back in the day, you know. And you didn't even say good-bye when it was all over."

"You've come up in the world, Bunda, I'm glad to see," said Reinhardt. It was the first thing that came into his head, some way of pulling Bunda away from whatever path his little mind was set on following. "Police patrolman to Ustaše captain. Congratulations."

"You 'ad no right to do what you did up there, Reinhardt. Embarrassing me in front of my men. In front of them people." He curled his finger where it rested on the gorget, the Ustaše's cracked fingernail making the faintest of scrapes across the metal. "And you got no right to be getting mixed up with the likes of Mrs. Vukić. She's fucking royalty compared to you. She's ours. What you want with 'er, anyway?"

"Something I can do for you, Bunda?"

"You can drop dead, is what," the giant growled.

"Well, miracles can always happen, but if they do it'll be a long time after an Ustaše gives an order to a German soldier." Reinhardt could see his words moving turgidly through the Ustaše's mind, so he took the opportunity to slide out of his way. "If that's all, then, I must be going." The words felt ridiculous, formulaic and polite, but Reinhardt could think of no other way of getting out and past him.

"Something you need to understand, Reinhardt," said Bunda, his eyes following him. "This ain't the place it used to be. There's no rules now but what we make. Ain't no gettin' around or away from that. Ain't no gettin' in the way of it, neither."

"I will bear that in mind, Bunda," replied Reinhardt, with a lightness of tone he did not feel.

"You get the one warning."

"And that was it?" Bunda just stared back at him as Reinhardt tapped the driver on the shoulder, and the car moved away slowly, its wheels skidding on the cobbles.

4

The *kubelwagen* wound its way carefully down King Alexander Street, straight through the old town and on into the newer, Austrian-built sections. The road was treacherous, and the driver was forced to hold the *kubelwagen* to a juddering path down a pair of ruts carved through remnants of black and filthy ice, through the tears and potholes in its surface, the tires squelching through a slough of snow and sludge.

Despite the lateness of the hour, one side of the road was filled with soldiers, thousands of them it seemed, marching or standing or sitting in lines that threaded toward the train station, and evacuation. On the other, people struggled across sidewalks humped with sheets and blocks of ice and snow, or chunks of stone and rubble, walking splay-legged to avoid slipping, often bent almost double under heavy loads. Clothes were bundled tight around their bodies, scarves and hoods around faces that, to Reinhardt's eyes, seemed pinched and drawn with cold and hunger, and he remembered something he had read once. Something about how in winter the cold kept the rich in but drove the poor out, if only to keep moving to stay warm.

The road opened out as it passed in front of the State House, the ruts widening to several separate series that merged and divided, like train tracks. In the small wood across from the State House, several small fires gleamed, smoke drifting heavily through the trees, the shapes of people clustered close around them. Past the wood, the Marijin Dvor intersection was packed with people, a black mass of them, and the car slowed, allowing Reinhardt to see what it was that held them there.

It was bodies. Dozens of them, turning slowly from the cords from which they hung. Hanging from trees, from lampposts and signposts, some dangling from windows. Men, mostly, but a few women as well. Braziers and lights painted the bodies in a ghastly play of orange and black that made grinning masks of the faces of the corpses, masks that seemed to mock the onlookers as if with knowledge only the dead could comprehend. Ustaše ringed the scene, and the tension of the crowd was palpable, wives and children yearning after the bodies of those who were so recently husbands and fathers. Reinhardt exchanged a glance with his driver, and then the car was into open space again, the long, white walls of Kosovo Polje barracks looming out of a rising mist. The sentry at the guardpost, muffled up tight against the cold, waved them through the barrier and into a vehicle park.

The vehicles parked around the walls were dusted with thin limbs and lines of clean, white snow from some recent fall, but the courtyard was an expanse of muddy grit across which the *kubelwagen* slid. Reinhardt and the driver heaved their baggage out of the car, mud caking the soles of their boots as they trudged heavily over to the entrance with the most signs outside it. He ran his eyes down them as he knocked the muck from his boots, found the sign to Feldjaegerkorps operations, and began their walk into the labyrinthine corridors of the huge barracks.

The corridors were gloomy and very cold, the ceilings and windows high, representative of the architecture of another era. Many of the windows were smashed or cracked, panes of glass covered in tape or hidden behind stepped piles of sandbags. The building echoed to the sound of hurrying men, shouted orders, the clack and clatter of typewriters and teleprinters, the jangle of telephones. They found the operations center, eventually. It was a huge room, the walls dominated by great expanses of maps and the floor covered in tables around which stood or sat dozens of soldiers and officers. The air was full of the noise of conversations, orders, the staccato rhythms of one-way exchanges on telephones and radios, and thick with cigarette smoke and the smell of bad food, wet clothes, and unwashed men. A lieutenant pointed them to a door across the room, beyond which was Feldjaeger operations.

"Reinhardt. There you are," said Colonel Scheller from behind his desk. He was frowning at a map of the city. "You're just in time. Staff meeting. I was about to send a search party out after you." He waved Reinhardt to a chair. "Cigarette? So?" he asked, as Reinhardt lit up, then sat.

"I got told today that everything east of the last line is 'Indian country,'" Reinhardt said. Scheller snorted, gave a wry smile. "We made our last sweep here," said Reinhardt, pointing out his unit's patrol route on the map with his cigarette, "and we found . . . something. Not sure what to make of it."

"Those deserters?"

Reinhardt's mouth twisted around a mouthful of smoke. "Could be. I just don't know. Three dead bodies. Probably German. Evidence of at least two units. It could be them."

"Frenchie mentioned something else?"

"A massacre of civilians. Refugees, by the looks of them. Executed by firing squad."

"The deserters?"

"Who knows, sir," sighed Reinhardt.

"Well, if it was them, they're on their own, now. Army command has ordered no more movements east of . . . east of . . ." he said, peering at the map. "Ahh, bloody hell, I can't get my tongue around these names. Here," he stabbed a fingernail on the map. "Donje something-or-other. From there"—he traced an arc south across the main road to the east, along which Reinhardt had arrived in the city that afternoon—"to here." A point to the south. "Everything east of that line is, as you say, Indian country."

"So that's it, then," said Reinhardt, quietly, watching the smoke spiral up from his cigarette.

"That, as you say, is it. And Frenchie tells me you've been scaring the local wildlife?"

Reinhardt started, pulling his mind back from thoughts again of that girl in her father's arms, and the man with the goatee. "Sorry, sir?"

Scheller grinned. "Barely five minutes into the city, and you've upset our staunch allies."

"The Ustaše?"

"None other." He waved a piece of paper. "Official complaint about your behavior."

"Bloody hell," murmured Reinhardt. "They didn't waste much time."

"No," said Scheller, chewing softly on the left of his bottom lip, as was his habit when thinking. "There's a lot going on, it would seem. Come!" he called, as there came a knock on the door. Two Feldjaeger officers stepped inside, the other captains in the unit, Lainer and Morten, together with a pair of Feldgendarmes—one of them a general, Reinhardt saw, as he straightened up—followed by an army captain.

The general was squat, almost as wide as he was tall, with the pugnacious set and build of a bulldog, all chest and a flat, belligerent face and narrow little eyes with which he blinked around the room. The other Feldgendarme with him, a major, had an altogether different look: tall, slim, slicked-back hair, but a nervous slant to his features as he looked askance at the general, as if expecting him to make a mistake or say something wrong.

"Gentlemen, this is General Herzog, commander of military police forces in the Sarajevo area." There were murmurs of greeting, exchanges of names that the general took in with a flat, expressionless face. "And these are Major Neuffer, who has been assigned as our liaison officer with the Feldgendarmerie, and Captain Langenkamp, army liaison to the Ustaše. I know it is late, but now that the whole unit is in the city I have asked the general here to give us his assessment of the situation, as it is his men we will be supporting. He has kindly agreed. General," said Scheller, indicating chairs drawn up around a low table, "please, be seated."

"Well, you are all welcome to Sarajevo," said Herzog, blinking his little eyes around the table as an orderly slipped into the room with a tray of sandwiches and coffee. "Not that I asked for you. But you're welcome all the same, and we'll find you gainful employment, don't you worry. Just don't go abusing that vaunted Feldjaegerkorps authority around me and my men. I'll not stand for it. You'll forgive my bluntness—actually, I couldn't care less if you forgive it or not—but I do believe honesty and forthrightness are the best ways to start a new relationship."

Reinhardt glanced around at Scheller and the captains, wondering if they felt as nonplussed as he did.

"That said, I want us all on the same page regarding the situation because we're going to be, pardon the expression, fucking busy. Gentlemen, our position here in Sarajevo is precarious. Over thirty-five thousand German troops, and many tens of thousands of our allies, are all but surrounded. We have one functioning railway on which to move, which leads north, through Visoko to Zenica, and on to the border with Croatia, where it is coming under threat from the Soviet forces massing around Belgrade. The line south to the coast was cut when the Partisans took Mostar on the fourteenth of February. The Partisan front lines have been reported as close as seven miles away . . ."

Reinhardt listened with only one ear, chewing softly on a sandwich with an all-but-tasteless piece of meat and cheese inside, thinking of that man with the goatee. What was it about him? What instinct was it stirring? Was it being back here, he wondered, sipping black coffee, and wishing for a cup of the Turkish brew he used to drink on Baščaršija? That conversation with Benfeld rattled around inside his head. Could murder still mean anything, after all that had happened? Because it had been committed, up there, in that forest. Just as it had been committed in places like it across the sweep of the continent. As always, his mind shied away from thoughts like that, unwilling, unable to comprehend what had been done, what they had witnessed, these past years, but here it had been done under his nose, almost. What chance, he wondered, of doing something about it . . . ?

". . . therefore, the evacuation by rail is our priority and is proceeding day and night, with troops being moved up to the station on a rolling basis. Finally, in addition to the Partisan forces massing around the city, within Sarajevo itself there is increasing Partisan activity—sabotage, espionage—all of which is being managed by cells of operatives. These cells are allegedly under the control of a senior Communist Party operative known only as 'Valter.' He is, for want of a better word, a cowardly and cunning son of a bitch whom I would like to catch and string up by his balls. However, this touches upon our Ustaše allies. For that, I hand over to Captain Langenkamp."

At mention of the Ustaše, Reinhardt stuffed his musing to one side and paid attention. Langenkamp had, perhaps, seen just a little too much of the Ustaše. He sat very still in his chair, hands folded on the table in front of him, and spoke very quietly as if from very far away. As if he sought to put distance between himself and the world.

"The Ustaše are in a most delicate position. Their hold over Bosnia is all but gone, and they are now concentrating their forces on defending the borders of Croatia itself. In addition, the Ustaše are increasingly affected by the emergence of factions that are forming around various territories, each led or held by a particular personality. For instance, the Ustaše in Sarajevo are under the control of General Vjekoslav Luburić. General Luburić is renowned as quite single-minded in his devotion to the Ustaše cause, and unmerciful to those he considers weak in its defense, or who have betrayed or compromised it. He has around him a coterie of six to seven men, his lieutenants, men like Svetozar Trpić, Jovan Buzdek, and Ante Putković." Reinhardt frowned and shifted at the mention of that name. "They exercise total impunity in how they run the city. Putković, in particular, is responsible for security in the city itself, and for the recent wave of arrests, on no particular grounds, of dozens of people. He is actually known by his *nom de guerre* of The Gambler, as he carries a set of dice that he uses to determine what punishment is meted out to prisoners or suspects. Just today, there was a mass execution of some eighty people, with the bodies hung up in the trees around the Marijin Dvor area.

"The Ustaše's capacity as an effective fighting force in Sarajevo is very low. It is questionable the extent to which they are still following orders from Zagreb in any meaningful way. As they grow weaker, they seem to be growing more desperate and out of control in the way they govern what little territory is left to them, with an increase in the use of terror, corruption, and brutality." Those ought to have been the Ustaše watchwords, thought Reinhardt—to go along with their ridiculous triptych of "knife, revolver, bomb"—and most certainly this Langenkamp had seen a little too much of all that. Reinhardt could see it in the man's eyes and the rigid set of the tendons in his neck. Ustaše liaison. Reinhardt could imagine few jobs more distressing and degrading.

"I would add one piece of intelligence. It seems a purge may be about to take place within the Ustaše in Sarajevo. There are rumors that some of the more senior Ustaše have disappeared, possibly deserted, and General Luburić is allegedly furious, suspecting treason and betrayal."

"Nevertheless," Herzog interrupted, impatience writ large across his boxer's face, "despite their weaknesses and internal divisions, they remain our allies. Our *allies*, gentlemen," he said, rolling his spiky little eyes around the group. "As our allies, they have ruled out any kind of accommodation with the Partisans, and the two groups seem set on a fight to the death, with no quarter being asked or given. The Ustaše are paranoid about Partisan infiltration into the city, and regularly conduct sweeps and arrests in an effort to break up the Partisan cells and capture or kill Valter and his commanders. They are utterly obsessed with him.

"And for good reason. Make no mistake, gentlemen, Partisan infiltration is very real. Those fuckers are everywhere. You have all heard by now, I think, of the rather audacious coup they carried out recently. The theft of the army's defense plans, two days ago, from right out of the locked safe where they were held, in this very building."

"Hats off to whoever did it," said Scheller, to a general murmur from the assembled officers. "That was a hell of an operation."

Herzog frowned at Scheller, though he nodded. "We tried to keep it a secret, and officially it still is. However, too many people got questioned, and too many things now need changing as a result of the theft, and it has been chaos. To make matters worse, the officer in charge of drafting the plans, Colonel Wedel, committed suicide yesterday, increasing the rumors and worsening the confusion. Back to you, Langenkamp."

"Our dealings with the Ustaše proceed on a delicate basis," Langenkamp continued, as if Herzog had never spoken. "With the evacuation, we are under pains to ensure they do not take the wrong impression, and believe we are abandoning them completely. That would lead to unpredictable consequences for our troops here, and across Croatia. In addition, Ustaše activity in the city, even if it is causing problems for our occupation and evacuation, has been given an implicit seal of approval by the general officer commanding in Sarajevo, General Kathner. Lastly, for your information, I have a counterpart in the Ustaše, a Captain Marković. Should you not be able to locate me, you may request his assistance. Thank you," he finished, ending as he had started, with his hands folded on the table and his eyes focused somewhere else.

There was silence after Langenkamp had finished, and Reinhardt wondered whether any of the Feldjaeger had an inkling of what awaited them out there, with the Ustaše. "Captain Langenkamp," he said, leaning into the silence, feeling the weight of Herzog's eyes boring into him. "You mentioned an Ustaša called Ante Putković. I wonder, did he used to be in the Sarajevo police?" Langenkamp nodded.

"Friend of yours, Reinhardt?" asked Scheller, eyebrows raised over the rim of his coffee cup.

"Not exactly."

"So you'll not be wanting to run into him again, I'd think?" Reinhardt's mouth opened, but he did not know what to say to that. "Hold that thought, then, Reinhardt. Let's listen to Major Neuffer. Major, please," said Scheller, indicating he had the floor. With his smoothed-back hair, wide cheeks, and a pinched mouth stitched across his narrow chin, Neuffer suddenly reminded Reinhardt of no one so much as the old Kaiser, Wilhelm II.

"Thank you, Colonel. I would like to take this opportunity to welcome you and your men to the city, and say that we are counting on your assistance to maintain order within the ranks. We are very happy to have you here with us," he said, though he looked, like Herzog, anything but happy. The major went on longer in that vein, a formalistic and formulaic litany, with only a few real pieces of information and intelligence sprinkled through it until Herzog grunted at him to "fucking get on with it." With flushed cheeks, Neuffer informed them that the Feldjaeger were to be deployed at certain hot spots, such as the train station and the main barracks here in Kosovo Polje.

"Colonel, if I may," Reinhardt spoke up. Scheller nodded. "General, sir, what is the role of the German forces in maintaining law and order within the city itself?"

"I would like to reiterate what Captain Langenkamp has said about the Ustaše. They remain our allies, and as such, it is our duty to assist them or, failing that, to not hinder them in their operations. Our responsibility is to ensure that our men maintain good discipline pending their evacuation, and to put the fear of God into them if they step out of line. Except in matters of strategy, and in operational security, and in those touching directly upon our troops, we have no authority over the Ustaše."

"Meaning, sir?"

"Meaning that law and order in the city is the almost exclusive preserve of the Ustaše."

"'Almost' exclusive? Meaning . . . ?"

Herzog frowned, clearly annoyed by Reinhardt's questioning. "Meaning we leave them the fuck alone."

"Meaning we leave them alone to do whatever damn thing they want?" asked Reinhardt, who had been irked by the general's dismissive profanity into slipping one of his own into his words.

Herzog's eyes narrowed. "And remind me just who the hell you are?"

"Reinhardt, sir."

Herzog turned his squinty eyes on Neuffer, who nodded. "Reinhardt. Right. Colonel," said Herzog, addressing Scheller, "this is precisely what we were afraid of. I must bring up the actions of Captain Reinhardt earlier this evening, about which we have received a written complaint from the Ustaše, and a report from one of our own people."

"Who would that be?"

"An officer who observed Captain Reinhardt's dealings with the Ustaše."

Scheller cocked an inquiring eyebrow at Reinhardt. "There was a Feldgendarmerie unit there at that checkpoint earlier this evening, sir."

"And what cause for complaint did Captain Reinhardt give, sir?" Scheller asked.

Herzog's mouth moved, and Reinhardt could not tell if he found the question distasteful, or the whole thing funny. "Captain Reinhardt got in the way of things, shall we say. The natural order of events." Scheller cocked his head, inviting Herzog to say more.

Neuffer shifted uncomfortably. "If we might return to the matter at hand . . ." He paused, as if inviting Herzog to say more, but the general remained silent. "Such unilateral actions as Captain Reinhardt's, going directly against the wishes of the Ustaše, are detrimental to our smooth relations and operations in this city. I have been asked for your assurance this will not happen again."

"Quite," said Scheller, his chin sunk on his chest. He looked up at Herzog from beneath his lowered brows, looking calm and reasonable, but those who knew him—and Reinhardt was starting to read his moods—could see the annoyance that was on the verge of turning to anger. Scheller was, as Reinhardt had learned in these past months, a man intensely loyal to his subordinates. He expected a great deal of them, but he gave a great deal back in terms of trust and responsibility and freedom of action. "We must all hope Captain Reinhardt, and indeed any of my men, not be faced with such situations."

"Too fucking right," Herzog grunted. "A rule of thumb, gentlemen. Think of it as colors. Our jurisdiction begins and ends with those in field gray. We have no authority over those dressed in black. And on that, I'll leave you to it, shall I? Neuffer's your man if you need anything. Best of luck and all that," he said rising, tugging his tunic straight, and then something seemed to change in the way he stood, and spoke, as if he suddenly stood in focus. "This is no picnic, gentlemen, and although it may seem like the worst of times, this is a prelude. Sometimes, you know things have to get bad, sometimes really bad, before they get better. These, gentlemen," he said, jutting his chin at the Feldjaeger, "these are such times, and this is such a place. When they look back, they'll look at this place, these times, and they'll wonder at the caliber of the men who lived and fought through it all." Herzog paused at the door as Neuffer held it open, looking back at them. "And with that, gentlemen, I wish you luck."

"Right, lads," said Scheller when they were alone. "Morten, be a good chap and reach that bottle out from the cabinet." There was quiet as Morten poured four glasses of brandy, and then they sat back, lighting cigarettes. Each of them, it was clear, was thinking of General Herzog. Reinhardt exchanged a glance with Morten, who raised an eyebrow as he glanced at the door. "Here's what I want. I want us all out of this city intact. I don't want anyone lost if we can help it. Not for this dump—you'll excuse the reference," he said, nodding to Reinhardt, who raised his glass back, "and not for these psychopathic Ustaše, either. So, we back up the Feldgendarmerie where they ask us to, but particularly at the train station. Things can sometimes get out of hand there, apparently."

"That's to be expected, sir. Men can go a bit crazy so close to a way out," said Morten.

"Quite. I want a few of our own patrols out, as well. I don't know how long we'll be here for, and I want our own eyes and ears and feel for the ground. Lainer, you take care of that, will you?

"Reinhardt, I'm taking you off operations. I want you on the staff here, and I want you liaising with army command. You know the city. I want your experience at hand if Lainer's and Morten's boys call in, or need intelligence."

"Sir," began Reinhardt. He looked at the other two captains. Both of them were, as was normal for the Feldjaeger, highly decorated and immensely experienced combat officers. Lainer was given to sporting a rather rakish appearance with his hair permanently combed back from a widow's peak, and Morten was somewhat piratical with a patch over his left eye. It had not been easy to win the respect of these men. Reinhardt was still not sure he had it, feeling that they all looked sideways at him, wondering if they thought him weak, or not tough enough, and sometimes the urge to tell stories of his days as a storm-trooper in the first war—to show them he was once as young and strong and hard as them—was powerful, but he stopped himself, not wanting to be seen as someone living in the past. Not some old man holding up the bar with stories from a bygone era. "If it's because of the Ustaše . . ."

"It is and it isn't, Reinhardt. I'm relying on you to make sure we navigate these waters. Which means, I want you focused, here. In fact, get yourself off. I want your after-action report on your patrol on my desk before midnight. Then get some sleep. You're on duty as of oh six hundred tomorrow morning."

5

For most of that following morning, Reinhardt's time was devoted to operational details of the Feldjaeger's deployment, liaising with the army commanders in charge of the ongoing evacuation. The Feldjaeger were deployed in the train station for the most part, where their reputation preceded them and where trouble had died away considerably since their arrival. They had been perceived as being so successful that calls had come in for their presence from several other areas where soldiers were billeted or barracked, and where tension was rising high as men's thoughts bent ever more sharply toward their seat on the train, and when it would be.

Dealing with those requests, rotating the Feldjaeger in and out for rest, was tricky but rewarding, and Reinhardt found his knowledge of Sarajevo coming back in useful as he directed Feldjaeger units around the city, and further afield, into the rear areas and out along the roads leading west and north toward Visoko and Zenica. All the while, twisting across his mind, the forest, three burned bodies, a corpse with a goatee, and a young girl in her father's arms. And behind all of them, the Ustaše. Bunda at the checkpoint, the primeval size of the man, the fear he engendered. Reinhardt found himself stroking the gap in his teeth, then clenched his jaw in anger.

"There's a judge wants to see you."

Reinhardt started, looking up and around from the duty roster he was correcting, then getting to his feet. Colonel Scheller stood behind him, a slip of paper in his hand. He waved Reinhardt back into his seat, and hooked a chair and sat down himself.

"A judge?"

"Judge's name is Dreyer."

Reinhardt frowned. "*Dreyer? Marcus Dreyer?*"

"And you know this Dreyer how?"

"If it's the same Dreyer, then he and I go a long way back. We served in the same unit together in the first war, then he became a judge in Berlin when I was a policeman. I lost sight of him in the late 1930s; then we were posted together to Norway. Turns out he had quit the judiciary and gone back into the army." Dreyer had been a good friend to the police, and a good friend to Reinhardt himself. The two of them had come under the same kinds of pressure from Germany's new masters, to conform, to adapt, to toe the line. Dreyer had given in before Reinhardt, if what Reinhardt had done to stay in the police longer could be countenanced as resistance. "I lost touch with him again after that. I'd heard he was in Russia. What's this about anyway, sir? Why does he want to see me?"

"Apparently, he's read your report from yesterday, and he wants to talk to you about it." Scheller stopped, chewing his lower lip, lowering his head to look at the paper held in his thick fingers. For all his formidable size and energy, Scheller was desperately tired. Major Hassler had been killed in Montenegro and not replaced, and although Reinhardt had covered some of the major's workload, much of it had still fallen on Scheller.

"Yesterday's report?" Reinhardt frowned.

Scheller shrugged. "You'll find out. Get going, Reinhardt. Take my car and driver."

Reinhardt wound his way back through the hallways, through the scrum of men and swirl of noise and back out into the cold. Mercifully, Scheller's car had a hard top and sides, and was thus warm. The driver trundled it past the lines of waiting troops, through the weaving streams of smoke from their fires, and then the car was pulling up at the State House, the old Austro-Hungarian building. Hurrying out, past the salutes of sentries on duty and through the echoing foyer, Reinhardt remembered coming here to speak with Captain Thallberg of the secret field police, back when he was investigating Marija Vukić's and Stefan Hendel's murders.

Following directions upstairs, past the old secret field police offices, he came to the section occupied by the army's judicial service. He paused, hesitating, feeling for a moment like an interloper, or worse, like a penitent. He shook himself out of it and pushed the door open, stepping tall into the office, and finding it empty. There was a murmur of voices from across it, from down a short corridor that ended in a half-open door, a harsh quality to them as if men were arguing. He walked up to it and knocked. The voices cut off, a stentorian *"Come!"* echoing from the other side.

The office was unlike any other judge's office Reinhardt had been in during his police career. No shelves of rich and paneled wood filled with legal tomes, no carpet, no leather armchairs and shaded lamps. This office was cold, spare: a desk, a couple of mismatched hard chairs, a gramophone in one corner standing next to a camp bed that had been hastily made and with a prodigious dip in the mattress. And rising from behind the desk, a man with a smile creasing a look of surprise off his face. He was big and bluff, breasting across the room like a galleon under sail.

"Gregor? *Gregor!* By God, it is you, man!"

"Marcus. Major Dreyer, sir." Reinhardt took the other man's hand, acknowledging his rank. He smiled back, but it was a sudden nervousness he felt more than any pleasure at seeing what was indeed an old friend.

"Bloody *hell*, Gregor! I'd heard you were here, but had no . . . idea, this was . . ." He stopped, his hand gesturing at the Feldjaegerkorps gorget around Reinhardt's throat.

"You get used to it, sir."

The other man in the room cleared his throat, a polite smile on his face as he looked between them. He was a tall, thin man in a well-tailored uniform, a pair of spectacles held in long fingers, like a pianist's. The man had a smooth head of silver-white hair, two spots of color on his cheeks, and an expression of erudite surprise and query on his face as he looked at Reinhardt, head to toe.

Dreyer turned, an arm extending to include him. "My manners, I do apologize. Reinhardt, this is Judge Felix Erdmann. A redoubtable jurist and my superior here."

"How do you do, Captain," said Erdmann.

"How do you do, sir. I am sorry for interrupting, only there was no one in the outer office."

"Not at all, Captain." Erdmann smiled. "I gather this is a happy reunion, Dreyer?"

"Very much so," said Dreyer, grinning at Reinhardt. "The captain and I go way back. We were in the first war together. He must've saved my life half a dozen times. And then he did it again in 1940, up in Norway. Pulled me off a sinking ship at Narvik after the British had destroyed it."

"My goodness!"

"And we were colleagues in Berlin when the war ended."

"Oh, really?" Erdmann's head tilted toward Reinhardt inquisitively. "You are a lawyer?"

"I was a policeman, sir."

"A policeman? Of what, exactly?"

"A detective."

"Indeed?"

"Reinhardt was one of the Alex's best." Dreyer grinned, proudly. "Fancy meeting him here!"

"Indeed," murmured Erdmann, again, a faint smile on his face as he brushed the frames of his spectacles across his lips.

"Sir, I wonder whether you might give the captain and me a few minutes to reminisce?"

"But of course, Dreyer. Of course," said Erdmann. He glanced at his wristwatch, an elegant bend of his arm. "Let us pick this up again on the hour? In my office? A pleasure to meet you, Captain."

The door clicked shut behind Erdmann, and Dreyer ushered

Reinhardt over to a pair of mismatched chairs. "Tell me. What's been happening to you? And for God's sake, drop the 'sir'!"

Reinhardt looked Dreyer over, from the dark green piping on his rank to the Knight's Cross at his throat, the Winter Campaign medal slanting red across his tunic.

"Cigarette?" Dreyer held out a metal cigarette case, its body lacquered silver and ivory, and he lit Reinhardt's cigarette with a matching lighter. Dreyer smiled as he saw Reinhardt's eyes on it. "The contents aren't quite up to scratch," he murmured, as he lit his own cigarette. "Damn things are all paper and precious little tobacco."

Reinhardt watched Dreyer's head tilt forward and down to the flame of his lighter. His eyes caught on the deep lines etched into the judge's face, the red veins that forked in broken tributaries across his nose. As Dreyer's eyes opened, Reinhardt's darted elsewhere, focusing furtively on his own cigarette, then lifting, following the smoke he blew at the ceiling.

"Drop of this?" asked Dreyer, holding out a flask. From the edge of Dreyer's breath, it was not his first but much as he was tempted, Reinhardt dared not. It was a weakness he dare not give in to as he once had, not so long ago. "No? You weren't so averse up in Narvik!"

"No. I wasn't." Despite his reserve, a smile cracked the corner of Reinhardt's mouth.

"That's better!" Dreyer grinned. "Well, don't mind if I do . . . ?" Dreyer took a long swallow, and his eyes were on Reinhardt when his head came down. "What's been happening to you, Gregor? Last I heard, you were running Partisan counterintelligence down here. With the Abwehr." Reinhardt nodded. "Wasn't there something to do with a general? I heard you got a bit roughed up."

"That was sorted out," he said, shrugging with his mouth.

"What happened, though?" Dreyer put an ashtray on the table, heavy, amber-colored glass done in complicated curves and inlaid metal.

Reinhardt sighed. "I was told to investigate a pair of murders. A general was implicated. He was killed. In action. But my investigation upset a lot of people. I got questioned about my role in events."

"Who did the questioning?"

"Who didn't?" Reinhardt snorted, a cynical edge to it he did not like but could not help. He ran his tongue around his teeth, probing that gap where the interrogators had knocked one out. "The army. Gestapo. The Ustaše wanted a go at me but didn't get the chance."

"They thought there was more? To the general's death?" Reinhardt nodded. "Was there?"

"There's always more," said Reinhardt, looking away, out the window. Something did not feel right. Too many coincidences, perhaps. Or perhaps he was still too suspicious of things that seemed good, but were not. He took a hard pull on his cigarette, flaring it red. "But it wasn't what they thought or wanted. They left me alone eventually. Reassigned me to an operational unit."

"And now here you are, again. A Feldjaeger, no less."

"It was a surprise to me, too."

"And tell me, what news of your son?"

Reinhardt's mouth tightened, and he gave a tight shake of his head, tapping his cigarette into the ashtray. "None. Nothing. Friedrich is presumed lost at Stalingrad."

"Ah, God, Reinhardt." Dreyer's hand came up to rest heavily on Reinhardt's shoulder.

Reinhardt nodded, paused, dragging the words out, wanting to ask, wanting to know, but not wanting to know too much. "What are you doing now? Last I heard you were in the USSR."

Dreyer nodded. "I was. With 2nd Panzer in Russia. Then 4th Army."

"I see you've been busy," Reinhardt said, pointing at his throat, looking at Dreyer's. "Not a lot of judges get to earn one of them."

"This?" Dreyer's hand rose up to his Knight's Cross. "This is what you get for . . . Never mind. Eastern Front. That's all that matters."

"And now?"

"War Crimes Bureau."

Reinhardt raised his eyebrows. "War Crimes Bureau?" he repeated.

"For my sins," muttered Dreyer, his eyes bright on Reinhardt as he tilted his head for another pull at his flask. "Nothing to say? People usually have something."

Reinhardt pointed at the flask. "I see you're still collecting."

"What?"

"You always did like that kind of thing."

"Art Deco?" Dreyer smiled, his eyes on the flask. It was a beautiful object, the lines tapered and flared, the mat of its body scrolled with lines of bright metal. "Yes, it's a nice piece."

"That too," said Reinhardt, pointing at the ashtray. "And your cigarette case and lighter. I'm surprised you still carry this stuff around with you."

Dreyer shrugged with his mouth as he stubbed his cigarette out. "We all have our little things, I suppose. Like that watch you always carried. What was it?"

"A Williamson."

"I haven't seen you with it."

Reinhardt shook his head. "The Gestapo smashed it."

"I'm sorry to hear that. It meant a lot to you, I remember."

"What brings you down here?" Reinhardt asked, prodding the conversation back on track.

"The Ustaše," Dreyer said, shortly, his eyes on Reinhardt. "There's a feeling in Berlin, in some circles, that we should look into the more—shall we say—egregious activities of our allies. In expectation of certain . . . eventualities." His eyes were heavy, probing. "You take my meaning, I'm sure."

"You don't need to spell it out," said Reinhardt, excitement building up.

"Needless to say, there are those in the army command here who find that a waste of time. Not only a waste of time, but a betrayal, of the Ustaše, of our shared principles and ideologies."

"Erdmann?" Reinhardt guessed.

Dreyer shrugged, picked up the ashtray, and walked back to his desk. "Erdmann possibly. The man's a ferocious disciplinarian, for all he hides it behind that erudite exterior. Others are worse. I am not, shall we say, exactly the flavor of the day, here, and just about any investigative work is impossible with the current situation." He lifted up a cardboard folder, extracting from it a piece of paper. "Your report. It interests me."

"Why would that be?" Reinhardt managed, quietly.

"I've a strong feeling you came across something I've been looking into for a while, now."

"What do you want, then?"

"Tell me about yesterday. In your own words."

Reinhardt nodded, thinking of a man with a goatee and a girl in her father's arms, and a small space opening up inside, some small connection to a long-ago past. "We came across a massacre in the forest. Two sets of killings. A group of civilians, and three other bodies. I think they were soldiers, but I can't be sure. The civilians had been shot while the other three had been shot, then burned.

"Both sets were a cover-up, I think, with the civilians murdered because they saw or heard too much. I found three survivors. An elderly couple, and a boy. I can't prove it now—if at all, really—but the Ustaše had something to do with it. I know they were up in that area, and then they seemed very concerned when I brought down the survivors. The area is close to where the Partisans now have full control, so whatever it was that took them up there, it was important, and whatever it was they did," he said, remembering what the defense line commander had said about them being in a roaring good mood, "they were happy about it."

He stopped as Dreyer gave a tense little smile, barely a lift of the skin around his eyes, and held up a hand. Reinhardt breathed, aware and embarrassed he had been talking fast, intently, as he sometimes used to about a murder case, and he felt a high thrill unfolding deep inside. "Tell me about the Feldgendarme. The major."

"The *Feldgendarme*?" Dreyer nodded. Reinhardt's mind floundered, lost down a different path. "What . . . what about him?"

"You met him at that checkpoint. Run by the Ustaše. Tell me about him. How he seemed."

"How he *seemed*?"

"How he seemed," Dreyer agreed.

Reinhardt frowned, sitting forward with his elbows on his knees. "Let me get something straight, Marcus. You are a war crimes judge. You are here . . ." He paused at Dreyer's movement of his hand, a placatory palm raised to ward off who knew what evil. "You are here on Berlin's orders, to examine certain allegations concerning the Ustaše, and you have read a report of mine that mentions them that is of interest to you, and you ask me to describe the behavior of a Feldgendarmerie major in an army penal battalion?"

Dreyer nodded.

Reinhardt sat back, crossed a leg, and shook another cigarette from his packet without offering one to Dreyer. He lit it, blew smoke to one side, and waited.

"The major's name is Erwin Jansky. I first came across him in late 1941," said Dreyer, eventually, his voice flat. "In Poland. Several times, in connection with black market affairs. Then rumors of weapons and ammunition being traded to local resistance fighters in return for treasures, artwork. Something like that. He turned up in an investigation into a Polish resistance massacre of German soldiers. Except, I'm pretty sure it was something else. It was the black market. A 'business transaction' that went very wrong. Someone covered it up, and whoever killed the Germans made it look like the Poles did it. A village was shot to death in reprisal for that one . . .

"I almost had him, but nothing came of it. Like I said. He was clever. Witnesses disappeared, or retracted testimony. Units moved on and apart. The blame fell—rather conveniently, as I said—on local civilians." Dreyer paused, swallowed, then continued. "I could never build a case against him. I lost sight of him. Then again, in Greece, last year, he resurfaced. It was the same sort of thing as Poland. This time there were rumors of a large sum of gold, bullion taken from the central bank. A cover-up that left many others dead. No direct proof. Again. But I'm sure he was in on it."

Reinhardt sat and listened to Dreyer's flat tone, and thought about those refugees up in the forest, and pictured a Polish village in flames, a gyre of crows above it.

"If you've no proof, why do you think it's him?"

Dreyer nodded, his eyes down. "It . . . I had a witness. In Poland. And again in Greece. But they were killed. And . . . Jansky . . . he had, he has, a way . . . of talking to you. Of needling you with the truth that only you and he know."

"And that is?"

"That he gets away with murder. This is why, I ask, Gregor, what did you see?"

"Did he seem like someone who had just committed murder?"

Dreyer's eyes squinted in frustration and he shook his head. "Yes. No. How did Jansky seem, to you?"

"I was a policeman long enough to recognize a leading question from a jurist, Marcus," Reinhardt replied. He reached back and took the ashtray from Dreyer's desk, gritting the cigarette out. "Tell me straight out what it is you suspect. Or what it is you want."

Dreyer had the grace to smile. "Touché, Gregor." He looked elsewhere, and his mouth moved once or twice before he seemed able to summon up the words he was looking for. "It is hard to actually say what I suspect."

"We are friends, Marcus. I won't mock you," said Reinhardt. He looked at Dreyer, saw how his eyes were heavy, as if worn down by the weight of something seen and unable to forget.

"Help me, Gregor." Dreyer loomed suddenly close to Reinhardt, as if searching for something, and Reinhardt found himself leaning backward away from him, searching for a way past the heft of Dreyer's presence.

"Catch Jansky?" Dreyer nodded. "At what? What do you have on him? What evidence?"

"I know. I don't . . . Threads, Gregor. Pull hard enough . . ."

"It might unravel. I know, Marcus. It's worked in the past. But the past is not here."

"Please, Gregor . . ."

"Marcus, it's not that I don't want to help you, but how can I?"

"*Please*, Gregor."

"I can't help you. This isn't Berlin, my friend."

Dreyer's eyes swiveled up heavily. "What does that mean?"

"It means we no longer have those luxuries of law, or process, or procedure to guide and protect us. It means we are out on an edge, Marcus, and we survive by balancing upon it. I can't . . . I can't see how sacrificing that edge can help. For what cause? For a Feldgendarme who may or may not be corrupt?" Reinhardt shook his head, though it pained him to do it, to see his friend pushed so far down, and his words only helping him to push him further. "Be realistic," he said, pausing before the sudden, stark expression of need in Dreyer's face. "What is it you're not telling me? Marcus?"

Dreyer's face twisted, a twitch pulling the side of his mouth down, as if a word weighed so heavily in there. "I've been after Jansky a long time. I've been . . . ridiculed, shall we say, for my interest in Jansky. But I know . . . I *know* . . . he's as guilty as sin."

"I don't doubt it, Marcus. But—"

"It's hard to trust people, Gregor. Trust them with what you know. Or think. I thought . . . I want to trust you."

How to say this? Reinhardt struggled. How to argue a point you do not believe, he thought, sadly, remembering his conversation with Benfeld up in the forest. Murder was murder, was it not? Dreyer believed this Jansky might have had something to do with it. He saw smoke, and there might be a fire, but there were so many fires, now. The whole world ablaze, and where did Dreyer's flame fit in that vast conflagration? Sometimes, it was just best to cut things short, and so he rose to his feet. "I'm sorry. I don't have the time. I don't have the resources. I don't have the . . ." Authority. He bit the word back, but they both heard it, that wretched symbol of the world they both inhabited. Reinhardt sighed, looking away, eyes running blindly into the corner of the room, and seeing instead a logged-out swath of forest, seeing it fading away.

Dreyer's head lowered to his chest, and he seemed to fold in on himself. Reinhardt left him there, pinned by whatever weight bestrode his mind, and walked back out through the offices, past an orderly who rose to his feet, past the open door to Erdmann's office, where the judge glanced up from a sheaf of papers, and back outside, pulling the winter down inside as far as he could.

6

"Sir. *Sir!* Wake up, sir."

Reinhardt dragged himself out of sleep, blinking up at the ceiling . . .

"What?" he asked, through a gummed-up mouth, turning to see who had woken him up. A Feldjaeger corporal stood by the camp bed.

"Colonel Scheller's orders, sir. You're to report to him in operations, immediately."

"Fine, fine," said Reinhardt, sliding his legs over the side of the bed. "What's going on?"

"There's been a shooting. Two of our men are dead, a third wounded."

Working the sleep from his mouth, Reinhardt walked quickly through the halls of the barracks, back to operations, following the Feldjaeger corporal. By his watch, it was just past three thirty in the morning, and the corridors were quiet. He had been asleep no more than a couple of hours after finishing his shift, and his head felt jagged, full of broken glass.

Scheller was finishing up a telephone call when Reinhardt arrived. He handed over a piece of paper. "That address. Now. There's a Feldgendarmerie car waiting for you."

"What's happened?"

"One of our patrols got shot up. I want to know who and why. Soon as you can."

"Who called it in?" Reinhardt scanned the address. Somewhere in Logavina. He walked quickly to Scheller's map, confirming his memory that it was one of the old Ottoman neighborhoods on the north side of the city, quite high up.

"Feldgendarmerie. They heard the shots."

"What were our men doing up in Logavina?" He frowned, the jagged edges inside his head shifting, smoothing, as he came awake.

"Ask Lainer. He had the patrol schedule."

"He's there?"

"He should be. And so should you. *Move!*"

Reinhardt ran through the barracks, back out to the courtyard. A *kubelwagen* was waiting with its engine running, a Feldgendarme behind the wheel, and Benfeld smoking a cigarette. The lieutenant crushed the butt out as Reinhardt came out, and opened the back door of the *kubelwagen*.

"Mind if I come?"

Reinhardt shrugged as he ducked into the car. "If you've nothing better to do, by all means."

Benfeld grinned and skipped around to the passenger seat, looking none the worse for wear after the day he must have had. The driver gunned the engine, and the vehicle took off fast, out of the barracks and back toward the city. The front end skipping across the cobbled ice around the Town Hall, the *kubelwagen* hauled itself up Sagrdzije Street, then onto Logavina, working higher into Sarajevo's fringes, up to the street the colonel had identified, slowing as it came to a Feldgendarmerie checkpoint thrown across the road. Beyond it, a couple more vehicles, including an ambulance, were parked. Lights bobbed up and down, the glare from flashlights as men moved around a *kubelwagen* immobilized with its back left corner against a wall, pointing up the hill, a stone's throw beyond the Feldgendarmerie checkpoint. One or two lanterns were held by, it seemed, civilians, who stood huddled and shivering against the side of the road under the guard of a pair of Feldgendarmes.

Reinhardt left the car behind, walking quickly up past the checkpoint, pointing to his armband as a couple of them made a move to stop him. He recognized Lainer's silhouette against the lights, the tall Feldjaeger standing stock-still, his hands gripped behind his back. He turned as Reinhardt came up alongside him, nodding.

"Good. I'm glad you're here. This is a fucking zoo. Maybe you can start to make sense of all this."

Reinhardt looked at the car, at the man moving around it, at the ambulance, medics shifting the surviving Feldjaeger onto a stretcher.

"This is a crime scene, Lainer," he said, for the second time in two days. "Scheller asked me to take care of this. So I'll take care of it. Agreed on that?" Lainer's jaw bunched, but Reinhardt knew it was just the stress. "Very well. Then just trust me." The other captain nodded, and he seemed to deflate a little, as if shedding a burden.

Reinhardt stepped forward, made his voice as deep as it could. "All you men, stop what you are doing. Immediately. IMMEDIATELY!" There was stillness, and one or two flashlights swung toward him. "All flashlights, aimed at the ground, thank you." He took a step forward. "My name is Captain Reinhardt, Feldjaegerkorps. As of this minute, I am taking over command of this situation. With the exception of the medics, anyone who is not called Reinhardt, please come and stand behind me. Now, please. NOW!"

Men walked and shuffled past him in the darkness, flashlights painting the cobbled street in little crescents of light and dark.

"Thank you. Is the Feldgendarme who called this in here? Yes? Step forward that man, please." A Feldgendarmerie sergeant came to attention, two privates with him, rifles over their shoulders. "Your name, Sergeant?"

"Ibel, sir."

"Tell me what you saw and did."

"Yes, sir. We were manning the checkpoint in Pirin Brieg, thataways," he said, pointing toward the east, "near where the mosque is, when we heard what sounded like an explosion. We weren't sure, like. It were muffled. More of a thud. And there was a glow, quite bright. It went out quick, and we couldn't figure out where it had come from. But a few minutes later, we heard a burst of gunfire, then, quite soon after, a few more shots. And we were pretty sure it had come from here. So me and these two, we come up, and we find the *kubelwagen* in the street, just like it is."

"And then?"

"Well, I check the passengers, and I see there's three Feldjaeger, and one's still alive. There's no one around on the street at all. So I send one of my boys back in our *kubelwagen* to the checkpoint to call this in, and me and the other lad we wait up here."

"What did you see? When you were waiting up here?"

"Nothing at all, sir. The street were dark. Completely silent."

"Was the car's engine running?"

"No, sir."

"Did you walk up the street?"

"No, sir. It were dark. It were just the two of us. If it were Partisans, we felt better down by the car. And we could look after the wounded lad, like."

"Did you hear anything? Voices? A car? A truck? Footsteps? Anything at all." Ibel shook his head to everything. "So, then reinforcements arrived?"

"Yes, sir. More of our lads. Some pushed up the street without seeing or hearing anything. The rest of us began to knock on doors. We wake up the few still living here, roust them into the street, start questioning them. Nothing doing, for now. They can't hardly speak a word of German, and we've no translator. And then your lot turned up. The captain, here, and his men. Then you."

"That's it?"

"That's it, sir."

"You sure?"

"Sir."

"Did you touch the bodies, Sergeant?"

"Well, yes, sir. To check if they were alive."

"Did you move them?"

"Only the wounded one, sir. We got the wounded one out. We left the two dead ones. It was Günsche's idea to leave them," he said, indicating one of the privates. "He said any investigation would want to see where they died. He did right, then, did he?"

"He did right," said Reinhardt, directing a tight smile at the Feldgendarme private. "You familiar with this street, Sergeant?" The Feldgendarme nodded, his lips pursing. "What goes on here, normally?"

"Not much, sir. It's part of our patrol sector, but we don't come much. Most of the houses up here is empty. Damage, you see. Just up there, the Allies dropped a load of bombs, so the street's all ruined. And it's a bit close to the mountains, so people is afraid of Partisans. And anyways, they're building some defense works up there."

"Who is?"

"Construction troops and the like. There's a work site up there." The sergeant indicated the top of the street. "Couple of KEEP OUT signs, some material in a locked shed. A bulldozer."

"What are they building?"

"An anti-aircraft battery, something like that. At least, they was. They've not been there the past couple of days. Not since . . . I mean, since the defense plans . . ." The sergeant paused, sidled closer. "Is it true, sir? 'Bout the plans? That they've been stolen?"

"Thank you, Sergeant," Reinhardt said, avoiding Ibel's question. "If you remember anything else, be sure to let me know." He looked over at Lainer, at Benfeld standing just behind them. Time to move. "Lainer, get a couple of your men to stand guard down here. No one gets past until I say so. Frenchie, you can help me. First thing, find me a flashlight, please." He glanced at the sky. The moon was not far off full, but it was hidden behind a rumpled sky of low cloud, only a silvery glimmer any proof it was up there. "Second, get on the radio, see if we can scrounge up some light. A searchlight or something like that. See if the air defense people have one on a truck we could use. And then get us a translator. Get on to operations. They should have someone." Benfeld nodded, passing Reinhardt a flashlight already lit, then ducking away. "Lainer, I don't know what we'll find, seeing as the scene has been trampled over the last half hour. And I don't know if the shooters are still here. I doubt it, but you never know. So, just follow my lead. All right?"

Reinhardt walked slowly up to the car, playing his light across it. The *kubelwagen* was starred with bullet holes, rosettes of bright metal, and the windshield was shattered, only triangular shards left clinging to the frame. The firing had come from the front and sides, it seemed. It had really been poured into the vehicle, riddling its occupants, and probably—hopefully—killing the front passengers instantly. The two Feldjaeger sat slumped with their heads back and mouths open, as if they were staring up at the night sky in wonder. The fronts of their uniforms were soaked red from multiple bullet wounds, and their skin, where it was exposed, had been shredded by flying glass from the windshield.

"Poor fucking bastards," Lainer grated. "To think they'd end up shot to pieces, like this. Bader survived Stalingrad, and Pollmann . . ." He trailed off.

Reinhardt tuned Lainer out, shining his light inside the car, the flashlight's beam refracting and sliding over the thousands of pieces of glass coating the interior. There were no good ways to go out in a war, he knew—other than in a hospital, doped up on morphine, maybe with a pretty nurse holding your hand as you went. There were three assault rifles inside the car. One on the floor in the back, one racked behind the driver, and the third standing between the front passenger's knees. Their equipment was, from what he could see, in order. Helmets, gorgets, webbing, pouches, bayonets. He reached in, thumbed back the catch on one of the magazine pouches to see three spare magazines. A flashlight was clipped to the passenger's webbing and the driver had a compass on a lanyard around his neck, a nice piece, edged in brass. Both men wore Iron Crosses on their tunics. In their breast pockets, they both had their *soldbuchs*—their pay books— and wallets with a few Reichsmarks and some *kuna*, the local currency, in them.

He craned his neck in farther, seeing the key in the ignition. He wobbled the gear stick. Neutral. The hand brake was not engaged. Worming himself back out, he shone the flashlight at the *kubelwagen*'s rear, where it rested against the wall. The car had crunched into the flaky stone of the wall. Bits of stone and cement dusted the ground, and the rear light was cracked. Looking forward, he saw that the *kubelwagen*'s front wheels were turned slightly to the driver's left. He turned his flashlight on the ground around the car, moving the light slowly and finding a shell casing, the brass winking up at him from the folds between the cobbles.

Two sets of gunfire, the sergeant had said. A heavy burst, then shots.

Wheels turned. Neutral gear. The car had probably rolled backward after the driver had died, which meant they had been shot farther up.

Reinhardt motioned to Lainer to walk on the other side of him and began to move slowly up the hill, swinging his flashlight from left to right and counting off the steps. He passed twenty when his flashlight picked out a gleam in the road ahead, then a second, a third, a slew of them. He knelt by the first, picking up a brass shell casing. He craned his neck around at the sound of quiet footsteps, and Benfeld dropped to his knee next to him.

"What do you say, Frenchie?" he said, softly.

Benfeld picked up one of his own. "Nine-millimeter," he said. "There's a bloody lot of them," he muttered.

Reinhardt shone his flashlight in a wide arc. There were two broad groupings of casings. "One shooter to the left, one to the right." He aimed the flashlight straight up the hill. "There. More. Three shooters, probably. One to either side, one in front. Nine-millimeter casings. Probably MP 40s. Say three full magazines. About ninety-six rounds."

"Bastards," grated Lainer.

The three flashlights were not much help, but Reinhardt was able to make out the general shape of the street. There were gaps in the houses up ahead, walls tumbled out and down across the cobbled road, roofs caved in or gone completely. This must have been where the bombing had hit the street, Reinhardt thought, his feet crunching across pieces of stone and masonry. Up ahead was a white signboard, red letters printed across it. KEEP OUT—CONSTRUCTION ZONE, a line of timber trestles marching across the width of the street as if to emphasize the point. The bulldozer the Feldgendarme sergeant had mentioned was parked up ahead to the left, side-on to the street, its blade resting almost against a house that, probably, was due for demolition. Just beyond it stood a small wooden hut, the whole thing wrapped in a heavy chain, presumably to secure whatever materials were stored inside it.

Beyond the sign, the street seemed to end. The houses on either side were gone; the whole expanse, what he could see of it, was graded flat except for two mounded depressions. Those were probably the bases for the anti-aircraft guns the sergeant had mentioned.

Dead end, Reinhardt thought, *except if you were on foot.* On foot, you could escape across that construction site, move farther up the hill, or melt away into the houses to either side. *If it was Partisans, they could do that with their eyes closed*, he thought, remembering the way he had been led that winding, circuitous route through the old town to that meeting with Dr. Begović in his safe house, the Partisans taking every precaution before delivering him to the man who was Senka—"The Shadow"—the man the Gestapo had most wanted to lay hands on. Not for the first time, Reinhardt wondered where Begović was, what had become of him, wondering as well if this new Partisan, this Valter, had replaced him.

But if you weren't a Partisan . . . If you were something else, or if you had a car, or a truck, the only way out of here was down. Back past that car you had just shot up. Which meant someone in that crowd of townspeople had to have heard or seen something.

Which also meant something had pulled the Feldjaeger's attention up here. This was an isolated part of town, unless they wandered up here by accident, new to the town, not knowing where they were going.

"Lainer. How long had those three been patrolling?"

"Past two days."

"Up here?"

"Hereabouts."

Reinhardt looked down the hill, at the firefly play of light at the bottom of the street. You would have to know these streets to navigate them on a night like this, he thought. Not to mention, run no risk or fear of being stopped. But the Feldjaeger, he thought, turning back, aiming the spike of his flashlight's beam in front of him, had stopped for something, or someone.

One of the trestles was awry, and there was a gap between it and the next one. There were no marks on the ground Reinhardt could see when he played his flashlight over it, but he passed through the gap easily, standing on the other side, looking at the bulldozer, then at the house.

There was a door just to the left of the bulldozer's blade. Rather, it was an opening, with no door in it. Reinhardt held the flashlight well out to the side of his body and aimed it into the house, peering around the frame of the door, his head jerking back at a reek that pushed out of the house, a stab of something sulfuric, a rotten-egg stench. Pushing his head back in, it seemed to be one room, empty of any furnishings, with another door on the far side. He drew and cocked his pistol, the sound harsh and metallic in the still air. He heard Lainer and Benfeld do the same, then stepped slowly into the house.

The floor was wood and the boards creaked under his feet. He took two steps, a third, then gave up trying to walk quietly, concentrating instead on what he could see. The floor was covered in dust and debris, and there were clear marks in it. Footsteps, drag marks, all leading across to that other door. He pointed at the floor, then at the door, and Benfeld and Lainer moved to flank him as he paused, then pushed it open.

There was darkness on the other side, and then Reinhardt saw the steps that led down to what had to be a basement. Pointing the flashlight down, he saw the wear on the steps, bright shards and splinters standing across the flat sheen of old wood, and something else. Something dark red, almost brown, smeared here and there. He walked down, the stairs creaking alarmingly under his weight, a smell of damp and oil rising to meet him, that reek from upstairs fading away.

He stepped off the bottom step, swung his flashlight's beam across a floor of beaten earth, pounded flat, and then his light froze.

There was a confused play of shadows across the basement's walls and floor as Lainer and Benfeld clattered down behind him, but their lights steadied, and the three flashlights shone full and bright upon the bodies that lay there.

"Reinhardt, just what the hell is going on here?" grated Lainer.

The basement was low, and none of them could quite stand upright under the wooden beams holding up the ceiling. Reinhardt shifted sideways down toward the bodies and knelt, playing his flashlight slowly across them from left to right. There were five bodies. All men, and all quite savagely mutilated. Their faces had been smashed, their noses and mouths caved in. The flashlight gave the wounds a terrible depth and darkness, like holes that had been dug down into places that should never have been seen. On top of the matted red ruin of their faces, their foreheads were cratered, each one, with the starred exit point of a gunshot. Heaving one of the bodies over, and feeling a sudden and unexpected sense of déjà vu, he saw the hole in the back of its head.

"Reinhardt," Lainer said, again. "What is this?"

"These bodies were never meant to be found." Reinhardt looked up at the two officers, their faces seemingly suspended in midair, lit from beneath, ghoul-like. "Somehow, your men must have come across this. Or across the edge of it. This is a cover-up. At least, it was meant to be. And, in terms of cover-ups, this one is, to put it mildly, excessive."

"And that matters?"

"It matters, Lainer. It might give us an indication of who did this. Who would want to hide something like this? Who stands to lose from this being found?"

"Well? Can you tell?"

Reinhardt held up a placatory hand, forestalling Lainer's protest. "I will do my best for you, Lainer. And for your men."

From upstairs, there came the creak of wood, a confusion of voices, and then someone called out.

"Benfeld, get upstairs and see what's going on. I don't want half the army traipsing around down here."

"What do you want me to do?" said Lainer.

"Can your men keep this place secure?"

"Yes."

"Then only those I allow down here may come. Anyone else . . . Well, it's about time we used our vaunted Feldjaegerkorps authority to tell others to get lost." The tiniest smile fissured Lainer's taut features. "You should go and do that, now."

Lainer nodded, turned to leave, then paused. "Anything you need, Reinhardt. You tell me."

Left alone, Reinhardt sat back on his heels, his mind ticking over, slowly, then faster, his tongue stroking that gap in his teeth. Five head shots. Five bodies here. Three more up in that forest clearing. Shot the same way, but then burned. Evidence destroyed. But not here. He looked up at the wall, up at the ceiling, seeing, imagining, that bulldozer up there. This house part of a construction zone. The wall coming down, rubble burying all this, obliterating it, as if it had never been.

"They were shot. Then their faces were smashed in," he said, talking to himself. The wounds to the faces had not bled, meaning they were caused after death. "Then they were dumped here to be buried. Someone . . ." His mind ticked over, gears clicking and moving, thoughts shifting, moving around pieces of a puzzle he could not know the shape of. Someone had gone to a lot of trouble to try to dispose of these bodies. He flexed the arm of one of the bodies, or at least tried to. Rigor mortis was still present. Meaning this man had died sometime in the last day or so. Crabbing from one to the other, he checked a limb on each of them. They were all the same, which meant they had all died at roughly the same time.

"You poor bastards," he muttered to himself. He drew back the sleeve of the body nearest him. Ligature marks. The flashlight made a mockery of colors, giving everything a flat, sepia tone, but Reinhardt guessed they would stand out livid, purpled, like bruised fruit. There were ligature marks on all the bodies, he saw, as he checked them one by one, evidence that their wrists had all been bound. He examined their hands, finding most of them hardened and callused.

As he shifted one of the bodies, its foot sagged, and a shoe fell off. Reinhardt paused, staring down at the man's foot, where the toenails glistened in the light. No socks, he realized. "Who the hell . . ." he muttered as he shifted down to the man's foot. Who would wear no socks in weather like this? "Someone who might not have time to put them on," he answered himself, taking off the other shoe, imagining the pounding on a door, a man rousted from sleep, dragged out into the night with only the clothes he had on. Then he frowned. The two shoes were not the same.

Looking more closely at each of the bodies, he examined the clothing. None of the men were dressed for the outdoors. None of them were dressed in clothes that seemed to fit. Laces were undone around the bulge of feet too large for the shoe, or shoes had no laces at all. Sleeves and trouser legs were too short, or too long. There were stains on them, and some of those stains were blood, almost certainly, but Reinhardt could not match up the stains to any wound on the men's bodies. In one case, a shirt was ripped across the back, the frayed edges crusted in blood, but there was no injury on the man.

He wiped his light slowly across the room. In one of the corners, the bare stone of the walls was mottled dark with overlapping spatters, like handfuls of paint thrown upon the stones. Squinting closer, he counted five such clusters, and the ground was fouled and scuffed beneath them.

"Five bodies," he murmured to himself as he swung his light back.

"Five sets of clothes belonging to someone else. Ligature marks. Gunshot wounds. Disfigurement."

"A real riddle, sir." Reinhardt turned quickly in surprise. He had not heard the stairs creak as Benfeld came back down them. "We have visitors upstairs. Feldgendarmerie. New ones. From a penal battalion. Say they have jurisdiction here, as their men are working on this construction site. And the Ustaše have shown up, with a policeman in tow. Lainer's keeping them back for now."

"Who would be missing five men, Lieutenant? Or put it another way, who would need to hide the identities of five men?"

Benfeld pursed his lips as he shook a cigarette from a packet. He shrugged, a tight little movement. He looked very tense, his arms close to his side. He swung his cigarette up to his mouth, his forearm swiveling close to his body, and drew hard on it. The red glow spread across his face, so much gentler than the yellow glow of the flashlight.

"What do you need, sir?"

"Give me one of those, for a start," said Reinhardt, tucking his flashlight under his arm as he lit a cigarette from Benfeld's. "Then get these bodies out of here. I want them taken down to the military hospital. You take care of it. Go with them, and find a doctor. I want the bodies examined, and then autopsied."

"Autopsied? Yes, sir."

"Any news on my lights?"

"None. I wouldn't hold your hopes up for it, either."

"What I wouldn't give for a camera and some photos," Reinhardt muttered to himself, angry when he realized his tongue was stroking that gap in his teeth. He walked over to the bodies, taking one last look at them, at the way they lay. "A *penal* battalion, did you say?" he asked Benfeld, turning suddenly. The lieutenant nodded, a small, tight movement. Reinhardt's mouth pursed, and then he followed Benfeld up the stairs and out into the chill air. Outside the house he stopped, checked by that smell, that rotten-egg stench. He followed it up the side of the house, his flashlight's beam breaking over rubble and stone, a wall that tumbled down into the dark. The smell was stronger back here as he peered into the neighboring house, which had collapsed into itself. A strong sulfuric reek, and something else. The smell of burned wood and stone, and beneath it all, a furtive layer, like charred meat. He had smelled this before, in Belgrade, and in Vienna, after an air raid.

He climbed carefully up over a slew of rubble, moving his flashlight slowly until the light settled on a swath of blackened rock and stone, and nestled at the bottom of it, a twisted cylinder of metal, bent and rippled by some extreme heat. Reinhardt leaned, putting his hand close to it, feeling the echo of residual warmth, wondering if there were any more of them out there, and remembering this place had been bombed not so long ago.

"There," he said to Benfeld, who had followed him out. "That's what's left of an incendiary flare. The Allies drop them during their raids to mark their targets for them. I'm guessing the killers must have triggered it by mistake, and that was the light and noise that woke the neighbors and brought the Feldjaeger up here." He stepped back down the spill, his feet clacking softly on loose stone. "Tell everyone to be careful. There could be all kinds of unexploded ordnance still lying around."

Back down the street, his foot kicked a shell casing that went ringing off into the dark, to where the checkpoint had been set up, and where flashlights and headlights made a confusion of shapes, angled shadows and pools of darkness. Lainer called to him, backlit by a car's lights.

"Reinhardt, over here!" Several men stood with him, a pair of Feldgendarmes—one of them Major Neuffer, the liaison officer with the Feldgendarmerie—and an Ustaša. A fourth man, standing somewhat back from the others, was dressed in a rumpled suit and overcoat. "Reinhardt, you remember Major Neuffer. And this is Lieutenant Brandt, from the 999th Balkans Field Punishment Battalion. It seems we're in his way." The lieutenant was a thin man, his gorget hanging from a scrawny neck. The red triangle of a penal unit was stitched to the arm of his coat. He seemed familiar.

"Come now, Captain," said Neuffer. "He didn't state it in quite those terms. A nasty business, it seems, eh, Reinhardt?"

"What do you want, Neuffer?"

There was a pause, as if Neuffer had been put out by Reinhardt's forthrightness. "It's not so much what I want, Captain," he said, emphasizing the rank ever so slightly. "It's what others want, and need. Lieutenant Brandt has a job to do. And this is Captain Marković, Ustaše liaison to the army, and Inspector Bakarević of the Sarajevo police. They also have a job to do."

"What might those be?"

"I have an anti-aircraft installation to complete, Captain Reinhardt," said Brandt. Reinhardt cocked his head, slightly, looking at him, realizing he had seen him the day before. At the Ustaše checkpoint, in the car with the Feldgendarme major.

"It's a bit early in the morning for construction work, isn't it?"

None of the Feldgendarmes replied to that, but Marković stepped forward. "Captain, you have bodies up there? Then, respectfully, I put it to you that this is the job of the police to investigate," he said, indicating Bakarević, a thin man with only a frizz of hair that ran over his ears and around the back of his white head. The inspector kept his eyes level, but Reinhardt could see the man's discomfort. He was a civilian, a Muslim by his name, caught between the sharp edges of jurisdiction, between what might be right, and what might be acceptable. Once, Reinhardt might have felt sorry for him. Once, Reinhardt had *been* him, but that was a long time ago. He felt a sudden lightheadedness, a vertigo tilt as if he looked down on this and could not take the air at such a rarefied height. He took a deep breath, calmed himself, and realized the feeling for what it was. Power. The raw exercise of it. That he and Lainer—and Benfeld, for that matter—had the mastery of this situation. Not because they were more fit for it but because of who they were.

"I think not, Captain Marković."

"And why would that be?" barked Neuffer. He seemed to pull himself together, rising up to his inconsiderable height, his chin bunching up tight. The Kaiser, Reinhardt thought, puffing himself up in front of his men. "Why exclude the police from this?"

"I have two dead Feldjaeger, a third wounded. I have reason to believe their deaths are linked to the others. Therefore, it is one case, and it's mine, until such a time as my colonel says otherwise."

"This kind of unreasonableness is *precisely* what I was afraid of, and what I was warned about," complained Neuffer.

"Someone's been doing an awful lot of forewarning about me, Major. Care to enlighten me?" Neuffer said nothing, visibly simmering. "Then let me tell you, the first minutes and hours after a crime has been committed are the most important. I will not have this crime scene corrupted if I can avoid it."

Marković snorted. "Oh, come now, Captain. It's quite obvious what's happened. It's the Partisans."

"Yes." Neuffer leaped into the narrow breach afforded by the Ustaša. "The Partisans. It would be just like them."

"And you wonder why I want to keep some level of control over this?" Marković and Neuffer looked confused. "You've seen nothing. Examined nothing. And yet already you are jumping to conclusions. However," said Reinhardt, switching tacks, hoping to keep them off-balance, "I admit a little help would not go amiss and I'm willing to cooperate. My lieutenant here can show Inspector Bakarević the bodies before we move them to the military hospital for autopsy. He's—"

"The *military* hospital, Captain?" Marković interrupted. "Why, may I ask?"

"I want a military doctor to examine them."

"Why, Captain?" asked Neuffer, scudding along in Marković's wake.

"I will get to that part shortly. As I was saying, the inspector is welcome to share in the results of the autopsy, and I need help in questioning the locals. There's a few of them, and they must've heard something."

"Indeed. Sharing of information, it's the best way forward," added a relieved-sounding Neuffer. Such a formulaic little man, Reinhardt thought, again.

"That is most reasonable of you," said Marković. "The inspector will view the bodies. I will take care of talking with—"

"Thank you, Captain, but I would rather the inspector take care of that as well." Not that Reinhardt was under any illusions that whatever Bakarević learned he would not pass on to the Ustaše. He would. It was how men like him survived day to day.

"Captain, are you suggesting anything?" That from Neuffer again.

"Suggesting nothing, Major. I just don't see the need for Ustaše involvement."

"And why not, Captain?"

"General Herzog said our involvement ends where the field gray ends. Well, those Feldjaeger wore field gray. Everything else follows from that. It's ours and I see no need for the Ustaše."

"It is all right, Major Neuffer," said Marković. "I can understand the captain's thinking." The Ustaše began giving orders to a desperately uncomfortable-looking Bakarević. Reinhardt had no great faith in the ability of the inspector to elicit anything worthwhile from the locals, but they would at least survive interrogation by him. Having the Ustaše do it was an uncertainty he could not countenance.

"And what of me, Captain?" interjected Brandt. "I've got fifty men waiting for work, and a timetable to keep."

"It'll keep, Lieutenant," snarled Lainer. "It's only earth. It's not going anywhere."

"Sir . . ." began the Feldgendarme lieutenant.

"Your bloody convicts'll just have to wait until we're done." The big Feldjaeger was a formidable sight in anger, and he was angry now. "Right now, fuck the hell off out of here."

"Captain," protested Neuffer, although he too seemed taken aback by Lainer's anger. "There's no need for such a tone." There was a stiff movement to one side—Benfeld, taking a step backward.

"You think?" spat Lainer.

"Gentlemen, I just need a little patience from you all. Then Lieutenant Brandt will be able to go ahead with his work. Lieutenant Benfeld, will you escort the inspector?"

With that, the group broke apart, and Reinhardt watched Benfeld and Bakarević walk up the hill, their silhouettes blurred against the yellow glow of their flashlights. Reinhardt walked away from the tangle of vehicles and the competing demands of men and their factions, needing a moment to himself. He lit a cigarette, pausing around a deep lungful of smoke, trying to feel the way ahead from now on, his mind playing with those pieces of the puzzle he had been dealt.

The trucks from the penal battalion were drawn up to the side of the street. The backs of men mounded the canvas sides of their load beds, there was a low mutter of voices, and he realized he had seen those trucks yesterday, stopped in front of the Ustaše checkpoint.

"Kreuz? *Kreuz?* Are you bloody wandering about, again?"

A shape was coming up the street, flashlight stabbing the darkness between the trucks. The light tilted around, blinding him.

"Ah, sorry, Captain." The shape resolved into a Feldgendarme sergeant, a red triangle patch sewn on his sleeve. "Like keeping track of a flock of chickens with this lot."

"There's no one here, Sergeant."

"Right, sir. With your permission?"

"Carry on, Sergeant."

Reinhardt continued his slow walk into the darkness, his mind still tilted around that realization of the power he wielded, and the fear he had always felt inside whenever he came anywhere near anything like it. Once, long ago, he had known something similar, reveled in the respect and fear a stormtrooper's reputation afforded him, but he had left that man behind, and had never wanted to be him again.

Just for a moment, he felt something deep inside, a sudden serpentlike coiling. As if something old and hoary had turned over, giving him a glimpse of a darker nature, mud-smeared and with the mad rolling eye of an animal gone wild. He shivered, conscious of himself in a way he had not been for a long time. He turned back up toward the lights, and for the first time in a long time his thoughts bent into the future, alert and alive, like a hound that had caught an elusive scent, and a feeling coursing through him that the hunt was afoot.

PART TWO

All Are Not Huntsmen Who Can Blow the Hunter's Horn

S tanding on Kranjčević Street outside the hospital under a low, overcast sky, Reinhardt took a last pull on his cigarette, then flicked the butt away. He pushed the smoke out, washing his tongue around his mouth and wishing for something to drink. The night had been very long, and he had gotten no sleep. The dim morning light illuminated nothing, least of all the confused jumble in his mind. He took a last, long breath of cold air and walked up the steps, past a cluster of medical orderlies and nurses all smoking under the entrance's portico. From the snatches of conversation he heard before it all died away at his approach, they were locals. Most of them averted their eyes, but one of them looked hard at him before looking suddenly away as Reinhardt pushed open the wooden doors, their squeak and squeal following him into the hospital's lobby, where he slowed, thinking of those orderlies, the way that one who had looked back seemed suddenly familiar. Something in the way he had been standing, in the set of his eyes. He was about to go back outside when he saw Benfeld waiting for him, the Feldjaeger leaning back against the wall with his arms folded and eyes closed. As Reinhardt hesitated, Benfeld's eyes slit open, then widened as he straightened.

"What do you have, then, Frenchie?" Reinhardt asked, still of two minds about going back outside to find that orderly.

"The bodies got here, all right. Finding a doctor was something else. I had to swing some weight to get done what you wanted done," he said, stifling a yawn, and murmuring an apology as he did so. He indicated an orderly waiting nearby. "He'll take us to the doctor. How did it go up there after I left?"

"About as confusing as I thought it might." Bakarević, the inspector, had taken a look at the bodies in the basement, made no notes, asked no questions, and had then left the house to conduct a series of halfhearted interviews with the people living in and around the street. Between the inspector's German, which was poor, and Reinhardt's stumbling Serbo-Croat, they had made slow headway. No one really wanted to talk, which Reinhardt could understand, but not accept. Toward the end the interviews had resembled interrogations, with Bakarević shouting and Reinhardt pushing and prodding, but all it had elicited them was a confused picture of a quiet night shattered by gunfire, then more silence. Some had said they heard a car, others a truck. Some said the killers spoke German, others were not sure. From most they got tears or protestations or just dumb insolence. The one thing they got from all of them was fear. They were frightened of Reinhardt, of his uniform, but they were more scared of Bakarević and the threat that lurked in his shadow, the fear of the Ustaše. That, above all.

At the end of it all, pooling what information they had, they had constructed a rough timeline of what had happened. At around three in the morning, everyone had been woken by a muffled explosion. Some had said it was more of a hissing sound. Witnesses had reported a bright light and the sounds of men cursing, which must have been the incendiary flare the killers had accidentally triggered. Then silence. Like good survivors, they had all hidden, hoping for whatever storm it was to pass over. Most had stayed hidden, but one person said she had heard the Feldjaeger's vehicle climbing the street, reporting quite accurately the sound a *kubelwagen*'s engine made in low gear. Then there was gunfire, a lot of it, and a handful of people had heard hurried footsteps. There had been voices, most agreed, but no one could or would agree on what had been said, nor even what language. Shortly after the gunshots, another vehicle had driven away.

"Nothing more than we could have guessed for ourselves, really," Reinhardt said, summing it up. "Shall we?" he asked, pointing to the orderly, still thinking that one of those who had been standing outside had seemed familiar to him. Benfeld nodded and the orderly crushed his cigarette under his heel and muttered, "Follow me." He led them into a maze of corridors, Reinhardt feeling, remembering, how much he hated hospitals. The sight and smell of them, the way they seemed to be eerily quiet, or shatteringly noisy, never anything in between. This one was noisy. Shouts and calls, a clatter of doors, and somewhere, someone was screaming as the orderly led them down several flights of stairs into the basements. The air became cooler, the sounds of their footsteps echoing back hard from the bare concrete walls and running ahead of them like heralds.

The orderly indicated a door, muttered, "Wait in there, please," and was gone. Opening the door onto a gust of cold air, Reinhardt saw it was a morgue, and one in much demand. A row of steel cabinets squared the wall on one side, but bodies were stacked on the floor and on tables around the room. Reinhardt spotted the five bodies from the house, one on a dissection table, the other four laid out close together on the floor, all naked.

"They haven't been autopsied? Why not?"

"Sir, it was all I could do to get a doctor to look at them. Anything more . . ." Benfeld shook his head, his lips tightening up. "You may have better luck than me."

Despite the cold, there was a faint miasma in the air, of rot crossed with something chemical, and Reinhardt and Benfeld both lit cigarettes at the same time. They looked at each other self-consciously a moment, and then Benfeld gave a sheepish grin. Reinhardt smiled back, shifting his weight onto his right leg. His left knee was very sore, a night spent running around having done it no favors.

"Pretty awful place," Benfeld said, quietly. The bodies might have agreed, thought Reinhardt, immediately hating the thought. Morgues did that to you. Made you think inane things, like imparting thoughts and feelings to the dead. He walked over to the bodies, looking at them in proper light for the first time. The bone-pale pallor of their skin made their wounds stand out so much more. The mutilations to the faces were awful to look at, matted red and slivered with white where teeth and bone showed.

"Where are the clothes?" Benfeld pointed to a heap on a table. "Anything?"

Benfeld shook his head as he walked over to them and pulled a threadbare cardigan off the top of the pile. "Only this. There's half a name tag on it. Looks like 'Kapet . . .' something-or-other. Rest of the name's gone. The rest of the clothing gives us nothing, except it's pretty obvious none of it was theirs."

The door banged open and a doctor walked in, a young-looking man in a white coat spotted and smeared with blood, and a stethoscope around his neck. He glowered at Benfeld, then turned bloodshot eyes on Reinhardt.

"You're the captain?" Reinhardt nodded. "You know your lieutenant here was making an absolute bloody nuisance of himself all morning? Well, it's bloody outrageous. We've enough trouble keeping the living alive without worrying about what might or might not have happened to the dead."

Reinhardt offered the man a cigarette. He looked desperately tired, his eyes circled in gray.

"Did the lieutenant tell you what happened? That three of my men were murdered last night close to where these bodies—those five there—were found?"

"And I should care about those three men why?"

"No particular reason," said Reinhardt, leaning forward to light the man's cigarette. "But this investigation is important, Doctor."

"Important enough to pull me away from other duties?"

"The longer you argue, the longer you'll be away," said Reinhardt, not unsympathetically. He recognized the man's protests for the form they were, and knowing the doctor needed to protest he was happy enough to give him the time to get it off his chest.

The doctor walked over to the body on the table, then ran a cursory eye over those on the floor. He pursed his lips as he looked up at Reinhardt. "You really needed an examination of these men? It's pretty bloody obvious what killed them."

"I know what killed them, Doctor. Dr. . . . ?"

"Henke," said the doctor.

"I know they were shot first, then mutilated, Dr. Henke. I want the best idea of who they were."

"Who they *were*?" Reinhardt nodded. "Were they even soldiers?" Reinhardt shrugged. "I don't know. My guess—"

"Well, if they weren't soldiers it's not my business," interrupted Henke. He sucked his cigarette red, then stubbed it out in a jar. "Why the hell didn't you have them taken up to the city hospital?"

"Doctor, please. I have my reasons."

"Next time, give them to someone who gives a shit, Captain. Preferably to someone who has had more than two hours' sleep in three days."

"Doctor . . ."

"Not to someone who may need to operate at any moment, and can't afford a mistake no matter how tired he may be."

"I understand, Doctor."

"I wonder."

"I needed this done by someone I could trust. That good enough?"

"Flattery, Captain?" asked Henke. He blinked slowly, as if he could push his exhaustion down and away, then nodded. "Very well," he said. "Give me another cigarette, and we'll see what we can see."

Squinting around the smoke spiraling up into his eye, Henke picked up a clipboard and ran a finger down a page of scrawled notes. "Very well," he breathed out around a long puff of smoke, looking at the bodies and back to his notes. "Much of a muchness, really. Five men, all between the ages of thirty-five and forty years of age, I'd say. Average height. Except for him," Henke said, pointing at the tallest of the corpses. "Six foot three inches, that one. Weight. More or less average for estimated age and height, although none of them would have tipped any scales. Not exactly malnourished, but they weren't high on the hog when they were alive. They were in generally acceptable health. Acceptable for this time and place, of course. Signs of vitamin deficiency on the nails. Lack of calcium. Teeth in generally poor shape. A couple of them had some dentistry done at some point. Prewar stuff. Quite good work.

"The bodies themselves . . . Fairly nondescript. No tattoos or any distinguishing marks of that sort. No birthmarks. A couple of scars. This one"—Henke pointed with his foot—"has what looks like shrapnel wounds on his back." Reinhardt motioned, and Benfeld turned the body over to reveal a cluster of ridged little scars. "Hands show signs of extensive manual labor of some sort, with a fair bit of scarring and callusing. Marked difference in color between faces and torsos, between hands and arms. They were probably men who spent a lot of time outdoors."

"Anything conclusive from the shoulders, or the right hands?"

"Such as?" yawned Henke.

Reinhardt demonstrated. "If they were soldiers, they were likely riflemen, and likely right-handed as are most people. So, their right shoulders might show callusing, or bruising, from the recoil and weight of a rifle. And their right hands"—he demonstrated—"might show callusing on the forefinger, from the trigger, and the gap between thumb and forefinger, from the stock."

Henke nodded, yawning, again. "Yes. I see. No, nothing like that. Or if it's there, it's inconclusive. Moving on. Ligature marks on all their wrists. Tied up before death. Bruising to their knees. They were all quite extensively manhandled after they were killed. A lot of postmortem bruising and scrapes, consistent with a body being dragged around. Picked up, rolled over, that sort of thing."

"That would fit with what they were wearing, and where they were found," murmured Reinhardt.

"Indeed. Now, the cause of death. Single gunshot to the back of the head. Right at the nape. Exit wound through the forehead. Some bruising in the scalps would indicate their heads were forced forward by someone's hand in their hair to expose the nape." The doctor paused, and Reinhardt knew all three of them were imagining that, their minds conjuring up images of the particular hell those men had gone through in the last minutes of their lives.

"What about the mutilations?"

"Postmortem as well. Quite some time afterward, in fact. Done by a blunt object wielded with tremendous force. There's only a few blows—in most cases, two or three—on each man. It takes someone with a lot of strength, or a lot of skill, or both, to inflict those wounds." Henke yawned, looked up and down his notes. "And that's about it, Captain."

"Lividity?"

"Inconclusive. The bodies were obviously shifted around a lot."

"Time of death?"

"Rigor mortis is gone. I'd say they were killed about a day and a half ago. No more."

"An autopsy will tell us more," said Reinhardt, knowing how little the doctor would want to hear that.

"An *autopsy*? Are you serious?"

"Very."

"What the hell would you know, and want to know, anyway?" snapped Henke, tossing his clipboard down and walking around the table.

Reinhardt put a hand on the doctor's chest as he made to walk past. The man felt light, almost weightless. "I used to be a policeman. I know something of how these things work. I have an idea of who they were, but I need an autopsy to confirm it."

"Like *what*?"

"What they ate, and when they ate it."

"Oh for God's sake, Captain," sighed Henke. "They'll have eaten the same shit as the rest of us in this dump."

"Maybe. Please, Doctor. It's important."

"So you keep bloody saying."

"If I have to, I will invoke Feldjaegerkorps authority."

"Look," Henke said, rubbing his eyes with the heels of his palms, "even if I'd agree to do it, I'm not doing it now. I'm no good to anyone. I need some sleep before I go on duty at midday, seeing as I didn't get much last night," he said, glowering at Benfeld. "I'll see what I can do tonight. If it's a slow night."

"Doctor . . ."

"It's the best I can do, Captain," interrupted Henke. "And don't even *think* about bothering any others. They'll give you shorter shrift than I did."

Reinhardt saw there would be no budging him. He offered him the packet of cigarettes. "The least I could do for your troubles."

"Indeed," the doctor said under raised eyebrows, but there was a hint of a smile in his tired eyes. "Check in with me tonight. You or your charming lieutenant. No promises, mind," he said, another cigarette waggling between his lips as he talked. Reinhardt lit it, and Henke nodded his thanks as he walked out. "Lights out as you leave," he called.

Reinhardt and Benfeld followed the doctor back upstairs more slowly. As they climbed the steps, the noise of the hospital crept steadily back in until, as they opened the door at the top of the staircase, it swept around them. Reinhardt felt the ghosts of the past, suddenly, wanting, needing, to be out of there, and he walked faster than he would otherwise have liked, back outside into the chill morning. He paused at the bottom of the steps, trying to relax, before turning to look back up at the hospital.

Reinhardt clenched his jaw against the pain in his knee, and against the rage that surged not far behind it. In the bed opposite, the Austrian with the bandages over his eyes was weeping again, dry sobs, and Reinhardt stifled the urge to limp across and throttle the moaning bastard.

He reached into the drawer on the little table next to him and pulled out the watch. He held it by its chain, watching it spiral first left, then right, then left again, the light flowing up and over it and catching on the inscription on the back. With his thumb he stroked the cursive letters, then pulled the bedclothes up and threw an arm across his face. The fire in his knee began to subside, and he breathed easier, his thumb stroking the watch, thinking, remembering, and he did not struggle his mind to understand the contradiction of how the memory of that British trench could calm him like it did.

"It'll fall off if you keep playing with it."

Reinhardt jumped. It was that nurse, again. The one who was always needling him, about the war, about politics, about everything. "I wasn't . . ." he said, flushing red. He brought his hand out from under the covers, showing her the watch. She smiled, and it was something bright and vivacious.

"Much better," she said. "You should do that more often."

"Play with the watch?"

"Smile."

He had not realized he had smiled at all.

"Hopefully you'll have a lot more to smile about soon enough."

"What?"

"The war. It's over. It's finished," she said as she bustled around. He liked watching her, the economy of her movements. Nothing wasted. She filled his water jug, then began straightening the sheets, then stopped and looked at him. "No one told you? This morning, in fact. An armistice, they're calling it. Fighting stopped at eleven o'clock, today, this eleventh of November. And I'm sure someone somewhere was still fighting at five to eleven."

"Someone's got to be the last to die," muttered Reinhardt, but his heart was not in it. He stared at the ceiling, at the spiderweb tracery of cracks in the plaster. Over . . . ?

"Spoken like a true stormtrooper," the nurse said, sardonically. "Open wide." She stuck a thermometer in his mouth.

"It's really over?" Reinhardt mumbled.

"That's what they're saying. Lift up your head." She plumped the pillow none too gently, and he lowered himself back down. She paused, one hand on her hip, the other smoothing her hair back over her ears. Her eyes were gray, very bright and piercing as she looked down on him.

"What?" said Reinhardt, almost spitting out the thermometer.

"Just thinking. What's to become of someone like you, now?"

"Someone like me?"

"A soldier. Not just any soldier."

"A wounded soldier."

"Stop feeling sorry for yourself," she said, plucking the thermometer out of his mouth. "Things could be worse, for you. But they'll be better soon."

"Oh God," he sighed, "not your bloody manifesto again."

"Yes, my manifesto again." Her color rose, her eyes sparking. "You can laugh, or sneer, my friend. But someone like you ought to know that we can't go back to the way things were. Look where that got you."

Reinhardt had no reply to that. He just watched her put away her things, and as she turned to go, he felt as if he teetered on a high edge.

"What's your name?" She turned, her arms straight on the little trolley she pushed, her fingers spread wide and strong. "All this time, you've said everything else to me, but not your name."

The trolley rattled quietly into motion, and she looked over her shoulder, the sun catching on the curve of one cheek as she smiled.

"Carolin," she said.

"What next, sir?" asked Benfeld.

Reinhardt blinked, Benfeld's words snapping him back from that favorite memory, that first time the woman who was to be his wife had told him her name. His eyes settled on the steps where the orderlies had been talking and smoking. In his mind's eye he could still see that man who had seemed familiar to him, but who and where kept slipping sideways and would not come. Reinhardt blew out a long breath through puffed cheeks. "Breakfast? Then a think."

And then Reinhardt remembered. He remembered where he had seen him before.

On Baščaršija Square, outside the little shop where Reinhardt would have his coffee. He was pretty sure it had been Simo, the Partisan who had led him on that winding route through Bentbaša to meet Doctor Begović.

9

"Who would be missing five men, Frenchie?"

It was the same question from last night, and there was still no answer. Benfeld looked back at Reinhardt over the rim of his mug of what passed for coffee, here in the barracks mess.

"Five men," Reinhardt continued. "From what I hear of what's happening in this city, five bodies is not an unusual number to find. So why all this effort to hide them? Who were they being hidden from? Who would be missing five men?"

"The Ustaše?" Benfeld ventured.

Reinhardt nodded, his tongue stroking that gap. "The army?" he countered.

"The Partisans?" said Benfeld, eyebrows raised and lips pursed upward as if he expected a rebuke, but Reinhardt just motioned him to go on. "In Russia, it would sometimes happen with the Partisans there, or in the cities. Infighting. Fallings-out. Or some group not in line with whatever directive was the flavor of the month. Maybe . . . someone in the Partisans needed to get rid of someone. More than one person. Some faction taking over? But they can't afford to be seen to be divided? I don't know. Just a thought."

"Not a bad one." Reinhardt nodded. "But short of walking up to a Partisan and asking him, I don't know how we'd prove it."

"No, sir," said Benfeld, looking downcast into his coffee. Reinhardt watched him, glancing down at the Knight's Cross hanging around Benfeld's neck and wondering where this hero of Kursk lurked at times like these when it took so little to set him back.

"So let's look where we can, Frenchie. I want you to start going through after-action reports. Go back to the beginning of the week. The condition of the bodies would not indicate they were killed any later than that. Have a look as well on any lists of deserters. Men missing in action. Men taken prisoner. Things like that."

"Yes, sir." Benfeld nodded. "What about our duties, though?"

"It's cleared with the colonel. We can work on this, but not full-time." Captain Lainer had been the one to push on that, when Scheller had come up to the site earlier that morning. The big captain had still been fuming at the deaths of his men as Triendl, the third Feldjaeger, the one who had survived the shootings up in Logavina, had passed away. Lainer had pushed Scheller to release Reinhardt full time to investigating it, but it just would not have been possible. They all knew it. There was too much to do. Besides which, Neuffer was insisting on the Feldgendarmerie's view that the deaths could be left to the Ustaše to investigate, that German resources were best spent elsewhere.

"What makes you sure it wasn't just Partisans, Reinhardt?" Scheller had asked.

Reinhardt had felt Lainer's eyes hot on him. "You can't rule it out, sir, but this is what I see. I see three Feldjaeger with first-class equipment. Three StGs. Valuable weapons. Several hundred rounds of ammunition. Pistols. A good knife. A better compass. Money and identity papers. Medals."

"Your point?" the colonel had asked.

"None of it was taken. The bodies weren't even touched. Whoever did this was in too much of a hurry. Or couldn't take the risk that the equipment would be found and come back to haunt them. But I've never heard of a Partisan who didn't take the time to strip a dead German of at least his weapon."

That had seemed to seal the matter. The Feldjaeger would investigate the deaths of their own, Scheller had told a scowling Neuffer, and any assistance requested would be rendered.

Reinhardt swirled what was left of his coffee around in the mug. "You are on shift at the train station tonight," he said to Benfeld. "So try to get some rest before then."

"What about you, sir?" asked Benfeld, leaning back on the bench to pull his cigarettes out of his pocket, offering one to Reinhardt.

"I'm going to go and have a look at the 999th Field Punishment Battalion. Seeing as it's on their patch of ground we found the bodies. Something the matter, Frenchie?"

"Sir?"

"You squirmed when I mentioned the penal battalion, and not for the first time. I noticed it last night, as well."

"My brother is in a penal battalion. In Russia."

"I'm sorry to hear it, Benfeld."

The lieutenant's mouth twisted. "Ahh," he said, drawing deep on his cigarette. His hand shook where he held his fingers up to his mouth, and then it was as if a dam had broken, and words began to tumble out. "He was . . . he was always the silent one. Me, I could talk the back legs off a donkey. Except, he had this god-awful knack of opening his mouth at the wrong moment. He never learned to shut it when it mattered. At school. In bars. At work. He was always getting into trouble, or fights. That's why I'm here, you know," he said, taking another deep drag. "We're from Alsace, but we were never French, and after the first war the French never let us forget it. Heinz fell for all that . . . talk . . . about Germany, and the Germans, and he joined up. My father made me join up too. 'He's your younger brother, Max,' he said. 'You bring him home safe and sound. Keep an eye on him.' And I did, for as long as I could, and then he went and said something or other to some officer, and they had him in a penal battalion before you knew it. I couldn't do anything to get him out."

"You have news of him."

"None, sir. But I know his unit was in a sector of the front that was overrun at Kursk."

Reinhardt finished his own cigarette, dropping it into the dregs of his coffee, feeling for the younger man's pain, but unable to make that small leap, to reach out beyond himself. "I am sorry to hear that, Frenchie," he said, feeling how inadequate such words were but unable to offer more, unsure even if Benfeld would accept anything from him.

"No, sir. It's me. It's nothing. Let's be getting on with it, shall we?"

Reinhardt took a car and driver and ordered him up to the old Ottoman fortress atop Vratnik hill. It was a steep drive, up through the wreaths of a light mist, and the car lurched up slowly, wheels skidding on the cobbles. They swung past the squat bulk of the old Visegrad Gate and followed the old city walls down to the Vratnik fortress, right at the end of a flat ridge of rock. There were Feldgendarmerie on duty at the gates, gorgets shining brightly in the wintery light on top of long, leather greatcoats. They waved the car forward, and a sergeant ran hard eyes across Reinhardt and his driver as he scanned their identity papers.

"Feldjaegerkorps? Your business here, sir?"

"To see the commanding officer or the chief of staff. I'm not expected."

"Chief of staff'd be best," said the sergeant, and then he cracked a morbid smile. "You'll have to wait a moment, though. He's inducting a new batch of recruits. In the courtyard."

There were two groups of soldiers standing at attention in front of the battalion's command post. One group was obviously of officers. He could see it in their bearing, the cut of their uniforms, and in the disbelieving air several of them had, as if they expected to wake at any moment from a bad dream. From somewhere deep inside he pitied them, but just at that moment the door to the command post crashed open and a major of the Feldgendarmerie stomped out in front of the two groups of soldiers, his gorget bright at his throat.

It was the same major from down at the checkpoint, the one who had spoken to Bunda, who had made the Ustaša back down. His name was Erwin Jansky, Dreyer had said. At the checkpoint, Reinhardt had noted the man's bearing and demeanor, the barely concealed edge of contempt. Up here, the man was in his element and no niceties bound him. There was a manic gleam in his eyes as he paraded back and forth in front of them, drawing the suspense out, feet pecking the ground as much as walking on it. From the command post a second officer stepped out, a colonel, looking old and sick, and a third officer that Reinhardt quickly realized was General Herzog. The general and colonel conferred quietly a moment, and then the general made a solicitous gesture and the old colonel nodded, stepped back.

"Soldiers," the general all but bellowed, his voice raw and harsh. He ran his sharp little eyes across the two groups. "I have only a simple message for you. You were all found guilty of offenses against the military code of conduct. You have all been sentenced. But your services are once again required by the Fatherland. You are being given a second chance. A chance to redeem yourselves. I suggest you take it." His eyes stabbed across them, back and forth, looking through them. "Take this chance to wash your names clean. Take this chance to do great deeds again in defense of the Fatherland, and in defense of our great cause." He nodded, stepped back. "Report as your names are called out."

Jansky slid up from behind him, standing before those Reinhardt had identified as officers.

"Well, look what a bunch of fucking retarded traitors the good Lord has seen fit to dish up to me today," he barked, baring his teeth in what passed for a smile. The manic gleam in his eyes flickered brighter as he read from a clipboard. "Commies. Pinkies. Half-breeds. Politicos. Head cases. *Shell shock?*" he screeched. "For the love of God, isn't there an honest deserter, thief, or rapist in among the lot of you? Or are they all over there?" he sneered, jerking his head at the other group. His eyes suddenly hooked on Reinhardt's and he smiled, as if drawing him into some secret joke. Eyes in the two groups flicked between them.

"Well, what heaven sends we must endure. Who said that, Reinhardt?" Jansky snapped, swiveling in his direction. The general's eyes followed, lingered for a moment.

"Goethe," replied a startled Reinhardt.

"Goethe, *sir*," repeated the major, seemingly absurdly pleased. "Now, greater minds than mine have decided you are to be stood up in uniforms, again. Me, personally? I'd have just done what the Russkies do, and shoved a pair of grenades into your cells." He stalked up and down as he spoke, his eyes stabbing over the ranks. "But instead, they've given you to me. Me would be Major Jansky. And I would be the chief of staff of this battalion."

His eyes flayed across them, and for a moment his grin slipped, twisted. Jansky's face went still, then shuddered back to life. "So, boys, here you are. Soldiers again, they say. We have infantry. We have engineers. We have tankers," he said, winking at a man in the black uniform of the Panzers. "But whatever you were, whatever uniform you wore, old or new, now you'll all have one of these." He held up a red triangle. Just a red triangle, about the size of his palm. Reinhardt knew what it meant. Most of them did, here, there, men leaning back, recoiling from it, but others in the ranks were not so sure. "You know what this means, boys, right? *Right?* You!" He jabbed a finger at an overweight officer in the front rank. "Fatso. You know what this means?"

"How dare you refer to me in that manner!" the officer spluttered. "You will respect my rank and—"

The man was floored by a blow to the jaw. He sprawled on the cobbles, looking dazed. "I'll call you whatever the fuck I want. Fatso. 'Cause you're mine now. Get up. *UP!* So," Jansky seethed, his face leering into the officer's. "Do you know what this means?"

"No, sir."

"He doesn't *know*! Poor fat fucker. Reinhardt!" he cackled, his arm stabbing out. "Come closer, Reinhardt. Come. You know. You're a Feldjaeger. This, boys," he said, standing to one side, presenting Reinhardt with his arms as if he were a tailor's dummy, "this is a *Feldjaeger*. Something quite special. You'll learn. Anyway, Reinhardt, tell him. Go on."

"It is the badge for a penal unit."

"That's *right*! A *penal* unit. It means, boys, you belong to the 999th Field Punishment Battalion. Means you belong to me. Means whatever you were, whatever rank you had, you can forget. Means if you thought things were bad, boys, you're in for a surprise 'cause you're really in the shit now. You'll dig shit. Sleep in it. Walk through it. Eat it if you have to, and ask for seconds."

The smile froze on Jansky's face again, and then he looked down at his clipboard. "When I call your name, step forward. *Amelung, Peter*," he snapped. A prisoner stepped forward, coming to attention before Jansky, who looked him up and down before looking back down at his papers. "Get yourself to A Company. *Audendorf, Conrad*."

On it went, Jansky calling out the names, reeling off the assignments. The men in the ranks dwindled to either side, chivvied and herded by sergeants and a pair of lieutenants until they were all gone, and Jansky was needling those eyes of his at Reinhardt.

"Something I can help you with, Reinhardt?"

"I want to talk about the murders of three Feldjaeger. Last night."

"Yes, I heard about it. What of it?"

"It happened at a construction site being worked on by your battalion."

"It happened down the street from it, so I understand. At three in the morning or some other ungodly hour."

"It didn't stop your men showing up at the equally ungodly hour of four thirty."

"That's true." Jansky grinned. "We drive them hard. No point to them being here, otherwise."

"Another five bodies were found in the construction site itself."

"There wouldn't be much point in just telling you to get lost, would there?" Reinhardt said nothing. There was no need; a Feldjaeger's aura and authority were right there, between them. Jansky's jaw clenched, and he nodded, the sharp edges he presented to the world seeming to soften. "How can I help you? Make it quick, please."

"We'll make it as long as it needs to be," said Reinhardt. Jansky's face went blank, and Reinhardt checked himself, wondering how much of this was him talking, and how much was Dreyer talking through him, how much of it was his friend's dislike for this man. It was easy, Reinhardt realized, to see something of Dreyer's fixation. There was something mesmerizing about Jansky. Like a wound, or a bruise, you could not help but probe and pick at. Like that gap in his teeth he could not leave alone. "I'd like to talk to the officer on duty at the site yesterday."

"That would be Lieutenant Metzler. I have to see the general off. Wait in the command post, and I'll send him to you."

Reinhardt stepped into the command post, where an iron stove shimmered in a corner producing far too much heat. The door to the commander's office was half open and, looking in, Reinhardt saw the old colonel with a handkerchief clasped to his mouth as he coughed. There was a musty smell of sickness from in there, a kind of tubercular stench. It reminded him of the trenches, of bunkers crammed to the brim with men, the whites of their eyes like arcs as the ceilings shook to the rolling thunder of a bombardment overhead.

Two men came to attention in the outer office: a sergeant behind a wide desk, and another man, a clerk, tucked away in the corner, almost hidden behind a red wooden chest. His desk was a rampart of piles of paper, forms, pay books, and ration cards, bastioned with ink bottles and jars of pens and pencils that seemed to wall him off from the rest of the room. As if he felt Reinhardt's eyes on him, the man glanced up, then seemed to hunch away and down, his arm curling protectively over whatever he was writing on like a schoolboy not wanting his homework copied.

"Who is out there?"

The querulous voice came from the colonel's office. Reinhardt and the other two men exchanged glances, and the sergeant made to close the officer's door but the colonel's hand came around the edge of it, spidery fingers blanched white at the tips as he held on tight.

"Colonel Pistorius, sir," protested the sergeant.

The old colonel ignored him, peering at Reinhardt and squinting at his Iron Cross.

"Who are you? You don't have the air of a condemned man to me."

"Captain Reinhardt, sir," said Reinhardt, coming to attention. "Feldjaegerkorps."

Pistorius frowned at him, clasping a handkerchief to his mouth as he coughed. He waved Reinhardt in, shuffling over to a long trestle table.

"Tell me then," Pistorius said, wiping his mouth. "How did it go? Outside."

"Sir?" asked Reinhardt, confused at the question. Behind him, the sergeant hovered in the doorway, unsure what to do, before closing the door quietly.

"How did my men perform, Captain? Outside."

"Creditably enough, sir."

The colonel's eyes lifted. They were bloodshot and watery, but there was a sudden glint in them. "'Creditably'? Careful, Captain. That sounds perilously like what an old-school officer might have said. Or a damn, obfuscating sergeant. Say what you mean, man."

"Yes, sir."

"Well?"

"It was a harsh welcome, sir."

Pistorius wheezed, his handkerchief blotting at his mouth and coming away bloody. "Harsh?" he managed.

"Personally, I was never convinced it did much to motivate a man."

The colonel blinked at Reinhardt's Iron Cross again, his neck thrusting forward, wattled like a turkey's and burdened with the gorget that swung back and forth like a tavern's sign. "Only real war was the first war, and the only real Cross is a first-war Cross," he muttered, sounding like nothing more than a crotchety old man musing in a dark corner while life surged past without him. He erupted again into a fit of coughing, his hand reaching blindly backward for a chair, collapsing back into it. Reinhardt looked at him anew, wondering who he was and where he had been. "What are you doing here?" Pistorius managed, finally, his eyes suddenly clear.

"Major Jansky is helping my inquiries into the deaths of three Feldjaeger last night."

"What's he . . ." he wheezed, his voice petering out. "What's he got to do with that?"

"Colonel, sir, is everything all right?" Jansky stood in the door, then stalked into the room, a mug of something steaming in his hands. He handed it solicitously to Pistorius, who took it gratefully, folding it against his wracked chest.

"Fine, Jansky, fine," Pistorius breathed, folding himself back into his chair. Whatever fire might have sparked the old officer to life, it was gone. Reinhardt stared at Jansky, who motioned out with his head.

"A brave, brave man," Jansky murmured as he shut the door, quietly. "By all rights he should have been invalided out, but he won't go."

A lieutenant of the Feldgendarmerie waiting in the outer office came to attention. Looking closely at him, Reinhardt realized he had seen him before as well, at the checkpoint in the car with Major Jansky and Brandt.

"Lieutenant Metzler," said Jansky.

"Major Jansky has told you what I want?" The lieutenant nodded. "Tell me about the construction site."

"It's an anti-aircraft installation, sir," Lieutenant Metzler responded.

"Go on."

"We were building site emplacements for four flak guns."

"Go on."

"We were tasked with grading the place flat. We had a section from an engineering company to help with the heavy work, bringing the walls down and such. A couple of demining people as well."

"Why?"

"Unexploded munitions, sir. The Allies bombed the place a few weeks ago. Could be anything left in there." Reinhardt nodded for him to continue. "That's it, really, sir."

The door opened and a sergeant put his head in the command post. "Major, sir. You're needed in the transportation unit."

"It can wait," Jansky said.

"Begging your pardon, sir, Alexiou says it's urgent."

Jansky sighed, his eyes on Reinhardt. "Can I trust you not to mishandle my lieutenant, Captain Reinhardt?"

"I'll give him back just as I found him, Major."

"Very well, then. Mind your p's and q's, Lieutenant," Jansky said as he followed the sergeant out the door.

"We'll do the same, Lieutenant. Outside, please." Reinhardt followed him out, unable to stay in that stifling room with its fungal reek. He took a long, low breath, clearing his lungs. The lieutenant watched Jansky go, feet stabbing the ground across the courtyard, over to a cluster of tents and the remnants of white Ottoman walls, then turned back to him, small brown eyes peering up at him from beneath bushy eyebrows. He had big, drooping cheeks, making him look like a hound. It made him seem hangdog harmless, but watching his eyes, and with a glance at the man's heavy knuckles, Reinhardt was not so sure.

"What time did you finish yesterday?" Reinhardt asked as he pulled out his cigarettes. "Smoke?"

"Thank you, sir, no. Umm, we finished at sunset, thereabouts."

"Why?"

"No point staying longer, sir. No light."

"Right. Notice anything unusual?" asked Reinhardt, lighting his cigarette and waving out his match. The lieutenant shook his head, inclining it slightly, making him look more like a dog than he usually did. "People hanging around?"

"No, sir."

"Someone there who wouldn't normally be?"

"No, sir."

"Vehicles? That sort of thing?" asked Reinhardt, building up the rhythm, keeping his eyes direct and level.

"Nothing, sir."

"Any trouble with the locals?"

"Never, sir."

"Any Ustaše poking about?"

"None, sir."

"So, it gets dark here early, doesn't it?"

"Yes, sir."

"About when . . . ?"

"We start losing the light at about seven o'clock in the afternoon."

"And you stop work?"

"No lights. Like I said, sir."

"No lights. And there's nothing else you could be doing up there?"

"Nothing."

"Nothing?"

"Just putting away tools. That kind of thing."

"You saw nothing and no one?" Reinhardt said, a little smile on his face, inviting Metzler to play the game.

"Nothing, sir," the lieutenant said, relaxing, those heavy fists of his uncurling slightly.

"What time does the sun come up?"

"About . . . six thirty."

"Six thirty. And it's dark before then."

"Yes, sir."

"Nothing to see. Nothing to be done."

"Not unless you want to go stumbling around in the dark," said Metzler, allowing a little levity into his voice.

"So what was Lieutenant Brandt doing there with fifty men at four thirty in the morning?" Light had begun flushing the dark from the eastern sky, graying upward from the mounded horizon, at around six o'clock as Reinhardt was finishing up at the construction site, and the sun was fully up around thirty minutes later. The lieutenant's mouth moved, and then he swallowed, and his fists bunched tight again. Reinhardt said nothing, letting Metzler work out the implications of what he had just admitted.

"I don't . . ."

"What might you have been doing at that time up there?" asked Reinhardt, tightening the screws a little.

"I don't . . ."

"Just think. Give me an idea," said Reinhardt, poking, prodding. "Anything."

"I'm sure I would have had a reason, sir," said Metzler, his eyes blanking out, and the whole of him tightening back up as if drawn tight by a thread.

"Amaze me, Lieutenant."

"I think you'd have to ask Lieutenant Brandt that, sir."

"And where do I find him?"

"I don't know, sir."

"Who might know?"

"Major Jansky, sir."

Full circle.

10

Reinhardt dismissed Metzler, telling him to find Major Jansky for him. He wondered he was not more frustrated than he was with this kind of obtuseness from men like Metzler, and wondered if it had anything to do with his being a Feldjaeger and had an expectation that he would be obeyed. He examined that thought a moment but decided to put it aside for later. He could ill afford his habitual introspection now.

He watched Metzler hurry across the muddy expanse of the inner courtyard. Old stone buildings stood here and there hard against the walls, the stables and barracks of the Ottoman troops who had once garrisoned this place, and mixed in with them or extending from them, more recent structures of brick and timber and canvas. Smoke drifted up from some of them, and a hammer rang somewhere. Over in the far corner, past where Metzler had gone, stood a row of trucks, men working around one of them, waist-deep in the engine compartment. A sergeant bawled at a group of men who were doing punishment drills along one of the walls, kneeling, crawling, running, falling face-first, rising again to the discordant rhythm of his orders. Not far from that, a group of men in mismatched uniforms holding shovels and picks was marshaled under the harsh bellows of a pair of Feldgendarmes, then loaded onto a truck, aided by kicks and blows from rifle butts. Reinhardt watched the truck rock past and out under the fortress's entrance.

Next to the command post was a stone building with a heavy wooden door. Moving without thinking, he pushed it open, stepping down into a long, low, darkened space, and immediately knew it for a barracks. Wooden bunks rose to the left and right, and the air was tight with the closed-in fug of sleeping men. There was a low susurration, slow and heavy like the tide, the breathing of exhausted men. A soldier by the door, woken by the light and cold, blinked open fuddled eyes, saw Reinhardt, and pulled himself out of his bed. The man's uniform was filthy, the bottoms of his trousers and the cuffs of his shirt caked in mud, and his eyes were sunk far back beneath the spare line of his brow.

"As you were," Reinhardt said, quietly. The man made no protest, just folded himself back into his bunk as Reinhardt backed outside, closing the door quietly, then followed the smells to the mess tent. It was largely empty inside, only one or two soldiers sitting at long, wooden benches and crates of iron rations—the army's emergency supplies—standing open along the wall of the tent. A cook was breaking the hard, all-but-tasteless black bread from the ration packs into a vat of soup. In the cauldron the water foamed and roiled, pulling Reinhardt's gaze, and a waxen shape appeared. A skull with a caprine eye stared gravely through ribboned flesh. It turned and sank away, bobbing up again as though eager for a last glimpse of this world. Reinhardt watched fixedly as the cook ladled soup into a man's bowl, then watched him find a table to sit alone at.

He ducked out of the tent and walked slowly over to the parapet, to a break in the saw-toothed line of the old Ottoman walls. The mist had lifted, and the edges of the low cloud were silvered by a weak sun shining over the western hills. Like a memory, the washed-out form of the city beneath was overlaid with another image, a sepia-toned recall of what it used to be. There was no color anymore. The town was, he thought self-consciously, rather like himself. Sarajevo used to stand proud, or at least unbowed. Filled with memories of better times, better masters. A rose, Begović had called it. A rose, in the shelter of her mountains. Bad times were transitory in Sarajevo, like her masters. Ottomans. Austrians. Ustaše. Germans. Coming and going. Forever flowing, rolling through, like the waters of the rivers that flowed through this valley, sometimes raging high, sometimes curling low, as the city and its people endured.

"*Hey*. Copper."

The voice was a low hiss. Reinhardt frowned, looking around for the voice. "Over here. Hey, copper. Share a smoke with an old soldier?"

A man was standing behind a pile of boxes and barrels, up against the wall. When Reinhardt saw him, the man backed farther into the shadows, his eyes and head shifting from side to side. He was a thin man, quite tall, in an ill-fitting coat, his hands and wrists hanging well below the edge of its cuffs. He smiled, a wet gleam of teeth.

"Got a smoke, Captain?" the man asked, again.

Reinhardt looked over his shoulder to see if anyone was watching, then stepped toward him, offering the packet. The man took a cigarette, smoothed it between his fingers, then under his nose. "Nice," he murmured. "Light?" The flared match Reinhardt offered pulled the man's face out of the shadows, all vertical lines, pinched, drawn, before the light faded out. "Thanks." The cigarette glowed, faded out, glowed again.

"I've heard of you Feldjaeger," the man said, quietly. He could not seem to stay still. "They say there's not much you can't do. D'you think you could get me out of this unit?" The man pointed at his tunic, where a red triangle was the only insignia he bore.

"Why would I do that?"

The cigarette glowed again. "I could make it worth your while, Captain."

"Go on, then." The man frowned, looking startled, but said nothing. "Cat got your tongue?"

The man winced, bouncing his weight from one place to another, and a grimace of a smile flickered across his face and was gone. "Cat's not got my tongue, but he's got my bloody balls. I reckon you're my ticket, copper. My big one. It's finally come in."

"I don't see a finishing line, do you? So, in your own time, which you'd better make quick, what is it you want to tell me? And what's your name, anyway?"

"Later." The man shook his head. "If you stop at the corner by Baščaršija, when you leave, I'll meet you there."

"Why would I want to?"

"You're a good copper. You might be interested."

Reinhardt opened his mouth to protest, but the man was gone, slipping backward and away. Reinhardt stepped back out into the open space of the courtyard. A group of men walked slowly past. They were dressed in German uniforms, but only a red badge adorned their tunics. They were stocky, heavy men, with dark skin and darker hair. They looked at him as they crossed the far side of the courtyard, an open appraisal, no hint of subservience, no acknowledgment of his authority over them. For some reason, Reinhardt felt a chill, and then the pressure of more eyes. Under an archway of dressed white stone, back in its shadow, another pair of men watched him, an enormous dog panting at their feet.

Reinhardt walked back across the courtyard to the command post. Jansky looked up from the orderly's table as he came in, and a little smile crossed his face.

"You're still here?" Jansky asked.

"I sent Metzler to find you."

"Oh? He didn't find me. But here I am. Working," he said, spreading his arms to encompass the room, with its desks and the sludge of paperwork atop them. "'*Even hell has its rights*,'" he said, looking inquiringly at Reinhardt, as if he challenged him to state the source of that particular quotation.

"Goethe," Reinhardt guessed, again.

"Indeed." Jansky cocked his head, birdlike. "I'm surprised to find you still here."

"I had a bit of a look around. While I was waiting for you."

From the desk in the corner, the little clerk's head peeped up from behind his red chest, then ducked back down. Jansky stepped closer, his mouth stretching in a wet gleam of a smile. "Let me walk you to your car, Captain," he said, placing a firm hand in Reinhardt's back. Reinhardt allowed himself to be steered outside, as much in surprise as from anything else. "I've been asking around about you," said Jansky, closing the door, rubbing his hands together briskly against the chill. He began walking over to Reinhardt's car. "I've been told that as you are leading something of an investigation into those Feldjaeger's deaths, you are to be afforded every cooperation. You've had that from me this morning, wouldn't you say?"

"Lieutenant Metzler was interesting, sir. If not as informative as I might have hoped."

"An accurate description of Lieutenant Metzler, Captain. *Limited* might best describe his character. He ought to have known why Lieutenant Brandt and his men were there."

"So Lieutenant Metzler did find you?"

Jansky smiled, something small and conspiratorial. "Forgive my little games, Captain. When you have spent as much time as I have around thieves and liars and blackguards, such as those men sent to serve in these ranks, well, I'm afraid truth is not always the best currency to use. I do apologize."

"Brandt said he was there for work. He said he had fifty men and a job to do."

"Lieutenant Brandt was there to collect some materials needed for work elsewhere."

"Where elsewhere?"

"Zenica, Captain," said Jansky.

Reinhardt stopped walking, feeling Jansky's hand fall away from his back. "Zenica is about eighty kilometers north of here."

Jansky nodded. "Which meant Brandt had a long drive in front of him, hence the early start. Zenica's where the next defense line's being built. It means the decision's been made that Sarajevo will be abandoned to the Partisans, but I'm not sure that secret's been shared with the Ustaše. Nor with our high command," he finished, with something of a portentous tone, as if to imply which of those two particular devils was the worst.

"It's no secret we're evacuating the city," said Reinhardt.

"No. But it's a secret we're giving it up without much of a fight. So, please, Captain? I know you need to conduct your affairs, but I would appreciate your keeping that information to yourself." His hand came to rest firmly on Reinhardt's arm. "Your word on this?"

Reinhardt nodded slowly, trying hard not to cringe away from Jansky's pincerlike grip. "Very well, then."

"If there's nothing else, Captain?" said Jansky, drawing himself up and away, suddenly, all hard and angular.

"Nothing else, sir."

"A pleasant day, Captain."

Reinhardt saluted and then walked over to his car. He stood by the door, lit a cigarette, and ran his eyes around the inside of that courtyard. Here, there, dotted around the walls, little knots of men—two here, three there—looked back at him.

"Baščaršija," he said to the driver, a corporal with an Iron Cross ribbon on his coat. He passed him a cigarette, then leaned over to light it for him. "Take your time about it. There may be someone to meet on the way."

"Right you are, sir," murmured the driver, hauling the *kubelwagen* in a tight circle out of the courtyard, out through the archway, past the Feldgendarmes in their leather coats around their brazier, and back down the winding road down the hill. Where the road joined up with King Alexander Street and Baščaršija ran down toward the Miljacka River, Reinhardt motioned the driver to slow, then stop, pulling the car to the side of the road. There was a food distribution underway, lines of people wound across the square, trucks with red crosses on them, and the place was full of people, an eddying swirl pulled in by the presence or expectation of help. He did not know how he would spot that man in all this, doubting he could have made it out of that fortress, anyway.

"Planning on staying long, sir?" asked the driver.

"Not long. I'm supposed to meet . . . *there*," said Reinhardt, spotting him. "Five minutes. Then blow the horn." He walked briskly over to the corner of the square, eyes tracking left, right, back up the road to the fortress, watching for something, anything.

"Copper!"

He turned at the hissed voice. The man was backed up into a narrow alley, his eyes and head shifting from side to side over Reinhardt's shoulders. He motioned Reinhardt deeper into the alley. Reinhardt paused, then ostentatiously released the catch on his pistol's holster and took several small steps in after the man. The place stank of human waste, of damp and rot.

"Got another smoke?" Reinhardt passed him one, then lit it for him. "Name's Kreuz," the man said, taking a long draw on his cigarette, exhaling through clenched teeth with his eyes flashing left and right. "How many penal battalions you come across, Captain?"

"This is my first."

"This is my second. I been a bad boy, Captain. But I did my time in the first one, got out, then managed to get myself straight back in. I'm what you might call a repeat offender, Captain."

"Makes me wonder all the more why I'm talking to you, then."

"Don't be hasty, Captain. Copper like you should know. Patience is the name of the game."

"It's certainly the name of some games. And why do you keep calling me 'copper'?"

Kreuz laid a finger alongside his nose, his jumpiness gone all of a sudden. "I can tell. I can always tell. You were a real one once, weren't you? Big-city copper. What was it? Hamburg? Berlin?"

"What is it you want?"

"Like I said, I want out of here before I get done in."

"Why would you get 'done in'?"

"'Cause people like me have a habit of sticking their nose in where it's not wanted. Occupational hazard, some calls it. Occupational therapy's what I call it."

"You're a snitch?"

"I'm that, Captain. A man has to live. And be true to his nature. And I been hearing things."

"Let me guess," Reinhardt said, losing interest. No one liked a snitch. He was talking to a man the Feldgendarmerie probably paid as an informant to keep an eye on what was being said and done in the ranks. "You've heard one too many things."

"I'm *serious*," Kreuz hissed, and his edginess was back. "The hiwis have been arguing. They're not happy."

"Is that supposed to mean something?"

"The battalion's riddled with 'em," Kreuz rasped, the sound drawing hard against the back of his throat. "How's a man like me s'posed to make a living if he can't understand a word of what's being said?"

"Kreuz, you're talking German to me, and I can hardly understand a word you're saying."

"Hiwis, Captain. They drive. They cook. They forage. The bloody battalion runs on them."

"Hiwis? *Hilfswiliger?* Foreign volunteers?"

"You could call 'em that. Started with the Greeks. Then the Albanians. We've got a few Serbs, some Bulgarians, a couple of Russians. But it's the Greeks and Albanians that are the worst."

"Worst for what?"

"Having things their way. The Greeks've a boss, called Alexiou. Some kind of old patriarch. Him'n his sons rule the roost. Live like kings for all the good they do." Kreuz drew furiously on the cigarette, twitching, a live wire needing to be grounded. He poked his head out around the corner, eyes flashing left and right. "Look, do you want to help me?"

"I thought you wanted to help me."

Kreuz giggled. "Right, right. Forgot that bit. Well, the hiwis've been arguing. Among themselves. And with some of the guards. I been told to . . ."

"Who told you?"

"The guards. The chain dogs. Bloody Feldgendarmes. Them that's supposed to be in charge of this. They told me to get in among them.

Find out what they're saying. 'Cept I can't understand it, can I? And the dogs won't take that for an answer. So they keep pushing, and I keep poking around, and I'm sure the hiwis're wise to me, now."

"Occupational hazard, seems to me," said Reinhardt, still wondering where this was going.

"And you would be right, Captain." Kreuz giggled, again. "Don't get me wrong, I get by doing what I do. Extra smokes. Easier work. First pick of the girls if there's any after the chain dogs get done with 'em."

"Get to the point, man," snapped Reinhardt, his mouth twisting.

"So the chain dogs are telling me to keep an eye on the hiwis, the hiwis are wise to that, and then the hiwis tell me to keep an eye on the guards. If I don't, I'll end up in a ditch somewhere, and I know they keep their promises like that. So there I am, hammer on one side, anvil on the other. And then this big-shot officer comes a'visiting, and the hiwis get worked up like I've never seen them . . ."

"Kreuz, wait. Wait." Reinhardt put up a hand, slowing the torrent of words. "This isn't making sense."

"I keep hearing a name. A couple of names. When the hiwis are arguing."

"What names?"

"Two names. Men the hiwis was close with. One called Berthold. The other called Seymer."

"Berthold and Seymer?"

Kreuz nodded. "Got another smoke?"

"No. What do you expect me to do about two names like that?"

"Look into it, Captain. Investigate." Kreuz took a deep breath, as if trying to control himself, but then it all seemed to fall apart around the edges. "Look, look. I did a bit of poking around on my own. Both of them are reported missing. Missing in action, is what they're saying. But I don't believe it. It's been over a week, now, and their *soldbuchs* is still in the command post."

"*Soldbuchs?*"

"*Yesss,*" Kreuz hissed, taking a couple of bouncy steps forward, making Reinhardt take a step back. "Their *soldbuchs*. They've vanished, but their books've not been handed in. You need to do that, right? When a soldier dies? So what're they keeping 'em for?"

Reinhardt frowned, thinking. "Drawing pay? Rations . . . ? Late with the administration?"

"Dead men's pay. Dead men's rations. Probably, probably. And I don't reckon it's the first time that's happened. Oh, *shit*!"

Reinhardt looked over his shoulder. A truck had drawn to a stop not far away, back up where the fortress road joined up with King Alexander Street. A group of men climbed down from it, looking intently across the square. Stocky, heavy men, dark skin and darker hair.

"That's 'em!" Kreuz wheezed, beginning to panic back there in his shadows.

"The hiwis? The Greeks?"

The man nodded, the whites of his eyes glowing white. "They can't see me with you. Listen. You're all I have. No one'll listen to me. I've tried. But this time I've got something. All right?"

"Sense, Kreuz. You're not making any sense."

Kreuz's face twisted in frustration, and he took a deep breath, his eyes tracking over Reinhardt's shoulder, craning to keep the hiwis in sight. "If you'll help me, I'll bring you something. Tomorrow. At the barracks in Kosovo Polje. This time tomorrow."

"Kreuz . . ." Reinhardt began, but the man was not listening.

"I tried talking to others. Tried talking to a judge, but the judge didn't seem to like me. Fancy that, eh?" Kreuz giggled again, and then it stuttered out, as if he swallowed it back.

"What judge?"

But Kreuz was turning and beginning to shift himself down the alley, the shadows seeming to reach out and pull him away. "Oh, God, one's coming here. Tomorrow, Reinhardt. The mess hall. Kosovo Polje barracks."

"*Wait!*"

Kreuz was gone, and Reinhardt could feel someone coming closer behind him. Moving on instinct, he unbuttoned his trousers and began urinating on a pile of sodden rags that, from the smell, others had used for the same purpose. Steam puddled around his ankles, and he resisted the urge to whistle, not wanting to overdo his act. Buttoning himself back up, he turned around. A soldier stood at the entrance to the alley, a swarthy man with a heavy shadow of beard on his thick jaws, and a red triangle patch bright on his tunic.

"A salute is customary to a senior officer," Reinhardt snapped. The man came to attention as Reinhardt stepped past him, his eyes glittering blackly. "I don't recommend the facilities, but they're all yours, soldier."

11

Reinhardt directed his driver back to the barracks, but they had not gone more than a few hundred meters when he ordered a halt. He sat in the car, looking straight ahead, feeling the driver's eyes on him, then made a decision. "I'm getting out," he said, as he checked his pistol's load, holstered it, then took his gorget off and stuffed it into his pocket. "You or someone else, come back for me in an hour and wait back at the square where we stopped. If I'm not there, try again an hour later."

"Yes, sir." The driver frowned at him. "If I may, what are you doing, sir? For if the colonel asks me."

"Following up on some ideas, Corporal," said Reinhardt. "Don't worry about me, I'll be fine. Give this . . ." he said, noting Kreuz's names on a piece of paper as best he remembered them, "to Lieutenant Benfeld. Tell him to do a search of administration, find out who they were. Tell them they were assigned to the 999th Field Punishment Battalion."

He left the car, standing by the roadside as it drove slowly away. He felt a sudden sense of isolation. King Alexander Street pulled away in either direction, straight, lined and bounded by two- and three-story buildings of flat, square façades. A steady stream of people were walking down it, and those on his side of the road gave him a wide berth, looking up at him from beneath lowered brows. A small convoy of army trucks crunched past, their drivers casting incurious glances his way.

He took the first side road that branched south, into the heart of the city where it was bounded by King Alexander to the north, and the Miljacka river to the south. He walked past the boundary between the old Austrian and Ottoman towns, the square blocks of the Austro-Hungarian period fading down into low walls of white stone and cobbled streets. He walked past the city market, the cathedrals—the Orthodox to the right on its little park, the Catholic to the left on its square—past the Husref Bey mosque, the covered bazaar with its vaulted stone arches and back across the edge of Baščaršija, skirting the crowd, and into the warren and twist of the streets around it. Despite the distribution under way on the square, it was silent in the metalsmiths' market, the stalls shuttered up, and the air felt still and dead without the tap and ring of their hammers and the bustle of their business.

At the Rathaus he swung right, walked back along Kvaternik Street, looking across the gelid roil of the Miljacka at the Emperor's mosque, and the old Residency building where he had been barracked two years ago, and at a tumbled swath of rubble where an Allied air raid had flattened a neighborhood. He walked slowly, not looking back despite the crawling urge to do so, but looking around, at streets smothered in refuse and choked with crowds of people that just seemed to eddy and flow, no purpose in their movement, their eyes lost somewhere in the past, or fixed on a future that might be no farther than the next street corner. In some places, men and women huddled in groups around fires built of rubbish, the smoke from them hanging heavy and low, tangling across the smells of damp and rot and excrement that sometimes rose up against the cold. Children slunk furtively along the edges of streets, from shadow to shadow, looking up at the world with little new moons of white beneath their dark eyes. Through it all, the Ustaše moved in their black uniforms,

like harbingers, and they moved in their own space, the crowds opening and parting around them.

The Ustaše were everywhere. On the streets, at checkpoints, and
in the few vehicles still running. He saw them eyeing up those who
went past, their gazes lingering, flicking on, switching back. He saw
arrests: a man pulled from the embrace of his family and bundled into
a car; a refugee beaten bloody and hauled away like rubbish. He saw
one killing, a man shot as he climbed down from a wagon drawn by a
slat-ribbed donkey and stumbled into an Ustaša. And once, he saw a
woman led away down a flight of steps into a cellar, her face glazed
flat. He caught the eye of the Ustaša who stayed up on the street. The
man flicked his chin up and head back at him—*What?* the Ustaša
seemed be saying, *What are you looking at?*—and the man's jaw
bunched as he sneered and looked away. They were everywhere, always in pairs, always with the stance of men looking for trouble.

These were end times, Reinhardt realized again. There was nothing
to lose, and all to gain for those—like these men—who chose to go out
and seize it for themselves, or in the name of what little that remained
to them as a state, while around them the townspeople passed on with
a philosophy that seemed to say what is not acknowledged does not
exist. The tenor of the streets was so different from the Sarajevo he
remembered. Reinhardt could feel it, as if the city were on the point of
breaking and that it might go either way. Break down under the terror,
crumple in on itself. Or break out, upward, against the Ustaše who
plagued them, and the Germans who stood by and allowed their allies
to rape and rend as they pleased, wanting only the space and time to
evacuate as many of their troops through the city as they could.

Sure he had established enough of a trail for a blind man to follow,
Reinhardt slipped past two men smashing up an old cupboard for
wood and eased himself into a bricked-up doorway. He was a patient
man and he needed time to think, so he stood there, hidden from
most, watching for anyone following. He lit a cigarette, looking up at
the slate-gray sky where it hung low and heavy over the city. He ran
his tongue across his teeth, thinking.

There was a rumble of thunder, far off, and he could smell rain on the air. He lifted the collar of his coat higher around his neck and pushed himself deeper into the doorway in which he stood, glancing left and right. He could not be sure anyone was following him, but once or twice he had sensed something. Just a shape, a stance, a way of moving. He had seen it once too often for it to be coincidence. Between moving his eyes slowly from side to side, he ran his mind over what he knew, what he suspected, the shape of what he thought was out there.

Bodies in a forest, bodies in a cellar, bodies on a street. Fire and mutilation, someone with something to hide. The Ustaše everywhere. A major in a penal battalion with a manic temperament. Opportunity for those who saw it. Even in times like these, some things had to be hidden, and not everything that needed to be hidden always could be. People talked. Eyes saw.

He screwed the stub of his cigarette out beneath his heel and waited a little more, his mind ticking over quietly to itself, and he let it take its time. His thoughts wound down, eventually, around a conclusion, a course of action, and he could see no other. As he moved, the wail of a muezzin crawled across the still sky. He stopped and listened, realizing he had not heard the call to prayer since he came back, and it was as if a piece of a puzzle he had not realized was missing slotted itself into place. Sarajevo without its mosques, without its muezzins, was not the city he remembered, nor, he thought, could it be the city it needed to be again.

He waited, listening to the lonely thread of the muezzin's voice until it faded away, then made his way back to Baščaršija. The distribution of whatever it was had finished, the trucks gone, but many people remained, waiting, listless, hopeful, and he caught a glimpse of a head of gray-blond hair spread across a black coat as she moved up and down and around the lines with a word here, a touch there, compassion and elegance. He waited a little longer, standing by the old coffee shop until he saw her go inside, back into the Napredak offices, the place where he had left the old couple and the boy he had brought into the city. Walking up to the door, she stepped back out and turned right, toward the Emperor's Bridge.

"Mrs. Vukić."

She started and turned, her eyes widening as they rose up to meet his. Her hand came up to her mouth in surprise, and he saw how the fear pulled at the corners of her eyes, as if she stared into a cold wash of wind, until recognition fluttered across her face. "Captain? I had—" She stopped, swallowing. "A moment, please. You gave me such a fright."

"I am sorry." He watched her calm, run her hands down her chest, fingers clenching at the fabric of her coat.

"What are you doing here?"

"I need your help, Mrs. Vukić."

"What with?"

"Those people I brought to you when I arrived in the city." She nodded, cautiously. "I need to speak to them."

"Why? What have they done?"

"Nothing. But I need to talk to them about what they saw. Or might have seen."

"In the forest? The massacre? Must you?"

"I am afraid so." He nodded, and she hesitated. "It is important. I would not be here otherwise." Still, she hesitated. "If I don't find them, others might. I believe they might be in danger."

"From whom?"

"From whoever murdered the others."

A last moment of indecision, and she nodded, a quick duck of her head. She smiled, but it was brittle. She seemed to gather herself, as if she folded in the ragged edges of her spirit. "Shall we walk, then? It's not so far from here."

They passed out of the crowds, and out onto the more open space of Kvaternik Street, next to where the Miljacka ran high and fast down its channel, the water a muddy froth. She led him down the street, and they walked in silence until she broke it with a question.

"Captain Reinhardt. My daughter," said Vukić. "You said . . . you would tell me."

"What is it you want to know?" said Reinhardt.

Vukić walked on for a few paces. "You know, Captain, they blamed you for the failure of the investigation into Marija's murder."

"The Ustaše?"

Vukić nodded. "I do not believe them. I mean, I did wonder, at first. But now . . ." She looked at him. "You seemed to be an honorable man. I did not think you did what they say."

"Cooperated with the Partisans? In bed with the Communists? Sabotaged the police's work? You mean all that?"

" 'And all that,' as you say," she smiled, and he smiled as well. "I do not believe it. But there is something unsaid between us, Captain. How it really happened. They never told me, they only told me you got in the way."

"Well." He hesitated, his tongue pushing at that gap in his teeth. "They were right, I suppose. In a way." She looked at him, waiting for him to go on. "The Ustaše were not really interested in finding who killed Marija. They were more interested in finding a convenient outcome, and perhaps to kill two birds with one stone. So they wanted to . . . assuage the political pressure they were under to find someone, anyone, to accuse. And they saw the opportunity to strike what they perceived as a blow to the Partisans, to the Communists. So they arrested someone they said was a Communist agent, and they tortured him into confessing."

"They said you were involved in his death?"

"The agent's? No. That was the work of someone else. A police doctor, who was also a Partisan. He put that poor man out of his misery. And also, I suppose, got rid of a security problem. Also two birds with one stone . . ." He trailed off.

"And you? In the middle of all that . . . ?"

"Me? I was . . ." How to explain it to her? "I was . . . I was lonely. In despair at the pass my life had come to and for what I had done, and not done. I despaired realizing how far you could stray from yourself when all you do is try to survive. And I saw in Marija's investigation a chance to do something right. To do the right thing. For myself. But also for her. She deserved the truth. Not some warped version of it. So did the man killed with her, one of our officers. And I suppose my path led at right angles across the Ustaše's. I followed my investigation but ruined theirs."

"And? Who killed her?"

"Not the Partisans. Or the Communists. Although God knows they both wanted her dead. It was a German officer. He did it out of loyalty to his superior, with whom she was having an affair. Marija had found out this officer was a Jew and was going to expose him. She took . . . pleasure in detailing what she was going to do. This officer . . . Are you sure you want to hear this, Mrs. Vukić?" She nodded, tight-lipped. "He thought he had beaten her to death, but when he sent his subordinate back to clear things up, the subordinate found her alive, and he was the one who stabbed her to death. Out of panic, at what she might do. And because he was terrified of her."

"You found him? This man?"

"I did. His superior killed him. Then he himself was killed in action."

"My God," she whispered, looking down into the water. "Poor Marija . . ."

Reinhardt said nothing, remembering the things he had learned about Marija Vukić, the passions that had driven her, that had driven the things she had done.

"They gave her a hero's funeral, you know. I got a medal. A husband given to the cause, and a daughter . . ." Her voice hitched. "Ustaše royalty, they call me. But they were just using her, weren't they? They never really bothered to find out what happened." She stared across the water, allowing the wind to sting at the tears that welled up in her eyes. "We were so different, her and I . . ." She trailed off, swallowed, and pushed at the tears with the tips of her fingers. "She was a monster, wasn't she? Just like my husband. But they weren't always. You have to remember that. There was once a time . . ." She stopped, her voice seizing up, and she sobbed quietly, her shoulders rounding around her grief.

"It's the regrets, isn't it?" she said. It did not sound like a question to Reinhardt, and so he stayed quiet, watching her. "Not being able to say good-bye. Holding on to a last image. Wondering if it was the wrong one. You have those regrets, Captain? Of things left unsaid. Undone."

He did not know what it was about this woman, what effect she had on him, but unbidden a memory surged up, and he could only observe as if from afar the way it felt natural to share something he had held private for so long. "Carolin, my wife, died of cancer. At the end, when she was in the hospital, I would come to her each night. I would hold her hand while she lay dying and talk to her. Sometimes she would smile, perhaps manage a few words. Sometimes she slept." He thought he might keep his voice steady if, somehow, he imagined it belonging to someone else. "But the morning she died, I was . . . sleeping. My head was there on her bed. When I woke up, her hand was on my shoulder. She had woken before she died, seen me, and always, ever since, I've wondered . . . Did she maybe try to talk to me? I had always wanted to be there for her, and instead I slept right next to her as she died. I had been working the night before. I was tired. And . . . I had been drinking . . ." Vukić was looking back at him, her eyes very bright and blue in the pale of her face. "It was the only way to face my work. And I think to myself, the last thing my wife saw," he whispered, forcing the words, wanting them out, "was her . . . *drunk* . . . of a husband snoring at her bedside."

He stopped. He had never told anyone of this. Not Brauer, his friend and partner in the Kripo of some twenty years. Nor, as much as he should have, his son Friedrich, estranged, lost to him, now, a corpse somewhere on the Eastern Front. He looked down at Vukić as she wiped a tear away. His throat felt raw, as if someone else had been using it. Which, in a way, was true.

"You know, a gentleman should not reminisce about his past loves in front of another woman."

"I'm sorry."

She laughed, sniffed back more tears, and he smiled to see her as she fussed through her pockets. "No. It's me. I should not make light of such things." She blew her nose on the handkerchief she managed to find at last, and then she took his arm in hers, and it felt natural there as they walked. "Now, you are here again. The same man? Or different?"

"Different. The same. Full circle. Back to where I was two years ago. Alone. Surviving," he said, staring up at the slate glower of the sky, weighing what he had said. They walked on, and then she paused, looking back across the river at a clutch of vehicles parked in front of a villa with a white façade. Ustaše stood around the cars, talking, smoking, or wandering up and down the rows of people, women, mostly, outside the house.

"What is that place?"

"That is the Pale House," she answered. He looked down at her, and she turned her head toward him, although her eyes remained fastened on the house. "Maks Luburić's headquarters," she continued, her eyes coming around to meet his. "It is a terrible place. Come away. Please."

There was a rising wind behind them. The air felt wet and cold, and still there was a rumor of thunder somewhere over the mountains. Vukić led the way to where the old couple and the boy were lodged, on through the city's aimless shuffle, her arm still in his, but he could see how she walked gathered tight around herself, wrapped around whatever memories his words had stirred, and so he left her to them, matching her step for step until she slowed outside a low building and said, "Here we are," and they both stopped as they came abreast of the door and saw it broken, folded in around the splintered wreck of its lock.

12

Vukić took a step forward, then stopped at Reinhardt's hand on her arm. He drew his pistol and stepped quietly inside. Closed doors stood to either side of a staircase that went straight upstairs. He looked at Vukić, and she motioned up, her eyes very wide and bright. Reinhardt took the stairs carefully. At the top, two more doors opened off a narrow landing, only the one on the left was gone, pale fractures of wood slicing the frame where the hinges had once hung. The door was tilted into the room, cracked and shattered across its middle.

Vukić pushed up behind him, her breathing high and short. She peered in, then ducked back out and crossed the landing to knock softly at the door opposite. Reinhardt stepped into the room, his eyes circling around. There was a pair of rolled mattresses in one corner, an old wood-burning stove, and a narrow window with one of the panes stuffed by rags gone stiff and filthy, the frame jammed shut. The stove was stone cold, a small pile of ashes inside it, two plates, two forks, two tin cups, a knife and a warped metal pot atop it. He thumbed through a pile of blankets, finding a suitcase beneath them, *Blagojević* stenciled across it. Crumpled on the floor behind the door was a man's jacket and a tattered woolen cap.

From outside he heard voices, Vukić's and someone else, then someone on the stairs, and as he turned to go he saw a smear of blood, low down, by the door. He stepped back onto the landing, seeing Vukić at the bottom talking with a woman dressed all in black. The woman snatched her eyes up at Reinhardt, and she was backing away, a handkerchief clutched around her fist, and Vukić was going after her. Reinhardt stayed where he was, waiting to hear their voices, then came slowly down the stairs.

Vukić was standing in the doorway of one of the downstairs apartments, the woman tilted around her door. Her eyes rolled at Reinhardt as he came into view, and it was only Vukić's hand on the door that prevented her from closing it. She talked softly to the other woman, calming tones, and the woman straightened a little and came out from behind the door.

"She says they were taken yesterday evening. The Ustaše came for them."

Reinhardt looked past Vukić at the woman. "Ask her, please, can she describe them? Can she describe the leader?"

Reinhardt watched the woman as Vukić translated, saw the panic tighten across her features and she was shaking her head, tears welling up in eyes gone huge and dark with fear.

"She can't. She won't," said Vukić, looking at Reinhardt. Her expression was soft, no recrimination in it, but the point in her voice was clear to him.

"Did the police come?"

The woman shook her head to Vukić's translated question.

"Please. Ask her just to name one thing about the Ustaše who came. The leader," Reinhardt said looking at the woman. "He was big? *Veliki?*" he asked, raising a hand up high. The woman stared at him, her head shaking, quivering. Reinhardt cast his mind back to that checkpoint, the Ustaše with Bunda. Just men. Only Bunda had that definitive size. "Please. Just one word. Anything."

Vukić murmured quietly at the woman, soothing tones, and then the woman swallowed, a careful movement, her eyes fixed on Reinhardt with the whites showing all around, and her finger made a slow line down the side of her neck.

"A scar," he remembered, suddenly. He looked at Vukić, urging her to translate. "There was one with a scar? A scar," he said to the woman, pointing at his neck, drawing his finger down its side, to his collar, as Vukić said, "*Ožiljak*," and the woman's eyes met his, and she nodded. He smiled, opened his hands, and stepped back.

"*Hvala*," he said, thanking her, then turning to Vukić. "That's it. Please thank her. Tell her no harm will come to her. Tell her if anyone troubles her, she must ask for Captain Reinhardt. Feldjaegerkorps," he said, pointing at his armband. He did not know what good it would do. It might do some, and it was all he could leave her for her troubles.

Back outside, a glance at his watch told him his hour was almost up. "If the Ustaše took them, where would they have gone?"

"To the Pale House."

He looked back at her, looking through her, thinking.

"May I escort you somewhere?"

She nodded, and he offered her his arm again and they began walking in a silence that locked each of them into their own thoughts.

"Do you think they took the boy when they came for the elderly couple?" Reinhardt asked at last. Vukić's arm tensed against his side, but she said nothing. "I saw no trace of him there."

"What do you mean?"

"I saw nothing of his, only the old man's suitcase, hat, and coat. Cutlery for two people." Vukić blinked back at him with wide eyes. "I can place the old man there, maybe the old lady. What happened to the boy?"

"You are going to the Pale House, aren't you?" Vukić asked as they reached the Latin Bridge. Reinhardt nodded. Vukić's eyes searched his face. "Captain, this may sound strange, but . . . you have given me something important. I should like to give you something in return. After this, maybe later tonight, you might want to accompany me somewhere that may surprise you. No," she said, raising a hand, allowing a little smile to come to her eyes, "I will say nothing more. Only, come, if you can."

They looked at each other a moment, and then the city seemed to come rushing back in on him: the cold, the noise, the passage of people past them on either side, and the pinprick pressure of eyes that watched and measured. He had nowhere else he needed to be, he realized.

"I will come with you, then."

She brushed a wave of hair from her eyes, strands of blond and ash folding over her fingers, and put her hands over his. "Thank you again, Captain, for the truth of my daughter. And I will see you tonight." Though phrased as a statement, Reinhardt heard it as the question it was meant to be, and he nodded, again, listening as Vukić gave him an address off Kvaternik Street. He parted from her there, watching her walk away, folded tight into her black coat with the spill of her hair a moving curtain across her back in the wind.

He made swift time back to Baščaršija and caught the driver as he was about to leave, a shout and a hobbled run taking him the last steps. He let himself fall into the car's seat, his knee afire and his breath short, cursing himself for the shape he was in, and ordered the driver down to Kvaternik Street, to the junction not far from the Ćumurija Bridge, about where he thought the Pale House should be. The driver nosed the car through the maze of one-way streets and little alleys, the directions coming back to Reinhardt as much from memory as from feel, some long-lost finger to the city's pulse and ebb and flow of its traffic. Eventually, the *kubelwagen* emerged onto Kvaternik, and a quick glance to the right showed him the Pale House.

The car parked on the side of the street nearest the river, opposite an entanglement of barbed wire on crossed wooden posts. There was a passage through the wire and a pair of Ustaše stood on duty at it. They looked distantly at Reinhardt as he got out of the car, running his eyes up and over the building's façade, its heavy carvings and the deep recesses of its windows. Even where there were no drapes, the panes showed only the flat gray wash of the winter and no hint of what might be going on inside. Up on the line of the roof, crows stalked back and forth like men of the cloth, pretentious in the precision of their steps and the bobbing of their heads, peering down at the lines of women huddled close to the barbed wire. They sidled up close to the guards and the scrawled lines of the wire, hesitant, like creatures that knew only the whip but could not help themselves from coming closer to what hurt them.

Reinhardt straightened his coat, looked at the building's door, and began walking, fixing onto his face and bearing all the power and presence a German Feldjaeger should carry. The two Ustaše moved into his path and he leveled his eyes on them, not slowing, then pointing over their shoulder at something only he could see. They both looked—because they wanted to, because he *compelled* them to—and as they turned back he was moving past them, through the gap they had made, walking straight up to the steps leading up to the main door. At the top of the steps, another pair of Ustaše barred the way, and these would not be moved by appearances. He stopped before them, looking from one to the other.

"Who is in charge here?"

Neither of them said anything, but the one on the left made the slightest of moves, an instinctive drawing away, leaving space to the other man.

"I need to go inside," he said, stepping closer to the man on the right, fixing him with his eyes. The man stared back, apparently unfazed.

"No entry for people not knowing," the Ustaša managed, eventually, in German.

Reinhardt looked back at him. "Captain Langenkamp. Liaison officer." The Ustaša nodded, hesitantly. "Go and get him. Tell him Captain Reinhardt is waiting to see him."

There was a long pause, and then the Ustaša turned to the other one and passed an order. The second one went inside, the main doors thumping shut behind him.

"You waiting just here," said the Ustaša, pushing open one of the doors and motioning Reinhardt inside. The dark entrance seemed to suck at him as he walked inside, and Reinhardt could feel the terror and fear in the place as soon as he stepped inside. Reinhardt's breath began coming short and high, as if the building were closing itself around him, sizing him up, like a dog circles a stranger. Somewhere, someone was crying. Somewhere else, someone laughed. Little by little, the building seemed to open itself up to him, peeling back layer on layer.

"You waiting here," the Ustaša said again, pointing at another Ustaša slouched behind a desk with a telephone that stood in front of a wide flight of stairs. The guard looked Reinhardt over, then gestured disinterestedly at a corner of the entrance hall. Reinhardt did not know how long he waited until he heard footsteps coming down the stairs, and Langenkamp stepped heavily onto the floor of the entrance.

"What do you want, Captain?" No greeting, nothing.

"I need to find an Ustaša. I don't have a name. Just a description. Short. Dark-haired. Thin. A scar running down the left side of his face, from his ear."

Langenkamp frowned, eyelids flickering shut. "I am not sure I know of such a person. But my counterpart might. What has happened?"

"I need to speak to him in connection to an investigation."

"Investigation? Into what?"

"The deaths of those Feldjaeger last night and the arrest of a couple of refugees, one of them called Blagojević."

Langankamp nodded, motioned Reinhardt to wait. He walked over to the desk and picked up the telephone under the guard's still-disinterested gaze. He spoke once, twice, replaced the receiver, and came back over to Reinhardt. "We wait," was all he said, seeming to fold himself up and into a standstill. Though he said and did nothing, and though Reinhardt was not someone who sought conversation for its own sake, Langenkamp's stillness was profoundly disconcerting, such that he was glad to see an Ustaše officer step off the staircase and turn toward them, recognizing Captain Marković from the scene of the murders.

The Ustaša shook hands with Reinhardt, a noncommittal smile on his face. "Captain? It seems you are looking to speak with one of our men? May I ask why?"

"I need to question him, is all."

"About?"

"His role in the apparent disappearance of an elderly pair of refugees I brought into the city two days ago. Perhaps a boy as well."

"What role would that be?"

"They have vanished. Witnesses claim they were arrested by Ustaše and they described this man I would like to question quite accurately."

"When did this happen, do you say?"

"I don't 'say.' It did happen, last night."

"The names of these refugees?"

"I don't know. I only know the man was named Blagojević."

"Describe this Ustaša again, please." Reinhardt did so, Marković nodding, a polite smile on his face. "And the address where these arrests took place?" Reinhardt gave it. "Captain, I was made to understand you were investigating into the deaths of your men this morning. So why the interest in this rather unrelated matter?"

"Captain, are you fobbing me off?"

Marković frowned. "I am not sure I know that particular vernacular, Captain."

"Are you giving me the runaround? Are you trying to hide something from me?"

"I am not, Captain. I assure you. I am only trying to understand why someone like you would care for the fate of a pair of anonymous refugees and a boy, what connection it might have to your Feldjaeger. And why such an illustrious former detective—yes, Captain, your reputation has preceded you—would be looking for a particular Ustaša who, it seems, is missing."

"Missing," repeated Reinhardt.

Marković nodded. "Since last night. As well, there is no record of any arrest at the address you mention, nor do we have anyone by the name of Blagojević in our custody here."

"What about a boy?"

"We have 'boys,' as you say. None arrested last night. None brought in along with an elderly couple, as you describe. So you see, Captain, your questions raise more questions, none of which seem to have answers."

"Very well. Thank you, Captain Marković, for your time."

"My pleasure, Captain."

"Should this man . . . what did you say his name was?"

Marković smiled, and shook his head. "A neat approach, Captain. I appreciate your interest, but I will no more give you his name than you would give me the name of a German we wished to interview."

Reinhardt inclined his head. It had been worth a try, but this Marković was evidently not Metzler to be caught out by a little verbal sleight of hand. "Should this man show up, I would appreciate the opportunity to ask him a few questions."

"Of course, I make no promises, Captain Reinhardt, but I will see what can be arranged."

A few more words—expressions of interest into the progress Reinhardt was making with the Feldjaeger case—and then Marković was indicating that Reinhardt was to be escorted out of the building, Langenkamp coming back to life, folding out from his corner. As they reached the front exit, the doors thumped open and Jansky stalked in, hands behind his back as if he were conducting an inspection, a second German at his heels carrying a large, red chest.

The two of them stopped dead, Jansky's martinet air simply sloughing away. Reinhardt watched Jansky's face go blank, then recognition come over it as he realized who he had in front of him.

"Major Jansky," Marković said, coming to polite attention. He looked between the two of them. "It seems you already know Captain Reinhardt, of the Feldjaegerkorps?"

"We have met. Only earlier this morning. How do you do, Captain?"

"Well, Major, thank you."

"What brings you to Ustaše headquarters?"

"Captain Reinhardt was inquiring into the whereabouts of one of our men."

"Are you bringing the Ustaše into your inquiries now, Captain?"

"No," said Reinhardt, quickly, seeing Marković about to speak. "This is in connection with those refugees I brought down from the mountains. The ones you saw me with." The major nodded. "They've gone missing. An Ustaša at that checkpoint we met at may have had something to do with it."

"I see," murmured Jansky, his eyes steady on Reinhardt. "Captain Marković?"

"Of course, Major," said the Ustaša. "Go straight up. Colonel Putković is waiting for you."

"Reinhardt," acknowledged Jansky.

"I met an acquaintance of yours. Judge Marcus Dreyer," Reinhardt said.

Jansky's mouth straightened in a polite smile as he turned around. "How is he?"

"Interested in old cases, it would seem."

Jansky's smile widened, as if he felt the ground under his feet firming. "Far be it from me to criticize our judicial brethren, but Dreyer has a . . . reputation. He wouldn't be after a little help, now, would he? Hmmm?" He smiled, broader still. "Or else, better hope you've nothing in your past you wouldn't want brought out into the light. Times like these, you never know who your friends are, but your enemies— you can usually tell them rather easily." The smile folded back in on itself, back to that straight line. "I've always found that rather comforting. And as I often say, 'All are not huntsmen who can blow the hunter's horn.' You might remind Dreyer of that when next you see him."

With that Jansky strode off, hands clasped almost daintily behind his back, trailed by the other German who had entered with him. It was one of the two clerks from the penal battalion's office, Reinhardt realized, the one from the corner, almost hidden behind his rampart of paperwork. As the man walked past, he seemed to cringe away from Reinhardt, clutching his red chest close as he went by, something clinking inside it.

13

The sun was low in the west, a watery glow across the slate-gray sky, as Reinhardt sat in the barracks communications center, a shallow sheaf of papers at his elbow. They were all of the after-action reports Benfeld had been able to dredge up, going back a week. Reinhardt could find nothing in the dry prose of the reports resembling a pattern, or anything resembling any theory Reinhardt could devise. The front lines had been quiet, but it was the quiet before the storm. Everyone knew the Partisans were gathering, choosing their time, but with little to no armed conflict with the Partisans in the past week as well, even that angle of checking the reports, or looking for men lost or missing in action, was closed off.

There had been only sporadic contacts across the front line, no significant casualties, and no prisoners taken. There were reports of a handful of deserters and Reinhardt toyed with the idea of trying to match descriptions with the bodies, but he gave it up as unworkable. Instead he mused about the likelihood that those five bodies from the construction site could have come from different units and be mentioned in different after-action reports. In which case, he acknowledged to himself, it would be all but impossible to trace five different bodies through that paperwork with any hope of finding all of them in a cellar in a bombed-out neighborhood. Making matters worse, Benfeld's search of administration had found no sign of a Berthold or Seymer. There was one option, Reinhardt knew, though he had been reluctant to take it until now.

"Captain, sir. Your call has been placed."

Reinhardt followed the signals operator through to a small room with a telephone. The receiver was already lying on the table. Picking it up, he heard the click of the operator, and then a distant hum on the line.

"Hello? Koenig?"

There was a silence. *"Reinhardt?"*

"It's me, Koenig."

"What a pleasant surprise."

"I'm glad you think so. How are you?"

"Well, thank you. Not much changed since the last time we met."

"Well, it was dark then; you could have looked like anything," said Reinhardt, forcing a little levity into his voice.

"Well, I suppose the blackout must be good for something. And yourself?"

"Very well, thank you. I am in Sarajevo."

"Yes, so I understood."

"Koenig, I wish this were a social call, but I have a favor to ask."

The pause was slower, Koenig now reassured it was Reinhardt by the exchange of what they sincerely hoped were innocuous-sounding phrases. They were anything but and were in actuality their resistance cell's codes to reassure members that the person calling was not doing so under duress.

"Of course, anything I can do."

"I am trying to trace two soldiers. Their names have turned up in an investigation ongoing down here."

"What is it you think I can do?"

"Are you still on the staff of the Vienna Garrison?"

"Yes."

"I am hoping you can check army administration records up there for me, as you have access to personnel records from across the Balkans."

"I can try. What are the names and units?"

"I only have surnames. Berthold and Seymer," Reinhardt replied, spelling out the names. "They were both serving a sentence in the 999th Balkans Field Punishment Battalion."

"A penal battalion?" came Koenig's surprised reaction.

"Yes. And, one more thing. Anything you can find out about a Feldgendarmerie Major. Erwin Jansky. Currently assigned to the 999th."

"What sort of things?"

"Deployments. Service history." Reinhardt paused. "Disciplinary record."

There was a pause. *"How soon do you need this?"*

"Soon, Koenig."

"How can I reach you?"

"Through the switchboard here at the Kosovo Polje barracks. You can also leave a message for me with Lieutenant Benfeld, Feldjaegerkorps."

"I'll see what I can do."

"Thank you, Koenig. Good-bye."

"Good-bye."

He sat there a moment after he replaced the receiver, embarrassed at the stilted edge to the end of their conversation. He would have liked to share more with Koenig, just as he would have liked to ask after the others in Vienna, but the risks were too great for that. Instead, he glanced at his watch and saw it was nearly time. He walked back through the barracks, taking it slowly, pushing his mind past the scrum of activity in its halls, ignoring the men bundled in blankets along the corners of walls for want of beds. In the Feldjaeger operations room, he scrawled a note on his conversation with Koenig for Benfeld, then left for the car pool, where a *kubelwagen* was waiting for him. He gave the driver Vukić's directions, then slumped into its bucket seat as the *kubelwagen* shuddered its way around onto the long curve of Kvaternik Street.

"This is it, sir," said the driver.

Reinhardt started up out of his thoughts, if the confusing echo within his mind could be called such, the cold clenching tight and stabbing through his knee as he looked up and around. The car was parked in front of a pair of battered wooden doors standing open. Next to them was a handwritten sign on a large sheet of paper. *Čaršijska Posla*, it read. He frowned, trying to translate it as people walked past him and into the building. The happenings in the market? The doings of the bazaar . . . ?

It was a theater.

Reinhardt looked up and down the street. The sky hung heavy over the city, the smell of rain stronger, and the street faded away fast into the gloom. Leaving instructions for the driver to wait, Reinhardt walked up the steps and into a small foyer, packed with an eddying shuffle, a flow of people moving toward a tall set of doors in the opposite wall. Standing to one side, her ash-blond hair bright under a cluster of candles, Vukić laughed with a tall man, his gray hair awry and a red scarf thrown dramatically over one shoulder. The man looked askance at Reinhardt as he came in, sliding to one side to get out of the way of the people pushing in behind him, but Vukić's smile came easily, naturally, as she came up to him, her hands extended.

"Captain. I'm so glad you could come."

"A play, Ms. Vukić?" he asked, as he tucked his cap under his arm and folded her hands into his own.

"Call me Suzana, please," she said, nodding and smiling, looking back and around. It was a theater, or what passed for one. There was a burst of laughter from farther inside, and a warm glow, like candlelight.

"Come," she said. She stepped back, their arms coming up straight between them, and he gave in and followed her. "I must greet some more people and I had arranged to help. Please, go through. Go in. Enjoy it. Wait for me here afterward?" She smiled again, and then slipped away.

Reinhardt paused to strip the gorget from around his throat, sliding it into his pocket, and only then passed on into a large room with a low ceiling. The place was stifling in the dim light, braziers burning in each corner, and the room was packed with people—men, women, even a few children—sitting on rows of benches and lining the walls. Up at the front of the room was a stage, what seemed to be planks of wood raised up on something hidden behind a heavy, red drape. Reinhardt shuffled to the side as someone came in behind him, then smiled apologetically as he squeezed into a space between two men. Only one of them glanced at him, a flat, disinterested gaze. He leaned back against the wall, taking his weight off his left foot, and waited.

Eventually, as happens in crowds sometimes, a hush started to descend. People stopped talking, straightened, looked around and over their shoulders. A man came in to dim the lanterns and candles burning along the walls. Another man stepped out onto the stage, the man from the entrance with the red scarf, the boards creaking under his weight. He smiled out at the crowd, opened his arms to welcome them, and began to speak.

Reinhardt lost the details quite quickly. The man spoke fast, with an accent, but Reinhardt managed to follow the gist of it as the man thanked them for coming and explained something about the need to pause and remember other times. He was applauded off after a few minutes, and the play began as a woman in an Ottoman costume and bent under a heavy load shuffled onto the stage, followed by a man in what seemed to be an absurdly small waistcoat and oversized turban with a pair of slippers the tips of which curled up almost to his knees. The audience laughed as other characters appeared left and right in all kinds of dress, and began to set up what looked like a marketplace.

With lights out and his attention focused on the stage, Reinhardt slowly took off his coat, holding it folded over his arms. He gave up trying to understand the dialogue and was content to follow along with his eyes, his mind fastening on a word or phrase here and there. The audience clearly loved it, giggling, chuckling, and laughing uproariously as the characters skipped and stepped and shambled around their market. Merchants and mercenaries, an innkeeper and a man who ran a secondhand shop, a fancy lady, a beggar woman, the actors shouted and whispered and, from time to time, broke into song.

The action was maniacal, the words came thick and fast in blurs of color and speech, heavy with what Reinhardt understood to be Sarajevo slang, and after a while he stopped watching the play and instead watched the audience, let himself relax into them.

There was a ripple in the row of people at the back. Reinhardt glanced to the side, seeing a man stepping cautiously into the darkened room. The man's head craned around, left, right, a tiptoe bob of his head as he looked forward, looking for space to stand, no doubt, what little light there was limning the edges of his heavy beard. Against the raucous action on the stage where a chicken and its feathers were the subject of intense and prolonged bargaining, the man began to sidle down the back row, murmuring apologies as he moved, eventually worming his way into a space between Reinhardt and another man.

"*Oprostite, komšija, žao mi je,*" the man apologized, somewhat breathlessly, to Reinhardt and his neighbor. Reinhardt said nothing, not understanding and not following the whispered conversation between the newcomer and the man who had originally been standing next to Reinhardt. He ignored them, soaking in the mood and atmosphere in the room. The play meant something to them, Reinhardt knew, wondering again about the ability of people to come up with things like this at times like these until he stopped wondering about it and just became part of it, until a thread of speech he understood very clearly darted out of the night, whispered straight into his ear.

"Captain Reinhardt."

Reinhardt froze, then turned his head, slowly. He could not make out the features of the man next to him, only the glitter of his eyes from the lamps on the stage.

"Please come with me."

Something hard was thrust into his ribs, and a hand scrabbled across his holster, unfastened the catch, and pulled his pistol out with a dull rasp of metal on leather.

"Quietly. You first. Now," the man hissed.

Reinhardt stepped softly back along the row of people, feet slithering out of his way, and the man behind him whispering apologies, once exchanging some quiet joke with someone, until they came to the door to the foyer. Reinhardt opened it quietly as the man followed him out. A second man stood in the deep shadows by the closed front door, his face all but hidden in a scarf wrapped high around his neck. The two men exchanged glances, signals, the second man shaking his head as he glanced out at the street through rippled glass panes.

"This way," the first man said, pointing him across the foyer, toward a narrow door behind what used to be a bar, the shelves empty of bottles. At a nod from the man, Reinhardt opened the door onto a small room, bare of furniture. A third man stood there. Tall, blackhaired, a black coat hanging from broad shoulders, hands clasped one over the other in front of himself. It was the man Reinhardt had seen at the hospital, and at least one of the men he had been sure had followed him that morning.

"Hello, Simo," said Reinhardt.

"Captain," Simo replied, gravely, inclining his head.

"A bit dramatic all this, isn't it?"

"If it is, it would be the place for it, do you not think?"

Reinhardt smiled, but it all felt slippery, a hasty façade over the confusion he felt inside, a presage as if some great weight were about to settle around him. "Couldn't you have come to me in town? I gave you all enough of a chance earlier today to get close to me."

"We are doing it now."

"So? What is the meaning of this, Simo?"

"Somebody wants to see you."

"You've done this to me before, you know. Lured me off, took me to meet someone. To meet Dr. Begović. You told me that it would be in my interest."

"And it was, wasn't it?"

Reinhardt paused, sighed. "I suppose it was, yes. And just how is the good doctor?"

Simo inclined his head again, pursed his lips. "As well as can be expected, given the circumstances."

"You know, if he wanted to see me, there must've been easier ways than this."

"It is this way, Captain," Simo said, opening a narrow door behind him that, until he moved, had been all but invisible.

Déjà vu swept over Reinhardt, memories of that house in Bentbaša where he had met Begović, gained the help and respect of a man who ought to have been his enemy, and begun his journey toward reconciliation with himself and his place in this war. But he had always known—Begović had always known, as well—that that reconciliation would mean different things to different people. That the further its implications traveled from Reinhardt, the more ways there would be to understand it. The truth of Reinhardt's reconciliation was not immutable, and the shape and strength of it would be tested beyond that door, Reinhardt knew, and he was suddenly terrified that he was not ready. That he had not been ready these past two years.

These thoughts scrambled across his mind as he ducked through the doorway, Simo in front of him, the man with the thick beard close behind. They walked up a cramped flight of stone steps, the walls flaked with concrete and plaster. At one point, a wave of laughter swept over them, a shrill of high-pitched voices beneath it, and Reinhardt realized they must be over the theater. Then it was gone, deadened as the walls thickened and the steps flattened into a confined corridor that turned, squeezing them one way, then another. The floor became wood, and the Partisans walked quietly, carefully, motioning Reinhardt to do the same. More voices could be heard around them, nothing distinct, and then Simo was climbing a ladder, metal rungs bolted to a brick wall, and Reinhardt went up after him, the bearded Partisan hard on his heels.

The ladder ended in a flat floor of heavy-beamed wood. Reinhardt placed his elbows, then palms, on the floor and shrugged himself up into the dark space. Only a skylight gave any illumination onto what sounded and felt like an attic, the air bone-cold and layered with dust and mold and damp. Simo loomed in front of him, a big hand coming up to stop Reinhardt where he was, the bearded Partisan standing behind him at the top of the ladder. Simo said something into the darkness and was answered. A pause, and there was a metal scrape, then a buttery spread of yellow light as a lantern was unshaded, the size of the attic swelling out of the dark even as the details of its shape leaned backward into deep shards of darkness.

The lantern stood on a small, round table. There was a pair of mismatched stools to either side of it, and a group of men stood on its far side. Standing on the other side of the light, they were hard to make out, but Reinhardt caught the glimpse of light on metal and the dull fittings of weapons held across chests. One of the men standing closer to the light than the others walked forward, stopping by one of the stools. He was not tall, but he was thickset, his head topped by a scrub of close-cut hair atop a broad forehead, his mouth narrow beneath a wide, flat nose.

He sat, indicating the other stool for Reinhardt. Simo moved to one side, and Reinhardt walked forward to the table and sat. The other man examined him, his eyes glittering beneath the heavy, bowed line of his brow. He leaned forward, the light fitting itself more closely across his face, and Reinhardt saw he was very young, not even thirty years old.

"Captain Reinhardt," he said, finally. "Do you know who I am?"

"I can guess." The man's eyes widened fractionally, inviting Reinhardt to continue. "You are Valter."

The man nodded. "Vladimir Perić is my name. You are maybe only German to know that. I give you that, for trust. There must be trust between us, Captain," he said, his German heavily accented, his face very calm.

"Trust?" Reinhardt worked a mouth gone very dry, his tongue stealing into that gap in his teeth. It was very cold, and he suppressed the urge to shiver. "Trust would presuppose at least a relationship between us."

"A relationship we will have, Captain. You will do some things for me. I will trust you to do those things. You will trust me to give you some time to do them."

"I am not sure I understand, Mr. Perić. Are you telling me you expect me to work for you?"

"You already work for me. For our cause."

"That is not true."

"How is not true? Did you not discuss this with Muamer Begović?"

"No. *No*. We never talked about me working for you. I was—" Reinhardt paused, suddenly, desperately afraid, filmed with sweat despite the cold. "Begović understood. It was my choice. My . . . path to find and follow."

"Pretty words, Captain."

"Then ask him. He will tell you."

"Fine words but of no use to me, now. You are here. I have need of you." Perić was implacable, holding up a hand, a tight shake of his head behind it, stemming any counter from Reinhardt. "Only listen, Captain, and understand. You will leave here. I have no wish for killing you. But you will work for me. Must I make clear the . . ." He paused, searching for the word, his eyes drifting away, then back. "Must I make clear the implications to you? The wrong word at the wrong time."

"You are blackmailing me?" Perić cocked his head. "Threatening me."

"I am," Perić said, simply. "I am also offering you choice to act, and opportunity to act. Have you not been looking for this? Why else would you walk around so evidently in the old town, today? Why else would you let Simo see you at the hospital?"

"I will not betray anyone to you," said Reinhardt, shaken by how close Perić's words had come to the core of his own dilemma of how and when to actually do something about what he felt and believed in.

"Fine words again, Captain. Betrayal is never easy," Perić acknowledged. "But stop first to think. Some things and some people are worth betraying. You do not think? Of course they are. You would not be here, otherwise. But do not worry. I will not ask you for betrayal. Only listen, now, to what I have to ask to you."

"I will listen. Do you smoke? I have cigarettes." Perić nodded, and Reinhardt carefully took his cigarettes from his pocket. He lit two, passed one to Perić. The Partisan drew deeply on it, nodded appreciatively, then leaned forward slowly.

"So, Captain. Tell me. Where are the Ustaše all going?"

14

"This war is coming to an end," Perić said. "A new peace is coming. In that new peace, there will not be room for the divisions of the past. We will be one people. One united people." Perić paused, drawing on his cigarette, then flicked ash on the floor. "There will not be place for the Ustaše in that world. They will be wiped out. This is necessary.

"There can be no place of retreat for them. No place for them to run to. To regroup. To come back and haunt us. There can be no place of exile for them, like Italy before the war, or Spain, now. There can be no more assassinations by the Ustaše, like that of the king in Marseille. I have no illusions, Captain. Those we cannot kill on the battlefield, those we cannot capture and kill off it, they will run. We will not catch them all, and I care little for the little fishes. It is the big fishes I want. Them, they cannot be allowed to get away. They must pay for what they have done. And they must pay for who they have been. Am I making sense to you?"

Reinhardt nodded. Perić was implacable in the way he talked, his voice hypnotic in its slow, precise diction. He kept his head low down on those big shoulders, and his eyes focused just a fraction below Reinhardt's, as if they were skewed, ever so slightly, at a place just out of touch with this world. Like Begović, Perić was a man of the future, compelled to live in the present.

"Not long ago, maybe a month ago, we began to hear rumors. There were divisions in the Ustaše. About whether to stay here and fight, or to leave, to regroup. And there were discussions about other plans. Longer plans. Plans that looked beyond the here, and the tomorrow, and the week next, and looked more to the future. The kind of plans we were afraid of.

"About a week ago, three Ustaše vanished. These three are not three of those we would consider as little fishes. They are big ones. Very big. We do not know where they went. We do know that Luburić—him, you know, of course—was furious about this. There was almost a purge of the Pale House, but he was convinced to stop that by his superiors in Zagreb.

"At the same time those three vanished, we noticed someone at the Pale House. This person was coming and going. He drove a car, and wore a uniform, and both were of your army, but he was not the Ustaše liaison officer, Langenkamp. Him we know of. We wondered who he was, this man. He was no officer. He came at night, always. We followed him, but could not follow him back to where he came from. So we decided to stop him. We stopped his car, and took him. Unfortunately, he did not tell us much, but he told us some interesting things. Although he drove a German car and wore a German uniform, he was not a German. He was Shiptar. An Albanian. He had a tattoo, here, on his shoulder. An Albanian eagle, and the letters *SSVT*. They mean '*Shqipëria Shqiptarëve, Vdekje Tradhëtarëvet.*' 'Albania for the Albanians, Death to the Traitors.' The man was a member of Balli Kombëtar. You know of Balli Kombëtar?"

"Albanian nationalists, and anti-Communists. Many of them fought with the Italians, then the Germans, in Albania, and some of them fought in the SS Skanderbeg Division." Perić inclined his head, almost the only movement he seemed to make. "What did this man say to you?"

"He said little. Not much of it made sense, and we were rushed with him. He was not strong enough for the questioning. We did not want to alert the Ustaše. So we put him back in his car, we made things look like a car crash, and left everything."

"What uniform was he wearing? Can you describe it?"

"German," said Perić, his brows lowering again.

"What rank, or insignia?" Perić frowned, looking at Simo. "There had to be something," Reinhardt insisted.

"A patch. A red triangle," Simo said, and Perić nodded. "On the shoulder."

"I see this is familiar," Perić said as he stubbed his cigarette out on the table and left it there. "Tell me of this uniform."

"The red triangle is the symbol of a penal battalion," Reinhardt said. Perić frowned and shook his head, not understanding. "A punishment unit."

"*Shtrafbat*," Simo murmured. Perić's face lightened, and he motioned Reinhardt to continue.

"There is a penal battalion in Sarajevo, headquartered at the Ottoman fortress on Vratnik."

"Tell me of it."

"I do not know that much. It mainly does support work. Construction. Transportation. And there is, apparently, a large number of foreign volunteers in it. Which would explain the man being an Albanian. There are some in the unit. Now, let me ask you some things. Did the Partisans have anything to do with the deaths of three German soldiers last night, in Logavina?" Perić shook his head, that slight frown pulling his face down. "Did the Partisans have anything to do with a massacre of civilians in the forests to the east of the town, two days ago?"

"At the logging site?"

"You know of it?"

"The site or the deaths? Both. We attacked the site in the past."

"Why?"

"It was run by the German Army." This was news to Reinhardt. "We had nothing to do with those deaths. Why are you asking?"

"I was a policeman, Mr. Perić, as I'm sure you know. I am eliminating possibilities."

"You are investigating these deaths?"

"Murders. Of the Feldjaeger, yes, I am."

"Will it get in the way of what I ask of you?"

Reinhardt smiled, and it was something sardonic, an acidic twist of his lips he could not control. "Mr. Perić, I . . ." He stopped, searching for the right words. "You know, you are asking me to serve two masters, pursue two ends."

"Maybe they will not be so far apart as you think, Captain. If we did not kill those people—and I assure you we did not—it does not leave so many suspects."

There was a soft sound of movement behind Perić, and one of the men leaned forward into the light. *"Druže, trebalo bi razmisliti o odlasku. Ovdje smo bili predugo."*

"Sačekajte, momak," Perić said, holding up a hand and all the while keeping his eyes on Reinhardt. The man subsided back into the dark. "My men are worried we have been here too long. I need to leave, Captain. But you will find out where those three Ustaše have gone, and whether the Germans have had anything to do with it. And you will find what is this connection with a German penal battalion."

"Respectfully, how do you expect me to do that?" It sounded formulaic, protest for protest's sake. Reinhardt knew it, and Perić seemed to hear it, although his broad face remained blank as he stood up.

"You will find a way. You are a resourceful man, Captain. You must be, to be still alive and thinking the way you do."

Reinhardt stood as well, feeling a surge of anger, that impulse to push back at those who sought to channel him. "You claim to know a lot about me for someone who has just met me, Mr. Perić."

Perić looked back at him, and a smile chipped across the stone façade of his. "So, there is some spirit in there." Reinhardt flushed, as he was meant to, thankful the yellow lantern-light spared his coloring. "I know some. I can guess more. The rest, I do not care about. That is why I have trust, Captain. I trust you are a survivor. Although I think it is not what you want to be, I will use that for myself and for my cause. I believe, am I right, that Muamer and you once talked of something similar?"

Reinhardt nodded, saying nothing, biting back a remark that Muamer Begović and Perić were cut from different cloth, the doctor having been so much more attuned to Reinhardt's state of mind at that time, so much more sensitive to the restrictions Reinhardt felt around him.

"Nothing more? Then Simo will take you back to the theater. He will be back in touch with you shortly."

"You leave me no option?"

"None," said Perić, simply, and turned to go.

"Mr. Perić. A moment." Perić paused, looking back. "Where is Dr. Begović?"

Perić stared back at Reinhardt, his flat nose flaring out as he took a long breath in. "He is dead, Captain. Executed, after Operation Schwarz. He would not leave the wounded. And when the Germans overran the hospital camp . . . They shot them. All the doctors. All the nurses. All the wounded."

They stared hard at each other, each of them with a memory of that one man between them. Perić made to go again, and again he paused. "Perhaps . . ." He paused, though, whatever he might have said going unsaid, as if words could not bridge that sudden gulf of loss, and he turned and left, one of his men preceding him out a door, two more following.

Reinhardt stared after him, then turned as Simo tapped him on the shoulder, handing him a piece of paper. He glanced at it, noting the three names written on it—Bozidar Brkić, Tomislav Dubreta, Zvoni-mir Saulan—and then folded it, almost crumpled it, into his pocket.

"You knew? About Begović?" Simo nodded. Reinhardt felt empty, sick, even, at the news, even though he had feared such ever since the end of Schwarz, and the orders given to the German armies to take no prisoners. He had hoped, a small harbor he looked into from time to time, that the little doctor might have made it out of those forests alive.

"It is time to go, Captain."

It was just him and Simo on the way back down the crooked corridors and cramped staircases that threaded the walls and gaps between and through the buildings. Reinhardt took no notice of it, thinking only of what he had just heard, and that news of Begović, and he was surprised when Simo laid his big hand on his shoulder in that room behind the bar, and he noticed suddenly the bearded Partisan was there, his ear against the door into the foyer.

"Do not act differently, Captain. It will be noticed. Do not look for us. We will find you." Simo looked to the other man for the all clear, and when it came, he handed Reinhardt back his pistol as the bearded Partisan slipped back past them.

"I'm sorry, Simo. For Begović." Reinhardt paused with his hand on the door and turned, but the room was empty.

Reinhardt made his way back into the theater, back into the warmth of the crowd, but the heat was stifling—unbearable even—the words and laughter a buffet of noise he could not absorb, and could only suffer.

They said their good-byes on the edge of the woods where they overlooked the valley, where Reinhardt had sat and felt the new truths of who he was and what he needed to do settle over him. The front lines in this battle were still fluid, with Operation Schwarz merging and washing over the slopes of the mountains and the forests that cloaked them. The Partisans thought it would take at least two days of walking, of maneuvering, of twisting and sliding and backtracking through the forest, of laying low and burrowing into cover when needed, before Reinhardt and his escort would be able to make it to the point they had selected. They would leave him there to struggle down on his own, rejoin his lines, use the story they had concocted together, and hope for the best.

"It has been a strange road we've traveled, has it not, my friend?" Reinhardt looked across at Begović. The little man was desperately tired. It showed in his carriage, in the long lines drawn down the sides of his face.

"With stranger yet to come. Would it be strange to say, though, what I feel most is elation . . . ?"

Begović smiled. "The elation of truths revealed. I can remember feeling so. But truths need to be put to the test."

"And mine are still ahead of me. I know." Reinhardt breathed deeply. The British liaison officer, Major Sanburne, and his men had left the day before, following a Partisan brigade farther south as it looked for a chink in the German lines. Sanburne had been skeptical of Reinhardt's decision to go back. It was too risky, too foolish a use of a valuable prisoner, the British officer all for bundling him into a sack and sending him down to the coast to be picked up by the navy, shipped off to Alexandria and put to work there. But Reinhardt was the Partisans' prisoner, and the Partisans seemed open to what Reinhardt was suggesting.

"You know I am not your agent," Reinhardt said, again.

"I know it," said Begović. "But others will not understand the finer points. They will see you as an asset to be used. The time will come when they will want you. That will mean betrayal. Of your men to us. And no matter the circumstances, betrayal is never a step taken lightly. But it will be either that or the risk that you are exposed back to the Germans."

"And so the finer points of one's conscience run counter to the realities we live among," mused Reinhardt. It felt like a trite piece of homespun philosophy, but it stemmed from his elation and a drive to do something different. Anything different.

"The first thing you'll have to do is hide that grin," smiled Begović.

"Long faces are my speciality," said Reinhardt.

The play ended, pulling him back and up to the here and now. The actors bowed, the audience applauding enthusiastically. People rose to their feet, turning this way and that with smiles on their faces. Reinhardt shrugged back into his coat and slipped into the crowd as it shuffled out. An elderly woman next to him said something brightly, and he smiled at her, not understanding what she had said, another chink in his mood appearing as he felt himself distinct from the crowd, remembering he was not one of them and never would be. He stepped into the foyer, keeping to the walls, and sliding his shoulders through the people who milled across the room, couples arm in arm, friends, all talking animatedly. He kept his eyes distant and on the door, what he hoped would pass for a polite smile on his face, and found a corner to stand in and wait. People passed, some looked at him, he heard the word *German* once, twice, and could not help the guilty flush that swept through him, like someone had clapped something hot to the back of his neck.

"There you are."

He blinked, breathed, and saw Vukić standing next to him, a quizzical smile on her face. Reinhardt nodded, a smile coming of its own accord. "So? You understood it?"

"Some of it. Enough."

Vukić smiled at him. "I should introduce you to the playwright. He will be most amused."

"Please. Do not," said Reinhardt. Vukić looked at him quizzically. "I would not wish to be the object of any attention. Not here. Not tonight. This was . . . not a time for . . . Not a time for outsiders," he managed. Vukić cocked her head at him, that quizzical set to her mouth moving to her eyes. "I enjoyed it. But I think . . ." He paused, and she turned to him, saying nothing. "I think I enjoyed being with you all more," Reinhardt managed, after a moment. It felt weak, insufficient to the gift she had offered him, but Reinhardt's mind was still slung between Perić's attic, and that last memory of Begović, and the happiness he had felt in himself.

Vukić nodded. "That is important. That is one of the reasons Safet wrote the play. Safet Kafedzić. People kept asking him, 'Why, Safet? Why bother? Why risk it?' Because it *was* risky. You simply never know, anymore, what people will think and say and do about anything."

"And so why did he?"

"A reminder, he would say. He told me, he wrote it to maintain his sanity. And to remind Sarajevans who they were, who they are, and who they could be again."

THE PALE HOUSE   161

"And what is that?"

"A community," she said, simply.

There was silence between them. It was nothing heavy, or oppressive, nor one of those silences that demands to be broken. It simply was, and he remembered something Padelin had once said, the day he had gone to meet the detective at police HQ, the day after the police had lost their prime suspect in the murder of Marija Vukić. *There is the world, and there is Sarajevo*, Padelin had said. *A world of itself. Rules you never understand. A community you will never be part of.*

"I'm sorry?" said Vukić.

Reinhardt had not realized he had spoken aloud. "Nothing. Just something I remembered."

"About?"

"This city. Its community. Those who are outside it."

"It's a choice, sometimes, isn't it?" Vukić said. "Being outside something."

"Or a decision that is made for you."

Reinhardt needed suddenly to be away from here.

"I would like to thank you for this. For taking the time to show it to me." He winced inside, hearing himself so formal. So Prussian. "If you will excuse me, I wish you a pleasant evening."

She tilted her head, knowing something was wrong. "I am glad you enjoyed it." She paused. "If you are going through the new town, perhaps you will escort me home, Captain?" He hesitated a moment, then nodded. "Then let me get my coat."

Reinhardt kept coming back to Perić. Perić—Valter, as he was better known—was elusive in the extreme. The Partisans' best-kept secret. For Perić to have revealed himself like that, exposed himself to such risk, meant the Partisans were concerned, profoundly so. They would use all the tools in their possession, including Reinhardt. And after all, he thought to himself, was that so different from the way he had spent so much of his life? Being a tool in someone else's possession? Soldier, policeman, soldier again. A life in service, so why the fixation on independence, now? Was he still so enamored of a need to make his own mark, in his own service?

He needed air, and there was still a crowd at the entrance. It shuffled out, slowly, and he could feel something was wrong. The crowd pulled him out into the cold air and he drank it deep, wanting to wake himself back up. He paused on the steps. Someone had hung a lantern from a makeshift hook over the door, and his breath puffed up and away into its light.

Bunda stood at the bottom of the steps, lantern-light glittering in his eyes, looking up at him.

"Getting cozy with the natives, is you?"

Reinhardt said nothing. He walked down the steps slowly, Bunda's eyes following all the way.

"I 'eard you was 'ere. I been looking for you." The huge Ustaša leaned back against a car with two other Ustaše standing on either side of him. Reinhardt's back prickled suddenly with his fear, and he pushed his tongue hard into the gap in his teeth.

"Captain?" The light from inside the theater and from the lantern cast Vukić into sharp lines of light and dark so he could not see her eyes. The Ustaše straightened, even Bunda. He seemed to coil up and in at the sight of her, and something in the set of his gaze sent a flood of cold through Reinhardt. Vukić seemed to hesitate, looking back inside, then came down the stairs, the light changing, flowing and fading and pooling differently over her as she stepped out of the lantern's glow. "Is there a problem?"

"No problem, madam," said Bunda, slowly. "Only, we was asked to fetch 'im."

"Who?"

"'im, right there."

"He has a rank. Do him the honor of using it."

Bunda's lips furled in around his teeth. He paused. Breathed. "That would be 'im. Captain Reinhardt."

"Better, Captain. Thank you. Why?"

"Something to show 'im. And someone wants to see 'im. Someone you don't want to keep waitin', if you know what's good for you."

"An Ustaša?" Reinhardt asked. Bunda nodded. Perić flashed through Reinhardt's mind. Here was a golden opportunity, but it was so soon. Too soon. "Then as I am not at your beck and call, I think I must respectfully decline," he said, stalling.

"No, Reinhardt. You don't decline. You just come." The two Ustaše to either side of him straightened, and their hands tightened on their weapons. "No fuss, now. Not 'ere. Not with all these nice people around. Just come with me."

"Where?"

"Not far."

"The Pale House?"

Bunda smiled. "After I show you something."

"Who wants to see me?"

"It's a surprise," Bunda said. His face shifted, hardened. "Enough." He hauled himself upright and opened the car door. "We ain't about to 'urt you, Reinhardt. Don't be such an old woman. It's just talk. Your driver can follow. So just get in. 'fore I lose my temper."

"Very well," Reinhardt said, remembering Bunda as he stood at that checkpoint at the entrance to the city. He wanted to walk away but dared not. He felt the pressure of eyes all around him, the people gathered and bunched up around him on the stairs, in the theater, and the eyes he could only feel staring down at him from the windows along the street. "I will come with you."

"I sincerely hope nothing amiss will come to Captain Reinhardt," said Vukić, suddenly. "Or I will have words with General Luburić."

As Bunda inclined his head, a glitter in his eyes as he looked at Vukić, something feral lurking far under the cavernous hang of his brow, Reinhardt realized she had spoken in Serbo-Croat. "Wouldn't dream of 'arm coming to the captain, ma'am. Not seeing as 'e's your particular friend." He said it loud, and he said it for the crowd around them. If it was meant to wound, or embarrass, Vukić seemed not to notice. Reinhardt looked at her as if for the first time. She had drawn herself up, standing straight. She was half Bunda's size, yet she still filled the space around her with a confidence rooted in some calm authority. But the risk she was taking, standing up to an Ustaša. For a German.

Vukić put her arm on Reinhardt's sleeve as he made to move. "I will see you later," she said, looking at Bunda as she said it. Again, there came that feral look in the giant's eyes as she turned and walked away, straight-backed elegance, her long black coat flaring out over her hips.

"Now that," said Bunda, "is one regal-looking backside." Bunda smiled, locking eyes with Reinhardt. "Nothing to say, Reinhardt? In the car, then."

Reinhardt took a moment to tell his driver to follow. The Feldjaeger was standing behind his *kubelwagen*, an StG 44 in his hands. He nodded, safed his weapon, and started his engine.

Thus comforted by knowing he had at least some support, Reinhardt climbed into the back of Bunda's car as one of the Ustaše pushed in after him. The car lurched to one side as Bunda dumped his huge weight into the front and the driver fired up the engine with a ratcheting cough, followed by the stench of homemade fuel. The car rattled down the road, turned left onto Kvaternik, then right, across the Princip Bridge. People moved around them in the gathering gloom, hurrying home. Fog was settling in, drowning the tops of the buildings, and the street was studded with points and pockets of light from candles, flashlights, even a couple of brands that left halos of light as they bobbed away into the deepening evening.

"Where are you taking me?"

"Not far, don't worry. But there's something you'd like to see, I reckon. It's up here."

The car's engine whined as the driver put it at a steep hill, and Reinhardt realized they were in, or not far from, Bistrik, the neighborhood to the south of the Miljacka where he had previously been barracked. The car lurched into a right-hand turn, a white sign on a wall proclaiming Balibegovica Street, and stopped outside a house. Like a staged reproduction of the killings that morning in Logavina, cars were drawn up outside it, but they were all local, one or two police cars, and a truck with Ustaše plates. The car door was opened, and Reinhardt, followed by Bunda, went up to the front door, past a soldier on guard, and into the house, flicking on a flashlight as he went. The place was dark, the heavy wooden walls and floors drinking what little daylight was left. There was a stench, latrine thick, as he was pulled to the side, into one of the rooms that led off the entrance, and handed the flashlight. It might once have been a dining room but was now a place where men had been murdered. Butchered, in fact.

Reinhardt stood in the doorway, stock-still with his hands clenched knuckle-white around the flashlight. Around his feet coiled a tubular tangle of limbs, cloth stretched tight over the angles of joints. He thought there were four bodies there, heaped across each other, at least two of them in poses of deliberate sexual obscenity with each other. Reinhardt's eye stuttered across the punctures and slashes of mutilations, across pallid swells of flesh, past raw-edged butchery, a part of him beginning to tick over deep inside, storing up glimpses and impressions, before coming up to rest on Bunda. The Ustaša's eyes had a wildness to them, and his face was engorged as if he strained to take everything in he could. A flicker of movement over his shoulder was Bakarević, the police inspector, looking utterly miserable again.

"What happened here, Bunda?"

"The Partisans happened, Reinhardt."

Reinhardt turned, startled, not wanting to show it. An Ustaša stood in the shadowed doorway of another room. He was tall, and very big, his uniform strained taut over his height and weight, a black belt bowing under a vast spread of gut. He stepped a little farther into what little light there was.

"Hello, Captain," the Ustaša said.

"Putković," Reinhardt replied, remembering this man from two years ago, the leader of Sarajevo's police, remembering the embarrassment and humiliation Reinhardt had heaped upon him as he had torn through the Ustaše's excuse for an investigation into Marija Vukić's murder.

"That's *Colonel* Putković to you, Reinhardt," snarled Bunda, ever the lackey solicitous of his master's rights.

"Partisans, Putković?" Reinhardt asked around a dry mouth, ignoring Bunda. "How so?"

Putković smiled at him and gestured at the bodies. "They're Ustaše. All of them. The Partisans did that. It's what they do when they get hold of one of us. But we got one of them. Show him, Bakarević."

Reinhardt followed the inspector out into a patch of ground behind the house overgrown with high grass and weeds traced silver by the flashlight's beam as the inspector pointed to a lump in the grass. Reinhardt walked carefully over to the body, checking the ground around it with his flashlight. The body lay on its stomach, its arms flat to its sides and its face twisted high to the right. Its mouth and nose were almost gone, smashed away by some terrible blow, rendering almost superfluous the gunshot wound that holed its neck. The body was dressed in an ill-fitting uniform of dull brown, and a cap lay in the grass by its head. Reinhardt picked it up, turned it in his hands until he saw the red star of the Partisans sewn to the front. Despite himself, he grinned, an ironic twist of his mouth, looking up at the sky to compose himself.

It had been a woman. Reinhardt ran his eyes up and down the body, the memory of that forest crowding suddenly into his mind, and then the basement. He touched his fingers to the bullet wound. It had not bled, meaning it was a postmortem wound. Reinhardt made to heave off one of the body's boots, but it slid away easily from the leg, being much too large for the woman. The foot was bare, no sock. Reinhardt sat back on his heels, thinking of those five bodies from the construction site. His mouth twisted, anger rising slowly. He turned at a rustle in the grass, having almost forgotten about Bakarević. The inspector stood there like a penitent, a notebook flapping open from his hand.

"You . . . you were a detective. Before. So. What does this all look like to you?" Bakarević asked.

"It looks bad," was all Reinhardt could find to say.

Bakarević stared, then laughed. A high-pitched giggle that he gulped back. "Bad? *Bad?* Oh, you have no idea." His mouth moved soundlessly, and then his eyes slewed left and right. He looked like a cornered animal. There was something very wrong, here, Reinhardt knew. Something that went beyond the slaughter that had taken place.

"Tell me," he said.

Bakarević shook his head, stepping backward through the grass, and then he was gone, back inside the house. Reinhardt followed him in, turning a corner into the wall of Bunda's chest.

"You saw outside? The Partisan?"

"I saw her, Bunda."

"Fuckers. Using women. No shame. And look what they did to my men. Go on, look. No secrets, Reinhardt. Look at 'em, I said! What do you see?"

"Bodies."

"You see provocation," said Putković. "Look a little closer."

"Look at 'im." Bunda's flashlight stabbed at a body. "His eyes have been gouged out. That one. Eviscerated. That's the stench. It's 'is bowels. That one, engaged in *buggery*? On this one, and 'e's been . . ." The giant stuttered to a stop.

"Emasculated."

"That's a fancy fucking word for 'aving your balls chopped off."

"You wanted me to see this, so give me a moment, Bunda."

Bunda subsided back, his huge arms folded across the boulder of his chest. Putković stood quietly to one side, one of his meaty fists closed around something small, something that moved with a gentle clack of hard surfaces. Reinhardt shone the light into the faces of the dead, his stomach turning at the one who had been blinded, at the empty, bloodied sockets. Each of the heads he turned to the right, until he came to the one he wanted, running a soft fingertip down the ridge of scar that ran from the man's ear down his jaw, and under his collar. Squatting there, he ran the flashlight over the room, and saw the blood spatters leap out at him. Two of them. On the wall. At a height consistent with men being made to kneel and then shot in the back of the head.

"What do you make of that, then?" he asked the Ustaše, the light shining on the bloodied walls.

Bunda leaned in, then growled. "Least they didn't suffer, did they."

At least two of them did not suffer, Reinhardt thought as he stood, wincing at the pain in his knee. "Is this it?"

"You're taking this a bit lightly, aren't you?" rumbled Putković, and Reinhardt realized his position, all but alone up here, and his tongue shot into the gap in his teeth.

"Bet you weren't so fucking flippant when it was your boys lying in the dirt." Bunda seemed to swell even bigger, fairly suffused with his anger.

No apologies. Not for these men, even if he was alone up here. "What do you want from me?"

"It's important you see this, Reinhardt," said Putković. "It's important you know we have the same enemies. Now, let's go somewhere a little more comfortable, shall we?"

They went back outside. The street was very quiet, only the murmur of the Ustaše and police, a sentry's feet crunching softly in the dark. Reinhardt stood a moment, listening to what was not there, then climbed back into the car with Bunda. Ahead of them, Putković angled his bulk into another car, and then it was the same journey but in reverse, and the Pale House loomed out of the murk, edged by the forlorn huddles of people who waited against its walls, coalescing out of the gloom, then falling behind as the car passed them. Then they were slowing past guards with shouldered rifles, skeins of barbed wire wound around wooden trestles, and stopping in front of the doorway set back under an arch bracketed by a pair of heavy, wrought-iron lamps. Up on the roof, a crow cocked its head down at the street and cawed raucously.

Bunda shifted around in the front and smiled at Reinhardt.

The crowd fell silent as Putković stepped out of his car. The big Ustaše ran lazy eyes across the penitent crowd, and he lifted his fist to his mouth, brushing it with his knuckles as his fingers curled around whatever he held. He seemed to play with the crowd, no words exchanged, none needed, only a predatorial sense of ownership, as if Putković knew exactly the terms of the power he wielded, and whatever sufferance he allowed the crowd to have. He left them there, eventually, and Reinhardt followed Bunda back inside and up that flight of steps, the desk in front of it empty now.

The building pressed back in around him, different now, a dog with its teeth bared wet and white, as if no pretenses were needed with the darkness outside. Someone was screaming in the building. It was far off, dimmed by distance and walls and doors, but it pierced the rank air of the entrance, a shrill thread of agony. Behind a door came the meaty thud of something being struck. Putković and Bunda hauled themselves up the stairs, the giant breathing heavily, then prodded Reinhardt to the right, following Putković, past a man chained to a huge, metal radiator. Reinhardt could feel the heat sloughing off it as he went by, and the man writhed desperately against the cast-iron pipes, whimpering, his face scarlet as he shifted one way, then the other.

Reinhardt and Bunda followed Putković into another room, some kind of office with a huge wooden desk surrounded by mismatched chairs. Heavy brown drapes hung at the windows, and Putković moved to each of them, drawing them closed. There was a smell in the air, like something had been burned. Putković turned and looked at Reinhardt, Bunda moving over to stand next to him. Putković's eyes were very dark and flat, no sign of what he was thinking visible in them or on his face. The fingers of one hand moved rhythmically, a faint clatter as something shifted around between them.

16

"Leave us, Bunda." Putković ignored the crestfallen look on Bunda's face, waited until he had left, then gestured to a chair. "Sit," he said, his fingers moving again, and he rolled a pair of red dice onto a tabletop. "It has been a long time, Reinhardt."

Reinhardt took a long, slow breath. This day seemed to be getting longer and stranger the older it got. "You're The Gambler." Putković inclined his head. "You're in charge of the city's security now."

"You are well informed." Putković stirred the dice with his fingers, rolling them softly across the table.

Reinhardt shrugged, keeping his eyes on the Ustaša. "Know your friends . . ."

"Know your enemies better." Putković smiled. It did not reach those flat eyes. "Are we your enemies, Reinhardt?" he asked, scooping up his dice.

"What do you mean?"

"I mean, we did not part on the best of terms, last time. I admit that. And now you return, two years later, and you start where you left off." Reinhardt said nothing. There was something here to be seen or heard, that was clear, and Reinhardt was content to let this conversation spin out the way Putković wanted it to.

"A drink, Reinhardt?" Putković turned to a wooden cabinet of dark, carven wood, opening it to reveal a jumble of bottles. "What will you have? Let's have a rakija!"

Reinhardt wanted nothing to drink, and wanted nothing less than to raise a glass with Putković, but he remembered how sensitive people in the Balkans were about their hospitality. "A slivovitz, then."

"Good choice. I've a nice homemade one in here . . . somewhere," Putković said, hunching into the cabinet and clattering bottles aside. "*Evo, sprska rakija!* Here! Say what you like about the Serbs, they make the best slivo." He handed Reinhardt a glass of clear plum brandy. "Cheers!"

"*Živjeli,*" Reinhardt answered.

Putković guffawed, and they both sipped. The brandy was very good, dangerously so, a smooth, tidal flood from his mouth right into the pit of his belly.

"To your promotion, Putković." The Ustaša smirked his thanks. "What triggered that?"

"Actually, it was your old friend and partner, Reinhardt. Padelin. Remember him? You were bad news for him, you know. After you left, he changed. Sort of went into hibernation and came out a different man. Began to take his work seriously. Much too seriously. So seriously, he became a liability, right at the time when we needed unity around us. So when a group of us were offered promotion into the Ustaše, we left him behind. We'd had enough of the police by that point. There was nothing happening and no way to get ahead. Anyway, Padelin ended up making such a nuisance of himself he got himself purged by Luburić. Not long ago, in fact."

"Charming story."

"One of the last things I heard him say was, 'Putković,' he said, 'police work may as well be fool's work in this town.' And let me tell you, he never said a truer thing in all the time I knew him."

"Your German is much better."

Putković smiled, straightening. "Thank you. I have made efforts . . ." And then it was as if he remembered something; the smile was rinsed from his face, and his fingers began to knead his dice.

"What am I doing here, Putković?"

Putković rolled his lips around a large sip of brandy, his porcine eyes glittering. "I've a feeling we are operating under a misunderstanding, Reinhardt. You are under the impression that, at best, we are a bunch of ill-disciplined psychopaths, and at worst, ill-disciplined psychopaths who are your enemies, no?"

"That's about the size of it."

"We are nothing of the sort, Reinhardt. Not ill-disciplined, not psychopaths, certainly not your enemies. We are something much more. Your people, my people, we are a rampart. We have a duty to civilization, to the future. We have an alliance, your people and mine, a sacred alliance. There should be no mistrust between us, to ensure—"

"Oh God, Putković." Brandy sloshed from the glass as Reinhardt put it down. "You did not bring me here for a lesson in propaganda."

Putković's face reddened. He turned and poured himself another brandy, the bottle rattling along the rim of his glass. "Very well. No propaganda. No history. No whatever. Just some truth." He rolled his dice, ran his eyes over the numbers. "You are investigating the murders of three of your men. You seem to be linking them to more deaths in a forest. You seem to think the Ustaše had something to do with it."

"Go on," challenged Reinhardt, though he would have bitten it back if he could.

"You were shown the bodies of four of my men tonight. Murdered and mutilated. Whoever is killing people, Reinhardt, my people are suffering too."

"A bit too soon to make such an assumption, Putković."

"That my people are suffering?"

"I don't doubt that," said Reinhardt, a scornful edge to his words that he could not help. "I meant it's a bit too soon to be assuming the same people are doing the killing."

"There's such a thing as overanalyzing a situation, Reinhardt."

"There are such things as instinct and evidence, as well."

"What about the similarities between your murders, Reinhardt? The bodies in the forest. The ones you found this morning in Logavina. Should you not be interested in that?"

"How about, for instance, the dead silence up at that murder scene, tonight? Not a single inhabitant on the street. No one being questioned. It's as if there was no need."

Putković's eyes slitted. "But there was no need. The Partisans did it."

Reinhardt bit back on his feeling that only two men had been killed there that night and inclined his head, a sardonic tilt to the movement.

"I'll go one better, Reinhardt. We are the masters of this city. Law and order. Life and death. If I need something taken care of—and by that, I mean if I need someone arrested, if I believe someone is a danger, or must be removed—I order it done." He flicked his fingers and his dice pattered across the tabletop. "Like that! No skulking in the shadows. No leaving a trail of bodies. Just action. Did you see what we did at Marijin Dvor? Two nights ago?"

"The hangings?"

"The hangings."

"That was you?"

Putković nodded. "Was that skulking in the shadows? Was that hiding what we had to do?"

"There is killing and there is killing, Putković."

"What do you mean?"

"That some deaths will not survive scrutiny."

Putković snorted. "What must I do to prove to you we are the masters of this town?" he said, his tone almost musing. "That we have nothing to hide. Come. Let me show you."

Putković scooped up his dice and pulled aside an edge of curtain. He looked down into an inner courtyard, Reinhardt joining him at the window. Torches burned in stakes and from sconces, washing muddy orange light across mounded heaps stacked against two of the walls. Pairs of Ustaše moved across the dark ground with the lurching precision of men bearing heavy loads, their shadows flowing across the walls. As he squinted down, the low clouds flickered with silver light, and the shape of the courtyard stuttered, as though summoned reluctantly from the darkness. As thunder rumbled in its wake, Reinhardt's eyes struggled to make sense of what he had seen stenciled in the strobed light. Bodies, stacked like cordwood along the walls, the Ustaše heaving more of them atop those already there.

"Is it worth," Reinhardt paused, pushing back on the nauseous anger he felt, "asking what any of them did?"

"No. You still don't get it, do you? Who they were alive is not as important as the message they sent dead. What they did? It's what they might have done. It's who they were. I suppose all that matters is they were people who entered this building and never left it. I gave them a chance, some of them. The least I could do. I offer them a gamble. They name a number"—he clattered the dice across the tabletop—"and if it comes up, away they go. If not, not. So, you see, Reinhardt, what happens to our enemies. This is no secret. Only, perhaps, the scale of it."

"Do you think this can go on forever?" Putković frowned at him, Reinhardt thinking he would never have a better chance to challenge any of the Ustaše on what Perić had demanded of him. "There's nearly always a reckoning to be had, Putković. The war is turning. There's a new future coming, and it's not the future our leaders told us it would be. Wait, let me finish," he said, as Putković made to interrupt him. "What will become of the Ustaše? What will become of you? You surely aren't going to wait here for the Partisans to wash over you, and you surely can't think you can hold them off anymore. So where will all those like you run to?"

"If you wore black, I'd have your tongue for those words," Putković whispered, turning on Reinhardt, his dice crunched in his hand.

"But I don't wear black, Putković," said Reinhardt, matching him step for step, but it was as if there were some kind of magnetism between them that kept them apart. Something almost physical, visceral, an inability to get close to each other. As if in touching, colliding, they would cancel each other out. "I wear gray. And even if the colors are not so different, you and I, Putković, we are poles apart, and so I'll say anything I damn well please to you."

"Maybe I should still educate you further about the realities of this place. Come with me."

Putković shouldered open the door, thumping down the hallway, past the wretch chained to his radiator. He stopped outside a door, listening, one thick finger lifted theatrically to his lips as he turned to face Reinhardt. He opened the door, one heavy hand on Reinhardt's shoulder, pushing him in. Reinhardt's face twisted in disgust at the stench from inside. Urine and excrement and fear, and the iron catch of blood. He stopped, stepped back, and then Putković was up against him and there was nowhere to go but in.

There were two Ustaše in the room, and a man, a prisoner. A wooden baton rested on two tables that had been pushed quite close together. The baton ran behind the prisoner's knees, and the man himself was suspended upside down from it. The man was weeping, and choking on the blood and tears and mucus that flowered around his mouth and nose. With his hands tied behind his back, and his ankles tied to his wrists, he could do nothing about the state he was in, nor do anything against the blows an Ustaša was raining down on him with a rubber truncheon. The man's thighs and stomach were welted red, and the Ustaša was stripped to his shirtsleeves, sweat shining across his face. The floor beneath the pair of them was stained and dulled, the shine of blood freshly spilt atop a dull glaze of deeper red, almost brown, of older blood that had sunk into the room's floorboards.

The Ustaša paused in midstroke, the baton raised high.

"*Tko je ovo?*" the man panted, looking at Reinhardt framed in the doorway with Putković towering behind him.

"This?" answered Putković in German, shoving Reinhardt forward. "This is someone who needs a lesson in what it means to cross us."

"Well, he's come to the right place," the Ustaša answered back.

"And Sutko's the one to give the lesson," the other Ustaša quipped. They smiled and laughed, all of them, the one called Sutko giving a little bow and flourishing his baton as if it were a sword. Straightening up, the Ustaša pointed his eyes at Putković's fist. "Is it time?"

"Did he give his number?" asked Putković, pointing at the prisoner.

"The number twelve." Sutko grinned.

Reinhardt was suddenly and appallingly aware of danger, all

around. He breathed long and slow, sucking down the fetid air of that room, and made himself stand easy, his eyes roving lazily over the Ustaše, the man hanging from the baton. It helped if he stuck his tongue hard between his teeth. It bunched up his chin, made him seem contemptuous of what he saw.

Putković looked at Reinhardt, and something twitched across his face, as if he were disappointed. He walked over to the prisoner hanging upside down, reached down, and grabbed the man's hair. He lifted, pulled, the man's knees pivoting around the baton that ran behind them. The Ustaša looked blankly down at him, the man croaking and gasping on his own blood. Then he let him go, the man swinging back and then forth like a carcass in an abattoir, a new whine of agony escaping his ruined mouth. Putković weighed his dice in his hands, then opening and sweeping his fingers over the floor. The red dice rattled across the wood. He looked at them, then folded them back into his hand.

"Wrong number?" smirked Sutko.

"I'm afraid so," said Putković, looking at Reinhardt, his eyes flat, and then he spoke to the third Ustaša. "Finish it, Marin."

Reinhardt turned away, back to the door, only glimpsing the one called Marin bending over the hanging man with a long blade in his hand. Then the door was shut, and there was only the image, burned onto the backs of his eyes, and a sound, a gargled scream. He stood in the corridor, breathing hoarsely, staring at the man chained to the radiator, until the door opened behind him, and Putković stepped back out into the corridor. Their gaze cracked and ground together, and then Reinhardt turned on his heels and walked back to Putković's office.

"You see, now?" asked Putković as he followed him. "This is how it is."

Bile rose in Reinhardt's throat, choking off what he had to say, and it might all have gone even further downhill from there, but they were interrupted by a knock at the door. A pair of Ustaše stepped in at Putković's answer.

"Sir, General Luburić wants to see you before he leaves."

"At once. Wait outside a moment." When they were gone, Putković breathed out, very slowly, the dice shifting in his fingers again, visibly making an effort to calm himself. "I will send Bunda to you. He will see you out."

The door thudded shut behind Putković and, alone in the room, Reinhardt waited a moment, listening for voices, the sounds of foot-steps, then let himself go. One explosive breath out, a blind rake of his eyes across the ceiling. His heart slowed as he listened to the house, and he heard voices, a snatch of laughter. From outside, it seemed. He walked back to the window, looking down, seeing Putković standing with hands on hips next to another man. Crows lumbered across the corpses, and more lined the roof of the courtyard like black hooks against the now-pallid gray of the sky.

"All done, then?"

Reinhardt's heart froze solid a moment with fear. He had not even heard Bunda come back into the room, and he could not move, and then realized he had best make the most of it.

"What's that down there?"

The giant grinned. "Housekeeping."

Reinhardt swallowed, then let the curtain fall back. "You're wasted up here, Bunda. Man like you could shift two of those bodies at one go."

Bunda's face curled and shifted. "I don't do that no more."

"Right."

"What's that mean, Reinhardt?"

"Nothing, Bunda."

"Don't say 'nothing,' Reinhardt."

"You make the rules, now, right? You're an officer, now."

"What d'you mean, Reinhardt?"

Reinhardt stared back at the giant and, even though he stood in the heart of Bunda's power, he felt his fear of him slide away.

"That an ape is still an ape, though you dress it in velvet."

"What the fuck did you just say?"

"Thank God for the Ustaše, right, Bunda? Else you'd have been milking cows all your life . . ."

"Fuck you, Reinhardt."

". . . living in the country, where men are men and the sheep run scared."

"*Fuck* you, Reinhardt. I don't get off on no animals."

"What do you get off on, Bunda?"

"I can get *anyone* I want. *Anything*. 'Cause it's there to be taken."

"Because the city's yours, right, Bunda? Country boy made good. Taking out your frustrations on the city folk."

"Careful, Reinhardt. You're all alone here. And the general's leaving. The city's ours, now."

"Putković said you were to see me out, Bunda."

The Ustaša blinked at the change in conversation, his mind still lumbering down the track Reinhardt had laid before him.

"Going too fast for you, Bunda?"

"What d'you say?"

"I told you, Putković's orders are for you to see me out."

"That's Colonel Putković to you, Reinhardt."

Reinhardt said nothing, walking around Bunda's bulk back into the corridor, past the man chained to his radiator. He heard Bunda's heavy footsteps pause, then a thud, an agonized gush of breath. He glanced back as Bunda lashed his foot again into the belly of the chained man.

"Bunda!" The giant's eyes glittered far back under his brows. "Putković said it was important, Bunda. But you have your fun, don't let me stop you. Up to you."

In that gloomy corridor, poised over the prisoner, Bunda was a form carved from primeval memory, the hulking apparition at the entrance to a cave. Reinhardt carried on down the stairs, his back crawling to have the giant behind him, hearing Bunda's footsteps thumping down after him. Reinhardt pushed himself outside, sucking down the night air, great gulps of it. He could not stay here anymore. The place was driving into him from all angles, and it was then he remembered the crowd, the people he had passed on the way in.

"Please. Did you see him?" An old lady held out a portrait, a sepia-toned window to another, happier, time. "Did you see my Selmir?"

"Bosko Jović? My husband. Did you see him?"

"Mirsad Huremović. The photographer. An elderly man?"

"Mohamed Spahić. From Logavina. *Mohamed Spahić?*"

"Hey, you. German." An Ustaša beckoned Reinhardt over, pointing out his car idling just the other side of the wire. The crowd followed him, and then they were all around him, holding up pictures, photographs, documents, sacks and parcels. Names came at him, of the men and boys of this town, the women their only guardians, now. The cries came at him thick and fast, urging, pleading, strident, and he felt himself slipping sideways in his own mind, overlays of the horror inside the Pale House jagging across the faces of the women in front of him, images of bodies stacked one atop the other and now only bait for crows. Dimly he heard the guards shouting, beating the women back, and then suddenly Vukić was there.

She took his arm, talking all the while with the women around them. He did not hear what she said, but space opened up around her, and there was something else other than desperation in the faces around him. There was respect there, even some affection, like they might once have given a noble. Vukić held his arm tight, pulled him gently from the crowd, and walked him to the car.

"What are you doing here?" Reinhardt asked.

"I was worried about you," Vukić said.

"Thank you," Reinhardt whispered to her, his throat tight. She said nothing, only smiled, and he took strength from it. "I'm sorry," he said, turning to the crowd and speaking in Serbo-Croat. He tried to take them all in with his eyes. "I didn't see any of them. I'm sorry."

"Go, now," said Vukić. "They will have to go themselves, anyway. It is tolerated, but it is well past curfew."

"Then let me take you home. At least let me do that."

She hesitated, then nodded, giving the driver an address near the line between the Austro-Hungarian and Ottoman parts of town. The car started off, and then Reinhardt froze, a pair of images jarring together like a bell that had been struck. He turned back, looking at the Pale House, seeing the Ustaše beating and chasing the women from in front of its walls, scattering them like geese.

"The goatee," he whispered to himself. "From the forest. *Stop!*" he said to the driver. He kept looking back, ignoring the other two, then finally swiveled his eyes to Vukić. "Back there. One of the women was holding a photograph of her husband. She called him . . . she called him Mira . . . Mirad . . . Something like that. A photographer."

"Mirsad Huremović," said Vukić.

"That's him. Her husband is dead. I found his body in the forest, at that massacre I told you of. How . . . how did he end up there, if she thinks he was taken here?"

Vukić's eyes were wide as she stared back at him, and then she slid to the side along the car seat. "Wait. I will ask her."

Reinhardt lit a cigarette as he waited, staring hard at his hand as it shook, willing himself to calm. Twisting himself back in the seat, he saw Vukić walking arm in arm with the woman who had held that photograph of a man in a dark suit, smooth brushed hair, and a neat little goatee beard. He watched as they said their good-byes, the woman walking away with another, Vukić hurrying back with her arms folded tightly across her.

"Her husband was taken about a week ago," she said, hunching herself onto the *kubelwagen*'s back bench. "You are sure he is dead." Reinhardt nodded. "She thinks he is still alive. A prisoner saw him four days ago."

"In the Pale House?"

"Yes."

Reinhardt faced forward, watching the woman walk past, head bowed, a hard truth awaiting her. He shook his head, took a last pull on his cigarette, and tossed it over the car door, nodding to the driver to get going again.

From the back, Vukić leaned forward to direct the driver, and her hand came to rest on Reinhardt's shoulder. She left it there as the car nosed its way through the streets, almost no lights to be seen, just the pulsing glow of fires, the light spilling and slipping here and there from doorways, windows, and stairwells. The car stopped at her word in front of a square building of Austro-Hungarian construction with three floors. Reinhardt climbed out as she did.

"Shall I escort you?"

"No, I . . ." She shook her head. "Thank you, that is not necessary."
The two of them looked at each other a moment.

"In there, in the Pale House—" Reinhardt stopped. "They are . . ."
He stopped again. "The people outside. Do they know?" *Do they know
what?* There seemed to be no words, and she lifted one hand and
cupped his cheek. Her fingers were small, and very cold as he covered
them with his hand. "Thank you, again," he said.

She nodded and turned away into her building. He watched her
disappear into the darkness inside, listening as her steps faded up on
wooden flights of stairs until he heard a door shut and he knew she
was home safe.

17

The desks outside Dreyer's office were empty of personnel, papers neatly piled up and sorted next to half-filled crates. Reinhardt stood quietly in the doorway to the clerks' office, wondering again if he had done the right thing in coming. There was a razor line of light under the door of that erudite judge's office, Judge Erdmann, nothing under Dreyer's, but there was a thread of music in the air. It was somewhat incongruous, but it was there and as he leaned his ear against Dreyer's door, he realized it was coming from his old friend's office.

He knocked softly, then again, harder, but there was no response. He opened the door, softly, onto musty darkness, and a soft, smooth trill of notes from a saxophone. A spreading rectangle of light flowed into the room, and there was a jerk of movement from the bed in the corner, and Dreyer rolled over. His face was red, puffy, and his breathing came high and edged with a ragged wheeze. Reinhardt's heart sank as he looked at him.

"I'm sorry," Reinhardt said. "I didn't think . . ."

"Reinhardt," Dreyer said, pausing for breath. "It's all right. Close the door. Here, on the desk. Put the lamp on, then help me get this off."

Dreyer was still wearing one boot, Reinhardt saw, as he clicked on the small lamp on the desk. Reinhardt heaved at it, and it sucked itself free. He stumbled a step backward as Dreyer rolled back onto his bed with a sigh, covering his face with his arm. He lay there breathing heavily, his belly mounding up and down, and then he struggled up onto one elbow and scrabbled around on top of a wooden crate that served as a bedside table.

"This what you're after?" said Reinhardt, lifting the hip flask from the floor.

There was a fleeting look of embarrassment on Dreyer's face, but he waved Reinhardt over, took the flask, and put it to his mouth. He drank deeply, sighed again, and lay back on the bed.

"Still don't want any, Gregor?" he asked.

"None for me."

Dreyer turned a bleary eye on him. "Not going all moral on me, are you?"

Reinhardt shook his head. "I'm not. But I've been there. Where you are. And it didn't do me any good, in the end." Reinhardt felt spread thin, utterly worn out by the pressure of the day, and knew it would not take much to tip him over the edge. He did not want to rediscover that part of himself that took solace in alcohol, nor did he want to be what he saw Dreyer had become.

Dreyer looked at him, blinked, turned his head up to the ceiling. "Oh, I doubt that," he whispered. "If you'd seen what I've seen, I think you wouldn't turn this down so easily."

"Why don't you tell me, then?" said Reinhardt, sighing, as he shrugged out of his overcoat and sat in one of the chairs, crossing his left leg over his right and rubbing his knee. "Tell me. Tell me what happened to you, Marcus." He wondered if he meant it. Behind him, so out of time and place, that saxophone played on, what sounded like a trumpet playing counterpoint to it, and he realized it was jazz. Prewar, American jazz, like they used to hear in the Berlin clubs in the old days.

"To make me like this, you mean?"

"I didn't say that."

"You didn't need to."

"And I didn't think it either. Marcus. Please. Don't . . . think . . . don't think I judge you. I don't. I wouldn't."

Dreyer giggled, suddenly, an incongruous sound from a man his size. He shook his head as Reinhardt looked at him quizzically, and he sipped from his flask. "Nothing. It's nothing. It's just I always find it funny when people use the word *judge* with me."

Reinhardt smiled back. "Seeing as you used to be one."

"Seeing as I still am one, if you can believe it . . ." He looked at the flask, sipped again. "A lot of people can't."

"A judge with a Knight's Cross. I remember you," said Reinhardt. He leaned back into the chair, one hand still kneading his knee, and closing his eyes. "First time I met you, a snotty-nosed kid. When was it? Winter of 1917? In France. You looked just like a lawyer. We figured you wouldn't last long. If the Tommies didn't get you, the cold would."

Dreyer smiled, sipped. "You . . . you took care of me, though. You. And Brauer. And Rosen."

"Always take care of the company quartermaster, was Brauer's motto." Reinhardt grinned, his eyes still closed. "I remember you in Berlin, afterward. Spic-and-span in that suit of yours. The one with the long tails. And the top hat."

"The penguin suit."

"Then came those judge's robes. It was a good day for the police when you got made a judge, Marcus." He looked at Dreyer. "And a better day for those of us proud to call you our friend."

Dreyer looked at him, and then his eyes crinkled back and his face sank in on itself. He fell onto his back again, his arm across his mouth. There was a silence, then his chest heaved, and he sobbed, his mouth ground tight into his arm. Reinhardt kept quiet, his own eyes blurring, as his friend wept and wept, until finally he calmed, and he lowered his arm, sighing long and slowly.

"Christ, I'm sorry. About that."

Reinhardt said nothing, only rubbed his knee.

"That knee still giving you trouble?"

"Always. What happened, Marcus?"

"The Nazis. The Russians. War. Life." Dreyer flipped open his silver cigarette case and offered it to Reinhardt. He took a cigarette himself and lit both with the matching lighter. Reinhardt looked back at him through a cloud of smoke.

"I'm listening, Marcus."

"The Nazis chased me out of my court in thirty-five." Reinhardt nodded that he remembered. "But I'd seen the writing on the wall and had made arrangements with old friends from the army, in the legal department, and they took me back in. After Norway, I went into Russia with Barbarossa, as a divisional judge with 2nd Panzer. Within a month of the invasion, we were up to our eyeballs in cases. Theft, arson, murder, rape, you name it, we tried it. Passed tens of death sentences, and carried most of 'em out. Dozens more sent to the stockade, or punishment duty. All signed off on by the general. General Heinrici. Toughest little bastard you ever saw in a general's uniform. He refused to pass on Hitler's Barbarossa Decree. That soldiers couldn't be tried for crimes against the civilian population. 'We'll have none of that,' he said, the old bugger. 'Courts will function as normal.'

"But it was like building a sand castle in the tide. Your little bit of it works, holds up. Principles, evidence, all that." Dreyer paused, hiccupped. "But all around, to left and right, in front and behind, you can't imagine . . . the things we were doing. Which were happening. And then Heinrici moved on to 4th Army, and the man who replaced him was a thorough-going Nazi. An absolute bastard. It all came to an end. 'No incompatibility with army discipline and National Socialist principles,' he declared. Theft, arson, murder, rape, you name it, we turned a blind eye to it. And no amount of booze would take away the taste of the day. Of knowing you were letting men . . . who . . . had done the most terrible things . . . you were letting them get away with it. With murder."

He fell silent. Reinhardt watched him, imagining the compromises Dreyer must have made with himself.

"The last . . . the last straw for me, was a man, a soldier . . ." Dreyer paused, drank. "Part of a unit accused of butchering the villagers of . . . some . . . flyspeck hovel. This soldier killed an entire family. Four generations. And then bayonetted an infant to its mother's breast. 'She was already dead,' he said. 'It was kinder to kill the child.' I mean"—Dreyer's head hung down—"I mean what *kind* of *fucked*-up world is that? What kind of *logic* . . ." He drank. "I requested a transfer to the front. I couldn't do it anymore. They refused. 'You're a judge,' they said," he mouthed sonorously. "'So just judge.' Just judge, little judge. Make the facts fit a National Socialist view. Then, it's all right to bayonet a child to . . . its . . ."

"Christ, Marcus," Reinhardt whispered, finally.

"Christ was nowhere to be found. I kept asking for that transfer. Pulled in every favor I had and finally got it. All I wanted was to die, because I was too afraid to put a bullet in my own heart. Suicide's a sin, right? Isn't that what they taught us in Sunday school? Suicide's a sin . . . How is it such seemingly inconsequential things—words, a belief—can still hold sway and influence in a world like ours, after what we've seen and done? I couldn't do it. I couldn't do it, so I gave the Russians every chance to do it for me. And they fucked it up." He laughed. "They *royally* fucked it up. Missed me every time. Instead I got this superhuman reputation. *Suicidally* brave. All that rubbish. I just wanted to die. So they gave me a medal. Then another one. Until it all came apart on me. I cracked. And they can stand many things, but a holder of the Knight's Cross who turns into a gibbering drunk they can't stand. They pulled me out. Dried me out," he snorted, waving the flask. "Assigned me elsewhere. And here I am. And that . . ." he said, upending the flask, shaking the last drops onto his tongue, "is that. That is what happened to me."

Reinhardt finished his cigarette and flattened it into the ashtray. "Where did they send you, after they pulled you out?"

"What?" mumbled Dreyer. His head rocked back as he considered the question, and he belched, softly and wetly. "Sorry 'bout that. My . . . friends . . . in the legal department. They put me in the . . . the War Crimes Bureau." He giggled again. "Talk about irony. Investigating Russian crimes against our side. A man would starve on the difference between us and them. It was a load of rubbish. Two bald men fighting over a comb. I put up with it about a year, then requested a transfer again. And here I am." Dreyer shook his head, screwing his eyes into the palms of his hands.

"Tell me again how you came across Jansky."

Dreyer raised his head, squinting at Reinhardt. "I told you."

"Tell me again."

"What?"

"Tell me differently."

Dreyer's eyes slid away, but Reinhardt had seen the dead light in them. "It was Poland. Just before Barbarossa. The whole country was crammed with Germans. There was a lot of waiting and a lot of tension. Men began looking for things to do. Jansky was in charge of a police unit in some wretched Polish town. Near the Russian border. I can't even remember the name."

"And?"

"And what?" Dreyer snapped, then seemed to remember something, perhaps himself, and he reddened and passed a hand across his face. "I'm sorry," he muttered. He moved his mouth, his tongue running thickly across his lips. "There was some sort of scam under way. I think it was trafficking in stolen art and treasure. Jansky had some sort of network moving the stuff back to Germany. Jewish art. Polish heirlooms. Things like that."

Reinhardt frowned at Dreyer. Something was not quite right, but he kept his doubts to himself, letting Dreyer ramble on. "There was some sort of falling-out. Dishonor among thieves. I came onto the case when we discovered a pair of dead Germans. Officers. They were known associates of Jansky. Subordinates of his." That was it, Reinhardt realized. Dreyer was rambling. This should have been clear to him. It was a seminal event, what had put Dreyer onto Jansky. There should not have been any *I think* or *some sort of*. Dreyer should have known this, but maybe it was just the drink, Reinhardt reasoned to himself.

"So you investigated?"

"The . . . evidence . . . pointed to a Polish resistance attack."

"And there were reprisals."

"A village was destroyed. All the men executed." Dreyer lowered his face into his palms.

Reinhardt waited, but nothing more was forthcoming.

"And Greece? I understand what you said, about Poland, about him getting away with it there. But for you to go all the way to Greece . . . ?

"Greece," said Dreyer. "The same thing. But bigger. Gold, this time. I found Jansky had gotten himself mixed up with a bunch of those Greek fascists in their security battalions."

"How did you hear about this?"

Dreyer's eyes rolled toward him, clawed veins reddening their edges.

"Through the War Crimes Bureau." Reinhardt waited. "You have to understand how these things work. I told you about Russia. The ridiculousness of it. Investigating their crimes in the middle of ours."

"Two bald men fighting over a comb."

"Right. Except, sometimes, we would launch investigations upon receipt of requests from the Allies. They pass cases through the Foreign Ministry. Through the Swedes, or the Swiss. Requests to investigate crimes against their soldiers. Their people. And sometimes we do the same." Reinhardt shook his head at the thought of it, of missives passed between chancelleries, the smooth paperwork of diplomacy in the midst of such barbarity. "The British and the Greeks—their government in exile, the one in London—passed a request through the Swiss for investigation into crimes committed by men in the security battalions. They were lunatics, most of them. Completely out of control. Raping. Pillaging. Massacring their own countrymen. You know of them?"

"Collaborationist units. Formed by the puppet government."

"The puppet government." Dreyer nodded. "The one we put in place. One unit in particular had seen the writing on the wall and were making their own arrangements. They robbed the state bank, something like that, during the retreat from Athens. Jansky had a hand in it. Helping them or something. Organizing it."

"How do you know this?" asked Reinhardt. Something was not right, he thought again.

"An informant," said Dreyer, shortly, burying his face in his hands again.

"What are you not telling me, Marcus?"

Dreyer swallowed. "Everything in good time, Gregor."

Reinhardt nodded slowly and stood, walking to the window and watching the dull, dim lines of his reflection in the dark glass. "Nothing is what it seems," he said, quietly, to himself, thinking of forests and photographers, burned bodies, executed bodies, Jansky and the Ustaše, Germans and hiwis.

Dreyer surged up, suddenly. "*What the fuck d'you mean?* 'Nothing is what it seems?' Things are *always* what they seem. Bayonetting a child to its mother's *breast* is what it seems. Lining people up and shooting them dead into a *ditch* is what it seems."

Reinhardt flinched back. Dreyer's voice had gone ragged, flecked with spittle, and his eyes were fixed in his head, staring past Reinhardt at some faraway place. Reinhardt regretted his words. He had meant them for himself. Perhaps as sounds to fill a space, but he should have known in that case how wrong they were. "I'm sorry," he said. "I didn't mean it that way."

"Whatever," Dreyer said, waving a hand. "Don't listen to me. Fat old man. Drunk."

"I've been there, too, Marcus." Reinhardt worked his fingers against and between each other, running his thumbs across his palms and feeling the cold sweat coating them. "Maybe not as far down that road as you, but I've been there."

"Yes? And how did you fare along that road? How did you make it back? Or didn't you?"

In the window, Reinhardt's reflection stared back at him, the curves and angles of his face like pale arcs. How to tell him? How to tell him of the conversion in that hut in the forest two years ago? He had never told anyone, and it had never come to anything, and anyway, was that not his burden to bear? How to tell him of a failed search for an act of resistance? How to tell him of the burden laid upon him by the Partisans?

"Nothing?" Dreyer closed his eyes and rolled back onto his pillow. "Maybe I was wrong, then. It seemed there was more to you. Turn out the light on the way out, would you?"

"I'll help you, Dreyer."

Dreyer breathed once or twice, then opened his eyes, staring up at the ceiling. "What?"

"I said I'd help you."

Dreyer hauled himself back up. "Why?"

"I think your case and my case are linked. This penal battalion has turned up once too often in the past couple of days. And Jansky's got a connection with the Ustaše. He was at a checkpoint manned by this brute of an Ustaše called Bunda, and Bunda paid attention to him. I saw Jansky again at the Pale House today, going in for a meeting with one of the top Ustaše."

Dreyer listened with wide eyes. "So, you don't think I'm crazy?"

Reinhardt frowned, leaning his head back. "I never . . ."

Dreyer waved it away, a lopsided smile hanging off the side of his face. "You are the first . . . first person to take me seriously on this. About Jansky. Thank you."

"Thank me later, Marcus, when we might have gotten somewhere."

Dreyer flopped back onto his bed, swallowed hard. "Gotten somewhere . . ." he repeated, "gotten somewhere," his face creasing up again, and his breathing coming suddenly high and ragged. "It's no good. It won't work." There was a glitter at the corner of Dreyer's eyes, and a panicked edge to his voice.

"It might. It will," Reinhardt said. "There's someone who can help. Someone inside Jansky's unit."

"Inside?" Dreyer struggled onto one elbow. *"Who?"*

"Someone I'm seeing tomorrow, an informant the Feldgendarmerie have in the battalion," said Reinhardt, sidestepping the question but wanting to give Dreyer something, anything, to keep him going. Give him some faith, some hope in the future.

Dreyer tilted his head at Reinhardt. He smiled, a sudden bright gleam. "Working together. It'll be just like the old days!"

Reinhardt would have smiled if he could, but those suspicions of Dreyer came creeping back up on him. That cold, reptilian feeling of something wrong. The music had ended, he realized; the gramophone had stopped. He got up to look at the record. "Duke Ellington?"

"That's part of my secret stash. Original imports. None of that Johnny and His Orchestra crap for me. When I leave this world, I'd want the Duke playing over my grave. Do me a favor. Take it off, put it away in that case. That one there. There's a dreadful recording by Hans Pfitzner by the gramophone. Put that on the turntable, would you?" He snorted a laugh to himself. "Camouflage, Gregor. Hiding in plain sight."

"It's late. I'm going to let you sleep. We'll be in touch tomorrow, all right?"

"More than all right, Gregor!" Dreyer threw his arm across his face, a smile pulling at his mouth. Reinhardt turned out the light, then crossed the room quietly. He listened to Dreyer's breathing go heavy almost straightaway, beginning to rasp at the back of his throat as he started to snore, and let the day start to sieve through his mind again. He had rolled with the punches as much as he could, feeling and guessing at the directions the blows were coming in. Somewhere in all he had seen today, the truth of what was going on was to be found.

"Nothing is what it seems," he mouthed to the darkened room, opening and closing the door quietly. He shrugged into his coat, then crossed the clerks' office with his head down and thoughts far away.

"A moment, Captain," a voice called out.

Reinhardt stopped, turned. The other judge stood there, his spectacles in his hand, his uniform immaculate, pressed and clean.

"It is Captain Reinhardt, is that right? Judge Erdmann. We met before. Yesterday, if you recall. I wonder, might you spare me a moment of your time? Do come in," he said, gesturing Reinhardt into his office. Although spare and spartan, and again nothing like any judge's office he had known in Berlin, the room was clean and tidy, all its lines straight despite the row of half-filled packing cases that lined one wall, *Court-Martial Office* stenciled across them. "A drink, perhaps?" Erdmann asked as he motioned to a chair. When Reinhardt shook his head, he hitched up the knees of his trousers and sat next to him, one leg elegantly crossed over the other. The judge smiled, showing even, white teeth, and Reinhardt's hackles went up. "You have been to see our friend, Judge Dreyer? It is rather late to be calling on him, would you not say?"

Reinhardt inclined his head. "The judge and I had some business together."

"It could not wait until morning?" Erdmann smiled again. "It is just that Judge Dreyer needs his rest. He is rather wrung out, he works so terribly hard. We all try to look out for the poor chap, for he spares himself nothing." The judge looked at him, an avuncular smile wakening a fine web of wrinkles that spread down from his eyes. "I should like to know what is so important you have to come here so late."

"I'm not sure I would be at liberty to say, sir."

"I am Judge Dreyer's superior, Captain. You can tell me. In fact, I insist upon it."

"I thought Judge Dreyer worked for the War Crimes Bureau?"

Erdmann cocked his head to one side, and his eyes narrowed to polite slits. "Indeed," he said. "Be that as it may, we still operate within hierarchies here, Captain, and Judge Dreyer is under my authority. So, I ask again, what did he ask you? Not something to do with the Ustaše, I hope."

"You 'hope,' sir?"

"It is a damnable business, Captain, investigating one's own allies, and at such a dire moment for them. And for us."

"Indubitably," said Reinhardt, dryly, unable to resist a poke at the judge and his austere manner of speech. "A most unpleasant tasking."

Erdmann's head cocked slightly to one side, again, the wrinkles deepening at the corner of his eyes as if he caught some echo of Reinhardt's sarcasm. "And so? What did Judge Dreyer want?"

"The judge requested my help with an investigation he has under way."

"Oh? Which one would that be?"

"One regarding a Feldgendarme officer."

Erdmann's lips pursed, and he frowned. "Ah. Would that by any chance be Major Jansky? I thought as much." He sighed, an eyebrow describing an elegant arc as it went up, and he brushed his spectacles across his mouth. "You could not know, I suppose, but those closest to him know this is his, shall we say, *cause célèbre*. It preoccupies him. At times, he becomes almost rebarbative in his focus upon it. It has become necessary at times," he said, his mouth twisting as if around something somewhat unpleasant, "to *humor* the poor fellow."

"I shall bear that in mind, thank you, sir."

"I do hope you will forgive him, Captain. I am sure you in the Feldjaegerkorps have more important things to do. Should it be so required, I would be more than happy to intervene with Judge Dreyer and ensure that you are left alone to concentrate on your work."

"That is kind of you, sir. Is that all?"

Erdmann nodded, considering. "Only, I wonder how very *fortuitous* it is for the judge that he actually has an investigator with whom to work. Well, I shall not keep you from your responsibilities anymore." He rose to his feet, a hand extended to guide Reinhardt to the door. "Thank you so much for coming, Captain. Do recall, however," he said, as he accompanied Reinhardt into the clerks' office, lowering his voice with a somewhat theatrical glance down the short hallway to Dreyer's office, "the poor fellow is not always himself. He has quite the problem with drink, although he does his very best to hide it. I admire him for that, and for carrying on after what he has endured in Russia."

"Are you saying, sir, that there is nothing to Judge Dreyer's interest in Major Jansky?"

"*Fixation* is rather the better word, Captain. Perhaps *obsession*. Judge Dreyer has a tendency to become positively splenetic when the subject of Major Jansky is broached. And, no, I would not say there is nothing, but I am not convinced there is quite the depth of malice there that Judge Dreyer feels there is. I have myself interviewed Major Jansky and had occasion to meet with him socially. Unquestionably, he is not someone I should want as a dinner guest, but he is an admirable fit for today's times. To be quite honest, I rather admire the chap, and of course his political convictions and principles are impeccable," Erdmann said, a hand gently placed in Reinhardt's back, punctuating his words with little silver gestures of his spectacles, held close to his mouth. "It is a devil of a task he has been handed with that penal battalion, not to mention a most important one, handling such undesirable elements of our armed forces, offering them a chance to redeem their crimes. Men such as Major Jansky should be supported, is my firm conviction, unless a fine reason can be produced otherwise." They paused as they reached the outer door. "Would you not say, Captain?"

"Innocent until proven guilty, sir? I would indeed."

"Quite, Captain." Erdmann's left hand went to Reinhardt's shoulder, and he offered his right to shake. The judge's hand was warm, the skin smooth and dry, and his handshake was firm. "You have my complete respect, Captain, for the work you do. You and your fellow Feldjaeger." He ran his eyes across Reinhardt's Iron Cross, the Honor Roll Clasp. "My door is always open to you and yours." A squeeze of Reinhardt's left shoulder, and the judge released his hand and stepped back from the open door. "A very good night to you, and I hope to see you again under more pleasurable circumstances."

18

Full night fell across the valley. Somewhere, a full moon shone, but its light strained to run the seams in the cloud that squatted over the city. Sometimes the clouds flickered with silver lightning, and the slopes of the mountains appeared, as though called up and created only then, for that moment, and only when they had fallen back into darkness did the thunder rumble.

His steps heavy with fatigue, Reinhardt made his way to the Feldjaeger's operations center, peering in around the door to see who was there. A sergeant sat at the radio, flipping slowly through the pages of a magazine, and Benfeld sat alone at the big table with the maps of the city, staring into the far corner of the room, a cigarette burning untouched in front of him. He looked very lost, and very young.

"Everything all right here?" Reinhardt asked, quietly.

Benfeld started, knocking over his cigarette. He lurched to his feet, brushing away sparks and ash. "I'm sorry, sir," he muttered. "You startled me."

"My apologies. So, all quiet?"

"All quiet." The sergeant nodded agreement from over by the radio. "And you, sir?"

"Been a busy day. I'll brief you tomorrow."

"The short version . . . ?"

Reinhardt yawned, leaning his weight back on the table. "A judge who may be able to help us out. The Ustaše who claim the Partisans killed four of their men tonight, and want to link it to our three men."

"But . . . ?"

Reinhardt nodded, yawning again. "But . . . I'm not convinced those four were all killed at the same time. Two of them were certainly killed at the location; the others I'm not so sure of. And there was a fifth body, a woman, dressed as a Partisan."

"Oh?"

"And for all that the bodies had been mutilated, there was not that much blood . . ." he mused, seeing the scene again, almost thinking out loud.

"Is that it for tonight, sir?"

Reinhardt started, realizing he had begun to drift off. He yawned and nodded. "For tonight, yes. I'm meeting a soldier from that penal battalion here tomorrow. It seems he might have something for us."

"We're investigating the penal battalion now?"

"It seems to keep popping up. You remember that judge I went to see the other day? It seems he's interested in its commander."

"In Jansky?" Reinhardt nodded, and Benfeld's mouth pursed, his eyebrows going up.

"Sounds messy, doesn't it?" said Reinhardt.

"It does. Who is the soldier coming in?"

"A man called Kreuz," answered Reinhardt, a third yawn almost cracking his jaw. "Did you get through with those after-action reports? Nothing? Did you include the penal battalion in that search?" Benfeld shook his head. "Do so. They've been in and out of the city, and they might well have had some action. Any . . . any messages for me?" Benfeld shook his head again. "Right, I'm for bed. We'll talk tomorrow." He paused at the door, his left leg dragging as he turned heavily. "I forgot. That doctor. Don't forget he owes us information."

Benfeld looked blank, and then his face came alight. "Right. Sorry, sir. I had forgotten. I'll get in touch with him."

Reinhardt sought the narrow cot in the small room he had been assigned, but sleep was hard in coming. Once, a long crackle of far-off gunfire stung him awake, straining his hearing into the night, but the firing faded away in a ragged sequence of shots, and no alarm rang through the barracks. Long into what remained of the night, and into the morning, he tried to steady his mind, and foremost in those thoughts was that penal battalion, the martinet stance of Major Jansky, a snitch called Kreuz, and a collection of foreign volunteers. Then thoughts of the Ustaše shouldered themselves in, black-uniformed, sentinels of some imminent end time, poles around which chaos flowed and from which it ensued. Then there was Dreyer, a friend, but some part of Reinhardt, some reptilian sense of something wrong, would not let him settle around him. Dreyer carried something in him, some cold fragment of the past, and Reinhardt was not sure he wanted to be there when it revealed itself.

The day had clamored past him. It was like trying to keep one's eyes on two balls at the same time, this investigation. His duties as a Feldjaeger, and his instructions—his license—to investigate the murders of those three men were not necessarily compatible, he was quickly coming to realize. Although he had considerable authority as a Feldjaeger, he could not simply abandon his Feldjaeger duties to pursue this case or barge in wherever he wanted. Evidence would not be found that way. It would vanish or change shape and place and time, and then those three Feldjaeger really would have died for nothing. These contradictions were threatening, already, to entwine him and render him immobile, the more so because he was not even sure what he was investigating, what was the outline of whatever lurked out there.

———————

Reinhardt slept, eventually, a cramped stretch of sleep that did nothing for the exhaustion he felt, and for the first time in a while he dreamed of Kragujevac, that winter field where the boys and their teachers had been lined up and shot into ditches. In his dream those two young boys, lost and alone in each other's arms, stared at him but then their eyes merged together, their bodies flowed one into the other, and it was the boy he had rescued from the forest and his little fists were full of earth. The boy lifted his hands and opened them and the earth turned to blood, thick and treacly, and it oozed through his fingers and spattered on a floor of mismatched tiles where Reinhardt's tooth rolled like an empty bottle atop a teetering deck, flailing from side to side.

Reinhardt woke with the light of a watery dawn as it spread slowly from the single high window in his room, bathed in sweat, but his breathing strangely calm. He made his ablutions, washed and showered in the echoing space of the communal bathrooms with a hundred other men, then made his way back to the mess hall. The cavernous room had come back to life. The kitchens rang and shook to the bustle of the cooks, and what passed for coffee was poured black and heavy into steel urns. He poured a cup and drank it standing by a window, smoking a cigarette. A train clanked past below, a troop train, full to the brim, armored cars at the front and back with men nestled behind sandbagged machine-gun emplacements. He watched it wind past, vanishing farther up the valley to the west, its smoke rising like a pointing finger in the still air, and wondered when his turn would come, and when Kreuz would show up like he had promised he would.

Kreuz did not come, but Langenkamp did. Reinhardt watched the liaison officer move woodenly across the room, placing items precisely on a tray and finding a place to sit by himself at the end of a long table. He watched him, considering, got bread, cheese, and jam for himself, another cup of coffee, and made his way over to where Langenkamp sat.

"Do you mind if I join you?"

Langenkamp's eyes came up slowly, and he looked at Reinhardt without much recognition. Then he swallowed whatever it was he was chewing and gestured loosely at the bench in front of him. Reinhardt sat and laid a piece of limp cheese across a slice of dark, multigrain bread.

"Thank you for your help yesterday." Langenkamp looked blankly at him. "At the Pale House. With Marković." Langenkamp swallowed again, nodded. "In fact, I was wondering about something and was hoping you could help me. What is your thinking, or feeling, about the Ustaše these days? What are you hearing, or what are they saying among themselves?"

"About?"

"The end of all this," Reinhardt said, quietly, watching Langen-kamp very closely, but his words—defeatist though they could be considered—had no effect he could see.

"The Ustaše are clannish," Langenkamp said, after a moment. "Those from Sarajevo. Others from Herzegovina, farther south. Those from Croatia itself. They do not always see eye to eye on things. The Sarajevo Ustaše, for example, were not happy with Luburić being sent in to oversee them. There was some resistance to that. And he purged quite a few of them."

"Which group is Putković a member of?"

"Putković is from Sarajevo. A small minority of the senior Ustaše are from here. They are very committed to the Ustaše cause. You have, I understand, met Colonel Putković."

"A committed man, as you say."

"Many of these Bosnian Ustaše, particularly from Sarajevo, seem to bear some kind of grudge against the city. They feel they were ex-cluded from the city prior to the war. From its life."

"And are getting their own back, now," finished Reinhardt. "You said three of them had gone missing? What were their names?"

"Three? When did I say that?"

"At the briefing you gave, on the first day we arrived here." Rein-hardt kicked himself, mentally, for mentioning "three." It was Perić who had mentioned three missing Ustaše. Langenkamp had only re-ferred to "a number," and it was on such small details that anything—an investigation, a secret, a conspiracy—could come apart.

"If you say so; I do not recall."

"Their names?"

"Bozidar Brkić, Zvonimir Saulan, and Tomislav Dubreta. Why?"

Reinhardt shrugged noncommittally. "Does anyone have any idea where they have gone?" he asked, feeling those same names on that piece of paper Simo had given him, feeling them as if they were burning a hole in his pocket. The cheese was disgusting, and Reinhardt spread thick, gelatinous jam across a second slice of bread. "Murdered? Deserted?"

"No ideas, and if the Ustaše know otherwise, they have not told me."

"What were they doing before they vanished?"

"Brkić and Dubreta were in internal security. The Ustaše equivalent of the Gestapo, I suppose. Saulan was the commandant of the prison."

"So . . . they all worked for, or with, Putković?"

"Yes. And he's got no idea, before you ask. He's as furious as Luburić about them."

"What else do they say?"

"Well . . ." Langenkamp paused, his coffee cup halfway to his mouth. "They say money is missing. Gold. Other valuables. Cash. Including cash sent down from Zagreb."

"Where is that gold and whatnot supposed to have come from?"

"The Ustaše have been stripping this place bare of anything worth taking for the last few years. Factor in corruption and extortion, and it all adds up, I am told."

"Tell me another thing, Langenkamp," Reinhardt said, taken aback by the captain's acerbic honesty. "How do they see their future?"

Langenkamp drank slowly from his cup of coffee, considering. "Will they fight to the death, like their propaganda says they should? It is anyone's guess. I would think not. But I have learned to be surprised by the Ustaše. You never quite know what they will do. And with that," he said, rising, "I wish you good day, Captain."

Reinhardt watched him go, dunking his bread and jam in his coffee in a vain effort to improve the taste, but the food tasted like cardboard, and the coffee was truly vile. He glanced around the mess hall, at the hunched shoulders and desultory conversation of his fellow officers, the monotony of the food, thinking that if this was what they were down to, they would be breaking out the iron rations fairly soon. He glanced at his watch. Kreuz was over an hour late for the meeting. Reinhardt had a few hours before he was on duty, and so he decided to go and find him.

He commandeered a vehicle and drove it up to Vratnik. He slowed on the road as it twisted beneath the steep tumble of the hill beneath the fortress's walls. Higher up the snow-shrouded slope, at a gap in the walls, he could see men looking down, the foreshortened lines of arms pointing at something. He slowed, stopped, tried to see what they were looking at. One of the men threw something, a rock, which plunged into a dip Reinhardt could not see from where he was. He heard a clack of stone, a faint burst of laughter from higher up, and a bird flapped up heavily into the air, cocked its head, and squawked raucously. It was a crow, perhaps. Or a raven, although Reinhardt did not know if those larger birds roosted around the city. He felt a chill as he restarted the car, a sense of foreboding that did not fade as he pulled up at the fortress's gates and asked for Major Jansky.

"Gone," was their sergeant's reply as he huddled over a brazier. "Gone to Zenica. With most of the battalion. Only the runts left, and we're s'pposed to be off tomorrow."

"Who is in charge?"

"That'd be Lieutenant Reche. But he's not here."

"Do you know anything about what's attracted the men to the walls?" The Feldgendarmes looked blankly among one another, shrugged. "Well, I'll have a look if you don't mind," he said, walking past them. He heard an intake of breath, a rustle of boots as someone moved, but no one stopped him. Inside, he could see and feel straightaway the fortress was all but deserted, the courtyard empty of vehicles, of material. Across its width, a small crowd had gathered around an old breach, where blocks of stone had once spilled out and tumbled down a steep plunge of brush-choked slope. He pushed through the men, angry mutters and queries fading away as they saw his uniform, his gorget, and space opened up and he looked down the slope.

There was a body in a dip in the ground, a handful of crows playing court around it, bouncing languidly from side to side and across it. The body lay facedown, the gray of its uniform blending well with the rock and icy snow.

"Anyone know who it is?" he asked, looking around. Men avoided his gaze, most looking away, mouths downturning in unspoken no's. A face caught his gaze, dark and swarthy, heavy cheeks under black eyes. "You," he said, pointing at one of the Greeks he remembered from Baščaršija. "You'll help bring it up. And you," he said, pointing at the nearest soldier. "Find rope. Long enough to get down there. Move. *Now!*"

He pointed at the Greek, then pointed over the wall. The man moved slowly, looking elsewhere for a moment as if for support or salvation, but none was forthcoming. He went reluctantly and, as Reinhardt climbed carefully over the wall, he understood it was not just an apparent reluctance to obey orders that made the man move slowly. The slope was treacherous, sheeted in scree and rubble and icy cold. He slipped, slid, caught himself, and his knee flared, and he grimaced down the slope, no one to see his face twist in pain. He moved as carefully as he could, following the other man down, until they crouched over the body, the crows watching them with cocked heads from safer perches. Reinhardt motioned for the man to turn the body over.

It was Kreuz. His skull had been caved in, a dark red ruin of a wound against his forehead.

Reinhardt looked at the body as he had once been trained to do. From top to toe, then back up, and for a moment he forgot the chill in the air, the wet stench of the fortress, the stiffness in his knee that never went away anymore. He saw the matted hair, the grimy crescents of fingernails, the filthy tunic, the greasy collar of a gray shirt. He saw how the wound on Kreuz's head had not bled. The front of Kreuz's tunic was frozen, a wide, dark stain of alcohol, the fabric caught in long creases. A broken bottle lay smashed at his side. He pushed back Kreuz's sleeves, then his trousers. The skin was unblemished. He opened his tunic, pulling up his shirt. His torso was bruised, sheeted with blood, crisscrossed with livid welts and long cuts, made while he was still alive. He heaved the body onto its back, but there was nothing there. Reinhardt looked at the bruising on Kreuz's torso, again, looking up the slope, wondering if it was the fall that had done that, or someone's fists. The body showed marked signs of hypostasis, the skin on Kreuz's front mottled purple with the blood that had pooled inside him once it stopped flowing. He was no doctor, but hypostasis was fairly reliable as an indicator and he had seen enough bodies in his time to estimate that Kreuz had been dead and lying here at least six hours.

"Who is Dreyer?"

Reinhardt frowned, started. The Greek was looking at him, crouched in an easy stance, squatting down with his elbows between his knees, his feet splayed out wide for balance. There was something immediately foreign but immediately natural about the way he lounged there, as if he squatted in the shade of a far-off, sun-kissed land, where life moved at a slower pace.

"Who is Dreyer?" the man said again, looking at Reinhardt with his dark eyes limpid in his sun-browned face. "Is not such a difficult question."

Maybe it was not a difficult question, but the answer had implications. All answers did. Certainly, the day was young, it had room for surprises, thought Reinhardt. Maybe he was tired, and maybe that made him reckless, and maybe he was tired of worrying about the shape of what was out there, so he sloughed off some of the weight of caution that bogged him down. "A judge," he said, finally.

"What kind of judge?"

"I will tell that to Alexiou," said Reinhardt, making the one throw he could, making it here and now with the man he had chosen, hoping it would hit something, and not just fall silently. He need not have worried, as the man's eyes went flat with menace.

"What do you want of Alexiou?"

"I want to talk to him."

"What about?"

"That is between him and me."

There was a call from higher up, and a rope unfurled itself down against the light gray sky, thumping to the earth next to them. Reinhardt wound and fastened it around Kreuz's ankles, then began pulling himself up it, hearing the Greek coming up behind him. At the top, breathless, he watched the men haul the body up. Reinhardt watched it come, seeing how the dead always lay at the wrong angle. Limbs were never meant to move that way. As if in death a body assumed a freedom it could never achieve in life. A last heave up and over the breach, and Kreuz's body lolled across the ground. Heads peered in and down.

"Drunk again," one of the soldiers said.

"Looks like he fell. Bashed his head in," said a Feldgendarme, kneeling and pointing needlessly at Kreuz's skull. "Stupid bugger."

"Couldn't'a happened to a nicer man."

"Anyone see him yesterday?" Reinhardt asked. Again, that space opened up around him, heads turning down and away. He looked for the Greek and saw the man walking away, toward an archway in the courtyard's walls. Reinhardt decided to give him time, and then he would go looking himself. "No one? Someone must have. I just want a when and where, otherwise I'll have this whole unit drawn up for punishment detail," he said, putting iron in his voice, challenging them with his eyes, his stance. "A time and place. That's all."

"Latrine block," said a voice. It was a skinny soldier, his hands hunched deep into his coat. Space opened up around him as Reinhardt walked toward him. "About midnight. He was in one of the stalls. Talking to himself. Like he usually did."

"What was he saying?"

"Nonsense, Captain. It's what usually came out of his mouth. Muttering and giggling about tickets and judges. Sounded like he'd won the lottery or something."

"Show me the latrine block."

The man's mouth fell, and then he nodded, sighing out through his nose. Reinhardt followed him across the courtyard, pointing at Kreuz's body and looking at the Feldgendarme. "He's all yours, Corporal," he said.

The man led Reinhardt to a sagging structure of wood and timber, the stench from which was eye-watering even before he ducked into it. The man pointed to a stall at the end, its door hanging half open in front of a hole in the sodden ground, a pair of duckboards all the support there was. The stench was appalling, and Reinhardt had to cover his nose and mouth with his sleeve as he pushed his eyes from corner to corner of the stall, but he could see nothing, and when he came back out into the fresh air the man was gone, but the Greek was back.

"You come," the man said. "Alexiou will talk."

19

Reinhardt was led through the archway into a small courtyard, trucks and cars parked tightly around it. Reinhardt followed the Greek around a half-track with no tracks sitting slumped to one side. There were men dotted around the courtyard, but his eyes were drawn to two big men warming their hands over a brazier in front of the entrance to what looked like it had once been a stable. They were twins, stocky, broad shouldered, thick black hair cut close to the blocks of their heads. They looked Reinhardt over, and then one of them glanced inside the room. There was a third man in there, sitting back in the shadows. Dimly seen, a hand gestured, and the twins stood aside, motioning Reinhardt to pass inside.

He squeezed past the brazier's glow, his skin pulling at its heat, then into the dimness of the room. The man sitting at the back leaned forward slightly, and Reinhardt could see immediately the resemblance the twins bore to him, such that it was obvious he was their father. Feeling self-conscious but feeling it was the right thing to do, Reinhardt extended his right hand to the man, who, after a moment, took it and shook. The man's hand was large, the skin warm and hard. It was a firm shake, one squeeze of the hand, and the man nodded slightly and sat back. He motioned with the other hand, and one of the twins pulled out a stool and offered it to Reinhardt. He sat, stretching his left leg out.

"My name is Captain Reinhardt, of the Feldjaegerkorps."

"Alexiou," said the man. He said something else, and one of the twins turned to Reinhardt and translated his father's words. "My father asks would you like coffee?"

"Only if it is Greek."

Alexiou smiled as he understood—a thin curl of his lips, but a smile nevertheless—though his eyes stayed flinty, and he and Reinhardt sized each other up as the twins busied themselves over the brazier. They sat in silence as the smell of roasting coffee filled the room, and the twins returned with mismatched cups. Reinhardt took his, turning it in his hands and lifting it to inhale the scent. His eyes closed a moment, and he was back on Baščaršija, the city moving toward high summer, and it was late afternoon, the square filling with people, with friends and families, the air thick with conversation. He opened his eyes, saw the old man looking at him, and he saluted him with the cup, taking a hot sip.

"Excellent. I thank you."

"My father says you are welcome," said the twin who had spoken. "My name is Kostas. I will translate for you. This is Panos," he continued, indicating the other twin. "Now, my father wonders what you would like to talk to him about."

"May we speak freely, and openly?" Reinhardt looked at Alexiou as he spoke, waiting until the man finally nodded. The man was a patriarch, and patriarchs expected a certain mode and rhythm of conversation, and if he expected deference, Reinhardt would give him that too. "Did you kill Kreuz?"

"No," Alexiou answered, finally, the word dropping into an aching silence.

"Do you know who did?"

"No. But I can guess." Reinhardt waited. "He was killed by those he served."

"By the Feldgendarmerie?" Alexiou's head came down in a slow nod. "Why?"

"I do not know."

"Kreuz was afraid of you. Of all of you," Reinhardt said, drawing the twins in with his eyes. "He was a spy for the Feldgendarmerie. For Jansky. He was afraid you would kill him for it."

"Better is the devil where you can see him, Captain. Kreuz knew and heard what we wanted."

"Who were Berthold and Seymer?"

All three of the Greeks leaned back, just slight movements, shifts of shoulders, tightening of necks. Alexiou's mouth twisted as he turned his head to one side to sip from his cup, keeping his eyes fixed on Reinhardt. "They were friends of ours."

"What happened to them?"

"They disappeared. About a week ago."

"How?"

"Working."

"Where?"

"In the forest. Outside the city."

"Where?"

Alexiou frowned, irritation unfurling itself across his eyes before he calmed himself. "At the camp for wood."

Reinhardt frowned at Kostas. "Camp for wood?"

"For cutting wood," Kostas nodded.

"The logging camp," Reinhardt said to himself, quietly. "Tell me about this camp."

"Nothing to tell. It was a place for taking wood. For the city. But it was unlucky work."

"Why?"

"The camp was attacked by the Partisans. Several times."

"Men went missing?" Alexiou nodded, slowly. "How many went missing?"

The Greeks looked among themselves. Panos said something quietly to his father. Alexiou shrugged, gestured with a jut of his chin, and Kostas turned to Reinhardt. "Four, maybe five men disappeared in the forest."

"Kreuz found out the deaths had not been reported," said Alexiou.

"That the men's *soldbuchs* were still here. They had not been reported missing. And that the books were with Thun, one of the men who works in Jansky's office."

"Who is Thun?"

"A snitch—it is the word?—a snitch, like Jansky. But good with papers."

"Who was in charge of the logging camp?"

"Lieutenant Metzler."

"Have other men gone missing?"

"What kind of question is that, Captain? This is war. Men go missing. This is a punishment unit. Men will go missing here, first. Who will care? Who will count? And now," Alexiou said, leaning his elbows on his knees, "you talk. Tell me of Judge Dreyer. What is he?"

"A war crimes judge," said Reinhardt, after a moment's consideration, watching the man's face. There was no reaction he could see.

"War crimes judge. What is this?"

"He works for the War Crimes Bureau. An investigation unit," said Reinhardt. "It reports to the armed forces high command."

"You work together?" Alexiou pointed at Reinhardt's armband.

"No. It's different. The bureau researches allegations of war crimes. By anyone, allied or enemy."

"And then what?"

"If there is evidence, military courts launch proceedings. Trials," he said. There was a reaction then, a flare and pinch of the man's nostrils. "Why are you asking me this?"

"Kreuz told us some things about you, Captain. Jansky told us some things. We found out some more. You were a policeman. You still are," Alexiou said, glancing at Reinhardt's gorget, pausing to drink. "I will tell you some things, Captain Reinhardt. Things you may find interesting. But first, I will ask you, are you ready to deal with the devil?"

"With you?"

"With me."

"I will listen," Reinhardt said.

"I can maybe give you Jansky," said Alexiou, a calm blink belaying the weight of his words. "This is what this judge wants, is it not?"

"Go on."

"We are Greeks who enlisted in the German Army, as we felt we could no longer live in our own country," said Alexiou. It was said simply, but the deeper meaning was there, the deeper truth that they were collaborators who had backed the wrong cause and were now paying the price for it. Said simply, it was a fact, like a rock in the road. It just was. It could not be moved, shunted aside. Only acknowledged, then contoured.

"We have been with this unit for some time, Captain. We were the first foreigners to join it. Nearly a year ago, in Greece. We needed a place of safety, and although it may sound strange to you, this place was it. If you like, I took the chance—for me and my family, and those others outside who are loyal to me—to hide away. To hide in plain view, if you like, to wait for another day, and I paid good gold for that privilege. Alas, that day never came. I used to think it would, but anyone who says there is a brighter time coming for our cause is dreaming. Now, I am no longer involved in the councils. In the decisions. Look at us. Everyone has gone, except the runts. We are last to move. Even the Albanians come before me."

"What do you think is going on?"

"I do not know."

"I heard of an Albanian who was killed, recently. In a car crash. He was from Balli Kombëtar." The Greeks went still, all three of them staring at him. "What do you know of that?"

"Nothing. What the Albanians do is not our business. They are pigs."

"What about the Ustaše?"

"What of them?"

"What do you hear?"

"They are pigs, too. We are all pigs, rooting in the dirt, eating shit, not able to see past our nose. I do not know the whole shape of what is happening, but what I see I do not like. This place no longer has the welcome of before, and now, I fear I must find another place for my people. I am tired of being ignored, of just being fed words. Words that are supposed to fill some hole, as if anyone but my sons could know the shape of the hole that fills me. Words that are supposed to kindle a fire in me, words that are supposed to recall the great blows we struck against the fucking leftists and the weaklings and the Communists who would have sent my country to ruin. Words that are supposed to describe the great things we will still do, if only we are patient. As if a warm handshake and a pat on the shoulder and praise is any substitute for action. You give such to a dog, Captain, not to a man."

Alexiou paused, and though his voice remained calm, his anger was palpable. He sipped from his cup, his eyes far away. His sons looked past each other, round-shouldered around their own cups.

"Who is it who tells you these things?" Reinhardt asked.

"I do not know," Alexiou answered. "Some fucking Germans. You all look and sound the same to us. One spoke like . . . like a fisherman. Harsh. Swearing. One spoke like a priest. That is when I knew. Always when you have no more need of us, this is when the big words come out."

"Did Kreuz tell you about Dreyer?" Alexiou said nothing. "If he didn't, who did? Was it Jansky?" Reaction, the nose flaring, pinching. "It was Jansky. Ask yourself, why would he do that? What does he want you to do with that information?"

"I do not know, and I do not care."

"You should. Maybe you should think why you are still here when the others have gone."

"I do not march to Jansky's music anymore. Now, I must consider how best to act for my people. I have a deal for you. I will give you something. But you must look away." Alexiou leaned forward, his cup tiny in his thick fingers. "If you can promise Dreyer will leave us alone, we can help give Jansky to him. We know things, and we are still close enough we can find new things. But you get nothing for nothing. For what we have, you must deal with the devil, and I think men like you find that hard."

Reinhardt turned the coffee cup around in his fingers, gently tilting it so the liquid ran away from the grounds. He lifted it, sipped slowly until the taste went gritty and sour. "I can do that," he said, looking at the sludge of grounds in the bottom of his cup. "After all, it's not so hard. You can even get used to it," he finished, raising his eyes to Alexiou's.

"To fight injustice, you must sometimes commit it," agreed Alexiou, gravely, leaning forward and taking the cup gently from Reinhardt while Reinhardt seethed inside, as if this man could dream he could plumb the depths of what Reinhardt regretted. Holding the cup delicately, Alexiou tilted it and turned it three times, spilling out a thin stream of liquid and dark grounds, then turned it upside down onto a small saucer and sat back.

"Kreuz had evidence he wanted to give to me. Can you find it?"

"What was it?"

Reinhardt shrugged, slightly, his mouth turning down. "I don't know. But I suspect it was documents. Maybe even these *soldbuchs* you mentioned he saw."

"Where would he get those?" The three Greeks exchanged blank looks. "If he stole those, or if Jansky suspected he might have, I can understand he is dead now," Alexiou continued.

"Kreuz was last seen alive in the latrines. Could it be he hid something there?" The three Greeks exchanged blank looks again. "Or somewhere else in the fortress."

"You will meet with one of my sons, tonight. With Kostas," Alexiou said, indicating the twin who had been doing the translating. "You will meet with him at the Serb Orthodox cathedral. There is a small place next to it. On Strossmayer Street, by a tavern. There is an alley. Go there to the house at the end. He will bring something. Information. Or evidence, if we can find it."

"What time?"

"At nine o'clock."

Reinhardt nodded, looking from face to face. There seemed to be nothing else to say.

"Thank you for the coffee. And the conversation," Reinhardt said, rising to his feet. The twins rose with him, Alexiou remaining in his seat. Reinhardt extended his hand, and the old man shook it, his eyes grave and serious, as if he took homage.

"Captain." Alexiou's voice called him back. The Greek gestured at the coffee cup, upside down on its saucer. "Don't you want your fortune to be read?"

"Has it ever worked for you?"

Alexiou's mouth twitched in a smile. "No. Not really." But he leaned forward and turned the cup up. He looked inside, then up at Reinhardt, then shrugged with his mouth.

"Women and wealth?" Reinhardt asked. The twins chuckled, and a smile cracked Alexiou's imperious façade. "I'll just have to take my chances, then."

20

"I found out today that site in the forest was a logging camp run by the penal battalion," Reinhardt said.

Dreyer looked up from his desk, where he was putting files together. His eyes were bloodshot, his hair slicked back against his head. He looked terrible, like the drunk he was, Reinhardt supposed. "Meaning . . . ?" Dreyer asked.

Reinhardt's mouth tightened, and he slapped his cap against his thigh. "I don't know. But it was an unlucky detail. Men went missing on it. Supposedly the Partisans killed them, or captured them."

"But you think what?"

"I think its part of . . . whatever . . . makes this up. Whatever 'this' is," he sighed, and sat heavily in a chair. "How did we get from three dead Feldjaeger to men going missing in a penal battalion?"

"'Supposedly,'" Dreyer muttered, looking around at the piles of papers and boxes surrounding him.

"What?"

"They are supposedly going missing," Dreyer said, a self-deprecating smile on his face. "Sorry. It's the jurist in me."

"'Sorry'?" Reinhardt's brow furrowed, irritation lacing his voice. "Look, Marcus, you asked for help, I'm trying to give it to you. You seemed pretty convinced last night that this penal battalion is being misused by Jansky. Are you splitting hairs on me, now?"

Dreyer raised placatory hands as Reinhardt talked, coming around the table. "Sorry, Gregor. I'm sorry," he said, taking the chair next to him. "It's like I said, I've been on this so long, I can't believe someone believes me, and I suppose I'm . . . just acting cautiously."

"Where are those files, then?"

"I can't find them," said Dreyer, looking sheepish. He sat back, looking nervous. "It wasn't much, but I can't find it in all this mess. They're moving us out in a day or so. So everything is in boxes that needs to go." Dreyer gave a small smile, a cramped grimace.

"So tell me what you know."

"What I know . . . I suspect Jansky is still up to his tricks. Black marketeering, mainly. Other forms of corruption. As to the penal battalion, it was originally a combat unit, but they were decimated in Greece, then almost destroyed in Montenegro. Now, they do all kinds of stuff. Menial labor. Construction. Casualty collection. Transportation. The opportunities for corruption are significant."

"So what is it you suspect him of?"

"Misusing assets. In this case, now, his men. It's all he has."

"Like what?"

"Hiring them out. Extorting them."

"There's a fair few foreigners in that penal battalion. Greeks and Albanians, I hear. What do you know of them?"

"Turncoats and traitors to their countries, probably. Or just people who nailed their flags to the wrong mast. I heard a rumor some of them might be the remnants of a Greek paramilitary unit. The unit was mostly destroyed, but not all of its leaders were killed." Dreyer rolled back his head, staring at the ceiling, his hand going to his neck. "Gold," he murmured. "Always rumors of gold, but never any proof . . ."

Something clicked open in Reinhardt's mind, a bright sparkle of thoughts tumbling out.

"What's the best way to hide something, Marcus?" he asked. Dreyer tilted his head straight to look at Reinhardt. "I've been hearing it nonstop since this started. In plain sight. You hide something right under someone's nose."

"What're you saying?"

"I think Jansky's scam is he is offering protection—asylum, if you like—to anyone who'll pay for it." As Reinhardt said it, he felt it was right. It settled into and around him, and his pulse quickened as he began to work it out.

Dreyer's expression quivered as he stared back at Reinhardt. "What are you saying?" he repeated.

"Look at where his unit's been, and look who he's got in his ranks. Greeks. Albanians. Probably Montenegrins. People from all over the Balkans. People who can't stay in their own countries. Collaborators. Criminals. Opportunists. Soldiers who chose the wrong side. Whatever. They pay him, he gives them protection. He enlists them as cooks, drivers, clerks, cleaners, whatever, but not soldiers. They're as out of harm's way as it's possible to be."

"They *pay* him, and he looks after them . . . ?"

"You suspected corruption, right? You thought it was linked to *soldbuchs* and misappropriated pay? Well, you were on the right track, but you weren't thinking big enough."

"What do you mean?"

"I mean," said Reinhardt, hunching forward, his tone turning sardonic, echoing Langenkamp's words, "people like them—people like *us*, Marcus, if we're being honest—have had four good years to loot these lands bare. Think of the opportunities. *Think!* Works of art. Jewelry. Valuables. Properties. The resources of whole states."

"The gold," Dreyer whispered.

"The gold," Reinhardt repeated. "Stolen. Just taken. You just walk into the state bank and take it. Who could stop them, especially when they *were* the state? But the people, too. The victims. The refugees. The desperate and the lost. Everyone's got something to give, and if everyone gives only a little, it becomes a lot."

"My God," Dreyer whispered, again.

"Everybody. Every *body*, Marcus. Don't forget the dead. A watch. A ring. A bracelet. A necklace. A gold tooth. *Something.*"

"Everyone's got something to give." Dreyer's eyes seemed to flutter frantically, as if something were trying to slam shut inside him. His gaze swung, suddenly, down to his pocket, and he pulled out his flask and tilted it to his mouth. Reinhardt sat back, his heart still racing, thinking, watching Dreyer drink. It felt right. It felt *right*, but there was still something else, he felt, some part that did not quite fit, or was still missing.

"You think the Ustaše are part of this?" Dreyer mumbled, his eyes downcast.

"They'd certainly have motivation. Some of them, for sure." Reinhardt's pulse quickened again. Is that where the Ustaše were going, the ones the Partisans were concerned about? Bribing their way to some kind of safety in a German penal battalion?

"Could Jansky manage this on his own?" Dreyer asked.

"Good question. I've no idea. I suspect not. And one of those foreigners I mentioned to you—a Greek, probably a former security battalion commander—has had enough of Jansky, and wants out. He said he'll give you Jansky, as long as we let him go."

"Wait, *wait*." Dreyer shook his head, heavy jowls quivering. "What are you talking about?"

Reinhardt ran him through his conversation with the Greeks. Dreyer listened with wide eyes. "The upshot of it is, I'm meeting the Greek's son tonight. He's going to give me more information on Jansky. Hopefully, he'll be able to find out what Kreuz was going to bring me."

"And this Greek wants out?"

"He wants to disappear. He says he has the means to take care of himself."

"So those rumors of gold are *true*?"

"Probably. Who cares?"

"A lot of people, I imagine."

"But that's not the point, Marcus. We just have to let the Greek go."

"And he thinks I can arrange that?"

"Not arrange it. But he's scared of you. He doesn't want you coming after him."

"Why?" Dreyer frowned.

Reinhardt frowned back. "Because you're *War Crimes* Bureau, and he obviously thinks he's got something to answer for."

"So Alexiou thinks Jansky's got someone backing him up."

"Can you try to find that out?"

Dreyer nodded and swigged from his flask, wiping his mouth as he gasped at the wash of brandy down his throat. "But what about the *soldbuchs*, then? Where do they fit?"

"I don't know. I haven't even seen them, yet. For all I know, they don't exist."

"So what's . . . ?"

He cut off as Reinhardt raised a hand, head cocked, listening. There was a far off rumble, like thunder, but sharper, more distinct. He took an involuntary step toward the window, stopping himself in time.

"Artillery!" he snapped, backing away from the window as shells ripped overhead with a sound like tearing cloth.

There was a rumble of explosions, somewhere in town. Another salvo clawed across the sky, explosions echoing across the valley. From somewhere to the west came the answering crack of counterbattery fire, German guns firing back.

"It's started," breathed Dreyer.

Reinhardt nodded. "The Partisan offensive. They're firing from the north and east." Unspoken between them was what this would do to what they know knew, or suspected.

"I need to get back to the barracks," said Reinhardt. He paused at the door, something skittering along the edge of his mind. Something they had said, but when he reached for it, it trickled away and he knew if he kept after it, it would vanish. "When I saw Jansky at the Pale House yesterday, he said something. He said to tell you, 'All are not hunters who can blow the hunter's horn.'"

Dreyer looked up from the papers, swallowed, and tipped his head back for his flask again. "Bastard," he muttered. "That's what he said to me in Poland. The last time I saw him, walking away scot-free."

"He rather likes his classical quotations, doesn't he?"

"He does," said Dreyer, his mouth twisted. "But now I've got you. I was never a hunter. But you are."

"So, no pressure, then," said Reinhardt, ironically, awakening an answering grin from Dreyer, but it fluttered lightly across his mouth. "We'll be in touch."

Outside, Reinhardt scanned the area quickly and saw smoke rising from the train station. Most of the soldiers were gone now; the queues of thousands that Reinhardt had seen upon first entering the city had been sucked away into the station and it was mostly civilians who ran and scurried and cowered for shelter. There was another concussion of artillery fire from the German batteries on the south bank of the Miljacka, opposite the barracks, and then all was quiet except for a steadily increasing crackle of small-arms fire coming, if Reinhardt was not mistaken, from within the city, meaning Valter's Partisans were also adding their weight to the Partisan brigades around the city.

He made the drive back to the barracks quickly, the roads largely deserted. Inside, the hive of activity was heightened. A stream of soldiers was coming out of the barracks, arms heaped with papers and folders, and either loading them onto trucks or tipping them into fires made in upturned oil cans where flames licked up at the air. In Feldjaeger operations, the room was full and Scheller, Lainer, and Morten were all bent over a map of the city.

"This is it, Reinhardt," said Scheller, motioning him over. "Two more days. Three at the most. And then the Partisans have this place to themselves. Our orders are in. If the lines hold, we pull out the day after tomorrow. Next stop, Visoko." He pointed at the map, indicating a small town northwest of Sarajevo. The west road from Sarajevo forked at Ilidža, one road continuing west, then south toward Mostar, but that road was cut off now. The other road turned north, through Visoko, on up the Bosna River valley in a meandering path past Kakanj, through Zenica with its giant steelworks, on to Doboj, and beyond that the Sava River, which marked Bosnia's northern border with Croatia.

Reinhardt listened with the rest of them to Scheller's briefing, the deployment orders—his own instructions were to move into the army's main operations center and act as liaison officer there—but his eyes kept meeting Lainer's, and he knew the big Feldjaeger wanted a result from him and he did not have one to give. When the briefing was over, Scheller took Lainer and Morten elsewhere. Reinhardt spotted Benfeld walking out of the crowded room, and he followed him after a moment, down the corridors to the mess hall.

"Frenchie!"

Benfeld jumped, his hand knocking the cup of coffee he held. Black liquid slopped across the table, and Benfeld muttered a curse.

"What's the matter with you?" Reinhardt asked, as he sat down with his own cup. Around them, the mess hall was a rumble of conversation, men running in and out, the kitchen a blast of heat and steam they could feel from here. "You've been jumpy since last night."

"Sorry, sir. Maybe I'm just tired."

"You can say that again," murmured Reinhardt. He sipped from the cup, his tongue and face turning. It was truly awful stuff after what Alexiou had given him, but he needed something with a modicum of stimulants in it. He felt he was running on empty, his stomach tight and twisted and a dizzy feeling in his head. "Where are you at with what I gave you? The names?"

"Nothing yet, sir."

"Nothing from Koenig?"

"Nothing, sir."

"Did you get hold of the doctor?"

"Yes and no," said Benfeld, busying himself with a handkerchief and the spill of his coffee. "He has been . . . busy."

"Busy? Christ. Did you go and see him?"

"No, sir. No time."

"The after-action reports? The ones I asked you about last night for the penal battalion?"

"Yes. Those I managed. At least some. There's nothing," said Benfeld, as he searched for a place to put his sodden handkerchief.

Reinhardt swung his legs out over the bench and pushed himself to his feet, giving his knee a rub as he did so. "You let me know what you find out before the day's out, Frenchie, all right?"

"Is it still important, sir?"

Reinhardt paused, hearing the note that ran low beneath those few words. A tone that sounded almost pleading. "I mean, with all that's going on. The evacuation. Do we . . . should we still be working on this?"

"I thought you were keen for this? What's the matter?"

"Nothing, sir," Benfeld replied, perhaps a little too quickly. "It's just that—I mean, it seems somehow . . . superfluous."

"Superfluous?" Benfeld wilted under the pressure of Reinhardt's eyes but it was not anger in them, it was introspection, a withering inward gaze sharpened by the ever-narrowing wedge of time before him. Was that what it was? What it had become? Superfluous?

"Sir?" Reinhardt shook himself out, realizing he had been standing there with his mind elsewhere. "Is there anything you want to tell me?"

"Time and loose ends, Frenchie. Things we don't and do have a lot of."

"Yes, sir."

"So sort yourself out. You sure you're not sick?" Reinhardt asked as he left the room.

"I'm fine, sir."

Like the days before, this one passed in a blur, but a blur with an iron edge. Men worked with the fervor of those who knew themselves condemned otherwise. Fights broke out in the train station, and the Feldjaeger were deployed into its halls to keep the peace. Ustaše units moved through the city in heavily laden cars and trucks. Many of their fighters were drunk, firing wildly into the air or across the façades of buildings, smashing and burning as if in some last frenzy against the city and its people. Heavy fighting erupted on the northern and eastern approaches to the city, Partisan brigades testing the mettle of the city's defenses. Shells landed sporadically in the city, mostly in and around the station and the sprawl of the barracks, but the German counterbattery fire was accurate enough to keep the incoming barrages down. That, or the Partisans had no wish to risk too much damage to the city. Not when they all but had it in the palms of their hands.

Coordinating security patrols, Reinhardt spent the day working with a dozen overstressed officers and NCOs on the details of the final pullout, trying to determine who would have the thankless task of being last out of the city. And always in the back of Reinhardt's exhausted mind was the meeting with Kostas. Somehow, he had to keep that, keep those shreds he had grasped with such difficulty from slipping away under the pressure of events. The possibility of maybe having to leave Sarajevo with none of this solved began to obsess him, and the hours ticked past, night falling across the increasingly beleaguered city, the rattle of gunfire coming from all around, it seemed. When it died away in one place, it started up somewhere else, and Reinhardt imagined Perić's men slipping and raiding through the city, adding to the rising havoc.

It was perilously close to nine o'clock when Reinhardt was finally able to get away from the army's operations room, and he knew he would be late. Moving fast through the halls, he knew he was teetering on the edge, more tired than he could remember being in a long time. He scooped up a mug of soup from a tureen in the Feldjaeger operations room and made his way to Benfeld.

"Give me good news, Frenchie," he said, hearing the peremptory tone in his voice, but too tired and too rushed to want to moderate it. "The names."

"Actually, something. A reprimand, from your friend Captain Koenig. For wasting his time."

"Koenig said that?"

"Yes, sir. He said his search found a couple of Bertholds and one Seymer, but none of them have ever served in the Balkans, and certainly not in a penal battalion."

"What?"

"Perhaps the names were not accurate?"

"Check again."

"But, sir . . ."

"Check it *again*, Benfeld."

"With Captain Koenig?"

"If you have to, yes. Or someone else. I don't care. Did Koenig say anything else?"

"Nothing, sir."

"*Nothing?* You're sure." Reinhardt frowned, not sure if he could mention his request to Koenig to look into Jansky's background. His tongue stroked the gap in his teeth. "The doctor?"

"Nothing, sir. I couldn't get over there, and I tried calling, but it's hopeless. The hospital's in the middle of being evacuated. Roads are busy, or jammed."

"That fucking doctor . . ." snarled Reinhardt, checking himself as he did so, seeing the consternation on Benfeld's face. He took a long breath and put a placatory hand on Benfeld's shoulder. "Nothing. I'm sorry." He snatched a glance at his watch, then risked a long swallow of the soup. "I'll see you back here in an hour or so, and we'll pay a visit to the doctor."

"Where are you going, sir?"

"I'm off shift," Reinhardt said.

"I know, but the colonel would like to know, I'm sure. In case of emergency."

Reinhardt laughed, a bitter quality to his mirth. "This whole thing's an emergency, Frenchie. I'm going into the city," he said, relenting, picking up an StG 44 and checking its action. "I've an appointment to keep."

There were no cars to be had, but on the edge of a screaming rage Reinhardt spotted a Feldjaeger patrol heading out and he hitched a ride with it as far as Zrinskoga Street, not far from police HQ, from where he could walk. Standing on the street almost alone, the town bathed under silvery light from a full moon, he hitched up the collar of his coat, checked all around, then walked fast north toward the Orthodox cathedral, a steady rattle of gunfire the only sound over the darkened city. Strossmayer Street ran along the back of it, totally in the shadow of the cathedral's towers and the pewter curve of its domes.

The address Alexiou had given him was next door to a tavern, one of the few that still catered to the city's people. Its doors and windows were shut tight, and the alley that ran down the side of it was very dark and narrow. Reinhardt shone a flashlight down it quickly, seeing nothing, and moved fast, banging his knee painfully on something as he went, hoping that Kostas had waited for him.

The Greeks' instructions had been to take the door at the end of the alley, which would take him up into a small apartment belonging to a family of Macedonian origin, thus trusted by Alexiou. Halfway down the alley, the door opened, and there was just enough light to show two men coming out. Reinhardt froze, then knelt slowly, listening.

The door shut and there was a whispered conversation, not a word of which Reinhardt could understand, but he knew from the intonation it was Albanian. A final exchange of words, and the men were coming toward him, and he had seconds to act. He laid the barrel of his assault rifle over his left forearm, angled the flashlight forward, and clicked it on, a sudden blaze of light that caught the two men cold. They blundered to a stop, hands coming up.

"Ku jeni?!"

Their hands were bloodred. Blood stained the front of their clothes and made dark stripes and spots across their faces, and a sudden cold rage coursed through Reinhardt.

The second one had a light and he turned it on, shining it back at Reinhardt.

"Kopil!" snarled the one in front, bringing a pistol out of his jacket.

Reinhardt fired two short bursts from his StG 44. The noise was blaringly loud in the confines of the alley. The men were flung back in a cloud of brick dust and spray of blood. Reinhardt clicked off the flashlight as shell casings bounced brassily onto the floor of the alley, moving as quietly as he could to a new position, and there he hunched down and waited, listening, trying to sink himself into the darkness. He had always been a patient man and knew that impatience had killed more soldiers than he liked to imagine. So he waited in the dark, letting his eyes adjust, listening hard. Unbidden, a memory came, of a mud-filled shell hole on the Western Front, his face ground into the viscous earth and his ears full of the hacking agony of a man who had not waited long enough for the gas to pass . . .

Reinhardt kept waiting, listening, trying to sink himself into the darkness, but eventually he drew a long breath, and it was followed immediately by a shiver, a trembling that shook him as he relaxed, slowly, the stress seeping out. A cold anger followed it, a flood of it gushing right through him from a hammering heart. He rose, wincing at the twinge from his knee, moving and feeling for the bodies. Still listening carefully, he clicked on the flashlight.

The two men were dead. He shone the light on their faces, recognizing neither of them. He swept the light up and down them. They were both dressed in baggy trousers and heavy sheepskin waistcoats worn over long, dark coats. Their cheeks were sunken beneath a scratch of stubble, and Reinhardt felt how lean they had both been as he ran hands across their clothes searching for something with which to identify them, all knobby joints and whipcord muscles.

On the first body, Reinhardt found nothing but two spare magazines for the small, blunt pistol the corpse still gripped in its hand. But on the second man, he found a knife, and felt something beneath the man's coat. He risked the flashlight a moment longer, finding a piece of paper wrapped around a leather packet. The paper was bloodied, and it had what looked like a list of names written on it.

He shoved it into his pocket with the pistol and switched off the flashlight, staring blindly up the alley, dreading what he would find up there. He opened the door carefully, risking another sweep with the flashlight, seeing a room at the end of a short hallway, lit by a steady glow from a lantern. He looked into what seemed to be a living room. The place was a mess: the table shoved to one side, chairs overturned, cups and plates and ashtrays scattered across the floor. There was a smear of blood on one wall, and Kostas lay beneath it, his shirtfront open and his chest covered in blood from a tangled lattice of wounds, not dissimilar to those that Kreuz had suffered.

"Shit," muttered Reinhardt. He turned his head to the ceiling and felt his face go, just for a second, into an agonized twitch. It felt like the stress of a battlefield, the visceral need to hunch down and away from the enemy, but knowing only movement would save you. Stop and you die, he knew, but that moonlit city was a haunted tangle of shadows and threats and he did not want to go out there.

He laid the assault rifle on the table, its grip toward him, and put the papers he had taken from the Albanian on the table. The paper was a list of ten names, all men. Next to each name was a series of six-digit numbers, no series alike. He unwrapped the leather packet, nose wrinkling at the ammoniac smell it gave off. Inside were *soldbuchs*—soldiers' pay books—three of them, the size of his hand. He looked at the top one, at its dun cover with its black eagle and swastika and heavy Gothic lettering, and wondered where on earth Kreuz had found such valuable documents.

He flicked open the first one. The place where the *soldbuch*'s owner's photograph ought to have been was empty. There was only the incomplete roundel of a stamp across the inside page, which once would have run across the picture. The book was not blank, though. It had belonged to a Sergeant Heinrich Keppel. Reinhardt flicked quickly through the pages, past the handwritten lines and faded stamps that recorded where and when Keppel had served, the injuries he had sustained, decorations received, punishments meted out. He paged quickly through the other two. They both had photographs and were filled in. From the quick glance he gave them, both seemed normal.

A fusillade of shots from somewhere outside snapped him around, pulling the assault rifle off the table. He needed to find time to think, and he needed somewhere safe.

Somewhere to think, and somewhere to be safe. His mind lurched back and forth between the two, and then steadied as he knew where he needed to go.

21

The door cracked open to his knock with a long sliver of golden light. A shape passed across it, paused. He felt eyes upon him. The door opened wider, and Suzana Vukić stared out at him, past him. She pushed her gaze into the darkness of the stairwell, then back to him.

"What do you want, Captain?" she asked, softly, almost whispering.

"I'm sorry," he managed, struck by the piercing glitter of her eyes. "I need . . . I need someone to talk to." She said nothing, and it was the pressure of her eyes that pulled it out of him. "I'm in trouble. I need some . . . somewhere to think."

"Did anyone see you come up here?"

"No one, I think."

She nodded, finally, opened the door wider, and kept her eyes down as Reinhardt came inside. She shut the door and brushed past him. "This way, then," she said, leading him farther inside, the robe she was wearing fluttering out behind her. The place was dark, with two doors opening off the hallway into shadow, and lit only by the wavering light of the candle she carried. It smelled clean but like so much of the city, the smells of damp and waste and refuse were there, inescapable. She ushered him into what passed for a living room: a sofa with a blanket folded on the back, and a pair of mismatched chairs drawn up under a table. An iron woodstove in the little kitchen adjacent gave off a ruddy warmth that helped take the chill off the air.

"Sit down, Captain," she said, before picking up the candle and walking out of the room, the light flowing out with her. Reinhardt shrugged out of his coat, stood the StG 44 in a corner, and lifted his gorget over his head. He put it carefully on the table, looking at it, then sat on the couch. As the light ran down the walls after her, he saw they were lined with bags and boxes, sheets draped over what he took to be furniture, pictures stacked against each other in a corner. They were belongings from another life, maybe from that big house up on the other side of the valley, the house where he and Padelin had interviewed her in a room with silver-framed photographs on a grand piano about the death of her daughter. There had been flowers, and an old dog. God, it was a lifetime ago.

He heard a clink of glass, and light washed across the walls as Vukić came back into the living room. She put a bowl of water, a cloth, and two glasses on the table before fetching a bottle from a cupboard, which she placed on the table as well, and the candle next to it. He shifted to one end of the couch as she sat next to him, drawing her robe tight and curling her feet up under her. The light in the room shifted as the candle flame steadied, shadows deepening, lengthening, then shortening, steadying. Her hair was down, as long as he remembered it from two years ago. It glowed in the candlelight.

"You should wash."

He looked at his hands, saw they were smeared with blood, dark crescents of it beneath his nails, whorled into his fingertips, caked and cracked across the backs of his knuckles. He soaked the cloth, wrung it out, then wiped his hands. He moved slowly, pressing hard, clouding the water when he rinsed the cloth out and taking it to his neck when she gestured to her own, and only when she nodded did he put it down.

Reinhardt began to shake, and did not know if it was the sight of her, or the stress, or both, but he did not even try to control it, and did not care that she saw. He heard the clink of the bottle, a liquid whisper as she poured, and then her fingers brushed his as she put a glass into his hand. His hand shook, and a little of what was in the glass slopped over his knuckle. He put his other hand over the wrist that held the glass, clamped down hard, and concentrated on himself here, now. On the drink. On the woman next to him, her eyes fixed on him.

Outside, close by, a gun fired. One shot, two, a burst. Someone shouted. Moving carefully, he brought the glass slowly to his mouth, breathed in. It was slivovitz. Plum brandy. He tilted the glass, wet his lips with it. The slivovitz burned, filling his mouth with warmth. He swallowed, sighed, and carefully put the glass back on his lap. He wanted it. More than he realized, but drink was not a weakness he intended to indulge again. Not after so long away from it. Not now. Not here. Not with her.

"Reinhardt, why are you here?" Reinhardt pulled his eyes from the glass and looked at Vukić where she sat, staring at him, the one side of her face golden in the candle's wavering light. Her eyes were steady on his, pinpoints deep inside them from the flame. "What do you want?"

"Someone tried to kill me tonight," he managed, finally.

"But you defended yourself," she said, a statement as much as it was a question.

Reinhardt smiled, a bitter twist to it.

Vukić stared back at him, uncertainty writ large across her face. "Who were they?"

"No idea," Reinhardt replied, shortly. "None." He looked up, past the candle flame, pushing his eyes into the dark corners of the room, into the black rectangle of the doorway. "There were two of them in a house where I was supposed to meet someone."

"You killed them."

"I killed them." He lifted the glass and drank again, deeper this time, and she drank with him.

"What do you want, Reinhardt?" she asked, again.

"I'm scared. I need somewhere. To think. To be with someone who knows nothing of this."

"Nothing of what?"

"Of any of this. Of killing. Or murder."

"You think that, Reinhardt? Really? Of me?" He looked at her, confused. "Such are the times. Such is the place," she said, gesturing at the window, the city beyond it. "Such are the people we share it with. That I shared it with," she finished. Her mouth tightened, and she looked away and lifted the glass and drank. There was a glitter of light on her mouth as she passed her tongue across her lips. She looked back at him, and seemed to see something that stirred her. "What?" she asked, light rippling up her hair. "Do I shock you, Reinhardt? Do I? Don't you remember to whom I was married?"

"I remember," said Reinhardt.

"Well, then . . ." she said, trailing off.

"I don't . . . know . . . anymore . . . I don't know what sort of man I am." He sipped from the glass again, deeper still. "I used to have a good idea. But not anymore."

"What did you used to be, then?" asked Vukić.

"I used to be a killer. As a soldier, in the first war. A good one, by any standards you chose to measure it. But then that war ended, and that man no longer had a place in my life. In any life. Too much passion. Too much darkness. Too much anger and ability and not enough direction. Too much to regret . . ." He looked through the candle again far away at himself lying side by side in that trench with the Englishman as he passed him the watch, then dying with his head slumped on Reinhardt's shoulder. "I used to thrive on all that . . . passion and . . . and respect—because we were respected, we stormtroopers—and then it was all taken away. It was all for nothing, it seemed. The war ended. We all went our different ways. Some found the Freikorps, and some the Reds. Some found a bottle and never crawled back out. Some just vanished. And Christ knows there must have been some who just went back to being normal, but I don't know how they would have managed that. I found the police. Or maybe the police found me."

Or maybe, a tinge of bitterness souring the edge of his thoughts, even back then he was being moved, a piece on a board. "And I came to love it. To need the control, the discipline, it implied and imposed. You had to think your way through trouble. You can laugh," he said, not that she was. Her eyes were steady on him, her face blank. "You can laugh that someone ever had such an idea of police work. But I did. It was what I needed. And I only once lifted a hand to a suspect. At the very end."

He stopped, looking at the glass and knowing it was so easy to just put it down, which was why he upended it into his mouth, wincing at the bite it left across the back of his throat. He closed his eyes and breathed deeply in through his nose, following the flow of warmth as it spread inside. Then he opened them, leaned forward, and poured a second glass. He glanced at Vukić, and she looked at him, then knocked hers back as well, holding it out for him to fill.

"And now?" she asked.

"Now?" His mouth twisted, and he drank from his glass. "I don't know. Somewhere along the way, I lost myself. The Nazis, this war . . . sometimes I just want to turn away and hide and let it all pass by. But a man I met here two years ago helped me to understand that was not an option. It's not choices you lack for in life, it's decisions. And I decided to change the way I . . . approached this war. But I was still hiding, and that younger me—he's tired of hiding. Of the lies, the frustrations. He just . . . he wants to tear people apart with his hands and piss on their graves." He felt a flush of embarrassment as he said it, and wondered if it was really him talking, or the alcohol. "I'm afraid I'm going to give in to the worst in me. I don't know if I can manage to be one or the other."

"And would that be so bad? To give in."

"Bad? It's . . ." He frowned, confused by her, by himself. "It's not who I am. Who I want to be."

"Who we want to be . . . What we end up being . . ." She sipped from her glass and ran her hand down her robe where it lay across her thigh, smoothing the fabric out. "It's not the same thing, is it? Who we want to be lives up here," she said, tapping the side of her head, "and the other lives out there, in the real world."

"Well, it's the one out here with us who worries me," said Reinhardt. He drank from his glass, remembering those Albanians. Two quick bursts. No consideration. No calculation. Just reaction. "I killed men tonight . . ." He trailed off. Vukić waited. "I killed men I probably should not have."

Vukić frowned. "Is there a difference?" Reinhardt looked at her, blankly. "In what you just said? Were there others you should have killed, instead? Or did these men deserve to die, but not by your hand?"

Reinhardt reached across and took the bottle, even though he knew he should not. He could already feel a tingle from the alcohol, so little was he used to it now, and he did not want to lose control of himself. He offered it to Vukić, but she cupped her palm over her glass, and so he poured a small measure into his.

"I don't know if there's a difference. I meant to say, it was wrong. I did something wrong."

"Did you come here for forgiveness, then, Reinhardt?" Again, he looked at her, startled by the tone in her voice. "I have none to give you, and I don't think you need it, or want it. For sympathy? I have so little of it left, and what do I know of what you did? Of what you've done. If you came for understanding for your losses, I can give you that. The Ustaše took all from me. They took my husband first, and gave me back a monster. Then he gave them my child and made her into something worse than him. So I could say, take what you need. Do what you must. But that's the easy way, isn't it?

"Listen to me . . . What do I know, Reinhardt? What freedom do I have? It's . . . What's important, anymore? I don't know, sometimes. And then sometimes, I think all that's important is this city. This community. It . . . we . . . deserve to come through this, after what we've been through."

"What about you? What do you want?"

"Ask rather, what do I deserve? What do any of us deserve?" She shrugged, looked away. "Does it matter? I play a role. I am a widow of a senior Ustaše," she said to the wall. "A man who died in glory for the cause. And so they, they put me in a gilded cage and I spend my days in black, because I am supposed to, mourning a man . . . mourning a man who . . ." She stopped, looked down. "Never mind. I try to work, even if they don't want me to, and I do my best for the people of this city, even if it is not mine, and I will never really be one of them. What little influence I have, I use for them."

Reinhardt smiled, gestured at the room with the glass. "You call this gilded?"

She smiled as well, the mood lifted slightly, but the smile was sad, rueful. "It's not the house in Bistrik, is it?"

"I remember that house. I remember the photographs. On a piano. I remember flowers in a vase, the scent they gave." Her frown faded. "I remember the coffee you served, with cardamom. And I remember you. I remember your elegance. Your poise. I remember . . ." He stopped. It seemed the pressure of her eyes had dammed up his words. He looked away at the candle, and then drank again, deeper still, the warmth buzzing through him.

"What do you want, Reinhardt?" she whispered.

"I just wanted to survive this war. I wanted to come out the other end. Alive. But I realized surviving wasn't living. It was just a way of hiding. I thought, once, I had found a way around that, but it has not worked out like I thought it would. And now, here I am. A Feldjaeger. More authority and power at my fingertips than any man should have. And I can't . . . I can't square it with who I think I am."

Reinhardt looked at his glass, took a deep breath, then drank what was left. He winced, teeth clenched, and waited for the burn to pass. Moving carefully, he put the glass on the table, and with one finger pushed it away. "I used to think it was enough that I would catch the guilty," he said. The glass moved with little fits and starts, jerking away, until it was at the end of his reach, sitting next to his gorget, each of the links of its chain a curlicue of light from the candle. He brought his arm back, rested his elbows on his knees, and clasped his hands. "Toward the end, in Berlin, when everything came apart under the Nazis, sometimes it would even be enough that I knew. That they knew I knew. Here, now, I know . . . I *know* the Ustaše are behind the killings I'm investigating. And I *know* they are setting themselves up to escape what they've done." Her eyes shifted, burned into him. "But it's just not enough to know anymore. It never was. And what I feel— when I'm not thinking of finding my way through to the other side of this war—is guilt. That I let people down. The man I was supposed to meet tonight. Those people in the forest. There was a girl . . ." He stopped as he thought of the girl in her father's arms and his throat became too tight and his thoughts too confused.

"You're too hard on yourself."

Reinhardt's mouth twisted, looking at the glass. "Maybe so."

"You are. And you did not come here for truths like that."

"No."

"What did you come here for?" Her voice was soft, the light from the candle inking the fine lines at the corners of her eyes.

Reinhardt knew it, then, the answer, but the words were so hard to say, and it was why he no longer wanted to drink. He wanted no excuse for his words, and wanted no cushion for if they did not work.

"To be with you. I came here for you."

She said nothing, only looked at him. He looked back at her, breathing high over the lump in his chest, that fear of rejection, and a fear of his own inadequacy, and that he no longer had a right to such things, but then her hand moved, tentatively. Her thumb slid gently across the top of his hand, fell naturally into the groove between his own thumb and fingers. He looked down, then up at her. She was looking at him, her eyes firm and direct, but they glittered in the low light, and he swallowed, slowly. He took her hand, pulled gently, and she came to him, sliding and curving down next to him on the battered old sofa. He wrapped one arm around her shoulders, his hand rising up to stroke her hair, and he turned his face into it, breathing in the scent of her. Slowly, gently, they relaxed against each other. He closed his eyes, and felt the world begin to fall slowly away.

After a while, she shifted slightly in his arms, and he moved with her. They were still, breathing in unison, in rhythm. He shifted, and she turned and lifted her head so her face was pressed into his neck. She kissed him there, a touch of her lips, another, firmer, longer. His lips found her forehead, and he kissed her gently. Their faces brushed, and they looked into each other's eyes. Their mouths touched, moved against each other, and her eyes fluttered closed. His followed, and it was only the sensation that was left, mouth against mouth, a sweet edge from the alcohol, and the rising sweep in his stomach like the deep breath before the plunge.

They broke the kiss after a while, and lay with their heads together. He kissed her eyes, tasting the salt of her tears, her brows, lifted his hand and ran it through her hair. She moved into him, against him, kissed his neck, his jaw. They kissed again, longer, their breathing coming deeper and faster, and Reinhardt gave in to that feeling, that vertiginous pull toward an edge he had not known or felt in so long.

She broke the kiss, breathing fast into his neck. She turned her head gently, one way, then the other, as if she debated with herself, then looked up at him. She kissed him with her eyes open, her fingertips tracing the line of his cheeks, and ducked her head down again. He kissed her forehead, sensing she needed that time with herself. "It's been so long, Gregor," she whispered.

"For me as well."

"Together," she said, raising her head and kissing him.

"Together," he said, softly, against her mouth. The plunge, the risk, of words once spoken impossible to take back.

She stood, suddenly, and for a frozen moment he thought she was leaving, but then she turned, looking down at him, and slipped off her robe. She shivered as she breathed in, then lifted the nightdress she wore over her head and let it fall to the ground. Reinhardt felt his breath go thick at the sight of her, and he stood up, cupping her face in his hands. "You are beautiful," he whispered, kissing her. She made a small noise in the back of her throat, and her hands came up to undo the buttons on his tunic. He shrugged out of it, then his shirt. He heeled off his boots, had a moment of panic at how he thought he must look and smell, then let the worry go as he stood naked next to her. They came together again, her palms smooth on the blades of his shoulders, his hands tracing the hourglass of her waist, the flare of her hips, and then she drew him down onto the couch, wrapping her legs around him, and the world was truly gone.

22

The first time was breathtaking, but over so much faster than he would have liked. Her eyes seemed to hold a question each time he moved inside her, and he wondered if his own eyes looked the same, or if there was an answer there in them and if she could see it. Sliding into her, raising himself above her, her breasts moving to their rhythm and their eyes locked together was too much. He found himself teetering on the brink, balancing on the cusp of feelings coming from deep within. She must have read it in his eyes and heard it in his breathing because she locked her legs tighter, pulling him deeper into her, and he shuddered at a release that had seemed to come from long ago as much as it had come from far within him. Eyes clenched tight, he buried his face in her neck. His breath sawed in his throat, a splinter of embarrassment scraping at the edge of his pleasure, that he had not been able to control himself better.

Her arms and legs came tighter around him, holding him in, and then he smiled into her shoulder, kissing her, and the smile became a laugh, self-deprecating. He felt her head turn, the quizzical set to her neck, and then she laughed as well.

"I'm sorry," he managed, after a moment.

"Well, you said it had been a long time . . ."

He lifted his head to hers, and they smiled and laughed again. Shifting on the sofa, they squirmed together until they found a new closeness, limbs entwined. He pulled the blanket from the back of the sofa over them. She drew his head against her, stroking his hair, and they fell asleep like that.

Some time later she woke him, her leg thrown over his hip and her hands moving across his chest, down to his groin. Her breasts were bunched together between her arms, heavy and soft, brushed by light and shadow, and he felt himself stiffening to her touch. She smiled into her kiss, her eyes glittering. Reinhardt kissed her back, and she opened her mouth, surprising him with her tongue, waking him further. He opened his eyes in surprise, found her looking back at him, a set to her gaze that sent a shiver through him. And then she surprised him again as she pushed hard into his mouth, then moved her hips, rising on top of him, then up and down. He gasped as he slid inside her warmth, and she gripped his shoulders hard as she ground herself down onto him.

He took her breasts in his hands, pushing her back and up, and pushed his hips up to meet her. Her face drew in and out of the candlelight as she moved, her hair swinging back and forth. Her eyes fluttered closed, and he felt her body stiffening and her breathing coming higher and faster, her hips grinding down harder and harder.

"Gregor," she managed, as her breathing hitched and she went rigid. She gasped, then curled over him, her hands clenched in his hair. He wrapped his arms tight around her, holding her down as he pushed up into her. She trembled, and he felt the muscles of her back soften, relax. And then, as he had done, she smiled as she nuzzled into his neck, and their smiles became laughter. It cleansed them, washed them clean, and they fell asleep again.

Later in the night, with the candle guttering low, he felt her leave his side and woke and saw the wobble in her balance as she stepped across the room, heard her catch her breath as she put her hand out to a chair to steady herself. She murmured something, some little admonishment, and he smiled. He turned in the warmth of the blanket, feeling the dip in the sofa where she had lain and the curve of his body. There were small noises from the kitchen, wood sliding over metal as she fed the oven. Moments later, she was back, her feet slipping across the floor, back into the warmth and shape of her space against him. She turned, lying with her back against his front, drew his hand around between her breasts, and they slept again.

He woke later, a feeling of utter lassitude running through him. Something had woken him, though, his mind circling down after some small sound. He woke easily, calmly, listening, his eyes drifting open and shut to their own rhythm. It was quiet outside. He guessed it was past midnight, and softly, slowly, his mind began to tick over. Thoughts began to circulate, possibilities, questions. What had happened, last night, at that house? Who knew of it? Who knew of the meeting? Who knew Reinhardt would be there? Very few people knew where he was to have been, and those few were all in the army, and nearly all of them in the penal battalion. Someone up there had talked.

He realized his earlier anger had faded, or subsided. Wound down tight within him. Compressed, like strata, beneath the self-doubt that, it seemed, could not be so easily done away with. If the passions of his younger days were not enough to remake him, still he could feel he was different. Yes, the anger had faded, the doubts were creeping in, but in turning inward he had turned backward, tapped that reservoir of memories and feelings, that younger version of himself. He could not let himself become that man again, though. That man had been too dangerous, too foolhardy, too out of control . . .

That was the man who had killed those men at the house. Two bursts. No consideration, only cold calculation. No remorse. Vukić had asked him if it was forgiveness he had come for, but it was not what he sought. He had been acknowledging a mistake. He should not have killed those men. They had had uses. Reinhardt had known that, but he had killed them anyway.

Sometime in the night, he realized, something in him had begun to fuse. Parts that had been separate for a long time. That part of him that yearned toward what he could do as a Feldjaeger, finding some echo of the man he had been when he had fought through and survived the first war's storm of steel. And then there was the other part, the cautious, creeping part, the part that wanted only to sidle and worm its way along, scrimping and miserly with what he thought and even more with what he said. He had measured those two sides so long, keeping that younger, rasher side down, he did not know what he would be like if he gave in and accepted himself as someone who could be both.

A soft brush of sound, maybe from the kitchen, and he knew it was that sound that had awakened him before. Somehow, he sensed Vukić was awake as well, and he ran a hand softly up her arm, whispered in her ear.

"Tell him it is all right."

She stiffened against him, and then her head turned toward him, her eyes very wide and dark.

"Tell him," whispered Reinhardt again, softly.

She sat up, wrapping her robe around her as Reinhardt pulled his trousers and shirt on. She walked quietly to the kitchen, called a name in a quiet voice. He heard her voice, soft, coaxing, and then she was coming back, and a boy had his hand in hers.

The boy from the forest.

Vukić brought him to the couch and sat, bringing him against her. The boy's eyes looked wide and white as he stared at Reinhardt, saying nothing.

"His name is Neven," said Vukić. The boy blinked and turned his head up to her at the sound of his name. She ruffled his hair, kissed the top of his head. "I could not leave him with the others. With the elderly couple. They were not his family, anyway."

"I understand," said Reinhardt.

"Did you know he was here?"

"Before I came?" She nodded. "I guessed. But it's not why I came," he said, sliding his hand along the back of the sofa to brush her shoulder, then her hair from her cheek. "How has he been?"

"He seems . . . all right. But he does not say much. I only know he lived with his uncle and sister. They had a little farm, and raised livestock that his uncle would butcher for sale at the market."

"Where did he live?"

"He does not know," Vukić whispered, brushing her mouth across the top of Neven's head. "Before the war, he had never been far from where he used to live."

"Who knows he is here?"

"No one," she said, laying her chin on Neven's head, her eyes far away.

"You know, they will not stop looking for him."

"I can keep him safe until the Partisans come."

Reinhardt looked at him, tilting his head down until the boy looked up at him. "Do you think I can ask him? About what happened?"

"Must you?"

"It's important, Suzana," he replied, a small thrill darting through him at the use of her name. She nodded, after a moment, and whispered quietly in Neven's ear. The boy never took his eyes from Reinhardt, though his head shook slightly, and his breathing came high and shallow, short little movements of his chest. Vukić held him, rocked him, and gave him his time, until the boy spoke, startling them both.

"Došli su kad sam bio u šumi."

"I was in the forest when they came," Vukić translated. "I was with Almira and Suljo, and I heard the cars, then the shouting. I wanted to run home, but my uncle always told me, if men came, if men in uniforms come, to run and hide and not to come back." The boy's eyes did not waver as he told the story. "But it was difficult. I could not stay away. There was my uncle, and my sister. So I came as close as I dared, and Almira came with me. I saw the men. They lined up my uncle, and my sister, and the others. And from their truck they took three men. They were crying, but they shot them, and they threw them in one of the houses. And then from their truck they took an old man, and made him stand with my uncle, and his friends. Then they killed them all. Then they set fire to the hut, and watched it burn. And then they left."

Reinhardt and Vukić exchanged a look at the boy's stark recital of the horror that had descended upon him and his family. He wanted so much to leave it at that, but could not, and his eyes asked forgiveness of Vukić as there seemed no way to ask it of Neven.

"Neven, I must ask you some other things," said Reinhardt, softly. "Did you hear the men say anything?"

"Some things. They were angry we were there. *'Why are you here?'* one of them demanded. They argued what to do. Then one of them decided, and he lined them all up."

"The ones they took from the truck. The three men they put in the house. What did they look like?"

"They were Germans. They had German uniforms."

"When did you arrive there, do you know?"

"We arrived two days before this happened. We were running. Our village was destroyed. We found the houses and thought we would be safe. They were empty. My uncle told us we would be safe there. The Ustaše would not get us there. But then Elma—she was my sister—she found the bodies and was scared, and everyone argued if we should stay or go."

"You found bodies?"

Neven nodded, solemnly. "Yes. We found two bodies. They were buried, but not deep. Wild animals had found them."

"You saw these bodies?"

"Yes. They were Germans, too. Elma was scared."

"I am sorry to ask you this, Neven."

"Auntie Suzana says you are a policeman." Vukić's eyes widened as she translated, looking down at Neven. The boy spoke to her, clear, simple words, and she smiled at him, but as he looked back at Reinhardt, she brushed the back of her hand across her face, the candle-light marking a wet, gold trail back from her eye. "Will you catch those men, he asks."

"I will do my best, Neven. I promise." The boy looked at him a long moment, and then the hard edges of his face disappeared, and his expression seemed to soften, and Reinhardt knew he was looking at the real boy. The boy who existed before the trauma of this war. "Do you think you can remember what the Ustaše looked like?"

"They were not Ustaše."

"Who were not Ustaše, Neven?"

"The ones who killed the soldiers. And then killed the others. My uncle, and my sister. The Ustaše only brought the old man."

Reinhardt paused. "Who was it killed your family, then, Neven?"

"They were Germans."

"How do you know?"

"I saw their uniforms. I could hear them. They sounded like you."

"They sounded like me?"

"They looked like you."

"Like me . . . ?"

Reinhardt froze as the boy's eyes fixed him, pinned him, and his finger came up to point at him. "They looked like you," he said again, and then his finger drifted away, pointing. Reinhardt followed its line to a buttery gleam of metal, leaned over to the table, and lifted up what Neven had seen.

"They wore this?"

Neven nodded, pointing at the gorget in Reinhardt's hands.

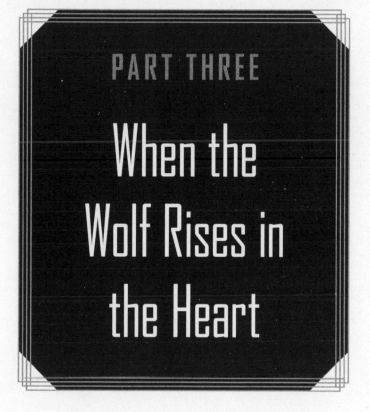

PART THREE

When the Wolf Rises in the Heart

23

Reinhardt stood at the window as Vukić took Neven back to bed. He parted the curtains slowly, looking out across the geometry of the city's rooftops. The sky was studded with clouds and—when they let it emerge—the moon shone down like a newly minted coin. It was a bomber's moon, glistening white, painting in pale shades the snow-shrouded slopes of Mount Trebević across the valley with its high valleys and coombs seeming to float in the night air. The city was very quiet now, only the sporadic crackle of gunfire from across the valley, shots that came in twos and threes.

He fished the bloodied paper and the *soldbuchs* from his coat, sitting back down at the couch, spreading them on the table. He stared at the *soldbuchs*, wondering where they had come from. All soldiers were supposed to keep theirs on them at all times. Failure to do so was a serious offense, enough to get you sent to a penal battalion these days.

He pondered that, then opened them one by one, flicking through the names and details within. Sergeant Heinrich Keppel, infantryman, born 15 August 1919, in Freising, Bavaria. Sergeant Georg Abler, infantryman, born 1 March 1922, in Marburg, Slovenia. Corporal Marius Maywald, tanker, born 19 April 1921 in Troppau, in Bohemia and Moravia. Personal information—height, religion, hair and eye color. All had served in a variety of postings and units before posting to a penal battalion. Fairly unobtrusive, run-of-the-mill soldiers. Nothing jumped out, although Abler seemed to ring a bell, or maybe look familiar, but he could not work out why. He knew no one called Abler, and until a few days ago he had had no idea of the existence of the penal battalion from which, presumably, these pay books had come.

He turned them in his hands, running his fingers over them, turning each page slowly. There was nothing untoward about the grimy covers, the softened edges to the pages, the looping scrawls in green and blue and black ink that a dozen company clerks in the same number of army units had left. They were in good condition, as mandated. Only the back cover of Keppel's book looked bloodstained.

He unfolded the note, the paper crackling softly, and read the ten names, noting for the first time the elegant lines of the handwriting that had set them down, rather old-fashioned in the curls and flourishes and slants of the letters. He rubbed the paper between his fingers, bending it a little, seeing how thick and fine it was. It was paper made by a craftsman, he realized, thick, silky paper made for a fine hand that knew how to handle a pen. No pooling or blotting of the letters. Was there a message here, too?

Georg Abler, Carl Benirschke, Otto Berthold, Bruno Cejka, Jozef Fett, Werner Janowetz, Marius Maywald, Jürgen Sedlaczek, Christian Seymer, and Ulrich Vierow. The names meant nothing to him. Neither did the six-digit numbers next to each name. Nothing. He let his mind relax, trying to see through to some kind of symmetry. He considered Keppel's *soldbuch*, then put it carefully to one side. What was left were ten names, and he had found five bodies at that construction site, and three in the forest, and Neven had said he had found two more, buried, and they had probably been Berthold and Seymer who, if Reinhardt could figure this out properly, had been the first to disappear. Ten names, ten bodies. Ten bodies, but only two *soldbuchs*. Three, if he counted Keppel's, but he still felt it did not belong. What the connection might be, he did not know and, hearing Vukić coming back, he piled them back together with the paper and put them back in his coat.

"What time is it?" she asked, coming to sit beside him.

"Two o'clock in the morning," he answered. "I should go very soon."

She ducked her head and nodded against her chest. He shifted over on the sofa and took her in his arms. She came softly, and they leaned back together, his hand running down her hair.

"What does it all mean?" she whispered.

"About Neven?" A little hesitation, and she nodded, and Reinhardt wondered if she had wanted to ask about the two of them. "I'm not sure. I suspect . . . I suspect some of the Ustaše are bribing their way into our ranks. I think that way they hope to escape from here."

She stiffened, raised her head to him. "How would escaping as a German help them?"

"I think they might be enlisting as what we call hiwis. Foreign volunteers. As such, they'll do mostly menial work. No fighting. They'd be as safe as could be. And once they're far from here . . ."

He fell quiet under the pressure of her eyes, and she picked his words up. "Once they're far from here, they can become themselves again." Reinhardt nodded, suddenly relieved when she turned the piercing glitter of her gaze down, and came against his chest, again. He stroked her hair, feeling something had changed.

He would have stayed there forever, he thought, but there was a day waiting for him out there, and there was no God to make the night longer just for him. He breathed deeply, and Vukić seemed to hear it for the signal it was. She straightened.

"You must go." She said it simply, as much a question as a statement. He nodded.

She heated water on the oventop, and left him to use the amenities on the landing, shared with the three other apartments on this floor. He went quickly and quietly, not wanting to meet anyone for fear of drawing attention to her, but he could not help but smile. Him, standing shivering in his coat and boots in a communal latrine, and the memory of the night he had just spent. When he came back, they stood on towels in the kitchen and washed. The war had changed him, he knew. The spars of his ribs and shoulders were clear to see, the muscle sheeted taut across his torso, wound cord-tight around his arms and legs. The ridged scar across his knee stood proud and livid. She still had the round-hipped and full-breasted mark of so many of the women of this land, but it seemed to him time and age and war had shaped her differently, as if the lines of her body still hewed to the proud stance of her soul and she was beautiful to him.

"What are you looking at?"

"You," he said, simply. She blushed and then smiled. He watched her, drinking his fill of her, wondering if this would be the only time, knowing it probably was.

When he had dressed, pulling on his soiled and dirty clothes, she came over to him with a little glass vial in her hand. She took the stopper and dabbed a little perfume on his collar, under his chin. "If they ask . . ." she said, then faltered, looked down. He put his hand under her chin and lifted her head gently, and she met his eyes with a sudden determination.

"I can say I was with someone," he finished for her. She smiled and nodded, her eyes suddenly wet, and he felt his own sting shut, and it seemed it was all too soon they were at the door. Her eyes were wide and full on his, and he felt his own were brimming with all he had to say, and no way or time to say it.

She ran a finger softly over his mouth, whispering. "No words. Later. If you need . . . If you want . . ." She blushed, again, her head shaking slightly at her own timidity in the face of what they had given each other that night. They kissed softly, and he wished it did not feel like it was the last time.

He went quietly back down the stairs and saw no one, the doors on each floor standing shut and silent. He paused at the entrance to the building, listening, buttoning his coat up against the cold and deciding where to go. He was loath to leave, feeling that the entrance was a threshold not to be crossed lightly, but the day was not going to get any younger. He had known it on waking, and it was as true now as it was then. More so.

He made to walk outside but paused, holding himself still. He did not know what it was, but he felt something. Somewhere out there, some part of the night was deeper, darker than it should be. A watcher himself, he could feel that something out there had eyes and saw him, and he folded himself back into the blackness of the entrance. Watching, waiting, listening, passing his eyes slowly across doors and arches and windows like inked squares on the coal outline of the street. Nothing moved, but he could feel it, some sense or vibration that ran at widdershins to the surface of the world.

Finally, he shook himself loose and made himself walk out, moving close to the walls. The city was very quiet, eerily so after the fighting earlier that night. Here in the Austrian city the roads were straight, some still bounded in filthy heaps of snow and ice and rubbish but empty of people. Still, he made himself change his rhythm, walking backward from time to time, checking behind, stopping to duck into a doorway, checking back, looking up at windows and across the street before continuing on. Above, the sky was rent dark blue and gray, the moon lighting the ragged edges of the torn clouds as they streamed above him on a chill wind that drove crosswise above the valley. He moved fast down Ante Starcević Street, still seeing no one, and finally up to the guard post at the barracks, and it was there he had the first inkling something was wrong.

It was not the fortified entrance that gave him pause. That had gone up yesterday, with the first fighting around the ring of the city's edge. It was the squad of Feldgendarmerie mingled with the soldiers on duty, the way their sergeant took a hard look at his armband, then asked for his *soldbuch*, comparing it to a handwritten list he held. His eyes froze, fixed Reinhardt where he stood, and he called over another of the Feldgendarmes.

"Hey. I think this is the one you're after."

The other Feldgendarme, also a sergeant, compared *soldbuch* and list, nodded, and with a motion of his wrist Reinhardt was bracketed by two more of them.

"What's the meaning of this, Sergeant?" Reinhardt's tongue stole toward that gap in his teeth.

"Orders, sir."

"Orders for what?"

"Can't say, sir."

"You will say more than that, Sergeant," said Reinhardt, planting his feet. There was a creak of accoutrements, the iron slide of weapons all around, as the Feldgendarmes backed away from him.

"Don't be foolish, sir," said the sergeant.

Reinhardt held the man's eyes, then nodded and followed him over to a Horch, where he climbed as ordered into the backseat. The car rumbled out of the barracks, back down Starcević Street, and pulled to a stop in front of the State House. There was a mob of soldiers on the building's front steps loading boxes of documents into waiting trucks. The sergeant escorted him inside, their footsteps clattering counterpoint to the jangling beat of Reinhardt's heart. He pushed his knee up the stairs to the offices he had visited only a few hours ago, the steps covered in pieces and scraps of paper, an overturned box piled into the angle of a landing, a spill of white documents across the floor the way a dealer might spread a deck of cards across the baize of a playing table. There were more men up here, Feldgendarmes, a few orderlies or clerks, and someone incongruous in a pair of striped pajamas, a hush that deepened into a flat silence as Reinhardt walked past, Feldgendarmes fore and aft. A Feldjaeger sergeant met them at the door to the judges' offices, he and the Feldgendarme sizing each other up like cats. "We'll take him from here," he said.

"All yours," said the Feldgendarme, turning and motioning his men out.

"Captain, sir," said the sergeant, quietly. "I'll need to take that."

"What's going on, Sergeant?" asked Reinhardt, equally quietly, as he handed over his StG 44.

"Colonel'll tell you, sir. Right away."

The sergeant led Reinhardt across the room, past desks and shelves empty of books and papers, boxes piled up against the walls, past probing eyes on heads that swiveled to watch him pass. A cold sweat broke out across his back. The sergeant knocked at Dreyer's door, cracked it open, and put his head inside. He ducked out after a moment, holding the door wide for Reinhardt.

Dreyer sat splayed in a chair, the left side of his head a matted and bloody ruin. One arm dangled down to the ground, a pistol on the floor under his right hand. His left arm was curled into his lap, the fist closed. He was in his shirt, the white fabric soaked with blood where his head lolled against his shoulder.

There were five men in the room staring at him. Scheller and Lainer stood at Dreyer's desk. Judge Erdmann was the third. The fourth man was Neuffer, from the Feldgendarmerie, looking—rather surprisingly—desperately uncomfortable. The fifth man was Herzog, short and stocky and glowering at him from beneath lowered brows like the belligerent bulldog he so resembled.

"This is Reinhardt?" the general grunted.

"This is Captain Reinhardt," answered Scheller. His face was very grave, and Reinhardt's worry grew. "Captain, you remember General Herzog, commander of the Feldgendarmerie in Sarajevo."

Reinhardt came to attention in front of Herzog's pugnacious stare, banishing Dreyer's body to a blur of white and red in the corner of his eye. "Where have you been these last few hours?"

"Sir?"

"Answer the question, Captain," said Scheller, firmly.

"I was on a . . . I was . . ." he reddened. He knew he would have to explain it sometime, but the words would not come. "I had a private engagement, sir," he managed.

"A woman?" Herzog snapped. "Convenient."

"Convenient for what, sir?" asked Reinhardt, now confused as well as worried.

"*This*, Captain," snorted Herzog, flicking a dismissive hand at Dreyer's body. "What the hell else?" The blood drained from Reinhardt's face, and he felt the ground tilt beneath him. "Nothing to say for yourself?" Herzog demanded.

Reinhardt's mouth moved, but nothing worked, his tongue stroking the gap in his teeth. Out of the corner of his eye he saw Lainer step next to him, and lean in and sniff.

"Well, he smells like he's been rolling about with a tart, that's for sure."

Reinhardt flushed, a prickling sweat breaking out all over him. Herzog sneered a chuckle while Lainer and Scheller remained expressionless. At least Erdmann and Neuffer had the grace to look embarrassed, but Lainer's throwaway comment had suddenly fixed Reinhardt, as if he had been rooted to the spot, and everything became clear, sharp, focused.

"Sir, am I under suspicion for the judge's death?" he asked, addressing the general, but also looking at Scheller.

"I don't know, Reinhardt," said Herzog. "You'll be relieved to hear, no doubt, that Dreyer topped himself. At least, that's the way it looks. Right, Neuffer?"

"Yes, sir," murmured the Feldgendarme. "Suicide. There's a note."

"There's a note," Herzog repeated, eyes fixed on Reinhardt.

Neuffer held out a piece of paper.

"*I am sorry. I cannot go on. Forgive me.*" Reinhardt looked up and around at the general, at the rest of them, and at the scrum of people at the door. "Potent stuff."

"A comedian, Reinhardt? I hadn't been told you were a comedian."

"Who found him?" Reinhardt asked. Neuffer blinked, and his eyes flickered to Erdmann. "*You* found him? When?"

"I'll be asking the questions, Reinhardt," Herzog interrupted, the judge's mouth closing on whatever he had been about to say. "You say you were with a woman—good for you, and I hope you gave her a good time so she remembers what you looked like—but from what I've been hearing, you and our judge here have been causing more than your fair share of trouble."

"Sir, I don't know what—"

"Quiet, Reinhardt," Herzog grated. "Speak when asked to. It's bad enough Dreyer was down here on his War Crimes Bureau business, stirring up trouble and discord with our allies, but then the pair of you had to go chasing shadows and besmirching the work and reputation of a man like Major Jansky."

"General, if I may," interjected Scheller, his face smooth. "Captain

Reinhardt was acting under my orders. I am sure he meant no disrespect or meant to cause any confusion."

"Admirable, Scheller, to stand up for your man. It's more than that, though." Lainer's eyes were flat as the big Feldjaeger stared at Reinhardt, but two red spots on his cheeks betrayed his anger. "I should like to explain one or two things to our captain, here. Him and his judge and their fairy tales. Thanks to him, I had to put down a bloody insurrection in the fortress tonight. Any idea what that might have been about, Reinhardt?"

"None, sir," he replied, although he had a sick feeling he did.

"On the contrary, I think you bloody well do. I don't know who the hell told you, or why the hell you thought it was a good idea to go poking around in a penal battalion under the command of one of my officers—an officer who, by the way, has my utmost confidence. But consider this a good old-fashioned bollocking, Reinhardt. You fucked things up. Royally. Smearing the name of a good officer and wasting his time. Getting up the collective nose of the Ustaše, who are the only thing holding this place together and are our trusted allies. Spreading rumors and dissension in the ranks. Yes, your little forays into the penal battalion upset a lot of people, and put some funny ideas into the heads of the wrong ones, to the point I had to put a dozen men against a wall and execute them tonight for attempted desertion and robbery. I lost two good men dead and six more wounded before I had the rebellion put down. Know what that's about, Captain?"

"No idea, sir."

"You're a fucking lousy liar, Reinhardt. You know damn well what it's about. Your Greeks attempted to abscond, tonight, with the best part of half a ton of gold. You wouldn't have put that idea in their minds, now, would you, because I don't think they've had an original thought among themselves since their mothers took them off the tit." Over Herzog's shoulder, Erdmann's face twisted slightly, as if in distaste, and the judge's eyes met Reinhardt's, an elegant shrug in them as if to say none of this was his doing. "I know you met them, Reinhardt. If I had the time, and if I were sorry enough about having had them shot, I'd drag you in front of a court-martial and rip the truth out of you. As it is, count yourselves lucky the Partisans are making that difficult, but if I hear one more bloody peep out of you, if your shadow so much as crosses mine, I'll ruin you, you see if I don't. Is that clear, Captain? Colonel? Clear to you? Control your officer, or have it done for you."

"Clear, sir," said Reinhardt and Scheller at the same time.

"Let's make a few more things clear, gentlemen," Herzog continued, a self-satisfied smirk on his face as he looked between Scheller and Reinhardt. "First, Major Jansky has my full confidence, as he does the confidence of Judge Erdmann, here. I will not have him bothered anymore by this sham of an investigation. He is a tough man, I know, but these are tough times, and it is a tough, tough job he has been given, to run that collection of crooks and pimps and misfits and make it a fighting unit, or at least a unit that serves a purpose.

"Second, I don't know why this man killed himself," he said, pointing a dismissive finger at Dreyer's body. "Personally, I don't give a toss. He was too weak for the times. That's no crime, I suppose, and I suppose he's relieved us the burden of having to carry his weak and sorry backside any further. But if there is an investigation—which there won't be—it will be the Feldgendarmerie taking care of it. There is nothing here for the Feldjaegerkorps," he finished, giving the last word an acid spin as he spat it from his mouth. "Is all of that clear? Let me hear that chorus of yeses, gentlemen," he said, with a smirk.

"General, I think that's quite enough," challenged Scheller.

"Fuck what you think's enough, Colonel." Herzog sneered, his eyes aglitter.

"I remind you, sir . . ."

"Don't even bother reminding me of your supposed authority, Colonel. Try to exercise it here, and I'll shove it right back up your arse. This is my town, these are my men, and these are my fucking times. Is that *clear*?"

"Clear, sir," said Reinhardt, loudly, hoping by volume to cover for Scheller, and distract him away from any confrontation with Herzog. The colonel's eyes, flat, dark pits, swiveled once to Reinhardt, then away again.

"Music to my fucking ears," chuckled Herzog, coarsely, staring at Scheller. Then his face changed, and he straightened up. "You will forgive my crudeness, gentlemen, I hope. It is just that sometimes I find it is the best way to make a point, and to have it stick. Understand me when I say these are desperate times and the last thing we need is division within our ranks. We are all very much in this together. If today is a ruin, tomorrow may be different, and we owe it to ourselves, and to the Führer, to pull through this. And not only that," he said, his bulldog stance tense, "but to plan for the future. When our enemies least expect it. Plan *now*. Here. Always remember, gentlemen, the Führer has a plan. He may not reveal all of it to all of us, but he has one. And it is beholden on us to try to think like him, act like he would, act like he would *want* us to." His glittering eyes stabbed at each of them, and Reinhardt wondered if it was madness he saw in them, or true belief, and wondered if the two were different. "Our enemies do not always do as we think, and so must we.

"With that, gentlemen, this is over. You have, I believe, your orders, Colonel Scheller. Pull out tomorrow for Visoko. And you, Reinhardt," Herzog said, thrusting himself up close to Reinhardt. "You stay away from Major Jansky, and stay away from his unit. If I hear of your involvement anywhere near him again, I'll have you stripped of your rank and assigned to his battalion." He guffawed as if he had just thought of it. "Wouldn't that be fucking poetic justice?"

24

Herzog strutted out, still laughing, Feldgendarmes pulled along in his wake. Erdmann slipped his spectacles on and walked quietly up to Reinhardt. "I am so terribly sorry for your loss, Captain," he said, extending his hand, placing the other on Reinhardt's shoulder. As before, his handshake was firm, the hand on the shoulder avuncular, his eyes intense.

Reinhardt's breathing suddenly came high and thick.

"Thank you, sir," he managed.

"I warned you, did I not, about all this? About getting involved with Dreyer's obsessions. About giving him hope. And now look. One of my best judges has taken his own life."

"Sir, if you don't mind, a question."

Erdmann's mouth straightened, and a little of the light in his eyes dimmed, but his hands remained firm on Reinhardt. "Ask, then."

"No," said Scheller. "No more questions. Enough's enough." He pointed out the door. "Back to barracks."

"Very well, sir. But if you would, I would appreciate a moment alone," he said to the question he saw in Scheller's face. "I would like a moment to say good-bye. He was my friend."

"Five minutes, Reinhardt," Scheller sighed. "No more."

Erdmann's hand tightened on Reinhardt's shoulder, a gesture of support, but it felt like an unwelcome weight. Reinhardt's shoulder shifted slightly, down and away, and something went across Erdmann's face, slithered away into his eyes. A last pat on the shoulder, and he followed Scheller and Lainer out of the room.

As Reinhardt knelt in front of Dreyer's body, he shook, suddenly, quivering off the edge upon which he realized he had been holding himself, where he had been holding off his grief. Reinhardt let his head drop, his hands gentle on Dreyer's forearms.

"I'm sorry," he whispered, although he could not really have said what he was sorry for.

Swallowing hard, not wanting to do it, he gently lifted Dreyer's head, one hand atop it, the other beneath his chin. Dreyer's jaw was soft, fleshy, folds of skin straightening and tautening as he moved the head, looking at the exit wound. He let the head down, then lifted Dreyer's hand, the one on his lap. Reinhardt peeled Dreyer's fingers open, revealing something that glittered in the light. It was a piece of jewelry, he saw, a brooch in the shape of an insect. A dragonfly, beautifully enameled in gold and green and blue, its wings slightly warped and bent where Dreyer's fist had closed around them. Pushing back the sleeve of his shirt, Reinhardt saw red welts at the level of Dreyer's elbow, stark against the pale skin. The other arm was the same.

He used a handkerchief to pick up the pistol, not stopping to consider the absurdity of trying not to contaminate what was not considered a crime scene, and sniffed the barrel. The weapon had certainly been fired, but there was no way of knowing if Dreyer had been the one to fire it. He ejected the magazine. One round was missing.

Dreyer's bed was rumpled, the blankets mounded in sharp creases, and the sheet hanging to the floor. He looked down at Dreyer's feet. He was in his socks, the fabric worn tissue thin at the toes and heels.

There was a scuff of cloth behind him. Reinhardt started, a jolt of cold going right through him, thinking he had been alone. Neuffer stood forgotten in the corner, screwing the heels of his hands into his eyes. Reinhardt frowned at the man dislaying such a gesture of weakness in front of someone Neuffer hardly knew. Neuffer's hands came down, his eyes red and wet, saw Reinhardt looking.

"This wasn't suicide, was it?"

Reinhardt froze, looked hard back at the Feldgendarme. "What makes you say that?"

"The fact that you're still poking around." Neuffer's lower lip curled into his mouth. "What have you found?"

"*Found?* Is this some kind of test, Neuffer?" The Feldgendarme said nothing, and Reinhardt pushed himself to his feet, irked at the thought that he was performing, but he walked over to the gramophone. The needle was lying in the center of the record, that "dreadful recording by Hans Pfitzner" as Dreyer had called it, and his eyes stole a glance at the case where the jazz records were. On the table, Dreyer's flask gleamed silver next to the ashtray. In the ashtray, stacked one atop the other, were Dreyer's cigarette case and matching lighter.

"Erdmann found him?" Reinhardt asked, frowning down at the brooch that shone in the palm of Dreyer's hand. Neuffer nodded. "Where had he been?"

"Dining with General Kathner at his HQ."

"*'Dining'?*" Reinhardt frowned. "With all that's going on . . . ? What does he think this is, a day at the races?"

"He said he came back, saw Dreyer, and called us in."

"Did he touch anything?"

"I don't know."

"What time did he say he came back?"

"Maybe around one o'clock in the morning."

Reinhardt had had Vukić's body curled against his at that time, and it already felt like a lifetime ago.

"What is it with those two men, Herzog and Erdmann, and Jansky?" Reinhardt darted the question at Neuffer, taking a chance on the obvious tension the man was under.

Neuffer blinked, pulled his eyes back from Dreyer's body. "Jansky? I mean, he works for them. With them."

"What does that mean?" asked Reinhardt, his pulse quickening.

"Herzog's his commander. And Erdmann's the one who reviews all the . . . all the disciplinary proceedings, confirms the transfers to the penal battalion. This wasn't suicide, was it?"

"It wasn't suicide, Neuffer."

"I mean . . . yes. No. I mean, how can you tell?"

Reinhardt looked at the Feldgendarme anew, wishing for some opening to push on with those questions about Jansky. Neuffer was clearly struggling with something, a far cry from the formulaic, obsequious behavior he had seen him display before.

"I saw Dreyer just yesterday, late last night, and he was fine," Reinhardt said. "In fact, he was happy. Or happier than he had been in a long time. He had something to look forward to. I know he talked of suicide, but he was too scared to do it. And he would've put the pistol to his heart if he could've. There are marks on his arms, indicating someone held him in the chair for someone else to shoot him."

He spoke calmly, interested to hear the academic lilt to what he was saying, as if he lectured a probationary officer or cadet back on the police force. *See, here, how the body lies, indicating the blow was struck from this angle . . .* He walked to the table, picking up the flask, a measure of something tilting around inside it. He noted how the light flowed across it in different ways, running blurred and heavy across the matte finish of its body, but glittering bright along the floral tracery that swept delicately across and around it. It was a beautiful piece. He slipped it into his pocket, his skin heating a moment as he felt Neuffer's eyes on him, and not knowing why he did it other than, perhaps, to lift it in Dreyer's honor one day.

"I've worked a few suicides in my time, and I never heard of one that got out of bed to do himself in. And he would never have gone out to that music." Reinhardt left it at that, letting Neuffer draw what conclusion he would.

"But, if there was nothing, no music, how would they have masked the gunshot?"

"Gunshots are not exactly a rarity at this time," Reinhardt said, dryly. Neuffer flushed. "Witnesses?"

"No one saw anyone. I mean . . . no one saw anyone . . ."

"Untoward?" Reinhardt finished. Neuffer looked miserable, like a wet cat with his slicked-back hair. "What does that tell you, Neuffer? It just tells you the killer was probably one of us."

"This was murder. Oh, God," Neuffer said, his eyes wrinkling themselves shut tight. "It's all going to hell, again."

"What do you mean, 'again'?"

Neuffer stared at the ceiling. "Nothing. It's nothing." His voice rasped, as if he feared being overheard. Reinhardt was again struck by the resemblance to the Kaiser. The way he had always seemed so unsure around his fighting men, the ones who had labored and fought and died for him in the trenches in the first war.

"It's something," said Reinhardt, making his voice softer despite the edge he wanted to put in it. "Tell me."

"You're a policeman. A proper one. I'm just a . . . stuffed shirt, compared to you. This," Neuffer said, pointing at Dreyer, "it's just like the other one."

"What other one?"

"Colonel Wedel."

Reinhardt kept his face blank as his mind raced over Neuffer's words. "The officer in charge of the stolen defense plans," he remembered, thinking back to the briefing, on the first day here.

"Yes." The Feldgendarme nodded. "Colonel Wedel. He killed himself, too."

"Tell me, Neuffer," said Reinhardt.

"We found Wedel dead in his quarters. He had shot himself in the head. There was a note as well. This was a couple of days after we had questioned everyone who had anything to do with the plans. We found nothing. No one and nothing out of place. It was like the thieves had just appeared and disappeared. No traces. Nothing. After all that, I thought then . . . I thought then that Wedel was the one. You know. When you have eliminated everything . . . whatever remains must be the truth."

Reinhardt nodded, reappraising his view of this man he had dismissed as a nobody, a flunky. "You said nothing?"

"I . . . tried. I suppose. But there was no proof and no one really cared. I mean, the theft of those plans turned everything upside down. And why? Why would he have done it? I talked to him, you see. The day he killed himself. I asked him if he had had anything to do with it. With the theft. I felt I could, you see. We knew each other, after a fashion. I asked him if there was anything wrong. Anything he wanted to tell me."

"And?"

"Nothing. Wedel just seemed to fade away as I spoke. Then, when he killed himself, I thought . . . I feared . . . I thought maybe I was the one who pushed him to kill himself. That if I had left him alone . . ."

"You blame yourself. You shouldn't. Maybe Wedel didn't do it," Reinhardt said, pointing at Dreyer. "*He* didn't. I'm sure of it. And if Wedel did do it, maybe . . . maybe he thought it was the only way out for him."

"What do you mean?" Neuffer whispered.

"Tell me something first," said Reinhardt, planting himself squarely in front of Neuffer. "What role does Erdmann play in getting men sent to the penal battalion?"

"A soldier must commit a breach of discipline to be court-martialed. These days, that can be over in a matter of minutes, and the sentence can be transfer to a penal battalion. The courts-martial have a presiding judge, assisted by two officers. The sentences are then supposedly reviewed by a senior officer who confirms or rejects them, and is sometimes advised by another judge."

"Erdmann is that judge?"

"And Herzog is usually that officer. They both have reputations . . . Discipline. Sacrifice. Washing one's sins away in the service of the Fatherland," Neuffer said, holding Reinhardt's eyes, with an acid spin to the words.

"They're believers?"

"Isn't it obvious? Them and God only knows who else, still. They all believe. They've always believed. And they'll never stop. Please. What did you mean? About Wedel."

"Maybe he *was* the one who took his own plans. But maybe someone forced him to and he couldn't live with it. Or he became a liability to whoever coerced him. Because I'll tell you what I think happened here, Neuffer. There were at least two men, possibly three. They just walked in here. Two of them held Dreyer down, in that chair, while the third put a gun to my friend's head and killed him. They didn't take anything. They didn't ask anything. They just killed him. Then they walked out. That means they were German."

25

They just killed him.

Reinhardt turned the words over and over in his mind on the short drive back to the barracks. The firing had started up again to the north, just beyond the humped line of the hills. The firing was still light enough, staccato bursts, but it was sustained, a rolling crackle across the lightening sky.

They just killed him.

He had needed to say them to believe it, he realized, as he followed Scheller and Lainer through the halls of the barracks. Neither of them had said anything on the drive back, nor during the walk through the barracks halls. Reinhardt's mind lurched back and forth, slopping around the thought of his friend sprawled dead in a chair, washing up against thoughts of Vukić, the boy, conjuring up images of the Greeks dead against a pitted wall, Valter sitting hunched over a table in a dusty attic, an Ustaša vanishing back into the darkness, the darkness flowing over him, the lines and curves of the man's face vanishing last.

He had to shake out of this, he knew, as they walked into the Feldjaeger operations room. So early in the morning it was still quiet, but there was a rhythm there, a hum to the place, and heads lifted here and there to watch them go past, Scheller thumping his door open with the heel of his hand. He waited until Reinhardt and Lainer walked in, then shoved it closed. He looked at Reinhardt, who took a long, low breath, steeling himself for what was about to come.

"So? Where *do* you stand with your investigation?" Scheller asked, finally.

"I don't have anyone in custody, if that's what you are asking, sir."

"That's what he's asking," grated Lainer.

"I don't know who killed your men, Lainer. I do know killing them was part of something much bigger, and it's got something to do with the activities of that penal battalion and its commander, a Major Jansky."

"The one you've just been ordered to leave the hell alone?" Lainer muttered.

"Go on," said Scheller, his eyes flat.

"It's complicated . . ." he began.

"Then make it simple," interrupted Lainer.

"I can't," Reinhardt shot back.

"Well, maybe if you spent less time with tarts, and more time trying to find who killed my men . . ."

". . . and it won't help if you take that attitude," Reinhardt slashed back, squaring up to the big Feldjaeger, his face burning again. Lainer's head went down and his eyes slitted, but he nodded after a moment, an appraising light in his eyes as if he had found something he had been looking for.

"Let's start at the beginning," said Reinhardt.

"Let's sit," said Scheller, pointing at the chairs. "Keep going, Reinhardt."

"The Feldjaeger were killed investigating a disturbance in the early morning at a construction site, which was being run by elements from a penal battalion constructing an anti-aircraft emplacement," said Reinhardt, looking at Lainer, then letting his eyes bring Scheller in. "The disturbance was probably the killers disposing of five bodies, all of which are unidentifiable. Although I suspect they might have been soldiers, I still don't have proof of it. Remember, we have no witnesses to what happened, only conjecture. Remember as well, the day before that, I came across a massacre in the forest, and I found what I took to be the three burned bodies of German soldiers, because of some uniform remnants at the scene. At the time, I thought I had found the bodies of deserters, because I found evidence that soldiers from different units were there, infrantrymen and artillerymen.

"I questioned Major Jansky about the construction site. His answers, and those of his men, were fairly consistent, and he was cooperative enough. But on leaving, one of the soldiers serving in the unit sought me out and swore he had information about foul play afoot in the battalion. I was unsure how to treat him, partly because the man was clearly unstable, and because he admitted he was a Feldgendarmerie informant within the ranks.

"Because I was thinking of the Ustaše as primarily responsible, I sought out the survivors of that massacre in the forest to see if I could get anything more from them. The Ustaše had come for them, first, and they had vanished. My inquiries at the Pale House . . ."

"You were at the Pale House?" Scheller queried, his brows furled.

"I was, sir. I went where the investigation took me," he said, willing the colonel to remember those same words he had said the first time they had met, in Vienna. "With Captain Langenkamp's assistance, I questioned the Ustaše and was told no one of the refugees' description had been brought in. I had the description as well of the Ustaša who arrested them, and was told he was missing."

He took a deep breath. The waters were deep and treacherous from here on—Vukić, Perić, Alexiou, even Dreyer—and he could not afford a slip. "Later that night, the Ustaše brought me to another murder scene—this is the third, after the forest, and the construction site— and showed me the mutilated bodies of four of their men, and claimed the Partisans had done it."

"Had they?"

"I very much doubt it. Too much was wrong with the scene. It was staged. And one of the bodies was the Ustaša I wanted to interview over the disappearance of the refugees."

"You think they killed one of their own men to stop him from talking to you?" Lainer asked, incredulously.

"I think they may have killed him because he was a liability," said Reinhardt.

"I'm still not seeing this conspiracy with the penal battalion or Jansky in all this."

"The construction site was being worked by the penal battalion. The forest site was a logging camp, sir. It was run by the penal battalion. That's why there was evidence of more than one type of soldier there, because men from all units get thrown into a penal battalion. And then a serving soldier in the battalion came forward to offer me information, but he was found dead yesterday morning."

"Bloody hell, Reinhardt!" exclaimed Lainer. "Remind me not to spend too much time with you."

"Lainer, be a good fellow, and give me some time alone with Reinhardt."

Scheller's face stayed impassive as Lainer's twisted, but he nodded and walked out of the office, shutting the door behind him. Then, to Reinhardt's surprise, Scheller leaned into a cabinet and clattered a bottle of slivo onto the table, two glasses bunched by the rims between his thick fingers.

"Reinhardt, is there any way of keeping this simple?"

"No, sir," said Reinhardt, watching the slivo flow into the glasses. "That's because I don't know what's going on. I suspect a lot, but have proof of little. I don't know who killed our men. But in investigating their deaths, I have uncovered something else. I am almost certain Major Jansky is involved in quite significant corruption, to do with selling a form of asylum to foreigners. In return for payment, he accepts them as foreign volunteers—as hiwis—into his battalion. He gives them menial tasks, and he keeps them out of harm's way."

"You suspect this?"

"I am sure of this," Reinhardt answered. "I spoke with one of these hiwis—a Greek, who I am sure served in their security battalions—and he confirmed he had paid his way into the unit as a way of escaping his country and throwing off any judicial pursuit after the war."

"This would be one of the Greeks you said you knew nothing about but that General Herzog had shot tonight?"

Reinhardt nodded. "I'm guessing they tried to make good their escape. With whatever they could carry. The Greek confirmed to me that Jansky had been paid in gold they had stolen, and there was still some of it left."

Scheller sighed, shook his head. "As if we don't have enough on our plates without something like this. I don't even know if we could start to investigate something like that . . ." He chewed his lower lip, softly. "What about the judge?"

"Judge Marcus Dreyer has—had—an interest in this Major Jansky, as the two of them had quite some history together. Judge Dreyer was convinced of Jansky's corruption and, before the three Feldjaeger were killed, he had asked for my help in investigating him. I had said no. But as the penal battalion and Jansky were appearing too often for coincidence, I offered him my help, which he accepted."

"And your help was such he decided to kill himself."

Reinhardt went pale. He felt the blood drain away, a hollow pit form where his stomach was. "That's . . ." was all he managed.

"Harsh?" Scheller had the good grace to look embarrassed.

"He was my friend, sir," Reinhardt whispered. Scheller made to speak, but Reinhardt shook his head slightly. "I've asked myself the same question, sir, don't worry. Dreyer was killed because of his connection to this . . . investigation. His theories about Jansky and my inquiries into our dead men overlapped. And because of that, he was killed. He didn't commit suicide."

"That's a stretch, Reinhardt."

"No, sir, it's not. He had done nothing different to deserve this. The only thing different was me. Somehow, me and him joining together meant we were a threat."

"What about you? You're a threat, and no one's taken a shot at you."

"That I know of," said Reinhardt, grimly, thinking of those two Albanians, and what might have happened if he had arrived just a few minutes earlier.

Scheller looked long and hard at Reinhardt, then sighed. "And that's where you are?"

"That's where I am. Except to add that I suspect some in the Ustaše are taking advantage of Jansky's 'offer.' Do you remember Langen-kamp briefing us on some of the senior Ustaše disappearing? Well, I wouldn't be surprised to find they have joined up as hiwis. And I met Jansky at the Pale House, on his way to meet a senior Ustaša."

"He sounds like a piece of work, this Jansky."

"He is. And this . . . this is where I start to wonder at all this. I ask myself, could he do what he's done, what he's doing, without help? Without help from someone higher up, more senior."

"What, like the two characters we just met this evening?" Rein-hardt nodded. "Christ. What the hell am I supposed to do with this, Reinhardt?" Reinhardt shook his head, not knowing what to say. Hav-ing recounted the whole thing, he was suddenly appalled at both the complexity of it and its vacuous nature, and that was without impart-ing what he had held back, like what Neven had said about the Ger-man involvement in the killings in the forest. There was a lot there, but not much to go on. Like the contradiction of his nature and his duty as a Feldjaeger. "Everything's coming apart in the city, and I need everyone here and now. I don't know if I can have you on this any-more." Scheller paused. "What? You've nothing to say? That's hardly like you."

Reinhardt found a smile for the colonel's dry attempt at humor. "First time for everything" he said, quietly. "I suppose I expected it. But I'm surprised, to say the least, that you accept what I said after what happened tonight."

"Don't get me wrong, Reinhardt," said Scheller, swirling his drink. "You put me in a bind. You should have kept me informed of what you were doing. But I have to say," he said, eyeing Reinhardt as he took a sip of his slivo, "Herzog is a complete arse." Reinhardt swallowed hard, choked, and coughed. "And when a complete arse like that says one thing, I tend to think another. Take a moment, get your breath back," he said, deadpan.

"Yes, sir," Reinhardt wheezed.

"Well, it's not that I want to do it, but . . . things being the way they are"—Scheller sighed—"it looks like we'll have to chalk Lainer's men up to bad luck. But when we're out of here, I want you to come and see me about this Major Jansky. Let's have a look at what you've got, and we'll see what we can do when things are quieter. Sound fair?"

"It's fair, sir," said Reinhardt, and was surprised to feel himself relieved. As if, in recounting what he had, what he knew, what he suspected, he had come to a realization that there was too much for one man, for this time and place. "Perhaps, sir, you'll allow me to wrap up a few loose ends."

"Like?"

"I have a few pieces of hard evidence, some names to follow up on, and a doctor who promised an autopsy on those five bodies. I would like to finish up what I can on those." And find some way to contact the Partisans and tell them where to find their Ustaše.

"I can't let you do that, Reinhardt."

"Just today, sir. That's it. A few hours."

Scheller worked his lips one against the other, keeping Reinhardt still with his eyes. "Why?"

That was a good question. Why?

Reinhardt realized that he had come to a simple truth during the night as he had lain in Vukić's arms. He had felt abandoned and ill-used since his epiphany two years ago, high on the side of that mountain, after his decision to play a different role in this war. He had searched for men who thought like him, and he had found them, and once again he had found choices, but once again made no decisions. He had been in search of a cause, but thought that cause had to be something grandiose. He realized now that he did not always have to have his eyes on the far horizon, on some goal or objective so much greater than him or his abilities, waiting for a summons, a clarion call to action. It was enough, Reinhardt now realized, that the cause be right to him, and be the right thing to do.

"Someone is committing murder, and . . . seeking justice for that has to be a cause worth fighting for," he said, finally, feeling suddenly the weight of Dreyer's death.

"Maybe dying for?" Reinhardt's mouth opened, moved, but nothing came out. Scheller shook his head. "Forget it. Nothing so grandiose. But sometimes, Reinhardt, it's worthwhile to remember we're not about justice. We're about discipline." The colonel sighed, knocking back the last of his drink. "Fine. I'll give you one day and a driver. And then that's it."

"Yes, sir. Thank you."

"How did Benfeld shape up?"

"Well, sir."

"You can have him, if you want."

"You'll need him, won't you?"

"If he helps you get the job done faster, take him."

"Very good, sir."

"Dismissed."

But at the door, as Reinhardt made to open it, Scheller called him back.

"Reinhardt? Can you guess who did it? Killed our men?"

Reinhardt paused at the door, his hand tight on the handle. "The simplest things are usually where the truth lies, sir," he said, turning around. "All these people—our men included—were killed because they knew or saw something. What they knew or saw . . ." He shook his head, and sighed, trying to navigate his tired mind around what he knew, and what he had to hold back. "If I had to guess, I would say the Ustaše. I can place them nearly everywhere this investigation has taken me. They almost certainly killed four of their own and weren't afraid to flaunt them to me. I'm pretty sure a few of them are taking the chance to get out of this war early. Maybe the five from that construction site were witnesses to their plan or were involved but got cold feet and had to be gotten rid of. I know they went after those witnesses to the forest massacre, which means those survivors saw something. And as it was the Ustaše who went after them, it stands to reason they were involved up in the forest as well. Everything points to them." Everything except the fact that, according to Neven, it had been Feldgendarmes who had shot those refugees in the forest, and the three men, and he still could not work out why they had done that.

And Dreyer had to have been killed by a German, but he could not understand that either, nor bring together the links between it all. It was there, just out of reach, he knew it, and given time he knew he could put it together.

"A falling-out among thieves," considered Scheller, softly, his eyes considering, weighing, and Reinhardt wondered if the colonel sensed his own unease, that he was holding something back.

"It could be."

"It could be a lot of things, is what I'm hearing. And what I'm hearing is we probably have to walk away from this. Even if it was the Ustaše, we've no proof."

"I'm afraid you are right, sir."

"I'll break it to Lainer. Won't it make him happy, us pointing the finger at the Ustaše and not able to do a damn thing about it."

26

They just killed him.

That litany was in his head, again, like a clock, marking down the time left him to make some sense of this.

"Who do we have on the main switchboard, and who is on duty now?"

The sergeant on duty at the radio blinked at his watch, then up at Reinhardt. "Corporal Ossig."

"Have you seen Lieutenant Benfeld?"

"Not for several hours, sir. I believe he's off duty."

Reinhardt walked away, back into the corridors, making his way to the barracks' main switchboard and radio room. He showed his identification to the guard on duty and asked for Corporal Ossig to be brought to him.

They just killed him.

This was bigger than corruption, or bribery. No matter how much money was being made on what Reinhardt suspected, he could not think why they would have killed him. Nor who the hell "they" were, and if he was not careful, he would start to be thought of as mad. Cracked. Obsessed. Like Dreyer. Dreyer had been considered a buffoon. He had been a buffoon with the thankless task of looking into the activities of the Ustaše. He had had a fixation on Jansky, about whom he suspected a lot but knew nothing. He had suspected a lot and known nothing for a long time. So why now? What had happened *now*?

Reinhardt had whispered he was sorry and not known why, but now he did. He was what was different. He had changed things. He had added something different, an edge to Dreyer's suspicions. He had skirted the edge of what Dreyer believed was out there, found evidence Dreyer had never known existed.

They just killed him.

Corporal Ossig was middle-aged, the image of a grocer—portly, solid, thinning hair combed over his head in damp strands, and a pencil behind his ear—but he wore the Winter Campaign medal and infantry assault badge on his tunic together with his Iron Cross, and a scar ribboned its way down the side of his head. He stood calmly before Reinhardt, not flinching when Reinhardt took his elbow and drew him to one side.

"I need to contact someone, as soon as possible, and I need to do so in confidence. Is that possible?"

"Yes, sir. Where is your contact?"

"Vienna. This is the extension where he is barracked," he said, handing over a slip of paper, hoping the details were still accurate. "You are to tell him Captain Gregor Reinhardt needs to speak with him urgently."

"You'll wait, sir?"

"Yes. Is it telephone or radio to Vienna?"

"We still have lines, so we'll try the telephone, first."

Reinhardt took a seat in a corner as Ossig vanished back into the communications center. He took the *soldbuchs* from his pocket, looking through them again, one by one, slowly, comparing them to his own. With the exception that his own *soldbuch* had no photograph— the older books, like his, were not required to have one—he could find nothing amiss in them. They seemed in order, and yet there had to be something. The very fact of how and where he had found them made that obvious, he thought, returning again to Abler's *soldbuch*, thinking how the photograph was familiar. He looked at it carefully: a thin man, narrow face looking to its right with a curve of ear visible, hair carefully parted, uniform collar buttoned up but hanging loose around a thin neck. He unfolded the list, read the names again in that flowing copperplate, the numbers next to each of them.

They just killed him.

Nothing. He could not make anything out. He put his head back against the wall, feeling sick, nauseated with fatigue, thinking that the last time he ate was yesterday, that quick mug of soup before he went looking for Kostas. He closed his eyes, and he dreamed hard and suddenly, a morass of images that came swirling up at him.

He stood in a forest clearing under a sky empty but for hanging black filaments, birds and scavengers that rode the high winds, gyring up and around and down, a frenzy of wings and raucous calls as they stooped and dived on something on the ground. He looked down and the boys from Kragujevac stood there, and they blended, merged into Neven, who held up a bloodied gorget in his two hands. An Ustaša loomed up behind him, and Neven was gone, the gorget falling slowly to earth, trailed by its chain, each link winking and moving. It landed gently on the body of a girl, lying as if asleep in the long grass, the chain molding itself to the curve of her shoulder.

The patrol made it back just in time, just as the weld between sky and land was loosened with the ribbon of the day's first sunlight. The tangled scrawl of no-man's-land etched itself across the light, the blasted angles of trees, the skirl of wire and the humped roll of the earth. Reinhardt knew they had to get into cover as otherwise the light would silhouette them perfectly to the British behind them.

Shoving the Tommy they had taken prisoner in front of them, the stormtroopers tumbled over the lip of their trench as first one shot, then a few more, then dozens blazed across at them from the British trenches. A machine gunner opened up from the bunker to the left, the noise deafening. For a moment all was pandemonium and then, as it always seemed to, as if by some unspoken accord, the firing dipped, then stopped, as if honor had been assured, and there was silence.

Brauer was the first to chuckle. Then Rosen. Lebert and Topp giggled like a pair of girls, and even Olbrich's normally taciturn face cracked a smile. The Tommy rolled furious among them across the bottom of the trench, his eyes ablaze above the filthy cloth they had gagged him with, and Rosen pointed at him and they laughed the harder for the man's outraged glare, and because they were alive.

They handed the prisoner over to the guard, watching as he was led away down the trench. At the point where a hole had been blasted in the parapet the guards shoved the Tommy to his knees, and they all bent double past the gap. Past the sign that said BEWARE—SNIPER, past the fluttering red rags and the skull that some wag had stuck on a pole and topped with a British tin helmet. They had christened the skull "George" in honor of Britain's king, and would wave it in the gap when bored, taking bets on whether the British snipers would stir themselves to take a shot at it.

"Oh, for Christ's sake, would you look at that," Rosen muttered.

They all looked. Squeezing to one side to let the guard and prisoner through, a soldier was struggling through the sludge of the trench's floor. His uniform was largely clean, save for the streaks of mud at knee and elbow where he must have fallen, and a pair of rich-looking leather boots climbed to his knees. He was a tall man, all gangly limbs, a round head perched upon wide shoulders. The patrol watched as the newcomer surged up to the gap in the parapet without seeing it, watching with the morbid curiosity of those inured to violence to see what would happen.

"Ten to one he doesn't make it," Lebert offered.

"Ten to one he does," retorted Olbrich.

"He won't," said Topp. "The Tommies are awake. He's got the sun behind him."

Reinhardt watched as the man gasped and staggered right into the gap, where he paused, straightened, and brushed at his uniform. There was a collective intake of breath from the patrol. The man *ducked his head as he picked a clod of mud from his tunic and a bullet slit the air where his skull had been a second ago. The man heard the crack of the shot and straightened, peering around, craning his head on his neck. Another shot whipped past.*

"Talk about the luck of fools or children," Brauer muttered.

"Will you for God's sake get down! DOWN!" roared Reinhardt.

The man looked at him, turning his head, and a third shot missed. The man's eyes widened as he realized what was happening and he flung himself to the floor as a fourth shot flattened itself against the back of the trench. From across no-man's-land, Reinhardt could hear the British jeering and laughing.

"You missed, you tossers," Reinhardt yelled back as he walked over to the man. He twisted his fist into the soldier's collar and hauled him to his feet. "What the fuck is the matter with you? Are you crazy?"

"No," the man gasped, his mouth wide as he looked helplessly at the ruin of his uniform. "Just new."

"Are you lost?"

"I'm looking for Lieutenant Reinhardt."

"That's me."

"Ah. I'm pleased to meet you. I'm Lieutenant Dreyer. Your new company quartermaster."

"A quartermaster's stirred himself to come visit us at the front?" Brauer frowned.

"A rarity, is it?"

"Somewhat."

"I understand these might be rare, too," Dreyer said, as he swung a haversack off his shoulder and pulled out a wooden box of cigars. There was a murmur of appreciation as he handed them around. "These really ought to be smoked as soon as possible. Plenty more where these came from, if only the gentlemen would ask no questions."

"If you've a bottle of brandy in there, I'll call you a saint," said Topp.

"Say no more," Dreyer quipped as a bottle came out of the bag, and the murmurs got louder.

Brauer saluted him with the bottle. "If you can manage this often, then you're worth your weight in gold."

"And he is a large lad," observed Rosen.

"Always take care of the quartermaster," said Brauer, sagely, as he drank deeply.

"What's the occasion, Lieutenant?" asked Reinhardt.

"None. Nothing. I assure you, no ulterior motives," Dreyer answered.

"What are you doing?" Reinhardt asked, again. "People like you don't normally come up here."

"People like me?" Dreyer repeated. Reinhardt said nothing, and Dreyer looked from face to face. The others had gone silent, everyone watching. "It's true, I didn't need to come. But how can you form objective opinions about a situation without experiencing it firsthand?"

"'Objective opinions?'" Brauer's face creased in incomprehension. "What are you, a lawyer?"

"Yes," Dreyer replied, simply. He breathed shallowly through his mouth, and coughed. "I needed to come. How else can I look after you if I don't know how you live?"

Reinhardt saw it then, that the man was terrified, and taking refuge in what he knew best. The patrol was silent, and then Olbrich leaned forward and clapped Dreyer on the arm, offering him the bottle. "Have some of this, it's really quite good."

There was a wave of laughter, Dreyer joining in sheepishly. He took a swig of the brandy, swallowed, and coughed. The men laughed again. With his mouth closed, Dreyer sucked a breath through his nose. He coughed again, his eyes popping wide as he snorted brandy through his nose, gasping for air. The others rolled about, laughing helplessly.

Reinhardt watched as Dreyer heaved air through his mouth, his eyes clenched shut.

"Are you all right?" he asked.

Dreyer shook his head. "It's the smell. I don't . . . How can you stand it?"

Reinhardt looked at him, then caught Brauer's eyes. His sergeant shrugged. They looked at each other: mud-smeared, festooned with weapons, unshaven, eyes like pits beneath the dark lines of their brows. Reinhardt let his eyes roam the heavy muddied walls of the trench, seeing it suddenly anew, like Dreyer would. The detritus and refuse and ruin, the flat, brown glaze of water where it dotted and pooled the floor, and there, just above their heads, the stark and blackened lines of fingers where a corpse's hand had pierced the bogged curve of the parapet. Reinhardt breathed deeply, as deep as he could, and only at the end of his breath did it catch on something. Some hint of the stench that Dreyer could barely handle.

He frowned, his mood darkening, and when the bottle came his way he turned it skyward and let the brandy flood his throat.

"Captain."

Reinhardt woke, his mind almost seared blank by his tiredness, and that tangled spasm of images. He blinked at Ossig.

"I have your call, sir. It is not your contact, but someone else. This way."

He escorted Reinhardt into the communications center proper, a long room that hummed with energy, long banks of radios with black buttons and white dials, a dozen operators with headphones hunched over them. Ossig led Reinhardt to a partitioned section with a radio telephone and left him to it.

"Hello?" Reinhardt said into the receiver.

"*Hello?*" came a voice back, made tinny by the seashore purr of the line.

"I am looking for Captain Hannes Koenig. Who is this?"

"*Who are you?*" came the voice back. "*Do you know the time?*"

"This is a friend of his. Captain Gregor Reinhardt."

"*Ah. A friend, you say. I am sorry, I have bad news for you. Captain Koenig has passed away.*"

"What do you mean?" demanded Reinhardt, his voice sharper than he would have liked.

"*I am afraid Captain Koenig took his own life.*"

"When?"

"Yesterday."

"When, yesterday?"

"Late in the evening."

Reinhardt sat in silence.

"Hello? I say, are you still there, Captain?"

"Did he say anything? Give . . . any sign of his intention?"

"It was a complete surprise," said the voice. There was a pause. "But *he left a message."*

"What . . . what did it say?"

"The strangest thing. It said something like, 'This is not all I am.' Something like that."

Reinhardt went cold. He must have said something to the man on the other end of the line, some parting courtesy, but he could not remember, he could only remember coming to himself sitting hunched over the telephone with the receiver back in its cradle. *"This is not all I am."* It was, if anything could be, the motto of the group Reinhardt had found, in Vienna. Their so-called resistance group. And if Koenig had written it, it meant they had been coming for him. He had done something to call attention to himself. That phrase was a message to the others. It was their way of using their deaths as a warning.

Reinhardt had put them on to him, he realized, a sudden drench of sweat washing out and over him. It meant what Reinhardt had found here, it reached as far as Vienna. If it reached that far, why not farther?

Just what the hell had he come across?

Somehow, he found himself back in the almost-empty Feldjaeger operations room. He checked his watch. Despite all that had happened, it was still early morning, not even five o'clock. On a table in front of him was the little stack of *soldbuchs*, and the sheet of paper. He had not even realized he had taken them out, and he leafed again through the little books, from tan cover to tan cover, over and past the entries in neat little hands that told the stories, to those who knew how to read them properly, of the soldiers' lives these books had belonged to. Some of it Reinhardt could read and understand, but he was sure there was something wrong in them; he was just not able to pick up on what it might be.

From outside the building came a roll of gunfire, starting slow, then picking up. Dull thuds of artillery rang bass counterpoint through it all. Men in the operations room exchanged looks, put their heads back down. Reinhardt sat and listened, but although the gunfire slackened, it did not stop, coming from the north, again.

Reinhardt felt himself sinking, as if he were starting to collapse inward into himself, and he knew he had to move before the world sped up to the rhythm of that gunfire and left no room for him. He knew he held one of the keys in his hands, but he needed someone to unlock it for him.

Despite the early hour, the barracks halls were as full as ever with the hustle of men and the bellow of orders. In the main operations room he found the directions he wanted, to the administration offices, although the harassed officer who spoke to him wished him luck at finding anyone there. When he arrived, Reinhardt found the officer was correct. The offices were empty, a slew of papers across the floors, tables and chairs in disarray, and a smell of burning in the air from a wastebasket that still smoked.

Reinhardt's face curled up in frustration, before another idea occurred to him, and he raced back through the tumult of the halls, back to operations. In one of the offices that split off the main room was military intelligence. His old stomping ground, he thought ironically. The suite of offices was full, a haze of cigarette smoke hanging over a dozen or so men all talking excitedly into telephones, radios, with each other. He caught the eye of one of the men and told him he needed to speak with someone in counterintelligence, preferably someone knowledgeable about documentation, or more precisely, forged documentation. An officer was pointed out to him, and Reinhardt crossed the room, weaving his way through a tangle of wires and limbs and boxes of papers.

"I need a favor," Reinhardt said.

The officer, a fellow captain, looked up from stuffing papers into a box, his eyes bouncing from Reinhardt's face to his gorget, flickering across Reinhardt's decorations, and plunging down to his armband. His eyebrows rose, and he straightened. "Anything for an esteemed member of our Feldjaegerkorps."

Reinhardt extended his hand. "Reinhardt," he said. "Got somewhere quiet we can talk for five minutes?"

"Prien," replied the officer. "I'll give you ten if you have a smoke. Over here." He pointed, leading Reinhardt to a corner of the room where there was a small niche in the wall. "What can I do for you?"

"I want you to look at something for me," said Reinhardt, as he lit cigarettes for them both. "Know anything about *soldbuchs*? I think I've got some forgeries here, and I would appreciate it if you took a look at them."

Prien's eyebrows went up as Reinhardt handed over the books. "Interesting," he murmured, flicking each of them open, quickly, pausing at Keppel's, his thumb stroking over the place where there should have been a photo. "And what makes you think they're forgeries?"

"We came across them during an anti-Partisan sweep," Reinhardt lied around a mouthful of smoke.

"If it's true, this could be a worrying development," Prien said, taking a magnifying glass from a pocket. "Give me a minute, let's see . . ."

Reinhardt watched as he examined each of the pages of the books, and his five minutes stretched to ten, and on. He kept his patience under control as Prien turned page after page, until he had worked his way through the three of them, and straightened up with a wince and a hand in his back.

"Well?"

"Well, these two," he said, holding up Abler's and Maywald's, "they're not fakes. They're originals, but they're replacements. See, here," he said, pointing to the top of the first page. "That number? It's the code for a replacement book. So, if they were being used for nefarious purposes, you would need to find the original records for which these are replacements."

"Interesting," Reinhardt murmured. "What about the other one. For Keppel."

"I'm not sure about that one. Other than that the photo's missing, there's nothing I can see wrong with it, or unusual. If it was part of some shady business it could be it was a trial run. Maybe they tried to rework it and failed. I mean, it's not impossible to forge entries, or alter them, but it takes time, and you'd need a pretty good forger and some special equipment."

"Or maybe they found a pretty good forger, and he didn't finish whatever he started."

"There's always that."

Reinhardt shook his head, his spirits deflating. "Well . . . thank you, I suppose."

"Hang on, hang on. There's a few bits and pieces that are interesting. Let's put aside this one—Keppel's—for a moment, and look at the other two." He spread them both open at the cover and first page. "All's in order. Serial numbers of the books, dog tag numbers, ranks, promotions, names, blood type, gas mask size, and military identification number. Nothing jumps out, right? Next pages, personal details, age, place of birth, height, physical appearance and distinguishing characteristics . . ."

"Abler had a scar," noted Reinhardt.

"Yes. It's mentioned later in his medical record. Shrapnel wound on the neck. But staying with these first pages, we have civilian professions—a plumber and a carpenter, apparently—next of kin . . ."

"Both blank," said Reinhardt, looking between them.

"Yes. No loved one waiting for them at home. Parents deceased as well, as there's nothing there either. Religion, both Catholic. Shoe sizes. Always found that one funny. And here is where we have further proof of these being replacements. Here, just above the unit notarization, we have the notation 'replacement for lost *soldbuch*,' and the signing officer." Reinhardt squinted down at the signature. "Don't bother. Signing officers usually sign like a doctor on a prescription.

Only a nurse can read it, and we don't have any nurses around. Got another cigarette?"

Reinhardt handed one over. "We can't read the name, but we can see the title. In both cases, it reads 'company commander.'"

"Doesn't mean much. Those things were usually put in with a stamp. Anyone could do it. No, what's interesting is this, here," he said, pointing to a faded stamp next to the company commander's signature, a round shape with Gothic text and an eagle and swastika, and at the bottom, the name of the unit. "Can you see?"

"'999th Field Punishment Battalion,'" said Reinhardt, his eyes flicking between the two.

"If you look on the first page, you'll see both Abler and Maywald of course started their military careers in different units. That's normal. Soldiers transfer. But in both these cases," he said, flicking to the pages in the *soldbuchs* that listed the soldiers' assignments, "they were sentenced to a term in a penal unit. Abler in October 1944, Maywald in January this year. But in both cases, these replacement books were issued within days of each other."

"In March 1945," said Reinhardt, nodding as he followed Prien's finger. The information was laid out, right there, but it took someone with a different set of eyes to point it out.

"You suspect foul play, right? Here's another interesting thing. These two are replacement books for soldiers who joined up, respectively, in 1940 and 1942. Back then, when these two joined up . . . do you remember how the old *soldbuchs* looked? The old *soldbuchs* . . ."

". . . did not have photographs," Reinhardt finished, thinking of his own book.

"Exactly. Photographs were introduced as a security measure in 1943."

"So, let me understand this," said Reinhardt, his excitement mounting. "These two *soldbuchs* are replacements for older books, either lost or destroyed, we can't know. Both the original books were issued prior to 1943, therefore no photographic correlation of the holders is possible between the originals, if they existed, and these. These were issued in March 1945, by the 999th Field Punishment Battalion."

"Correct," said Prien, around a mouthful of smoke. "And both these men are Volksdeutsche."

"Volksdeutsche?" Reinhardt repeated.

"Ethnic Germans, yes. Abler was born in . . ." Prien flicked back through the pages. "Here. Abler is from Marburg, Slovenia. And Maywald is from Troppau, Protectorate of Bohemia and Moravia."

"What are the odds . . . ?" It had been staring him in the face from the beginning.

"Whatever they are, rather low, I would have thought," Prien answered.

"Thanks, you've been very helpful. I don't suppose you've any idea what these are?" Reinhardt hoped, pointing to the six-digit numbers next to the handwritten names on his list.

"Nope, not a clue." Prien smiled.

"Ah, well, it was worth a try."

Prien nodded. "But him there," he said, pointing at a fellow officer, "he's a lawyer. He might know."

27

Everything was linked, Reinhardt knew. He had known that as a policeman. He had known it as an intelligence officer. Paper begat paper. Forms and rules created cages of procedure. A web that wove into and around and through your life, strand after strand. You had to know how it worked, and how to get around it, and where to look for the holes in it that ought not to have been there. Blocked on one path, you looked on another. A birth certificate, a high school diploma, a medical record, an identity document, a driving license, a police record, an army *soldbuch*, or a judicial record. These became links in a chain, a chain that made up a life, there to be read and dissected for those who knew how, and those who needed to.

Every army unit had a department for administration staffed by an adjutant, often a legal officer. Like the one Prien pointed out to him, a man with a fussy air. He had taken one harassed look at Reinhardt's paper and told him what those numbers were, and those numbers had led him here, to an all-but-abandoned section of the barracks, to a warehouse filled with packing cases.

Paper begat paper. It was a sludge that flowed from one desk to another. Some took a mania to it and could not live without it. Others hated it and did their best to ignore it. Others knew how to use it to beat the system it was supposed to serve, but whatever you did, the paper remained. Maybe filed, maybe hidden, maybe forgotten or misplaced, but it was there. You just had to know where and how to look.

The room in front of him was stacked with rows of crates and boxes, the wood colored dark yellow by the ceiling's dim electric light. Despite the cold, there was a warmth to the air, the smell of wood and varnish and paper. Of records, files, proceedings, case studies . . . It was all here, and although part of Reinhardt was astonished anyone would try to save this, another part of him knew the value of what he was looking at.

"Where are they, then?" Reinhardt asked.

The sergeant with him looked up and down at crates stenciled with numbers and names, back down at the sheaf of papers stuck to his clipboard. "Boxes from the State House should be here. There!"

The two of them heaved down half a dozen boxes, and the sergeant levered them open with a crowbar to reveal files in blue and yellow cardboard folders. The sergeant looked at it askance. "You sure you'll be able to finish, sir?"

"If it's in order, yes, Sergeant, and you give me a hand."

"Yes, sir, but . . ."

"Whatever it is, it'll wait. You take that box. We're looking for these files," Reinhardt said, showing him the paper with its numbers next to each name.

"Yes, sir," said the sergeant, just perilously short of a sigh. "What is it we're looking at anyway, sir?"

"Court-martial records, Sergeant."

"That'd be the files from the court-martial office, sir?" Reinhardt stopped, looking up, and nodded. "They're not here, sir. They're in the annex. It all came over from the State House earlier this morning. There was a real mess there last night. Someone got killed and it messed up the shipments. There's been hell to pay, apparently. Someone's been wanting them all morning."

It took a moment to register, but when it did, the sergeant stepped back from the look that must have been in Reinhardt's face, but he was past caring. He moved fast over to the sergeant, putting a hand on the man's shoulder, pushing him back into the row of crates.

"Who has been asking?"

"I don't know, sir. Honest. Someone on the phone. Gave the lieutenant hell until we found the boxes. And there was a Feldgendarme here as well."

"Show me this annex."

The sergeant took him back outside, past a squad of soldiers and impressed civilians heaving crates up into trucks, their feet squelching in the wet gravel of the courtyard. Around the corner, there was a long, brick extension to the barracks' main walls. The sergeant heaved a heavy set of sliding doors partway open, and Reinhardt followed him into the gloom of the extension. The building had a sense of space to it, and the brickwork was badly done, light stabbing through chinks in the walls and holes in the roof, picking through the web of rafters and crossbeams. The sergeant flicked a switch, and bulbs flickered lazily to life, the light wavering as if it had itself forgotten how to shine.

"Here, I think," said the sergeant, walking with his torso cocked sideways as he scanned the writing on a row of crates piled haphazardly, but then Reinhardt's breath quickened, and he stepped past him.

"Thank you, Sergeant, I have what I need."

The sergeant gave him the crowbar and left. Reinhardt looked at the three boxes. He had seen them before, he realized, neatly packed, in the office in the State House belonging to Erdmann. His finger reached out and touched the stencil that read *Court-Martial Office*, and he levered the first crate open. It was books, legal tomes and such. He pulled a few out, rifled through them to be sure that was all the box contained, then moved to the second one, heaved off the lid, and stopped, his breath shortening.

They were files, three stacks of them, each of them with the eagle and swastika, each of them with a name and case number. A six-digit case number. He lifted them out pile by pile and began to try to make some sense of the numbers, hoping for something sequential, and found one, which he pulled out of the stack. The number corresponding to Werner Janowetz. He opened it and found the proceedings of a court-martial. He scanned through the particulars of Janowetz. Volksdeutsche, from the Sudetenland. The charge was absenteeism. The verdict was transfer to a penal battalion. The 999th Balkans Field Punishment Battalion. He got to the unanimous judgment of the jury, and froze.

The presiding judge was Dreyer.

He read further, seeing the sentences confirmed by Herzog, advised by Erdmann.

He swallowed, put the file to one side, and kept going. He found two more in quick succession, understanding that in this, as in so much of this case, the trick was to hide what was being hidden in plain sight.

He found Benirschke and Sedlaczek's files. Both were Volksdeutsche, Benirschke from Slovenia and Sedlaczek from the Vojvodina in Serbia, near the Hungarian border, Reinhardt knew. Seymer was next, an Italian from the South Tyrol, and then Berthold, born in Romania.

All transcripts of courts-martial that led to sentencing in a penal battalion.

All with Dreyer as the presiding judge.

Not Erdmann.

He had been sure it would be Erdmann.

He felt sick. He did not know what to make of this, but he had all of a sudden a better idea of the shape of what was out there. It had come that bit closer, looming larger, that much more menacing.

A scuff behind him was all the warning he had. That, and a muttered curse, then an order.

"Stand up slowly."

"Careful. I do not want his blood all over the documents."

Reinhardt craned his neck around. Metzler stood behind him with a pistol, and behind the Feldgendarme was Erdmann, his erudite eyebrows arched over the silver frames of his spectacles.

"I said stand up."

Reinhardt stood.

"Turn around."

Reinhardt turned, slowly. As he turned, his right hand picked up the crowbar where it lay atop one of the crates and, still turning slowly, his eyes holding Metzler's, Reinhardt whipped his right arm into a swing at the pistol. The crowbar took the Feldgendarme full on his fist with a crack of steel on bone. Metzler's face crumpled, his arm going wide, and Reinhardt was swinging the crowbar back, stepping into the swing. Metzler got his arm up and the bar bounced up his shoulder and crashed into the side of his neck. The Feldgendarme's body seemed to fold in many places and Metzler collapsed like an empty sack.

Erdmann gasped, fumbled a moment at his holster, then turned and ran. Reinhardt threw the crowbar after him, end over end until it thudded into Erdmann's back and the judge staggered, stumbled, and fell sideways into a pile of crates that teetered and fell on him. He screamed as a case pinned him by the hand, squirming around the weight of it, his eyes wide with his fear as Reinhardt bore down on him.

Reinhardt heaved the crate off Erdmann, took the judge by the collar, and dragged him kicking and whimpering back past where Metzler wheezed unconscious on the floor, past the crates, into a darkened corner between piles of boxes.

"What does it mean?" he snarled, holding up one of the files. The judge said nothing, cradling his hand, and Reinhardt bunched the file into Erdmann's face, shoving it hard. Erdmann twisted his head, crying out. "What does it fucking *mean*?"

"You wouldn't understand, you fool," Erdmann managed.

Reinhardt twisted the judge's injured hand, and Erdmann yelped. "Try me. Why is Dreyer involved in this?"

Erdmann laughed, a cough of spittle and snot. "Your precious Dreyer. Not all he seemed, was he?" Reinhardt twisted his hand again, and Erdmann's face collapsed in pain, heels drumming at the floor. "No, please."

"Make sense, Erdmann."

"Blackmail, Reinhardt. It was as simple as that. We had something on him. He was ours, until he found you."

"What? *What?!*"

"All right, all right. It was money, Reinhardt. It is always money. He and Jansky were involved in something, I do not know what, back in Poland. Jansky cheated him, or something like that. I do not know. But Dreyer came looking to try to get his own back, and Jansky led him straight to us."

"Why did you kill him?"

"We did *not*, you *cretin*."

"What do you mean?"

"You were getting too close. He was using you to find a way out for himself. We sat him down, me and Herzog, and reminded him what we knew about him. Even if you found what you were looking for, we would still have him. We left him alive. He killed himself to implicate us. To make it look like murder."

"Why would he do that? *Why?!*"

"Ahhh, my *hand*."

"I said make sense, Erdmann, or I'll take care of your other hand as well."

"I will tell you. Let go!" Reinhardt shoved his hand away, Erdmann curling around it. The judge sagged back with relief, looking at Reinhardt through his spectacles lying askew across his aquiline nose. "He got cold feet, Reinhardt. He could not do it anymore. Because he was weak. He could not take the shame of what he had done. Not that we ever gave him a choice. He was ours."

"He was a war crimes judge. He couldn't . . . he couldn't have been mixed up in your affair."

"Did you ever check that, Reinhardt? No? Some policeman you must have been." Erdmann sneered, pushing his glasses straight. "He *was* a war crimes judge, until we took control of him. He spun you a tale. A tall tale. One he knew you would listen to. About the Ustaše. And you swallowed it."

"What the hell are you all playing at?"

"*Playing?* These are not games, Reinhardt. It's about preservation. It's about the future."

Reinhardt crumpled his fingers into Erdmann's lapels, dragging the judge up and closer. "*Preservation?* The *future*?! You *idiot*! It's *over.* It's finished. Can't you see that? There's no way back from this. There's no way back from what we've done."

Erdmann looked at him, suddenly calm, and then his mouth moved, as if he wanted to spit, his chin bunching. Reinhardt shifted back, then understood too late. There was a crunch, and Erdmann's eyes came alight.

"One people. One Reich. One Führer."

Erdmann gagged, and then his whole body tightened, as if bent on a bow. A gargled scream escaped his mouth on a white froth, and he sagged bonelessly to the floor.

Cyanide. Reinhardt's face twisted in disgust, but a part of him measured the extremity of Erdmann's act. Whatever it was, Erdmann could not fail it, even though it cost him his life. Reinhardt took a long breath, considering. Whatever it was, it went from here to Vienna, and it ran through the army at least as high as Herzog, probably higher, and it involved the murder of soldiers by other soldiers.

Reinhardt hauled a deep breath in, then prodded himself into motion. He dragged Metzler's body over to Erdmann's, piling the two together into that dark recess of the archives, then stacked boxes in front of them. It would not last forever, but would do for a while, he hoped, wishing Metzler luck in explaining himself when he regained consciousness. He risked a last check through the files, finding the remaining names from the list. He took them out and put them with the others, then hammered the lid shut with the crowbar. Stuffing the files under his coat, he calmed himself as best he could, but the roil in his gut grew too nauseating, and he doubled over, breathing harshly, willing it to happen, willing it to somehow cleanse him of what he had just learned and done. He dropped to one knee and retched, then vomited what little he had inside him, a caustic thread of bile and spittle, counterpoint to the acidic blight of the thoughts and images his mind summoned up.

Dreyer, his friend, asking for his help. "I *know* Jansky is guilty," he had said. Reinhardt saw it now; the all-but-open admission it was of Dreyer's own guilt.

Dreyer, the accomplice, reporting all Reinhardt found back to Erdmann, to Herzog, to whoever else was involved. How else had they known about the Greeks? And he remembered, a flash of memory, that last time they had talked, Dreyer mentioning Alexiou's name when Reinhardt never had. Dreyer had known. He had known who the "Greek" was.

Dreyer, taking the only way out he could. Some last desperate gamble, a gesture to the man he once was. A suicide that looked like murder. "I would shoot myself in the heart," he had said, had he only the courage to do it. "I would never go out to that music," he had said. All ways to arouse Reinhardt's suspicions, pull him deeper in, and further on.

Used. Manipulated.

All in plain sight.

Reinhardt stayed there a moment after the spasms in his belly subsided, wiped a sleeve across his mouth, and then walked out, his head as high as he could make it.

He kept it high, eyes focused somewhere far ahead, until he was back in the empty mess hall. He found a lukewarm cup of coffee and took a packet of iron rations from a pile of them by the door. He split the pack open, digging out the bread and jam, and then spreading all he had on a table. Three *soldbuchs*, the paper with the handwritten names, the files.

It all came down to the *soldbuchs* and the judicial files. He stared at the books as he chewed his bread and jam, trying to understand what they represented. Whatever information was in those *soldbuchs*, the military region from which these two men had been recruited would have backup information in the main registries, the *wehrstammbuchs*. You could change one thing somewhere, and it would not change something somewhere else. He realized, then, he was picking after process, looking for loopholes in a supposedly perfect plan. This—whatever this was, he thought, holding the two *soldbuchs* in his hand—did not need to be perfect. It needed to be good enough for a time and place, and that was here and now.

This was like no investigation he had ever conducted. He did not really even know if it was one. He had the shape of a crime, more than one, in fact. He had the names of conspirators—Erdmann and Metzler for sure, Herzog and Jansky probably, though his mind still turned from Dreyer. Without evidence, though, he had nothing to confront them with. The evidence he had, *soldbuchs* and trial transcripts, pointed in an unknown direction. They could damn or they could be explained, and so on their own they were just paper. He had just one witness, a frightened little boy who could not be pulled into this, a little boy who said he saw Feldgendarmes gun down other Germans, and something landed right in front of him with a crack of paper.

Reinhardt jumped back, startled, looking at the file that lay atop his evidence, and turned his head up and around. It took a moment before he recognized the man standing behind him.

"Dr. Henke."

"You know, for a man who had my sleep ruined for two nights in a row, you didn't seem particularly interested in what I found for you."

"I'm sorry, Doctor?"

"Yes, you bloody well should be."

The doctor collapsed onto the bench next to Reinhardt, his back against the edge of the table and his legs splayed out in front of him. His head went back in a gargantuan yawn and then rocked forward. Henke blinked once or twice, then looked at Reinhardt, then down at the file.

"That's what you were after, wasn't it? An autopsy of those bodies."

Reinhardt opened the file, fingering through five sheets of paper with handwritten notes.

"You did them?"

"You did ask so nicely, Captain." Henke's fingertips played against each other, and Reinhardt saw how his nails, and the folds of skin across the backs of his knuckles, were crusted dark, flecks and spots of something dark and brown. "And then you never came looking for them."

"I tried . . . we tried to contact you."

"Well, no one found me. You're lucky I'm a man of my word, and that I happened to be stopping here before continuing on."

"May I offer you a coffee?"

"You may." Henke yawned, again. He nodded his thanks as Reinhardt came back with a cup from the urn at the mess hall's entrance, lifting his eyes from the evidence on the tabletop and putting down the *soldbuchs*. "It's all there in the notes. Four of them had eaten the same thing at about the same time."

"What was that?"

Henke pointed at the packet on the tabletop. "Iron rations."

"Iron rations?"

"And some sort of broth of goat and tubers. Rather unappetizing, I would have thought."

"Goat?"

"Something wrong with your hearing, Captain? You keep repeating back to me what I say."

"I'm sorry."

"So you keep saying. But I'd say your suspicions were correct. They were probably soldiers. I don't know any other group of men who would have eaten the same thing at about the same time. The iron rations are rather definitive evidence, seeing as no one but us has them. Unless," the doctor yawned, again, "someone's captured a stock of them."

"The Partisans use Allied rations," Reinhardt murmured, leafing through the notes. Soldiers. He had guessed right, and it was good, he supposed, to have it confirmed although he had more or less assumed it from the evidence of the past couple of days.

"Is that who they were?" Henke nodded at the *soldbuchs*. Reinhardt picked up Abler's, opened it to the photograph. Something seemed to slide into place over it, and his breathing stopped, caught dead in his throat with a sudden surge of excitement.

"What do you mean, Doctor?" Reinhardt managed, after a moment.

The doctor tipped his mug back for the last of the coffee. "Just that.

I mean, granted, none of them have a face left, but these two could be matches for two or three of those bodies. Height, weight, hair color."

"Average."

"Average," Henke repeated.

In plain sight.

And he had it.

28

Dawn had begun to paint the sky, lighting the long edges of the clouds that hung low over the city. On the hills to the north, the crackle of gunfire was continuous, plumes of dark smoke smudging the slate sky, and there were reports coming in already of heavy concentrations of Partisan forces on Sarajevo's eastern approaches, probing attacks slicing into the German and Ustaše lines. The fighting was heavy, and the German and Ustaše troops still in the city as rear guard were already under deepening pressure. Making matters worse, Valter's Partisans inside Sarajevo were out in force, with bombings, sabotage, and ambushes flaring up across the length and breadth of the city.

Taking only the time to rush up to his room and throw some belongings into a canvas shoulder bag, Reinhardt ran out into the barracks vehicle park, his eyes searching for the car and driver Scheller had promised him was still there. He had left the colonel in the all-but-deserted operations room, most of the Feldjaeger having moved out to establish positions across the road to Visoko. Scheller's mouth had curled with displeasure at the thought of their orders, to round up stragglers and deserters, the lost and the bewildered, and pack them back into the front lines.

"Well, that would be why they call us hero stealers," Reinhardt had quipped, stuffing a pack of iron rations into his bag.

"Don't remind me," Scheller had muttered darkly, looking Reinhardt over. "You'll make it, I trust, Reinhardt. We can't wait. The lines are going to collapse before the end of the day. Well before, I'd reckon."

"I'll make it, sir," Reinhardt had said, checking the action of his StG 44, strapping on webbing and pouches, and picking up a helmet.

"Something happen to make you as giddy as a girl?"

"What?"

"That was irony, Reinhardt. Remember that? You used to be rather good at it," Scheller had said, his attention distracted by a messenger at the door. "Get going. Good luck."

Reinhardt found he did indeed feel light, focused. The truth of what he had discovered seemed to have liberated him from whatever slough he had fallen into. He had laid most of it out to Scheller, the words tumbling out and over each other as he ran the colonel through what he had found. What he now knew, and what he still suspected. He had had to tell him; there was no other way Scheller would have allowed him back into the city, and the colonel had sat stunned in his chair when Reinhardt was done, watching him pace back and forth like a caged cat.

He found the car and blessed the colonel for his forethought. He had thought a *kubelwagen*, but the colonel had scrounged up an armored car with a radio, a *panzerfunkwagen* with the bedframe-like antenna folded flat around the top of the vehicle's chassis. Standing in front of it was Benfeld, the big Feldjaeger straightening as Reinhardt came up.

"Frenchie," Reinhardt acknowledged, slinging his bag into the armored car, a wariness to his voice.

"Captain," Benfeld replied.

"Scheller's told you what it's about?"

"He said to keep an eye on you, watch your back. Captain Lainer had a few words to say as well, sir. Bader, Pollmann, and Triendl were ours. And anyway," Benfeld said, as he heaved himself up the side of the *panzerfunkwagen*, "we started this together, sir. I'd like to see it through."

Bader, Pollmann, and Triendl were the three Feldjaeger killed at the construction site who had started all this. Except that was not true. It was three other bodies, burned and abandoned in a forest clearing, that had started it. It was the body of a man with a goatee, and a dead girl. He slid his StG 44 into the cabin and narrowed his eyes as he looked at Benfeld. The lieutenant was tired. They all were, but it was something else Reinhardt was looking for. Some remnant or sign of the obvious pressure Benfeld had been under these past couple of days. It was still there, Reinhardt fancied. Something lurking in the corner of Benfeld's eyes, in the set of his shoulders. There was something more. There was a reckoning to be had, but not here and not now, Reinhardt thought, as the engine roared to life, the whole vehicle shaking.

"You'll have to hang on up there, Benfeld," Reinhardt shouted. "It's been a long time since I've driven anything . . . like . . . *this*," he said, each word punctuated by a grinding of metal as he tried to force the stick into first gear and finding it, the *panzerfunkwagen* lurching forward. He turned it in a wide circle around the edge of the vehicle park, then inched it out through the barracks' fortified entrance. He trundled it down to the main road, paused, then twisted up to look at Benfeld.

"You sure you are all right to come with me? No harm in turning back."

Benfeld peered down at him from the turret, his face backlit against the sky. "All's well up here, Captain."

"Right you are," Reinhardt muttered as he swung the vehicle onto the main road and floored the accelerator.

Most of the traffic was oncoming, trucks and cars filled with troops, a convoy of ambulances, a battery of artillery. Reinhardt slid the *panzerfunkwagen* close up behind a pair of trucks moving into the city, watched the pinched faces of the soldiers in the back, hunched around the uprights of their rifles. It could not be easy, heading up to the front when everything in them would be urging them the other way.

How did you ask a man to be the last man to die for a place like this, in a cause like theirs?

You did not ask, Reinhardt knew, as he surged the *panzerfunkwagen* out alongside the trucks and overtook them. You told him.

Reinhardt hauled the *panzerfunkwagen* right onto Kvaternik, following the sweep of the road next to the Miljacka. The streets were almost empty of people, but debris and detritus littered the sidewalk and spilled across the roads, and the windows of some buildings across the river showed the blackened traces of recent fire. He drove fast, drove straight, and pulled up in front of the Pale House without any difficulties.

Leaving Benfeld in the turret, Reinhardt hauled himself out of the *panzerfunkwagen*, pulling his assault rifle after him. On the pavement in front of the Pale House the barbed-wire entanglements had been pushed and pulled out of position. Scraps of clothing clung to the wire, belongings were scattered about: photo frames, a woman's bag, a lone shoe. The building's entrance was unguarded, the doors hanging ajar around the starred remnants of the windows. The foyer was empty and echoing; rubbish and junk patterned the stairs as Reinhardt took them two by two, up to the second floor, past the radiator with the manacles hanging from it, down to the end, to Putković's office. His breathing coming high and quick, he pushed the door open, nosing his assault rifle into the room.

It was empty. He followed the StG 44's muzzle over to the curtains that hung half open. The darkness hung heavy and slanted down into the courtyard, a handful of crows pecking their way disconsolately across the churned earth. Reinhardt stood and listened, turning slowly in the room. Gunfire crackled thickly outside, the thud-thud of artillery coming in staccato rhythms, but the house was still. Whatever spirit had inhabited it, whatever had moved it, had caused it to come up thick and menacing around him those other times, it was gone.

His heart thudded hard, beating after a sense of failure, a scent that was strong but fading. His eyes fell on the liquor cabinet. Some spark flared along his veins, a challenge to madness, and he pulled it open, his chin bunched tight with his anger. Breathing hard through his nose, he pulled a bottle out, his fist clattering others aside. A bottle of slivovitz, clear, sparkling.

"Say what you like about the Serbs," he whispered, his words a bitter echo of Putković's that night Bunda had brought Reinhardt here. He twisted the cork out, lifting the bottle, turning it to the light. "They make the best slivovitz." That challenge in his blood rose high, deafened him, and he tipped his head and sucked the bottle tight to his mouth, upending it. His mouth flooded, swelled, burned. He gagged, choked, flung the bottle away, and spat after it, the slivovitz spraying in crystal droplets through the heavy air. "*Bastard!*" he grated, as the bottle broke across the wall in a shatter of glass, and he did not know if he talked of himself or Putković, but he felt that challenge inside him subside and he knew, somehow, he had won something of a victory, if only against himself.

His feet crunched across the confetti spread of the smashed bottle as he walked slowly over to that second door that had caught his attention the last time he was here. The door was locked. There was no answer to his call, and he stepped back and fired a burst from his StG 44 into the lock. He shoved the door open through a smell of sawdust, then recoiled at the stench that flowed out over it. He waited a moment, hitched his assault rifle over his shoulder, and drew his pistol, crooking his arm across his nose.

The room was dark, curtains drawn against the pale dawn. There was a desk and a bed, a fireplace heaped with ash. A chest stood on the desk, a red chest, and what little light there was glinted across an array of small bottles and vials scattered around it. He swept the curtains back and dust and motes erupted up and circulated into the light, the shadows darkening the creases and curls of the body that lay beneath the window.

Reinhardt knelt by it, turning the body's head toward him with the back of his thumb. It was the soldier who had accompanied Jansky here that time Reinhardt had met him downstairs. The soldier who had been working up in the penal battalion's office the first time

Reinhardt had gone up there and had been carrying the red chest that now sat on the nearby table. His throat had been cut, and his face hung slack above the blackened crescent that slashed across his neck.

Reinhardt coughed, gagged on the smell, and hauled himself up and away, breathing deeply through the thick serge of his coat. He paused by the fireplace and pushed the muzzle of his pistol through the humped ash, raking back a collection of pieces and shards of . . . something. He knelt, fingering through them, lifting one, turning the edge of thick cardboard against the light, squinting at the darkened tan of its color. He took one of the *soldbuchs* from his bag, comparing it to the shard he held. His eyes swiveled to the case, back to the fireplace. He rose and pawed through the bottles and vials and powders that lay around and inside the red chest. He ran a soft brush across the back of his hand, pressed a stamp against a scrap of paper, thinking he had never in his years as a policeman come across a more complete forger's kit. He understood, now, the clerk's nervous nature, and why he had never seen him parted from that chest. He must have been a forger, a master at his trade, scooped up by those behind all this and now discarded.

He left the offices, walking back outside into the corridor, opening doors at random, but found nothing and no one. There was no sound, no movement. The house was empty, as if it had never been inhabited, used, and misused. He came down the stairs slowly and hesitated at the doors that led, he thought, out into that courtyard, down into the basements, and he backed away, feeling cheated.

There was nothing.

Reinhardt went back outside, blinking in the gray glow, watching the Miljacka spill past, watching a body undulate its way downstream, catch on a rock, and flop itself free. He ignored Benfeld's eyes as he threw his assault rifle back into the car, paused, and then wormed his way back inside.

"Anything, Benfeld?"

"Nothing, sir. Just a lot of noise."

"We've got to go a bit farther."

"As you say, sir."

"You fought in many cities?" Reinhardt asked as he hauled the armored door shut.

"I've done my share of street fighting, sir," Benfeld answered.

"Keep those eyes peeled, then."

Not that he needed to say it, but seconds later he felt the turret traverse, and the car juddered to the recoil of the machine gun, spent shells sparkling into the *panzerfunkwagen*'s interior. Benfeld said nothing, and Reinhardt asked nothing as he turned left into the angular warren of the Austro-Hungarian city, winding his way right, then left. The streets were still empty, but the pressure of eyes was stronger here, and then he was flooring the accelerator as windows exploded in puffs of smoke, and the car's armor rang to the percussion of metal. Benfeld cursed as he ducked out of the turret, but in seconds the danger was gone, and Reinhardt had wound his zigzagging way to the blank entrance he was looking for.

He twisted out of the car to the sound of heavy street fighting, the wind and distance ruining any appreciation of how far away it was, but dark silhouettes dashed across the mouth of a cross street a few hundred yards away. Reinhardt hesitated, then turned and ran inside, clattering upstairs. He paused, breathing heavily, then knocked softly, then again, harder.

"*Go away!*" came Vukić's voice, thread-thin through the door.

He knocked again. "Suzana. It's Gregor."

The door opened a sliver, and he put a hand to it, firmly, sliding his way inside, pushing it shut behind him. Vukić stood there, her eyes wide, flashing from his helmet to his webbing, to the assault rifle on his shoulder.

"Reinhardt. Gregor. I thought . . . What—what are you doing here?"

"I need your help."

"Are you all right? Is someone . . . is someone after you?" she rushed, her eyes flickering from him to the door as if she expected it to burst open.

He lifted his arms slowly and put his hands on her shoulders.

"I am fine. I am fine."

"Then what?" she breathed. And then she shook her head, and she pulled him to her. His arms went tight around her, his equipment pressing between them. "I was so worried," she whispered.

He turned his face into her hair, eyes closed, taking in all he could of her.

"I need your help," he said again.

"What?" she said into his throat.

"I need you to take me to Perić."

Vukić shifted her head, pulling it back. "To *Valter*? I don't know . . ."

She stiffened, made to step away, but he held her, gently.

"There's no time, Suzana," he said.

"I don't . . ." she said again.

"You do," he said, quietly.

"No."

"Suzana. How many people in this city know Valter's real name is Perić?" She said nothing, her eyes fixed on his. "I know, Suzana. Your work? The things you said about the city? About the Ustaše? How the people respond to you?"

"I . . . that's . . ."

"The things we said last night?" She blinked. "The theater?"

Something shuttered across the light in her eyes, and they gleamed coldly back at him. "What do you want?" she managed, finally.

"Perić asked me something," Reinhardt said. "He asked me about the Ustaše. What the future held for them."

"And?"

"And now I know."

"What do you know?"

"I will tell Perić. When you take me to him." She firmed her lips, those eyes staying flat and cold. "Suzana, there is not much time. I know you are working with the Partisans. I beg you. Please. Trust me."

She took a long breath in, then nodded, her face softening. "I am sorry, Gregor," she said, quietly. "Please understand, trust is not so . . . easily . . . won these days."

Reinhardt opened the door as she lifted her coat from a hook, then stepped out onto the landing. The light was dim, the shadows long and deep.

"Is it far?" he asked.

"Not so far," she answered, as she closed the door. "But Valter will be on the move, today, and . . ." She stopped, wide-eyed again, as Reinhardt raised his hand. He went still, freezing in place. There was a creak of wood, and the shadows at the end of the landing bunched and moved, and Bunda stepped out of the darkness.

29

Reinhardt's guts tightened with a visceral clench and that primeval gibber started up at the back of his mind at the sight of the huge Ustaše. It was the creature at the cave mouth. It was the arrow surge of ripples across dark waters. It was, he knew now, the watcher from the darkness, the one he had felt on the street, just earlier that morning. They recoiled backward from the size and power and the stink of him, begrimed, bloodied, smoke-darkened, his teeth gleaming across the blunt line of his jaws.

"What's this I 'eard about Valter, then?"

Bunda surged into motion. Reinhardt pushed Vukić back inside the apartment, yanking the door shut behind her. He hauled the assault rifle from his shoulders, but Bunda was too close. He swung the stock up at the Ustaša's head, but it thudded into Bunda's palm as his hands seized the weapon. Reinhardt did not even try to wrestle for the gun's control. Something took over, some battlefield reaction to move toward the enemy, and he ducked down, under Bunda's arms, and butted his head up. He felt the crown of his helmet burst across Bunda's jaw, heard the clack of teeth, and Bunda grunted. Reinhardt's arms reached up and he clawed his fingers into Bunda's eyes, feeling the giant's head rock back and shake from side to side.

But then Bunda's fist piled into the side of Reinhardt's head and his vision starred as his helmet spun away. He kicked at Bunda's groin, scrabbling for his pistol. Bunda grunted again around the thud of Reinhardt's knee, twisting and taking it on the inside of his thigh, and he slammed Reinhardt against the door, a web of cracks splintering away from the lock. Reinhardt felt the wood sag, and Bunda slammed him into it again. Reinhardt felt the twist of tension in the way Bunda held him, and knew a punch was coming but could do nothing except duck his head and lift an arm, and still the punch almost flattened the back of his head against the door. Bunda hauled him to the side and smashed the door open with his foot. The door crashed back against the wall and Reinhardt staggered backward inside, his arms windmilling for balance, and his pistol knocked against something and fell. There was a shattering pain in his knee as Bunda's kick swept Reinhardt's legs from under him and he crashed to the floor. Instinctively he rolled away, taking a second kick in a glancing blow across his back. He fumbled across the floor, then felt Bunda's hands come down on his shoulders and he was lifted, swung across the room to crash headfirst into the pile of boxes and belongings from Vukić's previous house.

He had never fought anyone like this. Never. Dimly, from somewhere far away, he heard Vukić screaming, and he turned his head, seeing Bunda laughing as he held her hand high and plucked Reinhardt's pistol from her grip. Still laughing, he backhanded her across the room to sprawl akimbo beneath a table. Summoning up a strength he hardly felt, Reinhardt drew his bayonet, forcing himself to his knees, to turn and face the giant.

Bunda's smile stretched wider as he looked at Reinhardt, at the bayonet that wobbled a child's scrawl in the air. He drew his spiked club from his belt, flicked it spinning into the air, caught it, then whistled it at Reinhardt's head. Reinhardt ducked, feeling the iron weight of its passage, but then the club was coming back and it buried itself in his shoulder. He screamed as he was knocked to the side, the bayonet clanging away somewhere into the bloodied darkness of his vision.

Reinhardt felt himself pulled across the floor and a band of ice went around his wrist. He felt a slap across his jaw and he gasped and wretched as Bunda poured slivovitz over his face. He spluttered back to life, one wrist manacled to an iron heating pipe that ran around the bottom edge of the room. Bunda smiled at him, his huge hand wound into Reinhardt's gorget.

"Wake up, Reinhardt, there's a good boy. Wouldn't want you to miss the show." Bunda tipped more slivovitz over Reinhardt's head, and it ran biting across his wounds and into his eyes. Bunda threw the bottle away, cocked his head at Reinhardt. "What did I say to you that first time, Reinhardt? You remember? 'This ain't the place it used to be,' I said. There's no rules now but what we make. Ain't no gettin' around that. Ain't no gettin' away from that. Ain't no gettin' in the way of it, neither. D'you remember? You do. I know you do. Bloke like you, he remembers things like that. What else did I say? D'you remember?" He pinched Reinhardt's jaw, shaking it from side to side with every word. "You *do* remember, *don't* you?" Bunda said, pursing his lips in a mother's mimic to a child. "I said she was fucking royalty. I said she was ours."

"No," Reinhardt slurred. His free hand came up, fingers arrowed at Bunda's eyes, but it was slapped away.

"*Yes*, Reinhardt," said Bunda, the light of madness in his eyes. "I said she's ours. I should'a said, she's mine. I deserve 'er. Fucking royalty. Airs and fucking graces. No time for the likes of me. but what's the point of being me if you can't take what you want, when you want it."

"NO!"

"*YES!* And a traitor as well. Fucking around with Partisans. I'm going to 'ave 'er before I leave this shithole, and you're going to watch."

Bunda stood, towering to his feet, and strode across the room. He pulled Vukić out from under the table, slapping away the life that came back into her. He hauled her to her feet, turned her, and bent her over the table. She really struggled, then, understanding what was to happen. Her back bowed up, hands flailing behind her until he cuffed her head down, and it thudded into the tabletop.

Reinhardt heaved himself against the manacle, helpless as Bunda lifted her skirts, tore away her smallclothes. He stood back, a broad smile across his face.

"Wasn't I right, Reinhardt? Is that not one regal-looking backside?" He slapped her, her flesh quivering away from the strike of his hand.

"Bunda, stop. *STOP.*"

"Why the fuck would I, Reinhardt?" He shrugged out of his jacket, winding his massive shoulders out of his braces. "Lie still, you," he said to Vukić, striking her head back down. He fumbled at his trousers, letting them crumple down around the trunks of his legs.

Reinhardt laughed, forcing it out around the fury that constricted his throat. "Is that all you've got?" he cackled, hoping to goad Bunda back over to him. "Big man like you? And there I was thinking it was true what they said about men with big feet."

Bunda reddened, but stayed where he was. "Funny man, Reinhardt. I'm going to fuck every 'ole in 'er, now. You tell me 'ow funny you find that." He turned and planted his fists into Vukić's hips, but she arched up, kicking, twisting, screaming, and Reinhardt echoed her, spinning, planting his feet against the wall, heaving against the bind of the manacle. It gripped tight, a fixed point to the sliding swirl of horror that cascaded through him. He pulled harder, yanked like an imprisoned animal, the bones of his hand blaring in agony. Behind him he heard Bunda swear at Vukić to lie still, but still she fought back, trying to slump herself off the edge of the table, although every movement weakened her. There was a meaty slap and Vukić made a little sound and Reinhardt knew her fight was over as Bunda laughed and his world began to crack, his vision fracturing into kaleidoscope blurs, and in one of them something moved.

He lifted his head, seeing Neven walk quietly over to Bunda, his uncle's heavy butcher's blade in his little fists. The boy paused behind the bunched strain of Bunda's legs, and then with both hands he stabbed and swept the knife across the Ustaša's left hamstring. Bunda gasped, jerked sideways, and Neven drew the blade across the other. Bunda's legs bent, quivered, and red lines opened across them. Thin, at first, then suddenly wide, blood sheeting out. The Ustaša grasped the table for support, and Neven drove the knife into his back, beside his spine.

Bunda howled, one arm swinging back as he arched himself around, searching for the source of the agony that tore at him. His fist caught Neven across the head and the boy was dashed to the floor, but Bunda's legs were going, going, and the giant toppled like a falling tree, bellowing, and his hand grasped for the knife where it stood proud from his back.

Heaving himself forward against the agony of his hand, Reinhardt hooked his fingers over Bunda's brow and dug as hard as he could for the eyes. Bunda bellowed again, his hands coming up, squeezing and tearing at Reinhardt's fingers, but Reinhardt pressed tighter, dug deeper, hauled harder than he had ever done as Vukić staggered back from the table, dipped to the floor, and rose with Bunda's club in her hands. A step, two, and she swung the club down into Bunda's groin. The giant went rigid, his scream cracking against his throat as his hands flailed wide and Vukić screamed in counterpoint as she sawed and heaved at the club, back and forth, as if loosening a stake from the ground. She ripped it free, as if from the grudging earth, flung it away, and collapsed to her side, reaching for the still form of Neven.

Blood pumped from between Bunda's legs. Reinhardt felt him weaken, the life flowing out of him, and then Reinhardt tipped slowly to his side, bile rising in his throat, and he vomited weakly. His breathing came high and hoarse but that primeval gibber in his mind began to calm and he lifted his head, wiping his hand across his mouth. Never. Not the trenches. Not the darkened streets of Berlin. Not the shattered battlefields of this war. He had never felt like this, fought like this, but the creature at the mouth of the cave was gone.

"The keys," he whispered to Vukić. "Please . . ."

She moved after a while, then dragged Bunda's jacket to her and pushed it over to Reinhardt. He found the key, holding his hand to his chest a moment after he freed it, then crawled over to Vukić.

"Suzana," he whispered. He touched her arm, and she shuddered up and away, a frozen angularity to her. Her eyes were wild, her mouth wide, but then she focused, her gaze clearing as she stared at Bunda's body. Reinhardt turned and saw that Bunda was still alive, looking at them, his eyes dark pits in the pallor of his face. Bunda looked down in incomprehension at the carnage of his groin, and then the thread of his breath went taut, stopped, and the blackness of his eyes fell in and away. Vukić sighed out, and she relaxed slowly into Reinhardt's arms, the two of them clinging to each other as Neven stirred, and the sound of battle filtered in from outside.

"It seems . . ." Vukić trembled, her arms tightening spasmodically around Reinhardt as she looked at Bunda's body, "it seems like forever that he was there. Always there. Always looking . . . at . . . me. I knew . . . I felt . . ."

"We cannot stay here."

Vukić nodded, rose unsteadily to her feet, smoothing down the twisted folds of her clothes. Neven rose with her, holding hard to her side. "A moment," she whispered, taking the boy out of the room with her. Reinhardt twisted one knee underneath him, tugged Neven's knife free, and pushed himself up. He paused, then lifted Bunda's jacket. He laid it over the table and dug through its pockets, his fingers closing around something smooth. He paused again, then took out a *soldbuch*. He stared at its tan cover, swallowed, then opened it, letting out a long, slow breath.

A picture of Bunda stared up at him, a profile in angle, the head turned to the right. His hair was combed, his face serious. On the facing page were all the particulars of a soldier named Carl Benirschke, from Marburg in Slovenia.

"I am ready."

Reinhardt turned. Vukić stood with her coat on, Neven close beside her. She pointed her eyes at the *soldbuch* as Reinhardt put it into his bag.

"Part of what Perić needs to hear," he said as he wiped the knife on Bunda's shirt. He looked at Neven, then offered him back the knife, but the boy shook his head, and Reinhardt put it carefully on the table, then holstered his pistol. He picked up the StG 44 from the hallway, then led them downstairs. She froze at the entrance at the sight of the armored car, shied back as Benfeld jumped down, his face narrowing as he took Reinhardt in.

"*Fucki* . . . bloody hell, sir. What the hell happened?"

"Never mind, Frenchie. We've got two passengers."

Benfeld's mouth worked, but he nodded. "It'll be a squeeze, but we'll manage."

"I must ride in the turret," said Vukić. She shook her head as both Reinhardt and Benfeld made to protest. "I must. If the Partisans see me, they will not fire. And we must hope any Germans or Ustaše will be too surprised to open fire immediately."

With much grumbling, Benfeld dropped down into the car, where he squeezed himself into the back. Reinhardt helped Vukić up, where she took two long strips of red cloth from her pocket. He gave her a last look, which she returned coolly, saying nothing, and he urged Neven into the car, the boy wedging himself behind the driver's seat. Reinhardt looked up at Vukić where she perched with her back against the turret rim.

"You need to head toward the theater," Vukić said. "I can't promise he'll be there. If he's not, we can ask."

Reinhardt drove fast through the narrow streets, his knee twitching painfully on the clutch and his injured wrist jarring on the wheel, hoping their luck would hold out, and although they heard a lot of gunfire, most of it was clearly to the east and north. Only once did they come across the remnants of any fighting, Reinhardt slowing and bumping the car over a meager barricade of rubble and paving stones where a handful of bodies in civilian clothing scattered across the road. Once, faces peered at them from the windows of a building at the end of the street, the slivers of rifles poking out and down, but Vukić shouted something and the faces cheered, arms reaching out to pump the air.

Reinhardt raced the car down Kvaternik, past the frothy skirl of the river, up to the theater. He braked at Vukić's shout, and men emerged from the side streets, heavily armed, to slow and surround the car. From inside, through the vehicle's viewports, Reinhardt watched their faces, dark with suspicion and mistrust even as Vukić talked to them, until a tall man stepped through their midst, and he recognized Simo. The Partisan called up to Vukić, and then his eyes swiveled to the viewports—all the Partisans' eyes did—a collective shift as men turned, tightened their stance.

Reinhardt turned off the engine and pushed open the door. He led with his hands, shifting his body awkwardly to climb out of the car to stand with his arms up and out. Even though they were forewarned, there was still a hush from the Partisans, men shifting away from him. Simo stepped in close, removing Reinhardt's pistol. The Partisan shook his head, something rueful in his eyes as he looked down at Reinhardt, eyes flicking to Neven as the boy slithered out.

"Impressive, Captain. And resourceful," he said, looking up at Vukić.

"I need to see Perić. I have that information he wanted."

Simo's eyes rose and his head went back, and then he nodded. "Your car stays here."

"I have a man inside. I don't want him harmed."

"If he does nothing foolish, he will not be."

"Frenchie." Reinhardt put his head in the car. "You stay put."

Benfeld's eyes were wide as he stared through the viewports, then at him. "Sir? What the hell is going on?"

"Unfinished business, Lieutenant. Stay put."

Reinhardt followed Simo into the building, Vukić and Neven at his side, a pair of Partisans bringing up the rear. The Partisans led him into the hushed warren of tunnels and passages, moving up and across and through buildings rendered silent by the noise from outside. At the top of the ladder, Reinhardt climbed awkwardly around his injured hand into that same attic where Simo had brought him the first time to meet Perić, the space brightly lit by the light that poured in from the skylights. Almost empty the first time, the space was a veritable war room now, with a radio and a bank of telephones, maps and charts festooned across the walls. The bustle of men froze as they saw him pull himself up behind Simo, and then the crowd opened out and Perić stood up from a table. The Partisan breathed out heavily, then nodded to the other men and the bustle renewed itself. He walked over to Reinhardt, his eyes narrowing as first Vukić, then Neven pulled themselves up into the attic.

"You have something for me?"

Reinhardt nodded, twisting his bag around off his shoulder. "I know where they are going. The Ustaše. The ones you are interested in." Perić's eyes lit up, his gaze following Reinhardt's hands as he pulled out three *soldbuchs*. Reinhardt opened the one he had taken from Bunda, his hands covering the first page, showing only the photo to Perić and Simo. "Who is that?"

The Partisans' eyes narrowed as they looked at the picture of Bunda. "*Picku materinu,*" Perić muttered. "That is Bunda."

"No," said Reinhardt, "it is Corporal Carl Benirschke. Who is this?" he asked, holding up a second *soldbuch*, one of those he had taken from the Albanians he had killed.

"That is . . . Pero Labaš."

"Wrong. This is Sergeant Marius Maywald. This?"

The Partisans reacted strongly. "That is Branimir Zulim. The torturer. Bunda's right hand."

"Wrong again. This is Private George Abler. But you don't have to worry about him. He's dead. The Ustaše killed him themselves."

"Are you sure?" hissed Perić, his eyes fixed on Abler's *soldbuch*.

"A scar down the side of his head and neck, here? He's very dead. I suspect Bunda killed him because Zulim had drawn too much attention to himself. He was the one," Reinhardt said, turning to Vukić, "who arrested the survivors of that massacre in the forest. The old man and the old woman."

"Bunda killed him?"

"And I killed Bunda."

"You killed *Bunda*?" Perić and Simo exchanged glances. "You killed Bunda. How? Why?"

"It doesn't matter," Reinhardt replied, feeling Vukić's eyes on him, and his stomach heaved, a heavy roll of memory at that fight in her apartment.

Perić fingered through the *soldbuchs*. "What does this mean, Reinhardt?"

"When you spoke to me of the Ustaše vanishing, I did not know what to think. You told me of the Albanians you captured, with uniforms with no insignia. I knew they were uniforms from a penal battalion, and I was already looking at the battalion because of my investigation into the murders of three Feldjaeger, and the discovery of five bodies near where they had been killed. I found out men were disappearing from this battalion. Just vanishing. Everywhere, it seemed, I was finding bodies, or hearing of people vanishing, and no one knew where, or how, or why.

"That same night I met you, the Ustaše were waiting for me downstairs." Perić nodded. "Bunda showed me four Ustaše he said you—the Partisans—had killed and mutilated. One of them was this Zulim, now called Abler. Bunda brought me to Putković. He showed me all the bodies in the Pale House, all the people the Ustaše had taken and killed, and he told me how, if he needed someone to vanish, he would just order it done and not hide it. All this showing, and all I could think was, 'What is he hiding?' I asked myself, what is the best way to hide something?" He looked from one to the other. "You hide it in plain sight. You hide it right in front of you."

"You . . ." Perić paused. "You are telling me the Ustaše are hiding by going into the German Army."

"More than that. I found out quite quickly that this penal battalion we talked of had many foreigners in it. And many of those foreigners had a past, one that would never let them be. I thought some of the Ustaše would take that same route, and I was right and wrong. Some are taking that route. Some kind of cabal, a small group. But they are not just becoming drivers, or cooks. They are becoming someone else." He took the books back from Perić, holding them up. "They are *becoming* these men. These men—the *real* men—were killed. Executed. Their bodies destroyed—by fire, by disfigurement—so their identities could be adopted by *these* men, these Ustaše."

"People would . . ."

". . . know? Who? Who would know?" Reinhardt forced himself to speak slowly, calmly, around the excitement he felt building up in him. "The men organizing this were clever. They chose their victims carefully. Volksdeutsche for the most part. Ethnic Germans. That would explain any accents, any doubts about a knowledge of German or Germany. They chose men who had no photographic identity, therefore no way to compare these photos. They chose men with no families. No wives, no children, no parents. No one waiting. And they chose men who had been consigned to a penal battalion. Men the world had turned its back on. But also men who, when the war ended, would elicit pity. Who would question a man sentenced to a penal battalion?"

Perić's mouth moved, but nothing came out. It was Vukić who took up the questions.

"Luburić does not know?"

Reinhardt shook his head. "He cannot. He could not allow it. He is a believer. Putković is not. When I pushed him to answer how he saw the future, he was evasive, and Luburić was furious about those three Ustaše who vanished first, the ones you told me of."

"But what of those organizing this, then?"

"I do not know," Reinhardt admitted. "I have met some of them. Some are motivated by faith, by ideology. A conviction that the reverses Germany and its allies suffer now are only temporary, and that if they are not then something must be preserved for the future. And some are motivated by money. This whole thing began with criminals who sought asylum in a place they thought no one would look, and they paid well for it. Somehow, someone began to extend that idea. To offer not just asylum, but identities. The Ustaše are paying too. Paying well."

"I cannot believe it," Vukić whispered. Reinhardt looked at her, and although she still held herself tight, as if wrapped around some inner pain, still she was at home, here, among these fighters. She had that air, as if authority and respect gathered around her. Perić glanced at her, and he shook his head as well.

"This must stop," he grated.

"It has," Reinhardt said.

"How can you know?" Simo demanded.

Reinhardt looked at the floor, feeling exhausted all of a sudden. "I stopped it," he said, simply, and as he said it he felt the truth of it, and it was good. "It worked for as long as they could hide it in plain sight.

But when I began digging, it began to come apart. I was asking too many questions, making too many links. They have ended it, I believe. I found their forger, dead. They had no more use for him. But it would have gone on. It would have gone far."

"Rats." Simo's face twisted.

"Rats abandoning a ship." Reinhardt's mouth twisted, no matter that he tried to give the words a sense of irony.

Perić held the books in his two hands, cocked his head as he looked hard at Reinhardt. "This is much more than we asked of you, Captain. Why have you done this?"

"Because this is not all that I am." Reinhardt shook his head, a rueful smile on his face. "For a long time, I just wanted to survive this war. But surviving was not living and for a long time, I dreaded being asked to die in this war. But living was not surviving. Eventually, I found people like me, who thought like me, but I would be lying if I said we accomplished anything. And then, here, I found that men—ordinary men, men who might have been you or I—were simply vanishing. As if they never existed. All that they were was just gone, and something else filled the space that had been theirs. I thought, then, someone should speak for them. Someone should remember them. Someone should . . . bring back at least the rumor of who they were."

He stopped, looking down, feeling embarrassed. "For the longest time, I wanted . . . I wanted to do something in this war. I wanted to strike a blow. A glorious blow, because I felt I would not survive, and I wanted to be remembered. Because this," he said, fingering his uniform—the Iron Cross, the eagle and swastika, the dirty gray of his coat and the brass gleam of his gorget, "is not all that I am. I am more than this. That," he continued, pointing at the *soldbuchs*, "was my act of resistance. That was my war."

"I must . . . I must decide what to do about this," said Perić, and Reinhardt glanced up at the tone of worry he heard in his voice. "I may have to ask you to help us more."

The three Partisans moved away, talking with their heads close together. Reinhardt watched them, caught Vukić's eyes a moment, and there was something in them, some grave appreciation of what he had done for them, perhaps, before she turned away. He fished his cigarettes from his pocket, leaning with one hand on the slanting beams of the roof and looking out of the skylight. His other hand, the one injured by Bunda, he cradled against his chest, working his fingers and wrist against the pain, working his jaw against the swelling he could feel coming on.

The window was open, and a cold wind slapped at his face and collar with the frenzy of an injured bird. The skylight was angled in such a way that he could see down the roof and look along a strip of the opposite sidewalk. To one side he saw the end of the street where the *panzerfunkwagen* was parked with its square antenna mounted in the upright position, the machine gun in the turret making an angled line at the sky. To the other side there was nothing, only an empty cross street. On the roofs as far as he could see nothing moved, and the sky was empty but for hanging black threads, birds and scavengers that rode the high winds.

He frowned at the sky.

Something was not right.

30

Reinhardt stubbed his cigarette out on the window frame. As he turned, he caught sight of motion, down the road where there had been nothing. He craned his neck out and saw trucks pull to a stop, men in uniforms piling out. He was not sure, but from here, they looked like SS troopers, and he knew a company of them had been left as part of the rear guard. A quick glance back at the *panzer-funkwagen*, and he pulled his head back into the room as the door burst open, and Partisans poured in.

The newcomers were all excitement, a raucous blare of information. Perić stood and listened, then straightened, and then he and Vukić and Simo were looking at him, and Simo was striding across the room.

"Did you betray us?" He gripped Reinhardt's coat, pulled him close. *"Did you betray us?!"*

"No! What are you talking about?"

"Germans in the streets. And Ustaše. All coming here. How would they know we are here?"

"I don't know!" protested Reinhardt.

"Izlazite svi!" snapped Perić.

The room exploded into motion at his order, Reinhardt watching maps coming down, weapons gathered up, last messages passed over the radio and telephones, and then the Partisans were pouring out of the room, out the door, down the ladder, out the windows on the opposite side to the street. Simo peered out the skylight, looking both ways, and when he ducked back in his face was grim.

"They are everywhere down there," he said, and his eyes flicked at Reinhardt.

"I had nothing to do with it," Reinhardt repeated. "Anyway, they do not know what you look like, do they?"

"No. But they might know what *you* look like," said Perić, ducking his head through the strap of an MP 40. "So this is good-bye, Captain. And thank you." He paused, then offered his hand. "Be safe, Reinhardt."

"I will go with the captain," said Vukić. Perić and Simo just nodded, and then they were moving. Simo handed Vukić Reinhardt's pistol, and he was following Perić out the window, and the space was empty, suddenly.

"Back the way we came," said Vukić. She handed Reinhardt back his pistol, and she was moving, as if she wished to preempt any word she and Reinhardt might have shared. She started down the ladder, Neven darting in front of her. Back down, back through the tunnels, the walls now echoing to shouts, orders, the stamp of feet and, once, a burst of gunfire and a woman's scream. At the hidden door, Vukić paused, listening. She turned to Reinhardt, her eyes wide, and Reinhardt heard it as well, the clatter of feet behind them, and Perić and Simo pushed into the small space with them.

"No way out," Perić breathed.

There were no words, only the labored breath of the Partisans.

"I can try to get you out," said Reinhardt. They looked at him. "I can take you prisoner. I am a Feldjaeger. No one will stop me or countermand my orders."

Perić's breath shuddered in and out, and the three Partisans shared an anxious glance. Then Simo nodded, and he handed his MP 40 to Reinhardt. Perić waited a moment longer, then gave him his, nodding that he understood. Vukić edged open the door. At her feet, Neven ducked his head out, then whispered up at her, and they slid out into the little room. Vukić's breathing came hard and fast; she looked at Reinhardt and then raised her hands, Simo and Perić doing the same. Reinhardt slung one MP 40 over his shoulder and gripped the second hard, motioning them forward. In the theater's foyer there was no one, and on the street outside, from the quick glance he gave, a squad of SS were lined up on the opposite pavement.

"Ready?" he whispered.

They nodded, then walked out, their hands high, Reinhardt close behind. He heard the shift of the SS as they turned toward them, and then Reinhardt raised a hand at their officer as he came forward.

"Halt there!" the man called, an Untersturmführer.

"My prisoners," Reinhardt called back, urging the Partisans on, seeing Benfeld's head pop up through the turret of the *panzerfunkwagen*.

"I said *halt!*" The SS barked an order, and his men broke into a ragged line, chasing after them.

"My prisoners, Untersturmführer!" Reinhardt snapped, turning and standing his ground. "This is Feldjaeger business. Butt out of it, unless you want more trouble than you can handle."

The Untersturmführer paused, frowned. A Feldjaeger's authority extended even to the SS, but the man could not let it go like that.

"Yes, sir. But who are they? What are you doing with them, anyway?"

"They are deserters."

"Deserters? Why don't you just shoot them? My men will be happy to oblige you."

"Thank you, Untersturmführer, your zeal is commendable, but I prefer a different kind of justice."

"And the woman?"

"Must I explain everything to you, Untersturmführer? Do you not have duties?" The other end of the street filled suddenly with Ustaše, doubling fast down toward them, and at their head was Captain Marković, his hair awry.

"Of course, sir." The Untersturmführer clicked his heels, inclined his head, and his arm came up. "Heil Hitler."

Reinhardt turned, prodding the Partisans on with his MP 40, and that might have been it, but another voice cut across the street.

"*Stop!*" Marković called.

"Keep moving," Reinhardt hissed to the Partisans.

"Untersturmführer," Marković's voice cracked behind him, "stop those men. Captain Reinhardt!"

"You know these people?" The Untersturmführer's suspicions were back.

"They are saboteurs," Marković shouted. His eyes locked with Reinhardt's and they were wide and wild, and Reinhardt knew he was part of it. "You must stop them."

"This is no concern of yours, Untersturmführer. Nor of yours, Captain Marković."

The Untersturmführer's eyes narrowed, flicking between the pair of them, and he made to unsling his weapon.

From an upstairs window came a shattering of glass and a sudden barrage of gunfire. The street around the SS was riddled with eruptions of dust and stones as bullets rang and burst around them. Some dropped, fell, lay motionless; others turned, swiveling up, vanishing behind puffs of smoke as they returned fire. Brick and glass exploded along the line of windows.

Simo and Perić broke into a run.

"HALT!" screamed the Untersturmführer.

"*Run!*" called Reinhardt, staying back, trying to stay between them and the others, the SS and the Ustaše. He fired his MP 40, stabbing a line of bullets into the street behind the Partisans' heels, as if opening fire on them. He turned back to the Untersturmführer, lifted his hand, and saw Marković heave something into the air, watched it tumble overhead, bounce off the wall and land with a wooden thunk. Reinhardt pulled Vukić and Neven to the ground as the stick grenade exploded. There was a short scream, and Reinhardt was rolling back toward the SS and Ustaše. Many were down, but the Untersturmführer was still standing, Marković behind him, and they were firing at him, the Ustaša's eyes crazed with a kind of blurred focus. Reinhardt took a moment, aimed carefully, and fired back, emptying the magazine. The MP 40 juddered agonizingly against his injured wrist, and the two of them were hurled backward as he stitched his fire across them.

The weapon clicked empty, and he dropped it, rising to one knee, shrugging Perić's MP 40 from his shoulder and unfolding the stock as a clutch of SS opened fire on him. The bullets clacked past as they fired, high and wild, and he was still and cold as he hunched into the MP 40, pushing it hard forward on its straps, aimed, dropped one, then shifted to a second, but there was a ripping shatter of fire from behind him as Benfeld opened up with the turret gun. Reinhardt collapsed flat as the air overhead was threaded thick with metal, the walls and pavement vanishing in clouds of dust and brick as Benfeld hosed his fire across the street, and the SS and Ustaše were tossed back and down.

In the sudden silence Reinhardt surged to his feet, let the MP 40 fall on its strap, turned, and hauled Vukić and the boy up. They ran to the others. The grenade had caught both of them from behind and shredded their clothing. Perić was dead, the back of his head pulped, and a huge pool of blood glistened beneath him, making islands of the street's cobbles as it flowed in sluggish twists away from his body. Simo moaned as he clawed at the street with his arms, one leg useless behind him. He hauled himself to his side, saw Perić, and cursed bitterly, biting back on his own pain. Reinhardt motioned, and the pair of them dragged Simo into a doorway, Reinhardt gritting his teeth against the pain in his wrist and his knee. Neven hauled on the handle, and the door creaked open onto a dark hallway. They pulled Simo inside as the boy pushed the door shut. Across the street, Benfeld made to jump down from the car, but Reinhardt waved him back.

Vukić and Reinhardt shared a flat gaze, and each knew the turmoil that screamed behind their eyes.

"You cannot stay here," she said.

"I'm not coming back, Suzana." She blinked, and her eyes glistened, suddenly. "But there's a circle I have to close. You can still help me. Both of you," he said, taking in Simo where the big Partisan blinked up at him from the floor.

"Tell me."

So he drew her close, and told her. She stiffened, then nodded as he spoke, and she relaxed into his arms. He pulled back, looking into her eyes, pushing himself down into them.

"You understand?"

"Yes. I think . . . yes, it can work."

"It must." He handed her the MP 40, then knelt to take Simo's hand. "Luck to you, Simo."

"And you, Captain Reinhardt."

Neven tapped him on the shoulder. The little boy was solemn, his eyes wide. Reinhardt extended his hand, and Neven took it, then tentatively wrapped thin arms around Reinhardt's neck. Reinhardt froze, then closed his own arms around the fragile span of Neven's shoulders.

Vukić walked him to the door. He brushed his fingers down her cheek. She blinked hard, and he opened the door, glancing up and down the street.

"Wait," Vukić said, slipping past him, craning her head up at the windows. She called something, her eyes wide, then called again. A voice came back at her. "You can go," she said, breathlessly. A last exchange of eyes, and he slipped out, running over to the *panzerfunkwagen*.

"Captain, what the fuck is going on?!" Benfeld yelled. "What the hell just happened?"

"Get back inside," he shouted at Benfeld. He ducked inside the car, hearing Benfeld clamber up into the turret. He pulled the door shut, pausing only to spare a last glance at Perić, where he lay in a puddle of red. The *panzerfunkwagen*'s engine exploded into life. Reinhardt paused, looked back at the street, at the bodies strewn across it, and drove the car the few dozen meters up to where Marković lay. Leaving the engine running, he slipped out of the car, his eyes stabbing across the shattered windows above. His fingers slithered across the Ustaša's body into the tunic pockets and pulled out a *soldbuch*, its cover matted red with blood. He backed away from the body. From windows above, pale faces peered down at him, tracked him back into the car. He dumped himself back into the seat, breathing heavily, and tore the car away from that street and the tumble of bodies that lay across it.

He drove the wrong way down Kvaternik, racing the river as it hurled itself along its rocky bed. Where the road joined with King Alexander Street at Marijin Dvor, Reinhardt merged the car into a broken flow of vehicles all streaming west out of the city. On a building, a red flag suddenly bloomed from a window; from roofs men and women waved crimson banners back and forth. A crowd of children shrieked as they hurled stones at the vehicles as they passed, and rocks clanged off the *panzerfunkwagen*'s armored sides. The edges of Sarajevo flickered past through the vehicle's viewports, the steps and pillars of the National Museum on the left, the long white walls of the barracks on the right, the graded lines of its roofs dark and gray beneath a smog of ash and fumes from the burning inside. A train was pulling out of the station as he sped past, its engine belching thick smoke in frantic bursts as it struggled to build up speed. Then the buildings were gone, and it was only open countryside to left and right, fields that spread and bowled up into the mounded lines of the hills to north and south.

Weaving in and out of the traffic, Reinhardt spotted what he was looking for and pulled the car off the road, bouncing it up a dirt track to where a low hill afforded a view back east. He turned the engine off, and there was a moment when there was nothing, no sound. He savored it, feeling the silence flowing up finally into the space he had made for it, and he climbed out of the car. He walked a little way, lighting a cigarette, one hand rubbing the swelling on his wrist, looking back at Sarajevo.

Under a tumult of clouds, the city lay under a gray pall of smoke that rose and eddied to the vagaries of the wind. The valley wore its shadows deep, the sun shining in great shafts through towering thunderheads, and these shafts caught the lines of the city in a luminous gray glow. Thick smoke lay to the north where the fighting was heaviest, the slopes alive with fire, tongues of orange flame that bled up into the sky. Beyond it all, the mountains lifted their folded shoulders in great furls of dark purple and green, the highest peaks still white with snow. He looked out across the rolling plain, over the chaos of vehicles along the thread of the road, saw how the colors of the grasses shifted as the wind and light passed over them, and heard the soft footstep behind him and the slow slide of a pistol's action.

"You have a choice, Frenchie," Reinhardt said, taking a long pull on his cigarette. He looked at the glowing end of it, where it flared brightly in the wind that flowed over this little hill, turned his head slightly to see Benfeld behind and to one side, a pistol held quivering in an outstretched arm. "You don't need to do what they tell you anymore."

"What do they tell me, Reinhardt?" Benfeld grated, and Reinhardt felt relief that Benfeld would talk.

"They tell you to look, and listen. To wait and watch. To go where they want, and do what they say." Reinhardt turned to look fully at Benfeld, the burning city etched across the dappled horizon behind him. "They say these things because they have a hold over you. What was it? Your brother?" Benfeld's eyes flickered wide, narrow, twitching back and forth, and his mouth moved, his knuckles tightening white on the pistol. "What did they say?"

"They said . . . they could take him out of where he was. From that penal battalion, on the Eastern Front."

"Who said these things, Benfeld?"

"A general. And . . . a judge. They said, if I didn't help them, they would make sure he never survived. They talked of my father, and my mother. They said they could do anything. The general, he boasted of . . . other things. Betrayals. The judge, he . . . blathered on about the future."

"Oh, Benfeld." Reinhardt shook his head. "You know that your brother is gone. Men don't survive penal battalions. Not in the east. It's what they're for."

"So what?" The younger man began to break down. "What could I have said? They knew everything. Everything about me."

"So you told them what I was doing?" Benfeld nodded. "Where I was going? All those things I asked you to do, you did not do them."

"Yes."

"You told them of Koenig."

"Yes."

"They killed him. He was my friend, and they killed him."

"I am sorry," Benfeld whispered.

"You used the radio in the city. You told them, you told someone, where I was."

"I didn't . . ." He stopped under Reinhardt's eyes, and the heavy glance Reinhardt put behind them at the *panzerfunkwagen*'s raised antenna.

"You couldn't even have known what I was doing. You could not even have known if it was about Jansky."

"They told me 'everything,' Reinhardt. *Everything* you do."

"So you radioed it in? To whom?"

"It doesn't matter. They just said to call in where you went. I'm sorry, Reinhardt."

"No, it's me. I suspected you. I thought you were the only one to watch out for, but there was another, and you slipped my gaze. If I had known the hold they had over you, I would not have brought you. You . . . we . . . cost a good man his life."

"That Partisan?"

"That 'Partisan' was none other than Valter, Benfeld, the Partisans' will-o'-the-wisp. Dead on the last day of his war. And now, you must make your choice."

Benfeld shook, his mouth bunched, and his eyes clenched shut. His forearm went up, and he placed the back of the pistol against his forehead. Reinhardt felt what was coming, and was close enough when Benfeld slid the pistol under his own chin. Reinhardt placed his hand over the gun, gripping it tight and shifting it just enough.

"That is not the way, Frenchie," he whispered. The two stood almost nose to nose, eye to eye. Benfeld strained at the gun; Reinhardt's wrist shook and throbbed. He felt Benfeld's strength through the strain of their arms and knew he could not stop him, whatever the young Feldjaeger decided to do.

"But it is. It is. It goes on forever, Reinhardt. How can you ever fight them?"

THE PALE HOUSE 329

"By taking apart what you see in front of you. Stone by stone. Brick by brick. Piece by piece. And before you know it you have a hole in a wall."

"What use is that?"

"A wall with a hole's not much of a wall," said Reinhardt, a wry edge to his voice, pushing, searching for some crack in Benfeld's misery. "It's not men we fight or move against. It's a system. It's men as pieces on a board. But you can only play the hand you're dealt."

"It . . . what does that even mean, Reinhardt?"

"I don't have all the answers. I don't even know if I make sense to myself. But it's about the beauty or danger of a system, Frenchie. Do you see? In a system, who is responsible? Who is to blame? And if you find no one man is to blame, whom do you seek out . . . ? You seek out the ones you can find. Start with that. Start small. The rest will come."

Benfeld wiped an angry hand across his eyes. "You sound so sure. I want . . . to believe you."

Reinhardt put his hand on the back of Benfeld's neck, butted their heads together. "Believe, Frenchie. I know where they are. I know what they've done. We can end this little bit. You and me, and the others. And you have already made your choice, on that street, when you covered me from the turret when the SS were firing at me. And you've made it here. Now."

PART FOUR

The Dead
Ride Quickly

31

The door creaked softly as Reinhardt eased it open. The room inside was empty, only a pair of battered tables standing against bare concrete walls. It was warm, though; the outlines of an iron stove in the middle of the room shimmered through the mirage of its heat, and there was that smell, that tubercular reek. He closed the door softly behind him, standing, listening. From the opposite wall, windows let in yellow daylight, a view through warped panes of a large courtyard bounded by high brick walls.

He walked slowly over to a door that was slightly ajar, pushing it open. Inside, that smell was stronger, and a shape lay humped on a camp bed, covered in a gray blanket. Reinhardt touched it with a finger, gently at first, then a little harder, and the shape rolled over, thin shoulders dropping to the bed, a skeletal head following. Eyes blinked up at him, and a hand came out from under the covers and touched the red band around Reinhardt's wrist, then the gorget hanging from his throat.

"It's you," the old colonel whispered. Pistorius.

Reinhardt nodded, unfolding the piece of paper with the bloodstain, and the names written across its fine grain in that flowing, old-fashioned script. The colonel's eyes blinked at it, then up at Reinhardt.

"You understood."

"Yes," said Reinhardt. "It was you. You sent Kreuz to me, as well, and gave him those *soldbuchs*."

"Yes," Pistorius breathed, struggling to sit up. Reinhardt slid a hand under his back, feeling the blade of his shoulders clearly through the colonel's tunic, but the man waved him away, collapsing back onto the bed and coughing. Pistorius turned his head, hacking wetly into a handkerchief already stained with red. "It was me," he managed, finally. "It was my last . . . throw . . . in this game of theirs. My last chance. When I saw . . . saw you, I knew . . ." His voice faded out.

"They used you, too."

"Yes. They used me. One . . . indiscretion. A woman. That was all. Used my reputation. And they said . . . they said they would keep my family safe. Safe. I was dying, anyway." Pistorius's eyes flickered open and shut to the tortured rhythm of his breath.

Someone came into the other room, a quick tap of feet. Reinhardt stood slowly, then paused as the colonel's hand plucked at his.

"Is it over, now?"

Reinhardt nodded, and Pistorius went limp in his bed, a small sigh escaping. He walked quietly to the door, then stepped softly into the other room. There was a man standing there, bent over papers on one of the tables. The man turned, and his eyes flared wide in panic. It was written broad across his face, just for a moment, before he looked past Reinhardt, searching for others. The two of them faced off, the air crackling between them, before Jansky turned back to his papers. "Captain Reinhardt. What a surprise. Is there something I can help you with?"

"Major Jansky, you are under arrest . . ."

"Oh, please."

". . . for the murders of George Abler, Carl Benirschke, Otto—"

"You are persistent, Captain Reinhardt, I'll give you that."

"You are a shit, Major Jansky. I'll give *you* that."

Jansky laughed. "Careful, Reinhardt. You're speaking to a senior officer."

"Major Jansky, you are under arrest for the murders of—"

"Oh, spare me, Reinhardt." Jansky sneered. "You don't know what you're ta—"

He stopped as Reinhardt flipped Keppel's *soldbuch* at him, flicking it like a playing card. "I can't figure that one out. What was it? A first attempt?"

Jansky opened the *soldbuch*, tossed it back at Reinhardt, where it flopped open against his boots. "A first attempt at what, Reinhardt?"

"That must have been when you were trying to forge the books, before someone hit on the idea of just issuing replacements." Reinhardt opened the bloodied *soldbuch* he had taken off Marković's body. The name on the book was that of Ulrich Vierow, one of the names from the paper the colonel had given him, but it was Marković's face that stared up at him in elegant profile. He snapped the book at Jansky, where it bounced off the Feldgendarme's chest. "You still needed the forger, I suppose. Signatures, stamps, some level of authenticity. You know Putković killed him?"

"Killed who, Reinhardt?" Jansky smiled, but it was taut and tight at the corners as he glanced at Marković's book, then tossed it aside onto the table.

"Your forger. He's lying dead in the Pale House."

"If you say so. I don't know what you're talking about."

"Why did you do it?"

"Do what?"

"Who shot those three men in the forest?"

"Which men?" Jansky turned away, rifling through his papers.

"I'm fairly sure it was you, and Lieutenants Brandt and Metzler. If you didn't know it already, Metzler's out of it. I left him for dead in the archives at the barracks, and Erdmann committed suicide. I found the trial transcripts . . ."

He broke off as Jansky whirled around, a pistol in his hand and his arm extending straight, but Reinhardt had seen it and had sidled closer to Jansky as the other man had his back turned. He stepped inside the length of Jansky's arm, gripped and held it under his own, and stripped the gun from the Feldgendarme's hand and threw it away. Jansky yelped as the pistol twisted free, and Reinhardt's elbow pistoned into his face. He staggered away but then surged back, his nose streaming blood. He wriggled and struck like an eel, all elbows and knees and hands like blades as he came at Reinhardt. The two of them traded blows, Jansky's fast, jabbing high and low, Reinhardt's more measured, heavier, using elbows and knees as he struck back with all the mounting frustration and anger he had been holding in, beating Jansky down until he swept his legs from under him and stunned him flat with a kick to the side of the head.

He stood over the Feldgendarme, breathing like a bellows and starting to feel the sting and swell of Jansky's blows where they lay over the ones Bunda had inflicted, feeling the cracked pain of his wrist most of all. Jansky pushed himself into a corner and slumped up into it, his eyes the rolling crescents of something beaten. The two of them glared at each other, and then Jansky leaned to one side, worked his mouth, and swore as he spat a tooth to the floor. Reinhardt watched the tooth bounce away, his mind jarring, and just for a moment he was back in that cell with the Gestapo and he envisoned his own tooth rattling across a floor of mismatched tiles.

"Listen, Reinhardt," said Jansky, a finger in his mouth as he felt along its new geometry. "You're a good investigator. Whatever it all is, you found it all out. Bravo."

"This is where it ends, Jansky."

"*What* ends?" Jansky laughed, blood dribbling down his chin, and he sniffed back on his nose.

Reinhardt breathed in, long and slow, pursed his lips. "Very well," he replied. He walked back to the door through which he had entered and made a wave with his hand. Moments later, Colonel Scheller's broad bulk cut across the door frame, Captain Lainer ducking beneath the lintel. The three Feldjaeger stared at Jansky, and the man's chin bunched, and he shifted with the nerves he must have been feeling.

Scheller glanced at his watch. "It is almost time, is it not?"

"Time for what?" Jansky asked, suspicion writ broad across his features. Behind the fan of blood across the bottom of his face, he had gone very white.

"Oh, I don't know. How about a roll call?" Scheller nodded to Lainer. The tall Feldjaeger strode past to the door to the courtyard, and Jansky quailed away from the look that must have been in his eyes. From outside, the strains of a bugle could be heard, and then the sound of men, hundreds of them, falling in across the courtyard, the sounds of their boots and the shuffle of their feet rising to an echoing din, then fading away.

"What are you doing? Reinhardt?"

"Putting an end to this charade, Jansky. Get up."

"Reinhardt," Jansky hissed, his eyes pinned on Reinhardt. "You don't get to have the cake and eat it. There are too many people in this."

"So there is something."

Jansky shook his head, eyes narrowing in frustration. "Most of these people are senior to you and me. So"—he ran a hand across his mouth—"pat yourself on the back. You've royally fucked things up for a lot of people. But just what do you think happens next?"

Reinhardt hauled Jansky to his feet and prodded him outside, into the luminous light of the early morning. Around the courtyard, the Zenica steelworks towered. Smokestacks and chimneys, girders and grids of reddened iron, and everywhere a stench of rust, and coal, and a granular feel to the air, as if it crept inside to coat men's innards with a flouring of dust and filth. Around three walls of the courtyard the men of the penal battalion were drawn up in ranks, a listless sense to their stance even though they stood at attention, but confusion in their faces as they looked at Scheller and Lainer, and behind them Jansky with his bloodied face, Reinhardt close against him. Scheller waved one arm, and the walls of the courtyard were suddenly lined with men, more pouring in through the gates, and the ranks of the penal battalion shifted, lost their cohesion as they bunched away from the newcomers. It was over in seconds, and the penal battalion was ringed with Feldjaeger.

"Gentlemen," Scheller called. "Roll call."

Reinhardt stepped forward in front of the men, running his eyes across them, looking for those faces he knew would be there, knowing he would only be able to recognize one of them. He took the sheet of paper the colonel had written.

"Corporal George Abler," Reinhardt called. "Abler?"

He stared around at the faces of the men, dumb and blank.

"Sergeant Carl Benirschke. Benirschke?"

Something. A shift in the way some men stood. He looked at Jansky. The major blinked back at him and shrugged, his lip twitching up in a sardonic twist.

"The dead ride quickly, Reinhardt."

Something clicked inside, and Reinhardt found himself quoting from some distant memory that unfolded itself like the page of a book, a stanza from Burger's poem, *Lenore.*

"*'Dost hear the bell with its sullen swell,*
As it rumbles out eleven?
Look forth! look forth! the moon shines bright:
We and the dead ride fast by night.'"

And the memory folded itself shut again. "You're not the only one who can trot out the classics when he feels like it, Major. Care to remind me how it ends? It ends in death, does it not?" Jansky went pale and swallowed. Reinhardt turned his back on him.

"Private Otto Berthold."

"Private Werner Janowetz."

"*What the hell is this?*"

The shout had come from the ranks. Reinhardt did not try to find who it was, hoping, wanting the conversation and confusion to spread, to get the men to lance the cancer that lurked within them themselves.

"Private Christian Seymer."

"Is this a fucking joke?" More men took up the call.

"Why would it be a joke?" Reinhardt pointed at one of the men who had shouted.

"Because they're fucking *dead*, that's why."

"Is that right?" Reinhardt called out, a ragged chorus of assent coming back at him.

"Fucking *Partisans* killed 'em."

"Vanished in the forest."

"Is that right?" Reinhardt challenged them, again.

"Fucking right, *hero stealer.*"

"Goddamn chain dog."

Reinhardt turned his eyes across the ranks of men, their mood wretched and cracked, turned his eyes until he found them, the hiwis huddled in a tight mass in a corner of the courtyard. He walked toward them slowly, feeling the weight of the men's attention shift with him. He looked across the hiwis, seeing how they stood stock-still, none of the movement or agitation of the others. He looked across them until he saw him.

"Sergeant Jürgen Sedlazcek."

There was silence, as the men realized this was no game, and there was an edge to the quiet, as if they scented blood.

"Sergeant Jürgen Sedlazcek," Reinhardt called again, holding the man with his eyes. Sedlazcek's trial transcript had noted he had been very big. The man did not move until Reinhardt indicated to a pair of Feldjaeger, and they hauled the man out of the ranks. Big, fleshy, an old uniform devoid of insignia stretched taught over his height and weight, and a black belt bowing under a vast spread of gut. "Sergeant Jürgen Sedlazcek," Reinhardt said, looking up into the flat eyes of Ustaše colonel Ante Putković. "Point out the others to me, please."

"Fuck off."

"I know Zulim is dead," Reinhardt said, holding up Abler's *soldbuch*. "Bunda got rid of him, on your orders, probably. He had drawn too much attention to himself."

Putković swore something under his breath. "Fucking Bunda. What a fucking bull."

"Yes, he was, rather. He tended to overreact with predictable regularity. He was the one who smashed in the faces of those five prisoners, I'm guessing, probably in a panic when you heard I was around.

Overkill, if you'll excuse the term. Doing that just drew attention to the fact they had no faces, and so of course I wondered why. Still, if you send a butcher to do a tailor's work, that's what you get."

"Go to hell."

"Bunda's dead, too."

"You're lying."

Putković went pale as Reinhardt took Bunda's *soldbuch* from his pocket, held it up.

"I watched Suzana Vukić rip his balls off, and I left him to bleed his life out."

"What?"

Reinhardt held up Marković's *soldbuch*. Then Labaš's.

"Point out the others, please."

"No."

"Bozidar Brkić. Tomislav Dubreta. Zvonimir Saulan." Putković blinked. "Do it quick, or I'll tell the men what you've done, and watch them rip you all to pieces."

Reinhardt watched the play of frustration on Putković's face, and then he turned and called something out. Three men stepped out of the lines, joining Putković. Reinhardt was about to speak when he saw something in Putković's eyes, some glitter of a secret suppressed.

Ten names, Reinhardt thought. Ten Ustaše. Four of them were dead. Bunda, Labaš, Zulim, and Marković. That left six, and four were standing in front of him.

There were two more, somewhere.

Reinhardt walked slowly along the ranks, his eyes flowing over faces, and then he saw him. It was the man's eyes that gave him away, shifting back and forth between Reinhardt and something on the far side of the courtyard.

"You." Reinhardt pointed. The man did not move. "You," Reinhardt said, again. The night Bunda and Putković had brought Reinhardt to the Pale House, he was the one who had been torturing the prisoner.

"Sutko."

The man swallowed and stepped out of the ranks.

"And you," Reinhardt said, swiveling his arm at a second man, half hidden behind a soldier. The man jumped, went pale. He had been there with Sutko that same night. He had killed the prisoner on Putković's orders as a demonstration to Reinhardt of the Ustaše's supposed power, and why they did not need to do their killing in secret. Reinhardt remembered the man's name. "Marin."

Reinhardt ran his eyes over them. Tall, short, slim, fat, blond hair, dark hair.

Average men.

Hidden in plain sight.

Reinhardt nodded to the Feldjaeger, and the six Ustaše were taken away, back into the command post. He walked back to Jansky, standing there thin and broken in the middle of the courtyard.

"The dead ride quickly, it would seem, indeed."

32

A truck drove away from Zenica, away from the pallid town that clustered around the steelworks. The Bosna River flowed north as the truck went south, a placid river, wide, bottle green, thin streamers of mist hanging like a man's breath on a cold morning. The river was bounded on both sides by low hills that rolled up and away from the road, shrouded in trees that plucked and pinched at the sky-line. There was a quality to the light, as if each branch and leaf of the thick forests that coated the hills had been picked out, shining and limned like the fine hair on a young girl's arm when the sun shines at the right angle.

Benfeld drove, the big Feldjaeger taciturn and unquestioning. Though Reinhardt's eyes watched the road unwind before him, his thoughts were back in the steelworks, in that office, hearing the thuds and groans from the other room where Lainer and his men had set about Jansky and Brandt. It was payback. Reinhardt understood that, although the man he had been—the man forged in police work, the man who had eschewed the child of the first war he had so recently been—would not have.

So he had sat and waited, smoked a cigarette and looked at a pile of ten *soldbuchs*, and the court-martial records he had found in the archives, but it was into himself he looked, into that rent that ran down within him, feeling the coiling within of something old and hoary, staring back into its eye as it rolled mad and bloodshot. It was there, gripping the rent inside him with mud-smeared fingers, as if it wanted to come out, but as if it were content to let him alone. As if what Reinhardt was doing satisfied its sense of right and wrong.

In the corner of the room, Scheller talked with a judge. Reinhardt had presented what he knew to him, the whole story, and the *soldbuchs*, and the files. The judge had clearly been panicked by the case, had wanted to take it as he would have wanted to grasp a shitty pole. Whether he would or not, Reinhardt found he did not care. His part was done. He had his hole in the wall, rubble about his feet, and enough light shining through for him to see something of the shape of the structure he had come across. He had no illusions he could do much more than he already had, and he wondered at the contentment this seemed to afford him.

"The *thrill*, Reinhardt," Jansky had said, his words mumbled through his lacerated lips when Lainer had finally let him out, led him stumbling blind to a chair and dropped him into it. Jansky's face had been swollen almost beyond belief, and he had sat hunched over to the side. In the chair next to him, Lieutenant Brandt's eyes were bloodied shut, and they bracketed a nose that was crushed and misshapen. Jansky had smoked a cigarette through the last two fingers of his hand, the others swollen and broken. "Getting away with it. Herzog and Erdmann and the others can believe what they want. For me it was the challenge, the thrill. The money helped, of course."

"Did you kill those three Feldjaeger?"

"Yes. Me and Brandt and Metzler." He cocked his head to his cigarette, pecking at it with his broken lips like a bird at water, something strangely effcte in his movements. "They found us up at the construction site. Bunda was with us, and a couple of his men."

"That was where you killed those five soldiers?"

"Yes. We'd shot them there when we found out we couldn't go

back to the forest, and left the bodies because even if we weren't working there anymore the site was still ours, and under our guard. We'd
have come up quietly during the day to bring that house down on
them. End of story. But Bunda was terrified of you and when we found
we had to get rid of the bodies in the city, he was even more scared. He
went berserk. You've never seen anything like what he did to those
bodies. He smashed their faces in with his club, and then he dressed
them in clothes he'd brought from the Pale House. He was like a boy
playing with dolls." Jansky giggled. "Playing dress-up, muttering to
himself. But then two of his men kicked over that flare and it killed
one of them—"

"Labaš?"

"Labaš." Jansky nodded. "Burnt him to death. And then your Feld-
jaegers showed up. You know the rest."

"You sent Lieutenant Brandt to try to clear things up."

"Waste of time, but we had to try. When he found out what Bunda
had done, disfiguring those bodies and triggering all that mess,
Putković was furious. He would have just put them in the Pale House,
mixed them up in all the other bodies, but it was too late. Bunda had
panicked, but then it got worse. Bunda sent Zulim to get those refugees, the ones you found, but that just made you more suspicious and
you came looking for Zulim, so Bunda panicked again. Bye-bye Zulim.
I mean," said Jansky, drawing on his cigarette, "those two were virtually inseparable, but Bunda was unstoppable. He was so fucking scared.
Putković is apoplectic at this point, and tried to make the best of it and
throw you a false trail, but no good. Bunda. What a moron. Ironic,
though, isn't it? That we should"—Jansky coughed, smoke splurting
from his mouth as he winced in pain and squinted bloodied eyes at the
judge—"that we should have been more careful listening to him. And
been more careful with those *soldbuchs*. Zulim's and Labaš's, when we
got them back."

The rest of it had come. Names, places, the genesis of the idea,
starting when Jansky had been approached by Alexiou, offered money
in exchange for being able to hide himself and his men in the ranks of
a unit no one would think to look in. Then, as the penal battalion

retreated shattered and broken through Montenegro, Herzog and Erdmann appeared to him one night, long speeches about the rightness of their cause, the need to preserve for the future. "I thought they were mad," Jansky had said, carefully stubbing out his cigarette, one hand supporting his wrist. "And they were, but they weren't going to take no for an answer. They brought that doddering bemedaled old fool of a colonel—Pistorius, that one hacking his lungs up in the next room—and said he would provide the respectability needed to make sure disreputable things could happily take place."

"To be managed by you," Reinhardt had said.

"By yours truly." Jansky had nodded. "Not that I had a choice. Herzog and Erdmann were nothing if not peruasive. And I was already halfway to their ideas anyway." He spoke of how the two of them had revealed to Jansky their knowledge of his corruption, of his selling asylum to the highest bidder, and winding him tight to their cause with cords of his own making. That was a surprise, Reinhardt acknowledged, that Jansky had fallen into their clutches as well. He had always considered Jansky an instigator of the scheme, not a pawn in it, and in a way that was true. Herzog's and Erdmann's cabal had roped him in, but Jansky had played along willingly. The thrill of it, Reinhardt reminded himself.

The first victim had been killed in Montenegro, his life taken for an Albanian from the SS Skanderbeg Division. Two more had followed as Jansky and the cabal perfected their techniques, but the forgeries were always tricky, even after Erdmann found the forger, dredged up from who knew where.

"Their *names*?" Jansky had stuttered when Reinhardt interrupted him.

"Their names," Reinhardt repeated. "The names of those men whose identities you took."

Jansky's eyes drifted sideways, rolling and bloodshot. "I can't . . . Roesing? Roese . . . ? And . . . Kaubisch? I really can't . . . remember." He trailed off at the look on Reinhardt's face, the fury boiling out of his eyes at the thought of those men simply erased from the earth.

Jansky talked on, and Dreyer reappeared, tried to resume his con tact with him. "He was pitiful," sniggered Jansky. "Thinking he had something on me, when it was the other way around." The iron jaws of the cabal and the web of blackmail closed itself around Dreyer and reminded him of that one moment of weakness in Poland, and he found himself presiding over courts-martial, but selective ones, targeting a particular type of soldier, and at that time, as the army began to crumble, there was no lack of raw material for the cabal's scheme. "And then we came to Sarajevo, and the feelers went out to the Ustaše, and oh my, were there takers for it!" Jansky cackled, pointing at the *soldbuchs*.

The Ustaše had provided the photographer, getting rid of him at the end in the forest. But the Partisans were pressing harder and faster than anyone thought, and time was short. It had been Jansky's idea to use replacement *soldbuchs*, instead of trying to add forged entries to existing ones. It had been Jansky's idea as well to "steal" the defense plans so as to cause confusion and accelerate the city's evacuation, with the subsequent compromising of Colonel Wedel and the pressure on him to accept responsibility for the "theft." It all came delivered in a mumbled monotone through broken lips except when Jansky laughed, remembering particularly ironic moments while, with one finger, he traced the pattern of the tabletop, his nail dipping into the whorls of the wood, sticking, moving on.

"Why these Ustaše? Why not others?"

Jansky shrugged. "I don't know. Herzog and Erdmann considered Putković to be worth something. In any case, there was no way they'd be able to shelter someone like Luburić, even if they could've convinced him. Putković was worth it, I suppose, and he was the one who brought along the others. His henchmen. His clan. And of course, it helped that they paid. Handsomely. Money up front, or no *soldbuch*." He giggled. "In any case, ten was about the right number."

"Ten Ustaše?"

"Ten Volksdeutsche." Jansky smiled, teeth like needles behind a scum of blood. "Dreyer was doing his best to round up as many as he could, but it was hard to find the right profiles. 'Specially ones as big as Bunda and Putković."

"Who is behind it all?"

Jansky had shaken his head. "I don't know. I don't know anyone other than Herzog and Erdmann."

"There are others."

"There must be," Jansky had replied, a sudden clarity to his words. "If you think about it, this might be happening everywhere. This, or something like it. We've a lot of friends to get out of harm's way. Or, you could think of this as a trial run. For something bigger and better." He had grinned at the thought. "Think of that, eh? What does that do to your policeman's soul?"

When Reinhardt had left, Scheller was involved in helping the judge find his backbone and confront Herzog, but the colonel had been doubtful anything would come of that. Outwardly, Herzog would suffer no consequences, Reinhardt knew. There was no proof linking him to the deaths, only Jansky's word against his, but Reinhardt consoled himself with the thought that the powerful suffered their own sanctions. There would always be rumors about Herzog, because Scheller would be sure to start spreading them. People would talk, there would be a loss of confidence, perhaps a transfer, and with any luck, someone—perhaps someone higher in the conspiracy than Herzog—would suggest to him a quiet way out, and perhaps that person would leave behind a pistol with one round in the chamber. For personal use.

Jansky would not talk, and in any case, Jansky was gone now, Reinhardt knew. Lainer would not let him live, and if he was honest with himself, Reinhardt did not care either way. The dead would ride no more, and although *Lenore* ended with a hint of redemption for its damned heroine, there would be none for Jansky. The trail stopped with him. Whatever Jansky said, the proof would not suffice to reel anyone else in. Herzog would be the judge's problem, and maybe Scheller's. Erdmann was dead. Whoever was in Vienna would remain nameless. The others, too, because there were bound to be others.

And that was all right, too, he realized.

The penal battalion would be broken up, the men dispersed. Most of them would go back to their original units, while the incorrigible cases would be sentenced elsewhere. The hiwis were—there was no other way to put it—in trouble.

It was an escape line Reinhardt had stumbled across, he knew now. Some way of rescuing something from the wrack and ruin of the war, a way of preserving something for someone's twisted vision of the future. Again, that image came to him of a ship that was foundering, sinking slowly and rolling belly-up in dark waters, its hull a squirming mass, rats abandoning ship searching for a chance—any chance—at escape. Some would drown. Some would strike away alone across the waters; others would find some way to survive, entrust themselves to a desperate lunge at safety.

Rats abandoning a ship. Someone throwing a lifeline.

A ratline.

There had just been the last question, the one Reinhardt had been loath to ask.

"What was it with you and Dreyer?"

Jansky had tilted his head back, the better to needle the slits of his eyes at Reinhardt. "Give me another cigarette, and I'll tell you. Dreyer came after me in Poland," Jansky had said, blowing smoke across the table. "A real terrier. He had witnesses to what we were up to, trafficking artwork back to the Reich, weapons to the Polish underground. We made the witnesses go away. Those we couldn't kill, we bribed quiet. You should've seen how hard he tried to get to us. Almost made you feel sorry for him."

He had drawn long and hard on his cigarette, eyes drifting to Brandt, where the lieutenant sat slumped with his head across his arms. "He found someone, eventually, a last witness. Probably wouldn't have done much, but we took no chances, made him an offer. And he refused. Then we made him another. And it's true what they say, that every man has his price. He didn't look very proud of himself, but he took what we offered. I told him not to take it so badly, that if he could not beat us, he might as well join us. He took a bribe." Jansky grinned, a cocky twist of his lacerated lips. "And that's when I told him, 'All are not huntsmen . . .'"

"'. . . who can blow the hunter's horn,'" Reinhardt finished.

"The army broke us apart, and he went one way and I went another. Never gave him another thought until he showed up in Greece, working for the War Crimes Bureau. He had heard something of what I had done with the Greeks, stealing all that gold, and he tried to blackmail me in return for a share. Poor bugger. He didn't have a clue what he was getting himself into. Before he knew it, they had him out of the Bureau and back into the army judicial service. He wasn't the same man, though," Jansky said, considering. "Russia had really screwed him up."

"What did you bribe him with? That time in Poland."

"You know that Art Deco rubbish? All that modern crap? He was mad for it, and we were up to our eyeballs in the stuff. The Poles had a real taste for it, particularly the aristocrats, and the Jews. All those artists and intellectuals. I laid a whole load out for him. Glasses. Vases. Ashtrays. Jewelry. Paintings. What did it for him was this flask by some Jewish artist. It mesmerized him."

Reinhardt looked at the flask where it lay against his leg, then up at the road as it wound on, almost empty, only the occasional truck or car hurrying north. Sometimes a village flashed past hard by the road, clustered around the spike of a minaret, or a hamlet lifted its roofs from the forest, but there was no one and nothing in them. The countryside was empty, the people vanished, knowing the war was about to roll over them, and Reinhardt watched the trees, wondering how it would look if, by some magic, he could cause them to vanish. What would he see, he wondered, imagining a host of people that would suddenly appear as if brought forth by his own will.

They reached the front lines at around noon, although *line* would not have been the description Reinhardt would have given the cluster of tanks and mobile guns he found at the crossroads near the town of Kakanj. The officer in charge had been warned of their coming, and they passed through without comment, feeling the eyes of the rear guard until the winding road hid them from sight. They stopped when they were out of sight of the Germans long enough for Reinhardt to tie red streamers to the truck's wing mirrors, and then they were moving again, slower now, deeper every minute into Partisan territory.

They found them just north of Visoko. A car was parked by the side of the road with a red flag flying from a makeshift pole that had been wedged into its rear window. A man straightened from where he had been smoking as the truck appeared, and climbed into the car, his arm emerging to wave the truck to follow him. They pulled in behind him until they arrived in a ruined hamlet with a truck drawn up across the road, a red flag draped over its bonnet. Partisans emerged from cover behind the hamlet's gapped walls. They were big men, some with closely shorn beards, and they carried weapons that looked well cared for. They were dressed in uniforms of green and brown, leather boots on their feet, and if their faces were dark with the grime of long journeys, they carried themselves like soldiers of the victorious army they were.

Benfeld turned the truck and reversed it so it was facing back north, and let the engine clatter into silence. Reinhardt climbed down and walked slowly toward the Partisans, his arms open at his sides until he reached a point midway between his truck and the Partisans, and there he waited. He stayed there, still, under the curious eyes of a dozen Partisan soldiers until he saw movement behind their truck, and two people passed onto the road. One was tall, walked with a limp, and leaned heavily on a cane. The other was a woman, dressed like a man in a dark blouse and trousers tucked into low boots, a pistol belted at her waist, looking curiously like a Russian. He watched her, drinking in the sight of her, at the wisps of gray-gold hair that escaped the knot she had bound at the nape of her neck.

The three of them stood together in the middle of the road, a peculiar tension molding the spaces between them. It was the change in the balance of power, Reinhardt knew. He had always been the interloper, but they had not always been able to stand tall before him like they did now.

"You kept your word," said Simo, finally.

Reinhardt pulled his eyes from Vukić and nodded, wondering if he looked as distant to her as she did to him.

"This way," he said, walking back to the truck. Simo and Vukić followed, and a handful of Partisan soldiers followed them. Reinhardt nodded to Benfeld, and he unfastened the chain that secured the back doors, then pulled them open, light pouring into the dark box of the truck's load bed.

Putković blinked against the glare, lifted bound hands to shield his eyes. Next to him, the five others did the same, lowering them slowly, squinting in confusion. Then, one after the other, the realization of where they were was swept away, replaced by fear that rose and bloomed across their faces.

The Partisans stared up at them with what Reinhardt could only describe as a ravenous hunger that could neither declare nor sate itself. As if, confronted by their enemies, now, at the moment of their victory, all their hopes and options had suddenly collapsed down to one point. To a single road, one they were loath to take, as if to do so would break a moment so long hoped for. Until Simo broke it, pointing at them, then down at the road.

"*Izlazite.*"

Putković climbed down and stood on weak legs, leaning back against the truck. Two others managed to get out themselves, but Sutko broke and cowered in the back until two big Partisans went in after him and cast him in a blubbering heap on the road. Simo stood before them, measuring them with the weight of his eyes.

"Franjo Sutko," he grated, looking at the one who had collapsed to the ground. "Bozidar Brkić. Tomislav Dubreta. Zvonimir Saulan. Nikola Marin." They flinched away from him though he did not move. "And Ante Putković." Simo nodded to his men, and each of the Ustaše were bracketed by Partisans and marched away. Only Putković delayed, digging his weight into the ground, his eyes on Reinhardt.

"You know what they will do to us. You know."

"I know," Reinhardt replied.

"You will let them?"

"I will."

"This is on your head."

"I know," said Reinhardt.

"On your head," Putković shouted over his shoulder as they dragged him away. "*Your head.*"

"A last time I must thank you, Captain," said Simo, exchanging his cane to his left hand to offer his right. "To your future, Reinhardt. May it . . . may it be the one you deserve," the big Partisan finished. He glanced between Reinhardt and Vukić, settled his cane back into his right hand, and limped away.

"Let us walk a little," Vukić said softly. His heart in his throat, Reinhardt matched her steps over to the side of the road, where she turned to look up at him.

"Are you all right, Suzana?" he asked. She nodded, ducked her head a moment, then smiled up at him, but it was tight, strained, and they both knew her healing would be a time in coming. "You look different," Reinhardt said. "But it looks right."

"Different times, now, Gregor," she said, simply. Neither of them moved, until Reinhardt's hand came up, brushing up her arm to her shoulder. Her hand came up and covered his. "Your hand. How is it?"

"Fine."

She ran her fingers over the swelling and bruising that mottled his wrist. "I . . . I told Perić about you."

"I know."

"I thought you could help us."

"I did. You were right."

"Was it real, Gregor? That moment we had. I am afraid it . . . it was not."

"I never used you, Suzana," he said, feeling it come out in a rush. "Neven, and the Partisans. I knew. But it was you I wanted."

"It was real," she said, an affirmation that seemed to lift her free of something.

He took her hand, raised it to his lips. "If we had that freedom, you and I . . ."

"It could have worked," she whispered, her fingers light against his cheek. "You could . . . you could come back with me."

"You have a city and a country to rebuild. You could not do it with me. It would color you."

"I don't care."

"You would come to care."

"Maybe when this is all over . . ."

Reinhardt gave a wan smile. "If we deserve it." She smiled as well, remembering their conversation that night. Only memories abide, and the first cut was the one that went deepest. But a clean cut was the best kind, and he kissed her eyes, feeling the salt of her tears. "May you find the happiness you deserve," he whispered against the curve of her brow.

He turned and walked away, feeling as if his heart were stretching out behind him.

EPILOGUE

D awn came with the Sava River shrouded in thick fog, and the world was pale and faint. Men appeared through it like apparitions, looming silent and insubstantial like beings only partially imagined. Along the surface of the river, the fog was so thick Reinhardt almost imagined that, were his heart light enough, he could step out and walk on it, and let it carry him somewhere else.

By the bridge, where they had pulled over, the Feldjaeger had started a fire. Reinhardt stood close to the blaze, watching the orange light slide over the scrollwork on Dreyer's flask as he tilted it to the fire. He looked up to see a company of Cossacks in German uniforms loom out of the fog as though called that instant from some other realm, a column of horsemen stepping slowly over the fields and onto the metaled road that led up to the bridge. One of them, a young man with broad cheekbones and eyes of flinty blue, leaned out of the saddle and spat as he saw Reinhardt. Riding close behind him, a Cossack sergeant—a *starshiy* with a magnificent curled mustache—cuffed the trooper hard on the back of the neck, let loose a stream of expletives in Russian, and nodded an apology at Reinhardt as he rode past, the horses clattering onto the bridge, many laden with women and children. Reinhardt watched them go, a people in exile, the ground shifting daily under their hopes and aspirations. There could be no future for them that was not grim, that would not end in blood and tears and betrayal.

Although the land was tilting slowly toward spring, frost still crusted the creases of the land a thick, shiny white, but where the horses had passed the frosty ground had turned to one trodden into slippery chunks and mud. Cars, trucks, horse-drawn wagons, tanks, half-tracks, everything and anything that could roll had been scooped up. The German retreat had passed over the land like a rake, uprooting all before and behind it while beside the road men marched and walked, emerging and vanishing from the mist. Somewhere, maybe south, maybe east, where the Russians were, artillery rumbled like distant wheels on a wooden deck.

The traffic on the road lifted, lessened, and then there was nothing, the only sound the steady hiss of the river beneath its veil of mist. The radio crackled with orders, and the Feldjaeger stirred themselves to move. Benfeld pulled a Horch up next to him, and Reinhardt stood a last moment by the fire, on the edge of its heat, then tossed the flask into the broken tangle of branches and coals. Feeling as if a weight had been lifted, he climbed into the car, his men boarding their own vehicles, chivvying the men they had rounded up—stragglers, the lost, the dazed, one or two certain deserters—into the trucks. All was silent, the men turned in on themselves, on the weights they bore that seemed to pulse the only truths worth conceiving. That they were still alive. That they had survived another night, with another day to come.

The car rocked over the bridge, past the engineers laying their demolition charges, and a curious sensation grew in him, a push-pull as if the land behind him were reaching in and tugging at a tight knot of memories, and pulled one out in particular. Two years ago, a molten sun setting across the knuckled mountains, and the realization that the truth one saw within was as important as, more important than what others thought. He had misled himself since that night, thinking he was owed more. Owed recognition, thanks, the chance to participate in something grander and greater than him. But that was not the way life worked. He knew it then, and he knew it now, but he had forgotten it along the way, too obsessed with his own survival while cradling his hurts and injuries, real and imagined.

And even if it beat to its own rhythm, in and out of time, a broken heart still beat. A body still moved. Responsibilities had to be met. Benfeld bumped the car onto the northern bank, into Croatia, the small column of Feldjaeger merging into a broken flow of men and vehicles, all moving west. Its verges strewn with the wrack and ruin of an army in retreat, the road paralleled the river before drawing away across fields where water threaded pewter lines across the sodden ground. The road wound its way up the crest of a long, low hill, and at the top, Reinhardt looked back, just once. The sun had risen higher, and the fog and mist had begun to thin and shred, vanishing like a receding tide and exposing the plain that had lain beneath. The land on the southern side of the river was flat, not the mountains he was used to, a hummocked horizon of hills and mounds that thrust up like islands, jutting like peninsulas across the soft spread of the mist. Against a far horizon, where no seam showed between land and sky, the sun flared and flattened up as if stricken, sucked up into the white sky in a flare of light that washed across the clouds.

The car crested the hill, pointed its nose north, and Bosnia was gone.

HISTORICAL NOTE

On 6 April 1945, four years to the day since German bombers attacked the city, Sarajevo was retaken by Tito's Partisans. They found a city reeling after four years of German and Ustaše occupation. Sarajevo's infrastructure was in ruins, its people stunned by the brutality they had lived under, especially during the last months, when the Ustaše's rule had veered toward the crazed and uncontrollable.

Sarajevo's Jews were all but exterminated, as were the Roma. Thousands of Serbs were killed or imprisoned, their properties confiscated, and hundreds more fled to the hills and to the ranks of the Partisans or the Četniks. The city's Bosnian Muslims, torn between the demands of their German and Ustaše overlords and their own visions of a future of their own, navigated a path to survival that involved a mixture of collaboration, tolerance, and resistance.

These years were among the worst in Sarajevo's history. Much of its commercial or industrial activity was stifled or shut down. Food was constantly in short supply. Outbreaks of disease such as typhus stalked the city. In the face of German and Ustaše disinterest and incompetence in making any attempt to run Sarajevo and provide basic services, the city's various charities and cultural societies filled the gap, providing vital and lifesaving assistance. The workers and volunteers of Napredak, Prosvjeta, and Merhamet did their best for their communities, often in the face of overwhelming difficulties, often in the face of official discouragement and even opposition, and it was not unusual for the charities' supplies or properties to be commandeered by the occupying forces. Although the city was stretched to the breaking point, the complex web that bound the different communities together frayed but did not break.

Exactly how many Sarajevans died during the war is unknown. The closest estimates come from the findings of a commission formed in 1981 by the city's veterans. It established that some 10,900 Sarajevans had died as a direct result of the war, the overwhelming majority of whom were Jews. As one Yugoslav historian wrote, they were hemmed into a city in which they could not live and that they could not leave. Thus cornered, and subject to every sadistic and nonsensical whim and vagary that legislation or fascist imagination could come up with, some seven thousand Jews perished during the four-year occupation of the city. This figure is made all the more sobering when one considers that it accounts for more than two-thirds of all Sarajevans the commission found were killed during the war, and for three-quarters of the city's prewar Jewish population. The abject conditions to which they were subjected were documented in detail after the war by a judge, Srećko Bujas, who was appointed as one of the trustees of the Jewish community by the Ustaše. Horrified by what he saw happening, Bujas did his best for Sarajevo's Jews. Motivated by his humanity, an agile and persistent negotiator, Bujas was personally able to save many among the city's Jewish population.

Of the other Sarajevans killed in the war, the majority were Serbs. Some 1,420 Serbs died or were killed, as well as more than four hundred Muslims and more than one hundred Croats. In addition, several thousand Sarajevans died serving in the ranks of the Partisans or operating within the city clandestinely as part of the Communist Party's resistance network. Serb and Bosnian Muslim refugees flooded into the city over the course of the war, to the extent that despite the years of conflict and deaths, Sarajevo's prewar population of some ninety thousand people had actually grown to something over one hundred thousand when it ended.

Of course, the deaths in the city do not include the deaths in the countryside, where the exactions of the Ustaše upon Bosnia's Serbs reached genocidal proportions, and from which tens of thousands of Bosnian Muslims fled at times equally bloody depradations of the Četniks. Furthermore, the war was not confined to Bosnia-Herzegovina but involved the whole of prewar Yugoslavia. By the end of the war, some 1.7 million Yugoslavs were dead, and the majority—approximately one million people—had been killed by their fellow compatriots in an internecine and fratricidal conflict, by Croat Ustašc killing Jews, Muslims, Serbs, Četniks, and Partisans; or by Partisans killing Četniks and Ustaše; or by Četniks killing Ustaše, Muslims, and Partisans.

Under the command of Vladimir Perić, known as Valter, the Communist Party in Sarajevo was the only organization to offer effective—if often only clandestine—armed resistance. Perić was an able organizer of urban resistance despite being in his very early twenties when he took over the Communist Party's networks in 1943. Notably, the Communist Party was the only organization that was able to bridge the ethnic and sectarian cleavages that the Ustaše and Četniks would not, or could not, cross. Added to strong links to the countryside in which the Partisans operated, the Communist Party also overcame the rural-urban divide that had been such a distinct characteristic of Sarajevo's history. Communist Party cells made up of five people—known as "fivesomes" or *petorke*—were active and instrumental in the final days of the occupation, disrupting German and Ustaše movements, defending key installations and cultural sites from damage, and liaising with the advancing Partisans.

It was during these operations that Perić was killed, under circumstances that are still shrouded in mystery, on the very last day of the city's occupation. This event added both to his myth and to the mythology of the Partisans' and Communist Party's activities, with his legend inspiring the classic film *Valter Brani Sarajevo (Valter Defends Sarajevo)*. Given the obscurity around Perić's death, I have exercised a touch of artistic license in order to involve Reinhardt in it.

By 1944, with the Germans and their allies in full retreat across most of Central and Eastern Europe, Sarajevo assumed an increasingly vital and strategic place. It was a key transit point for the German retreat, and the decision was made at the highest levels to hold the city at all costs. This meant increasing control over the city and its population and increasing the repression. In February 1945, the leader of the Ustaše, Ante Pavelić, sent Vladimir "Maks" Luburić to Sarajevo with orders to destroy the resistance movement. Perhaps best known for being the commandant of the notorious Jasenovac concentration camp, in which tens of thousands of Serbs, Jews, and others were murdered, Luburić was a committed Ustaše and a particularly imaginative proponent of state-sponsored terror. He was responsible for a substantial increase in the levels of repression with arrests, tortures, murders, and mass executions. Much of this was ordered or carried out from a villa on the banks of the Miljacka. It was called at the time "the house of terror"; I have renamed it "the Pale House." Its horrors were documented by, among others, an American journalist called Landrum Bolling who entered Sarajevo with the Partisans on 7 April.

What Perić hints at to Reinhardt—that the Ustaše could not be allowed to escape—does come true. The last days of the war saw several hundred thousand Croats—Ustaše, soldiers, and civilians—turned back into Yugoslavia by British troops at Bleiburg, on the Austrian border. Once back in Yugoslavia they were taken prisoner by the Partisans. What ensued remains a stain on Yugoslav history, as well as a sore that festered for decades, as the Partisans summarily executed tens of thousands of Croats and Ustaše, with tens of thousands more succumbing to ill treatment on forced marches to concentration camps.

Despite this carnage and the virtual extinction of the Ustaše as a movement, many of the Ustaše's fighters and most of its highest leaders abandoned their people and escaped the British and the Partisans, vanishing into the Austrian forests and mountains. Some were eventually captured, but some of the worst of them, including Luburić and Pavelić, eventually escaped using "ratlines," which is what Reinhardt stumbles across in Sarajevo.

I have not termed what Reinhardt finds as a "ratline" as such, as that description did not yet really exist. The ratlines were escape routes of varying complexity that mainly operated after the war to bring Nazis and other fascists out of liberated Europe to safety in other countries. Perhaps the most famous Nazi ratline was called ODESSA, run by SS Colonel Otto Skorzeny, but there were many more, with new evidence coming to light in declassified archives in Argentina and Italy of extensive state-sanctioned operations.

The destinations were often Frankist Spain or South America, and the Catholic Church—from individual priests, up to the highest levels of the papacy, and often using Vatican resources—played a depressingly central role in the ratlines' functioning. There is also evidence that the Allies, particularly the United States, were also involved in the escape of some of these individuals, particularly as postwar western and eastern tensions began to solidify into what would become known as the Cold War. Allied disinterest or involvement was certain; how else could someone like Pavelić live virtually undisturbed in American-occupied Austria until April 1946 before escaping to Rome, where he was sheltered by a network of Croatian priests in, among other places, a monastery that had been infiltrated by U.S. intelligence?

Whoever moved them, and however they were moved, the fact remains that hundreds, if not thousands, of Nazis and fascists, among them some of those most guilty of heinous crimes during the war, escaped Europe and lived peaceable and peaceful lives elsewhere. Whether their consciences ever troubled them, who can know. For sure, save for some notable exceptions—Luburić was eventually killed in 1969 by a man later alleged to be an agent of the UDBA, the Yugoslav secret services, and Pavelić was seriously wounded in an assassination attempt in Argentina and died in 1959 in Spain—and save for the efforts of some notable activists such as Simon Wiesenthal and the Klarsfelds, they were rarely troubled in any official capacity to account for what they had, or had not, done during the war.

By early 1945, the German Army was in full retreat across most of Europe. The war in the east was very different from that in the west, and the Germans had recourse to various forms of discipline in order to maintain order and cohesion in the field. Two of the most notable included the Feldjaegerkorps and penal battalions.

The Wehrmacht—the German armed forces—shared with the Soviets the unenviable distinction of incarcerating or executing the highest numbers of their own soldiers for real or perceived breaches of discipline. Although the 999th Balkan Field Punishment Battalion never existed, *strafbattaliones*—often translated as penal battalions— were indeed formed, sometimes under the control of the Feldgendarmerie, to which soldiers who had been sentenced for various breaches of military conduct were assigned. These units were often poorly armed and assigned to the most dangerous and menial tasks, including suicide missions such as leading or covering attacks, often against overwhelming odds, and the construction of front-line defenses under arduous conditions. Sometimes, soldiers who survived their terms were deemed fit to return to normal duties. However, as the war worsened, military tribunals came under increasing pressure to assign those sentenced to penal battalions. By war's end, it is estimated that tens of thousands of Wehrmacht personnel had served in punishment units. The survival rate is unknown but was probably not high given that those sentenced to them were considered as the lowest of the low.

The Pale House features a penal battalion, albeit one with a high percentage of foreign volunteers, or *hilfswiliger*—hiwis. These were men whom the Germans enlisted, or who volunteered, to serve in auxiliary or supplementary functions such as drivers, cooks, medical orderlies, and porters. The word now has an overwhelmingly pejorative nature, especially regarding the tens of thousands of Soviet citizens who served with the Wehrmacht in the USSR. *Hiwi* has almost become synonymous with them, but there were many such people from most of the countries the Germans conquered during the Second World War. Partly as a means of demonstrating the upheavals engendered by war, the novel includes hiwis who were gathered up in the penal battalion's retreat across the Balkans, a collection of Greeks, Serbs, Albanians, and Croats, all of whom had good reasons for not being able to stay on in their own countries after the Germans had gone. Alexiou and his men, for instance, had served in the security battalions formed by the German collaborationist government in Greece and had fought in a bitter civil war in which, like in Yugoslavia, the German occupation had been the trigger that fractured wide a whole range of prewar political cleavages.

The Feldjaegerkorps was created in November 1943, partly as a solution to the perceived inability of the Feldgendarmerie and other existing military police units to maintain desired levels of discipline. The Feldjaegerkorps accepted only officers and noncommissioned officers, and in order to be eligible for service soldiers had to have a minimum of three years front-line combat experience and have earned the Iron Cross Second Class. The authority of the Feldjaegerkorps came directly from the armed forces high command—the *Oberkommando der Wehrmacht*—and thus even the lowest-ranking soldier theoretically carried more power than an officer, and their authority extended even to the Waffen SS (the armed branch of the SS).

The Feldjaegerkorps's basic duties included maintaining order and discipline behind the lines, preventing retreats (especially those driven by panic), gathering and organizing stragglers, and rounding up deserters. Their duties, and the harsh environments in which they operated, have given them a mixed reputation. Without doubt, they could be harsh. Drumhead courts-martial and executions were not unknown. However, and despite their extensive powers, there is much evidence that they were far from needlessly brutal and could be tough but fair.

Three Feldjaeger "commands" were created: Commands I and II served on the Eastern Front and were all but destroyed by the end of the war. Command III was formed in Vienna and fought mostly on the Western Front. In an interesting detail of history, Feldjaegerkorps III was the last German unit to formally lay down its arms, in June 1946, with the U.S. occupation forces in Germany using it to help ensure discipline among German prisoners of war. Although there are no records of the Feldjaegerkorps having served in the Balkans, it seemed an ideal opportunity to detach a small unit and send Reinhardt there with them.

The War Crimes Bureau existed. It was a special section of the legal department of the armed forces high command formed to investigate reports of alleged Allied war crimes for the purposes of lodging diplomatic protests, war crimes trials, and for official government publications (also known as "white books"). The Bureau, including several of its senior staff, were the direct successors of a similar body formed in the Prussian war ministry during World War I. The Treaty of Versailles effectively cast all guilt and blame upon Imperial Germany for crimes committed during the first war, and the feeling was probably strong that the same was not to happen again. Although the Bureau's mandate did not exclude investigating war crimes committed by Germans, the majority of their work was devoted to investigating allegations of war crimes committed against German soldiers and civilians, and the vast majority of what they investigated occurred on the Eastern Front.

By all accounts, the judges who worked in the Bureau were exemplary professionals, largely uncorrupted by Nazism—that indeed the Bureau was something of an environment of opposition to national socialism, with several members executed for their roles in resistance activities—and they carried out their work meticulously and methodically. This does beg the question, however, as to how it was possible— or what mind-set was needed, or what bureaucratic environment had to exist—for these judges to carry out such careful investigations into alleged Allied war crimes in the midst of the staggering levels of official criminality being perpetrated under the Nazi regime? The irony can surely not be lost on us that as the War Crimes Bureau was not competent to investigate any accusations made against the SS, the greatest crime of them all—the Holocaust—passed them by.

Two books in particular were invaluable for describing the situation in wartime Sarajevo: Emily Greble's extraordinarily detailed *Sarajevo 1941–1945: Muslims, Christians and Jews in Hitler's Europe* and Robert Donia's *Sarajevo: A Biography*. I am indebted to both authors and to many other sources and books. Alfred-Maurice de Zayas's excellent *The Wehrmacht War Crimes Bureau, 1939–1945* was also of great use in outlining and describing the Wehrmacht's judicial systems. Eric Tobey's excellent *Soldbuch Anatomy* (dererstezug.com/SoldbuchAnatomy1.htm) was invaluable in researching the ways in which the *soldbuchs* were misused by Jansky and his cabal, as was the information on soldbuch web.com. Any historical inaccuracies are either just those, or the author's attribution of artistic privilege to alter facts, just a little . . .

Reinhardt's journey has taken him on a path of renewal and rediscovery, culminating in an act of resistance that he sees as fitting for the times within which he lives. He knows, however, that to come to that acceptance he has had to make accommodation with himself and what he has always thought is right. In siding with the Partisans over the Ustaše, he is conscious of what he has done. Reinhardt's war is not quite over, but more importantly, the peace that is coming will be as challenging as the fighting it ended. Reinhardt still has far to go until he, like so many others, can pretend to live in a time of peace.

Although he may not serve under his country's colors much longer, there is still much to live and fight for. Reinhardt will march again.